Praise for

RUNNING THE LIGHT

"*Running the Light* is a majestically bleak, hilarious, and bruising tour of regret, delusion, and the detonation of the soul. In Billy Ray Schafer, Sam Tallent has created one of contemporary fiction's more memorable self-destroyers, and it's a harrowing delight to witness him evade and then perhaps finally confront his truth. If there is a comedy club in hell and they have a merch table, this is the only book on it."

— **SAM LIPSYTE**, author of *The Ask* and *No One Left to Come Looking for You*

"A thrilling, nauseating, and painfully real depiction of what happens at length as youth, talent, and charisma sour, *Running the Light* is the best novel I've ever read about comedy but also about a particular strand of relentless hedonism. Sam Tallent is that rare thing, a funny person who can convey his funniness in fiction and do it alongside prose that will break your heart, too."

— **MEGAN NOLAN**, author of *Acts of Desperation*

"Brilliant writing . . . astounding . . . one of the best books I've read. Ever . . . the best fictional representation of comedy in any medium ever."

— **DOUG STANHOPE**, stand-up comedian

"A hell of a novel, too fucked up to miss."

— **RON WHITE**, author of *I Had the Right to Remain Silent . . . But I Didn't Have the Ability*

"You'd never expect this abomination of a man to write such beautiful prose, but Tallent has done it. Wow, what a book!"

—**SHANE GILLIS**, stand-up comedian

"A gripping, raw, brutal, messy portrait of the life of an out-of-control road comic, full of drugs, booze, blood, sex, and a few jokes . . . It reads like a heightened satire of a life on the lowest tier of show business, but I'm here to tell you it all rings true."

—**MARC MARON**, stand-up comedian and podcaster

"Chaotic bliss . . . vivid, electric . . . reads like cinema."

—*The Denver Post*

"Sam Tallent is one of the true originals. He's as much myth as man, like a character who wandered off the pages of a Jack Kerouac novel. But he's very real and full of real integrity that shines through in all his work."

—**CHRIS GETHARD**, stand-up comedian

"*Running the Light* absolutely nails the despair, futility, indignity, and perverse beauty of a life given over to stand-up comedy. The sad and the funny bleed so effortlessly into each other that you don't know whether to laugh or cry or check yourself in to rehab. . . . Ought to be required reading for every open-micer in America."

—**ADAM CAYTON-HOLLAND**, author of *Tragedy Plus Time*

"It feels unfair to compare a first-time novelist to masters like Denis Johnson and David Gates, but it's all here: despair, fury, nihilism, tenderness, lyricism, hope, dark new insight into the human condition. . . . As bleak and electrifying as anything by Cormac McCarthy."

—**MISHKA SHUBALY**, author of *The Long Run*

RUNNING
THE LIGHT

RUNNING THE LIGHT

A Novel

SAM TALLENT

RANDOM HOUSE
NEW YORK

For my mother, for teaching me how to read.
For my father, for teaching me what to read.
And for Emily, for everything, for always.

This book is dedicated to comedians,
but only the funny ones.

Eddie:
"Do you mean to tell me you could've taken
your hand out of that cuff at any time?!"

Roger:
"No! Not anytime—only when it was funny."

—*Who Framed Roger Rabbit*

For you, the day Bison graced your village was
the most important day of your life.
But for me, it was a Tuesday.

—M. Bison, *Street Fighter*

It was alright to be who he was, but others
would probably think it was terrible.

—Denis Johnson, *Angels*

FOREWORD

By Doug Stanhope

Sam Tallent's *Running the Light* with its protagonist, Billy Ray, is the best true-life representation of the Great American Road Comic that has ever been written.

And it's fiction. It would have to be.

Stand-up comedy has been largely ignored as an art form except at the highest levels, and even then its only focus is on the show. The ins and outs and lifestyles of any given working road comic are as much a mystery as the average day of a carnival barker or an aging Ice Capader to the average schlub on the street.

"You're a comedian . . . so, *how does that work*? Do you work on a circuit? Do you have, like, an agent? Do you travel as a group?"

And so on.

These are all legitimate questions for this oddball career, and this is another place where Tallent excels. It's been said that if you read any article or story about any subject that you are an expert on, you should count the number of errors you find and then assume that that is the case across the board with any subject you read. I am an expert in this field and at no point did I find anything that wouldn't be well within the norms of the business. No exaggeration, no stretching scenes into the unlikely. Every bit of this book reads like it is the fact-checked autobiography of a tired and debauched veteran comedian whose best days are behind him and even those weren't very good. And this is a comedy world you are most likely familiar with. This isn't Madison Square Garden or the Hollywood Bowl. This story resides in the Chuckleheads or the Snickerz strip mall comedy clubs of your towns, the local pub with barely a stage that does stand-up shows on Wednesday unless it's during the NBA playoffs. You've gone now and then, and one time there was a hypnotist that made you cluck like a chicken and oh boy, do the fellas still make fun of you for that one!

That kind of comedy where some comics spend their whole careers spanning every time zone, sleeping in comedy condos or in their cars at a Pilot Flying J on their way to the next run. Some adjusted to the lifestyle and some succumbed to it as in this case, Billy Ray.

Every comedian of any era knows at least one Billy Ray. For my generation there was John Fox. For John Fox there was Ollie Joe Prater. Not household names, but if the names come up in a green room, every comic is chiming in retelling urban legends and rumors in the angsty whisper of campfire horror stories. Perhaps today they would hold the tone of righteous indignation and fashionable outrage, but the tone doesn't change the underlying reasons that the Billy Rays of our world compel you.

You could call him self-destructive but as the story begins, you see the destruction was finalized years ago. He simply continues down the spiral staircase on muscle memory, booze fumes rising from the spent cartridge of his soul. I have known him and I have shared the stage with him. I've tried to save him and I have also assisted in his downfall. He's stolen my jokes and I still closed the bar with him. Several comedians have told me that they read this character as me. I read him as a down-and-out Ron White.

Most important, I was as engrossed by this book as anything I have ever read. The prose, the turns of phrase, the vernacular . . . all that shit . . . it is so brilliantly written that I found myself reading passages out loud to anyone within earshot on nearly every page.

Running the Light is the definitive book on road comedy, and Sam Tallent has created an instant classic in the same fashion Hunter S. Thompson did with *Fear and Loathing in Las Vegas*. And by that, I mean that they were both written by men wearing distastefully ill-fitting shorts.

RUNNING
THE LIGHT

BILLY RAY SCHAFER STEPPED OFF THE PLANE IN AMARILLO, Texas with twenty-six hundred dollars tucked down the leg of his black ostrich-skin cowboy boot. He walked to baggage claim slowly, jelly-legged and nearing lucidity, coming out from under the Xanax he snorted before the flight. He removed his suitcases from the conveyor belt and found a restaurant in the terminal that served alcohol. After three drinks he went outside to smoke until his ride arrived.

The club owner sent his son to carry Billy Ray the two hours to Tucumcari. The son had a wide pink face that smiled amiably the entire drive. He didn't care if Billy Ray smoked in the truck—not at all, just crack the window, please. As he drove, going fast, making short work of Texas, the son, a junior at the university in Albuquerque, remarked on the buildings they passed—peeling gray barns, rusted silos, long squat adobe houses baked the color of dried blood—detailing the different methods of construction and explaining how the architecture reflected the evolution of the Southwest as a region and the "resilient nature" of "these humble people." On the barren stretches, he spewed an eclectic barrage of regional facts: "Taos Pueblo was built one thousand years after the death of Christ"; "Sante Fe is the tallest state capitol city"; "New Mexico is home to more cows than people and more chili peppers than cows"—followed by a list of famous New Mexicans. While the kid prattled, Billy Ray flirted with sleep, barely listening, finding it hard to imagine any life, human or otherwise, being lived in this blasted expanse of teeming red desert.

Based on how fast he talked, Billy Ray wondered if the kid had any amphetamines. Uppers would be helpful for his continuance. He was reaching the edge of himself.

He'd flown red-eye from Memphis to Dallas, where he suffered a four-hour layover before switching planes. In Memphis he'd performed at a nightclub patronized by black professionals, the men attired sharply in tailored suits and the women, their hair elaborate, in velvet and satin. He was not what they wanted and they were vocal in their disdain. Before Memphis, he'd done two nights in Tupelo at a rathole called Tortugas Cantina. Tortugas, which the locals called Tugs, brought in comedians on the weekend, transforming their dining room into a comedy club with the addition of a stage comprised of a single wooden pallet. The shows were sparsely attended but the staff prided themselves on entertaining the comedians and, like most service professionals, they were flush with cocaine and generous in their hospitality. Before Tupelo it was Birmingham and Huntsville and Chattanooga, Tennessee, a riverboat in Knoxville called the *Smoky Queen Pearl* and a biker bar in Charlotte that kept a snake in a glass tank behind the bar and fed him on hamsters, twelve days continuous of Greyhounds, rental cars and the cheapest motels starting in Virginia Beach two Wednesdays ago, twelve days of bad food and free liquor and women with low morale, twelve days away from his apartment in Los Angeles—a one bedroom in Koreatown that was less an apartment than it was the address of a storage space where he slept on occasion. He'd been on the road more than two hundred days this year. The damage was cumulative, both physical and mental, a sense-dulling exhaustion that limited his scope of emotion to a callous and shapeless contempt. He felt like he was evaporating. Seven days to go.

They stopped for burgers at a drive-in where the carhops rode inline skates. The girl who brought their food appeared to be floating and Billy Ray registered her an angel until he saw her wheels. They ate off the tailgate, watching the clouds push and expand across the West Texas sky. When he was done eating he lit a Winston, but he could not enjoy it; the air was hot enough already.

For the rest of the drive Billy Ray shut his eyes. With no one to talk to, the son whistled to himself, the same fifteen notes repeating, and Billy Ray passed gas in protest, filling the cabin with the smell of his decay.

When they finally reached Tucumcari, they stopped at a liquor store and Billy Ray bought a six-pack of Coors bottles and a small bag of ice. He instructed the kid to deliver him to his hotel, where he checked in and stripped nude and, after filling a wastepaper basket with the ice and beer, he laid on the mottled mattress and let the air conditioner lick the sweat off his body. The kid had promised to return at six-thirty to pick him up and take him to the venue. In the downtime, Billy Ray tried to nap but he was too tired, so he cracked a beer and flipped the channels until he found a network playing a show he liked. In the show, film crews followed actual police on patrol, capturing low moments of low people: domestic violence, DUIs, solicitations, assaults. The show was his favorite; he found the sincerity of lives in collapse to be absolutely compelling. In one episode, a pair of fat deputies in Fort Lauderdale, Florida uncovered a kilo of cocaine on a routine traffic stop. Billy Ray watched with envy as the police sliced into the brick to confirm it was drugs. "We just ruined someone's party," joked the cops. When asked, the possessor of the cocaine claimed the kilo was for personal use. "Hell yeah," Billy Ray said and saluted the man with his beer.

The show that night was directly off the highway in a concrete roadhouse named Mingles. A banner hung on the face of the building announced BUD LIGHT PRESENTS MINGLES MONDAY NIGHT COMEDY RIOT. Pickup trucks dominated the patch of dirt out front that served as a parking lot. The kid parked away from them, behind the building. He insisted on carrying Billy Ray's suitcase. Billy Ray followed him in through a back door into a kitchen alive with the smell of potatoes frying in dirty oil, past the lone harried cook standing with his hands on his hips in front of one of three microwaves and continuing through a set of swinging doors and into a barroom lit in low red light, decorated in maroon and black vinyl and outfitted with pool tables, dartboards and an arcade hunting simulator.

"My dad will be in later," said the son. "Are you hungry? We got your dinner and whatever you want to drink. I've got to set up the chairs."

Billy Ray requested a whiskey-coke and a menu from the bartender, a stoic man of deeply wrinkled indigenous features, his skin clay-red, his hair blue-black. He drank his highball fast and ordered another. Nothing about Mingles encouraged mingling. This was an unwelcoming place, vaguely apocalyptic. Everyone looked like a bounty hunter or a gas huffer. They were a grim clientele, all of them unlucky, the sunburnt and scarred survivors of anonymous, intimate catastrophes. They reminded Billy Ray of science fiction, these deep desert mutants, of nuclear fallout and Area 51. Looking at them gave him anxiety. He focused on his drinking. By the time the show began he was quietly very drunk.

A few minutes after eight, the owner's son—whose name turned out to be Pauly—stepped to the microphone and introduced the opening act, a tall, thin man defined by an upright shock of stiff white hair. He wore a lab coat and went by the name Doctor Dixon Gorged. For thirty minutes, Doctor Gorged rattled off a combination of jokebook jokes and stolen material. Billy Ray identified bits by Hedberg, Carlin and Cosby among the bad doctor's menagerie, but the crowd didn't notice or, if they did, they didn't care, and Doctor Gorged ended his set to decent applause.

When the Doctor walked past him on his way off the stage, Billy Ray nodded, abiding custom, and offered the traditional obligatory acknowledgment: "Good set."

"Thanks. They're fun. Are you the headliner?"

"I'm up next."

The man extended his hand. "Wayne Hanson. I'm not actually a doctor."

"No shit," said Billy Ray. The man's hand was warm and moist.

The owner's son was uncomfortable behind the mic. He rocked back and forth. "Before we bring up your headliner, I just wanted to remind y'all—Bud Light drafts are two-for-one."

Wayne Hanson/Doctor Gorged lowered his eyebrows, smushing his face apologetic. "I wish I could stay for your set, but I have to work in five hours."

"That's okay, man," Billy Ray said, cinching closed his bolo tie. "I wouldn't watch me either."

On stage, the owner's son did his best to bolster the energy in the room, but his false excitement came off as pleading. "Are y'all ready for your headliner?" he begged, raising a tepid affirmation from the crowd. He talked louder: "I *said* are y'all *ready* for your *headliner*?" The crowd responded with slightly more enthusiasm. "I've been hanging out with this guy all day and it has been a hoot." He pulled a slip of paper from his coat pocket and read: "You've seen him on Letterman and Leno, Comedy Central and HBO."

Wayne Hanson's eyebrows hiked. "You did Letterman?"

"What's the matter?" Schafer sneered. "You never seen a big star before?"

"It is my sincere pleasure to bring him to the stage. Let's give a big Tucumcari welcome—here he is—Billy Ray Shatner!"

Bounding onstage to a wave of gentle applause, Billy Ray Schafer shook the boy's hand and snatched the microphone from the stand. "Keep it going for Pauly and that heartfelt introduction." He looked out at maybe thirty people distributed among eight circular cocktail tables. When he was setting up the room, Pauly lowered all the lights besides the ones pointed at the stage, rendering the crowd a collection of bodies without faces. Schafer knew there were more people at the bar, beyond his vision. It didn't matter: they did not need to be seen. They all looked the same.

He breathed in, he breathed out. Then he addressed the darkness.

"Tucumcari, how are you tonight? Who's drinking? Me too. Cheers.

You can't argue with two-for-one Bud Lights—someone's getting a DUI tonight. I heard in Tucumcari, for a sobriety test, the cops make you pronounce the name of this fucking place. Tucumcari—what the hell kind of name is that? *Tu-cum-car-i.* Whoever named this town was sneezing—'*Tucumcari!* Excuse me.' Jesus Christ. It must be an Indian word. I bet it's Comanche for 'middle of fucking nowhere.' Sounds like the nickname of a very demanding lover: Two Cum Carrie—she needs it twice or not at all."

What he lacked in innovation he made up for in execution, tenacity and volume. He operated with a defiant nonchalance that concealed his craft beneath a layer of manufactured effortlessness. He'd been doing it—doing this—for so long that after a certain, indefinable tipping point, he had them—he owned them—and it no longer mattered what words he said, only how he said them. The funny was in the timing, the pronunciation, the spaces in between. He wove in and out of prepared material, riffing at his leisure, and working the crowd ("I see a lot of Mexican couples in here. Sir, is this your wife? How long have you been together? Wow—seventeen years. Congratulations. Mexicans, y'all have the strongest marriages and I'll tell you why: because Latinas are fucking *scary*. Look at her—she's laughing because she knows. You ask a white girl for a divorce, she might sue you for alimony. Worst-case scenario, she slashes your tires. But shit, man, you ask a Latina for a divorce—she's liable to slash your *throat*. That's war right there! You know what happens when you ask a Mexican for a divorce? The fucking Alamo is what happens.").

He was excellent, an emancipator, a prophet, the microphone a relic in his hand; for the duration of his set, his was the only voice in the world. Santeria, cult ritual—jokes as incantations. What he said altered the listener, caused them to revert and devolve: they howled and grunted, they whooped, they squealed. Under his spell, they communicated without words, slapping at each other like lesser hominoids. Some cried, the joy welling up and escaping their eyes in the form of clear liquid and running down their faces gone sore from smiling prolonged.

For fifty-eight minutes, Billy Ray Schafer harnessed the protean, giving shape to that which has no form. It was a masterful performance that left the crowd liberated and buckling like convulsives. But for Billy Ray, while his attention was occupied, he operated autonomous of a sense of pride—while he was killing, Billy Ray Schafer was completely and hopelessly bored: he checked his watch, he thought about dinner. This task brought him joy no longer. He didn't hear the laughter anymore.

"Thank you, Tucumcari. Now let's get destroyed."

He stands in the back of the room behind a pool table displaying his merchandise. People approach to pay compliments. Some of them want photos, others just want to talk. He exploits their gratitude for an opportunity to push his wares: T-shirts, beer koozies, CDs—the merchandise is his lifeblood. This is how he survives. They thank him for coming, tell him he was amazing, tell him they needed that. They hug him goodbye. A few people ask how he wound up in Tucumcari, a common question in the small towns. He always gives the same answer—"I'm just following the money." It is a better thing to say than the truth: "Because life is pain and I am very much alive."

He signs autographs for no extra charge, scribbling in thick black Sharpie: DAVE, THANKS FOR THE DRUG MONEY! BRS or CINDY, THANKS FOR BRINGING THEM TITTIES GIRL! BRS. They tell him jokes and he pretends not to have heard them before. He gives them fake laughter, he gives them more of himself. When they offer to buy him liquor, he obliges. Beer chases whiskey. Tequila salt lime. He drinks until he is anesthetized. He asks them for cocaine.

Sorry, they say.

I can't help you, they say.

That's okay, he tells them. I can't help myself.

The bar becomes an illusion that requires all of his focus to maintain. He plays songs on the jukebox that make him feel more real: nobody else knows the words. He orders a cheeseburger, tips the bartender twenty dollars, forgets about it, tips him again. Conversations wear on. He begins to repeat himself. There are only so many things to say.

—————ᴍ—————

Near midnight, a man who claimed to be the owner pulled him away to a small storage room behind the bar. A bare bulb in the ceiling yellowed the chamber visible, illuminating a row of stainless-steel kegs lining the wall like the torsos of B-movie robots. A water heater hummed in the center of the room flaking paint. Hanging on the wall, a feedstore calendar laid open to a picture of a girl in a bikini lying sideways across bales of hay. *She must be itchy*, thought Billy Ray.

The owner's face was sharp, his sunbaked skin pulled tight, his nose an arrowhead jutting out of the middle of his head. The precise angular symmetry of his composition was disrupted by a black patch he wore over his left eye. His long arms hung to his knees, lumpy with muscle, the skin cobwebbed with faded tattoos gone all shades of gray. He looked nothing like his son.

"Do you need a check or is cash okay?" the owner said.

"Cash is just fine," said Billy Ray. "Better for taxes."

"I get it." He handed Billy Ray an envelope. "It's like you were never here." The owner pulled a baggie of white sand from his pocket, held the bag to the single bulb and flicked it twice with his index finger. "Nightcap?"

Billy Ray smiled. "I wouldn't want to be rude."

The owner opened the bag and spilled powder on top of the water heater and carved the mound into six thin scars with a pocketknife. He licked the blade before closing it then rolled a twenty-dollar bill tubular and handed it to Billy Ray. "Fire it up."

Billy Ray bent over and snapped his head back with a snort, disappearing two of the lines. The cocaine tightened the parts of him made loose by alcohol. Immediately he felt improved. They passed the bill between them, efficient in their consumption. When the first set of lines were gone, the owner chalked out six more.

"You got some good shit here," Billy Ray said, his lips completely numb.

"The guy last week couldn't get enough."

"Who was here?"

"Andrist. Something Andrist."

"Andy?"

"That's it. You know him?"

Billy Ray nodded. "Oh I know him."

"He's got a Hoover for a nose."

"How'd he do?"

The owner shook his head. "Bad."

"Really?"

"It was bad. He said something about the military that pissed a lot of people off. It got pretty ugly from there."

"Andy's not for everyone. His stuff is pretty smart."

"Too smart for this town. They hated him." The owner finished the last of the powder then licked the water heater clean. "But they loved you."

At last call, Billy Ray stepped onto the patio to smoke and count his money. Including the cash in the envelope, he added $430 to the lump in his boot. The bar emptied and he watched the last-call stragglers stagger across the parking lot, crunching the dirt beneath their soles as they hunted for their rides. He'd attempted to procure a bit of the owner's cocaine, but they'd exhausted his holdings, and now his blood begged for what it couldn't have. As was often the case at this hour, he didn't know what to do. In cities, no matter the night of the week, the party never had to end, but out in the Rest of It, in the remote, blank nowheres, the night had a way of dying just when he was feeling the most alive.

Hard white stars henpecked the sky, burning clearer in the fathomless black. It would be nice, he thought, to spend the night beneath this sky, to lie down in the desert and sleep with the snakes. As a young man, when he first began working the road, he spent many nights in a tent camped off the side of the highway. There was an overwhelming sense of adventure in the beginning, a thrilling desperado wanderlust that made each day special and new; he'd relished every night and the miles in between. Now, after twenty-six years, the romance was gone, replaced as it was in all long-term relationships with a fatalistic obligation: this is what I do and I'll do it until I'm dead. Tonight he would sleep indoors. His bones were too old for the dirt.

He was ready to ask Pauly for a ride back to the hotel when a girl approached from across the patio. Her pants hung low on her waist, exposing the points of her hips, an unlit cigarette dangling out of her pinched face. Redheaded and tomboy skinny, her mossy, dull eyes reflected little light. She appeared stagnant behind them, like she was staring out of mud. He recognized her from the audience. She had covered her mouth when she laughed.

She asked him for a light and he gave her his Bic. She asked him what he thought of Tucumcari and he told her he didn't have a chance to see much. "You're not missing out," she said. She offered to show him some things.

An hour later, inside of an IHOP bathroom, he had her bent over a baby-changing table, his thighs to her haunches, his fingers in her mouth. She was loud. "Yes," she said. "Yes yes yes yes yes yes yes." She was strong, eager. She pulled him inside of her and held him there— "Yes." He finished on her back.

Afterward, she ordered a waffle with whipped cream and he drank ice tea. They were the only ones in the restaurant but it took a while for her food to come. While they waited, she told him about her life. It was all very sad. She ate her waffle with a spoon. When she was finished, he paid for her meal and she drove him to his hotel.

"Don't forget about me," she said as he got out of the car.

"Never," he told her. He didn't know her name.

RENTAL CAR COUNTERS WERE ONE OF THE FEW PLACES WHERE his name still had meaning. Inside of them he felt special. He never had to wait in line.

"As you know, Mr. Schafer, your membership tier allows you for a free upgrade."

"I'll pass."

"Are you sure? With your rewards points, we could put you in a Mustang at no additional charge."

"I'll take whatever does best on gas."

"Of course, sir. My pleasure."

He had no palate for cars. A tool to be used, a conveyance; their design was of no interest to him. He never understood the appeal. He knew people that owned dozens of cars, motorcycles, boats, all of them insured and in need of routine maintenance, losing their value daily and rusting away like their owners. Things had never been his thing. He spent his money on more immediate gratifications.

The day was clear electric blue. Cloudless. Pristine. The undistilled sunlight bounced off the highway in shimmering waves: it looked like rain in reverse. In a brand-new maroon Toyota Corolla, he took the miles of ruined red earth at ninety miles an hour, pressing into the hundreds when he thought it was safe, relishing the speed, challenging the horizon. He stopped at a McDonald's for a large orange juice and married it to a quarter pint of vodka. He sang along to the radio whenever he knew the words.

He measured time in mile markers. Albuquerque was six exits long, Santa Fe was three. Once he'd thought that capital cities received their designation because they were the largest and most prosperous cities in their respective states. Then stand-up dragged him across the country, through Springfield, Albany, Carson City, Olympia, and he realized that he did not know much about the choosing of capital cities or about anything much at all.

In Raton he stopped at a diner for pork green chile and fresh tortillas with butter. While he ate, he called his manager, Randy "Red" Haberstadt, and left another message, saying he would call back tomorrow, same time, they had to talk about January, about the cruise ships: he was starting to get nervous. It was important to stay on top of Red and it had been a few weeks since they'd talked. The submission window for Carnival was approaching and he needed to know Red had sent in his tape. The boats represented thirty weeks of easy money. He couldn't do another year like this one.

He picked up a six-pack of Coors Banquet at a gas station moated by tables of Indian blankets and turquoise jewelry. A dinner-plate chunk of quartz caught his eye and when he stopped to admire it, a shrunken woman with a raisined face approached him from behind the table.

"Is beautiful, no?" She wore a rosary. As she talked she passed the beads between her thumb and forefinger.

"Sí," he answered. "Muy bonita."

"Or this." She selected a silver-plated necklace from among her riches and held it up to glitter in the sunlight. "So pretty."

"Auténtico?"

"Sí. Touch."

"No gracias."

"Sí sí. Tócalo."

"I see it."

"Tócalo."

"Lo siento, mamacita."

"Un regalo para tu amor."

"I have no amor."

He drove on, crossing Raton Pass and the volcanic mesas pushing spruces and Christmas firs from their rich, black soil, passing Fishers Peak and the sprawling walls of granite left over from the construction of I-25 and the closed exits to the ghost towns created by the interstate when it made the railroads obsolete.

Four hours after leaving Tucumcari, he arrived in Trinidad, Colorado and found a park near a river to get out and stretch his legs. He removed his boots and socks and locked his bankroll in the trunk and walked down to the water in his bare feet, concealing a beer in his pocket. He'd been slipped a joint the night before and while he wasn't big on dope, he figured with four hours between him and showtime, he had nothing better to do than get a little stoned. Part of the job was killing daylight. Spending too much time in a hotel room gave him a caged, static feeling that reminded him of jail. Boardwalks, movie theaters, shopping malls—in these places he whittled the excess hours off his days. But given the option, he preferred parks for the lack of crowds and the low price of admission and because he could loiter and smoke cigarettes and drink liquor from brown bags.

In the shade of a scabrous ponderosa, the bark cracked and eaten up with blight, he sat down and lit the joint and sank into the listless afternoon. The smoke was dense and smelled like gasoline and turned the water of the Purgatoire complex and beautiful. The river seemed alive somehow, sentient, the skin rippling and flashing like melted sunlight, a single purposed organism built of liquid glass, pulsing and reptilian, like a great blue snake shouldering the banks as it raked its belly along the riverbed. For a while he became preoccupied in his mind with the pronunciation of the word "salamander," repeating it to himself until the syllables lost all meaning. He cracked the beer and drank it and when it was empty he set an alarm on his phone and took off his shirt and laid down on his belly, stoned and tranquil and drunker than he expected, enjoying the contrast of the cool grass on his skin and the sunlight on his back. In the quiet of the fading afternoon, Billy Ray dozed off into a restless sleep, finding it difficult without a pillow to find a comfortable position and dreaming of a pattern of triangles and squares.

At seven, the alarm called him back from wherever we go and he woke up in the darkness thirsty and confused, unsure for a moment of this place in the world and who he was in it.

He drove to the hotel and checked in. Before he took a shower, he masturbated into the sink with the lights off so as not to see himself in the mirror. His reflection ruined the experience.

The GPS led him to a nondescript building on the outskirts of town. He pulled up slowly, unsure if he'd entered the correct address. He rolled down his window and asked a woman in the parking lot if there was a comedy show here tonight and she told him she didn't know, probably, she wasn't sure what all they had planned this year. He parked on the side of the building and left his merchandise in the car and walked around to the front of the building, a pre-engineered corrugated sheet metal kit-shed, bunker-esque and utilitarian and at home in the surrounding high desert. A plywood deck had been built onto the building, and a spotlight attached to the railing painted the valley below in pale, ephemeral light. Scraped out by a flash flood the year previous, the valley stretched out like a graveyard, a forgotten place, the bleak landscape bristling with tufted sagebrush and knobs of cactus and dried out, bone-white yuccas, the serrated leaves growing as stiff and sharp as ivory knives. Looming at the end of the valley, the Sangre de Cristos guarded the edge of the world; their enormity blacked out the moon.

The building was one big room. A thin galley kitchen ran along one wall, a bar along the other. Between them a hundred or so people sat at collapsible tables in plastic folding chairs. The walls were sheathed in faux-wood paneling that reflected the obnoxious fluorescent light screaming off tubes in the ceiling.

Billy Ray went to the bar and asked the man behind the counter if there was comedy here tonight.

"I think I heard something about that," the man said.

"Do you know who I should talk to? I'm the comic."

"That would be Dan."

"Do you know where he is?"

The man put down his rag and came out from behind the bar. "Let me see," he said, setting off into the crowd. The man walked with a bouncing limp.

While he waited, Billy Ray milled about the perimeter reading plaques inscribed with the names of dead men and the dates they were killed. One of the men was named Leslie Faggot and Billy Ray laughed.

"Mr. Schafer?"

Billy Ray turned around to find the barman standing with a squat, severe-looking man.

"Mr. Schafer," said the man. "I'm Dan Guntley. Welcome to our VFW."

Dan Guntley's title was sergeant at arms. A blocky, square-headed, taciturn man, Dan Guntley served two tours in Vietnam, and despite his age, he still appeared capable of violence. His movements were precise and unwasted and he shook Billy Ray's hand like he was trying to win a contest.

"Help yourself to the prime rib," Dan Guntley said, motioning to a table covered in potluck. "You can take a plate with you if you like. We always have too much." He put his hand on the barman's shoulder. "This is Dave. You already met."

Billy Ray moved his extended finger between the two men: "Dan and Dave. That's easy."

"Excellent. Dave will take care of you. Entertainment starts at twenty-one hundred hours. You'll go on at twenty-one and a half, right after plop-o. You are scheduled for forty minutes and we'll do the raffle when you're done."

"Did—did you say plop-o?"

"Yes sir."

"Is that a clown?"

"No sir."

"You never played plop-o?" asked Dave.

Billy Ray shook his head.

The two men exchanged glances. This seemed to please them. "Well, in that case," Dan Guntley said, "I won't ruin the surprise."

Billy Ray loaded a plate with macaroni and cheese and green beans with bacon and slices of white bread and a slab of prime rib as big as his face and ladled gravy over the entire mess. The flimsy plate sagged under the weight of his meal; the grease soaked through the paper. He carried his dinner to the bar and asked Dave for a whiskey-coke.

"No can do, partner. No liquor. We only got wine, Mike's Hard and Coors in a can, but we got a shitload of them and they're cold as death."

The beef was leathered, overcooked and underseasoned, but he ate it all and returned to the buffet for seconds of the macaroni and cheese. He knew comics that said they couldn't eat before they went on, that digestion messed with their show, but Billy Ray never had that problem, especially when the food was complimentary: as a rule, he took whatever was free and kept his eye on the rest.

The event tonight was a ticketed fundraiser for a charity that worked with military families. He estimated the average age in the room to be sixty-five years old. The men were loud, their posture impeccable. They tucked their shirts into their starched Wranglers and they tucked their pant legs into their boots and they stood bolt straight clasping their hands behind their backs as they agreed with each other, treading the surface, using many words to say nothing, waiting for their turn to talk. Their wives were quiet, sturdy women, plain without being homely, ChapStick, cheap earrings, lacquered but not polished. They wore their hair piled high into stiff meringues above soda can bangs or pulled back into ponytails that stretched their foreheads smooth and pinned their eyebrows incredulous. Like their husbands, they wore jeans along with denim jackets and hooded sweatshirts and souvenir T-shirts purchased on vacation and they donned their husbands' Carhartts to step outside and smoke Marlboro Lights and gossip about each other's kids. Nearly all of the men and a good portion of the women wore some kind of hat: ballcaps and boonies and beanies and berets and flat caps and patrol caps and camouflage visors, a few cowboy hats and he even spotted one deerstalker, all of them stuck with buttons and pins and medals and patches, commemorations signaling their ranks, platoons and battalions, the ships they manned, the aircraft they flew, identifiers of the lives they lived, reminders of what happened to them: brass scars. The only ones among them not wearing hats were seated at the table closest to the bar, a pack of long-haired young men and their dates, sad boys with men's faces who quietly drank beers at a steady pace, their blank eyes ringed in sleepless purple. They looked like they were tired of seeing.

Billy Ray had never been here before, but observing these people, he understood where he was. He knew them. He'd met them many times. Proud, generous, unremarkable, their faces big and red and tired, these were capital "A" Americans, the ubiquitous, stalwart, forgotten surplus. They would die here because they were born here, baptized and married in the same church, living the span of their lives within fifty miles of where they'd been pushed screaming into the world. These people populated towns that only existed on maps—Tama, Iowa, Demopolis, Alabama, Wyoming et al.—the faceless spaces between destinations. They spent their lives persevering, aware that they were waiting for something, but for what, they didn't know.

Billy Ray went outside and smoked a cigarette in the dark. He wanted to find some cocaine. Having some gave him comfort. It was palliative, a rip cord, an escape hatch: if the show was shit, he could always get high afterward. And if the show went well, why not celebrate with an old friend? That's what he told himself, but if he was being honest—in rehab they said it was important to be honest—he simply enjoyed being high on cocaine. It made him feel good and smart and special. There was nothing else to it: life is long and it was lonely out here.

After retrieving his merchandise case from the car, he went inside to find the crowd clearing tables and chairs from the center of the room. Two boys unspread a tarp in the middle of the linoleum floor and smoothed it flat. A grid had been drawn on the tarp to create a matrix of forty-nine squares. Spray-painted along the vertical axis were the letters *A, B, C, D, E, F* and *G* and across the horizontal axis numbers one to seven. The crowd crushed around the tarp, jostling for position and comparing slips of paper until the appearance of a big man from the kitchen dropped the room into reverential silence. The big man's beard hung past the bib of his faded gray overalls. He walked like he thought he was important. He carried a duck under his arm.

"Ladies and gentlemen," the emcee said into the microphone, "there he is: Mallard Fillmore." The big man walked to the center of the tarp and raised the duck above his head, an act of ceremony Billy Ray, completely confused, interpreted as sacrificial. The duck, an old mallard with a proud brown bosom, snapped at the man's wrist, drawing blood. The big man cursed and dropped the duck fluttering to the tarp. Billy Ray had never seen a duck indoors. This was a haggard specimen. Patches of dimpled skin showed through where its feathers had fallen out. The eyes trapped in its teal head indicated neither excitement nor petulance, only indifference, blinking flatly with a hostile stultification, a look of imminent degradation. Billy Ray knew it well: *Alright, motherfuckers, let's get this over with. I could be flying right now.*

"Here we go," said the man on the stage. "Who's ready to make some money?"

The crowd cheered.

"Alright, y'all. It's that time. One, two, three—plop-o!"

The crowd flared like a flame licked by wind. They stomped their feet and clapped their hands and slapped at the flat parts of themselves with their palms or barked or blew sharply into elaborate handheld devices that bleated like waterfowl and looked like kazoos. Others cooed sweetly, throwing bits of bread or kneeling with crackers in their outstretched hands in an attempt to influence the duck's movements, to draw it closer to them and away from the others, whispering, pleading. The surreality was spellbinding. Billy Ray watched like a man on drugs. The emcee's voice through the loudspeaker was barely audible over the chaos. ". . . where will he shit, where will he blow, whose luck will hit, we all want to know."

"Jesus fucking Christ," Billy Ray said, ascertaining finally the rules of the game.

Grace, do you remember me? I remember you . . .

Duck shit bingo.

I'm following duck shit bingo.

Condemnation has many names.

The crowd's collective fervor crescendoed when the duck waddled absently off the edge of the tarp and sat down to pick at a piece of bread. The onlookers whooped and howled and threw pieces of dinner rolls but the duck, nonplussed, stared on intransigent, defying their demands. Billy Ray wondered why the bird didn't fly away. For some reason, he thought he remembered hearing that ducks couldn't fly unless they were near water but that didn't make sense. Did the big bastard clip your wings, little duck, or did you forget how to use them? Cutting through the crowd, the big man went to toe the duck back toward the center but the duck took his bread and scurried farther down the tarp. Billy Ray smiled. Despite his embarrassment at being involved in this sideshow, he found himself rooting for the bird. In a strange way, he empathized. *Good for you,* he thought, watching the duck avoid the big man's boot. *You don't have to feed the pigs their slop, little duck. I do, but you don't.*

Eventually, the big man got his hands on the bird and walked it back to the free space and said something Billy Ray couldn't hear and the crowd laughed. When the duck finally shat, the crowd erupted. The watery green mess on space D-4 won two ticket holders one hundred dollars apiece paid by the big man who then tucked the duck back under his arm and waved to the crowd. He turned in each direction, bowing like a bullfighter, and the strange duo left to a round of hearty applause and the tarp was removed and the tables returned. Billy Ray checked his watch. Almost showtime. He wondered what the duck was getting paid.

Billy Ray went to the bathroom and stepped into a stall to piss. He was glad to be away from the people in the main room. Bathroom stalls were one of the few places he could be himself; they made him think about cocaine. Not including the toilet, he counted five surfaces in the stall on which one could measure themselves a serving of powder and snort it in private and not have to share. How fine that would be. Surely someone here had cocaine. He decided that after the show he would talk to the sullen longhairs by the bar. They looked like they spent time in the bathroom. If they didn't have cocaine, he would take whatever they had. He just needed something—anything—to help him get closer to right.

He shook off and zipped himself and stood at the sink trying to make sense of the face in the mirror. When he was younger, he knew he was handsome because women told him so. There was a time in his life when he had been fawned over, coveted. He remembered that face and the permissions it gave him, the strength in his jaw, the devil in his eyes. There was none of that left. He didn't recognize himself.

In the eighties, before his wife, he dated a girl who practiced Bikram yoga. On her birthday, he surprised her with a trip to Las Vegas to attend a weekend retreat and see the famous yogi speak. The night of the yogi's lecture, the girl convinced Billy Ray to accompany her in eating LSD. Under the influence of the drug, the yogi's lecture became a sermon of profound revelation. At one point, after hearing the yogi's stance on memory, Billy Ray shouted "Hallelujah!" and dropped to his knees and buried his face in the carpet. "No one remembers what they looked like yesterday, a week ago, last year. There is a version of us inside of our minds that does not correspond to our actuality, an idea of who we are that is unaffected by time or reality. Then, one day, you are confronted by the person you really are, the *you* you have become, the one who exists in the world, the one that breathes and shits and screams. And you realize: the people we think we are may never have existed. You were an idea, steam or smoke or wax. You destroyed the man you remember and in his place is you. You have become a stranger to yourself. You have become an impostor in your own skin. The man—*this* man—a living thing of blood and bone. Here he is. I am him but he is not me. I will never be the same because there is no future, there is no past. Some men are only here and now and that's all they will ever be." The yogi's words stuck in Billy Ray like arrows. They became a mantra of supreme importance. He carried them with him like a precious compass until one day he forgot.

He splashed cold water on the face in the mirror, watched the water drip. He breathed deep. *Goddamnit,* he thought. *I need some fucking coke.*

He left the bathroom to find the hall quiet, the audience seated and listening as a frail woman onstage spoke in a breathless whisper, the words coming in weak gasps, sounding hollowed out. Her clothes hung off her shrunken frame like rags from a leper. Clutching the podium with her thin fingers, bent and emaciated and completely bald, the skin of her head paled to translucence, she looked like a mantis, Jovian, a mistake of science escaped from a bunker. Above all else, she looked anything but funny.

"Over two thousand new cases of breast cancer are diagnosed every month . . ."

"What the fuck is this?" said Billy Ray, turning the heads of nearby tables. He scanned the room for Dan Guntley and located him at the bar.

". . . on the day they found my cancer, I was getting ready to welcome my first granddaughter into the world. I still remember how my son cried when I told him . . ."

"No way," he grumbled, quickstepping to Guntley. "Dan, hey, Dan," he said to the fire-hydrant-shaped man. "I thought I was on after the duck?"

Dan Guntley nodded as he tipped up a silver flask. Whatever was inside made his face lemon. "Yessir, that was the original plan, but then Sheila asked if she could say a few words about her charity, so I told her why not? She won't be on long."

Billy Ray looked at Sheila. Barely visible behind the podium, her wrists the same circumference as the microphone stand and the tiny bones of her skull visible under the harsh white light, she looked like she was stuffed with straw, like a scarecrow, neither dead or alive.

". . . but at this point, the doctors say that every day I live is a medical miracle . . ."

"Is that alright?" Guntley said, shaking the flask. "Cutty?"

Billy Ray tipped back the whiskey, filling his throat with iced heat. Dave slid another Coors his way. "Well, you know," he said. "I guess she's not the worst opener I ever had. I did a weekend with Gallagher once . . ."

". . . which is why I set up this charity: I wasn't going to let terminal cancer stop me from riding my horse, and neither should anyone else . . ."

"She's almost done," Dan Guntley said.

"I'll say," said Dave, and the three men laughed.

". . . cancer may have won the war, but if I have to die, I'm going down on my horse."

Billy Ray winced. "There's a better way to say that." He took another sip off the flask.

Sheila left the stage with the aid of her husband. Before he led her off, he stepped to the microphone to say that his wife was his hero and that he loved her and the room welled then burst with the compulsory applause due to a man and his dying wife.

The emcee came to the podium wiping tears off his cheeks. "Brave words from a brave woman. We're gonna miss you, baby. We're all gonna miss you very much." He struggled to compose himself as the crowd dabbed its eyes. "May God bless you, Sheila. Tell him to take mercy on us. We're giving him an angel." He honked his nose loudly into a red bandana and wiped his eyes. "Alright, alright. Enough bawling, y'all. Who's ready to laugh?"

No one, thought Billy Ray. No group of people had ever been less prepared to laugh in the history of laughter, organized or otherwise. Drowning a puppy would have been a better opener. Once, in the Florida Keys, he had worked with a Catskill fossil on a string of awful shows. Whenever one of his jokes didn't hit, the fossil would say, "Oy vey! The food lines at Dachau were warmer than this!" Billy Ray chuckled. Oy vey: fuck my ass. It was so unfunny he couldn't help but laugh.

As the emcee read his introduction, he stood by the side of the stage awaiting the sound of his name, focusing on afterward, doing the math in his head of how much cocaine he could buy, happy to know none of this mattered and that it would soon be over: in an hour he would be no one again.

"We feed him on watermelon all day until he can't help but shit his self."

Billy Ray sat at the long bar, afterward, listening to Mallard Fillmore's owner explain the finer points of plop-o as bowlegged veterans broke down tables and folded up chairs. The crowd vacated. Both Billy Ray and the man were waiting to get paid.

"We sell raffle tickets and guarantee a hunnerd-dollar prize, but we always sell more than one hunnerd tickets and we sell them for five apiece so there's always plenty of cream to scrape, and that's all tax free on top of the guarantee."

The man breathed in heavy wet rattles: sharp and raspy inhales, croaking exhalations. His face was porcine and round, his hair brushcut short into a precise gray diamond. The breasts draped over his massive gut jiggled whenever he laughed or coughed on the Pall Malls he burned. He smoked them down until they singed his fingers and through his fat lips, he sipped red wine mixed with Pepsi over ice through a straw. Calle ocho, he called it. "They let kids drink it in Spain." He said his name was Clarence, Clarence Wade—as if Billy Ray gave a hot shit—but everyone calls him Junior.

"Plop-o's the easiest money I ever made. And I know easy money." Clarence/Junior rolled his fat cheek up in a wink and grinned, revealing a mouth of purple stained teeth, each of them dead or dying. "Only thing better than easy money is easy women."

Billy Ray wondered from what movie the fat man stole this line. Maybe an old comic book. Billy Ray believed firmly that, beyond the age of thirteen, there are no original ideas. People talk like the things they see. After a certain age, nothing is new besides death. Billy Ray, hungry for more of the cocaine the fat man shared with him after he got offstage, bit his tongue and decided to fit in. "Any woman is easy if you have enough money," he said. The fat man bobbed with agreeable laughter.

"Shit. I'll drink to that." Clarence/Junior emptied his tumbler of cabernet and cola. His lips were the color of hematoma.

Like most Americans, Clarence/Junior enjoyed talking and disliked listening. The conversation was gapless. He talked fast, desperately unspooling his yarn, leaving himself nothing to weave. This was common: Americans thought they had a right to be heard. They viewed themselves important and integral and interesting, but after talking to as many of them as he had, Billy Ray knew the opposite to be true. In his experience, most people had on average one good anecdote and one good joke. That's it: two things to say and they repeated them whenever they had a pair of fresh ears. Oftentimes the anecdote wasn't even their own. Three hundred million people with six hundred million lines of dialogue, and Billy Ray Schafer had heard most the jokes. It was a shame. If only they knew what it was that made them unique. Then Billy Ray would never be bored.

Billy Ray had many failings, but he used his ears better than most. He learned to hear what was said at an early age: to make his father repeat himself was cause for a beating. He didn't mind listening because he didn't like talking all that much. At his core, he was just one more person with nothing to say.

Attention is manipulative; it made men trust him, seeing in the undisturbed pools of his silence a reflection of themselves. Women adored him for it: he inhaled their words like perfume and they rewarded his regard with their bodies—listening as foreplay, heed for head. He knew to be heard is an intimate act—to penetrate, to receive. Commanding a person's attention is to temporarily own their reality, thus sociopaths and narcissists coveted his company: he did very well at Hollywood parties. Before he was no longer welcome at such events, he always left with a pocketful of business cards.

Clarence/Junior snorted his sinuses clear, swallowed loudly and lit another cigarette. Billy Ray found the fat man repugnant. He wondered how he was still alive. Initially he was only interested in his drugs, but after talking with him, hearing the contentment in the pig-man's voice and the lack of spite in his words, Billy Ray was curious how much cash Clarence/Junior pulled in with his rolling waterfowl shit fiasco. The number must have been higher than Billy Ray's quotient—the question was by how much? Men are measured by their portion of the gate. Clarence/Junior was a shark-eyed carny with a diarrhetic duck and Billy Ray was the only white man to ever receive a standing ovation at the Apollo: he needed to know how far he'd fallen. Only then would he know exactly how small to feel.

"You sell a lot of merch tonight?" inquired Clarence/Junior. *Fucking carny*, thought Billy Ray. Carnies lived to talk merch. The fleecing was worth more than the money. The only difference between a carny and a gypsy is superstition and scarves. Billy Ray was not a carny. He took no pride in the amount of product he moved: selling merchandise postshow was a concession of his integrity (once in a moment of rare honesty, Billy Ray had confessed to his wife, "I'm not an artist. I'm just a traveling T-shirt salesman that dabbles in spoken word"). The duck man was only setting himself up to brag: they had shared a merch table in the back of the room and Billy Ray had done fine, no records broken—seven CDs, five or so shirts—but his sales were meager compared to Clarence/Junior's. The fat man sold hats and T-shirts emblazoned with a cartoon duck, its face puckered up and straining as it squats over the phrase THIS DUCK S*!@S MONEY and pictures of Mallard Fillmore "signed" by a webbed footprint stamped onto each glossy 8 x 10. He charged twenty dollars for one photo or three for forty. At one point during the frenzy, Clarence/Junior turned to ask Billy Ray for change for a hundred. As Billy Ray counted him out five twenties, the fat man said—without irony—"You gotta love showbiz," and winked his slow, dough-rising wink. It was at that moment that Billy Ray decided he hated him.

If it weren't for the cocaine they would have had nothing to talk about.

Billy Ray tried to strike up a conversation with the aged young metalheads in the back of the room, but they didn't bite when he mentioned an afterparty, most likely, Billy Ray decided, because they preferred downers—the black pupils in their blown-glass eyes were barely visible through the slits of their nodding eyelids—or maybe, Billy Ray considered, they didn't want to party with a fifty-two-year-old drifter who said things like "My friend Andrew Jackson is looking for some action." Whichever it was, the youths colded him, and now Clarence/Junior was his only option if he wanted to hurt less.

"I did alright for a bunch of farmers," Billy Ray said, tabulating numbers in his head. He sold around $150 worth of merchandise. "These people were wound so tight, they shit corkscrews. I was glad to get anything off them."

"I moved about six hunnerd," Clarence/Junior croaked.

You vulgar carny bastard, thought Billy Ray, his hand tightening reflexively around his Coors. He wanted to break the bottle and cut out the fat man's tongue and shove it up his ass, learn him some couth. Instead he said: "What's the duck's cut?"

The fat man smiled: "I just put it on his bill."

"Hilarious," Billy Ray said. He finished his beer and reached behind the bar for another.

From outside came Dan Guntley bringing the cold behind. "Gentlemen," he said, approaching with two envelopes in his hand, his gait rigid and rehearsed and ex-military. "I apologize for the wait."

Billy Ray stood and leaned against the bar next to Clarence/Junior. He knew the fat man would verify the amount on his check. Carnies always count the money, the tactless savages. Sure enough, he tore into his envelope as soon as Dan Guntley delivered it, his short arms working on the shelf of his belly like an otter prying a clam: $300—fifty more than Billy Ray's two and a half. Within him, the difference ignited a rage far beyond jealousy, an ignoble scarlet fury bordering on homicidal. The inequity demanded retribution: he envisioned a fantasy in which he drove to Los Angeles, killed his manager and then himself. At the very least this necessitated a long, serious conversation. He was better than this, even now, even him.

Dan Guntley shook their hands and told them they were locking up the building in twenty minutes. He thanked them and they thanked him and as soon as he turned his back, Billy Ray leaned over the bar and pulled a six-pack from the cooler. Clarence/Junior tapped his nose with his index finger: "One more for the road?"

Billy Ray stood up. "Is the pope a pedophile?"

Freshly cleaned, the bathroom was immaculate. It burned with harsh fluorescence. White light singing to white tile. The walls of the stalls were devoid of graffiti. The toilet sparkled with the luster of wedding china. It reminded Billy Ray of an emergency room or a rest stop: somewhere bad things transpire outside the purview of darkness. The sterility made Billy Ray anxious on top of his indignity. The pronounced cleanliness reinforced the depravity of their actions.

They entered separate cubicles. The fat man snorted twice, sounding like an animal at a trough. "Incoming," the man said, his pudgy hand reaching a paper parcel of cocaine over the top of the stall. Billy

Ray opened it and dolloped a lump onto the knuckle of his thumb and shoved it up his nose, filling his head with warm euphoria. That's better. He took another blast, too much, gagged, choking on the drip and retching like a house cat.

Clarence/Junior laughed. "I told you it was good."

Billy Ray worked Key West, Houston, El Paso. He knew great blow: he'd been unlucky that way. Quality coke smelled like permanent markers and flaked like fish scales and provided enough ego to rip God from the sky; it wasn't gray and it didn't crumble or taste like licked battery. The fat man's cocaine was not good cocaine but there was a lot of it, and that was good enough.

Clarence/Junior snorted loudly and spat a hefty wad into his toilet. "Help yourself to that. I think I'll take a shit."

Of course you will, thought Billy Ray. *Of course you fucking will.* Billy Ray heard an unclasping then Clarence/Junior's coveralls landing in a pile at his feet. The porcelain creaked beneath the fat man as he sat. He grunted, grunted again, then there was a thick, wet sound, like a bowl of chili spilled into a bathtub. Billy Ray threw up in his mouth. Bent in half, his face hovering inches from the toilet seat, Billy Ray wondered if he had ever detested another living soul as much as he despised the fat man in this moment.

"Oh boy," the carnie giggled. "I shouldn't have had all that clam chowder."

No, no he hadn't. This was the capacity of his abhorrence. He had to get out of here.

Eureka.

Fleeting clarity. He remembered where he was, who he was. He pondered for a moment. No. Go. Fuck it. Of course. He smiled sincerely for the first time all day.

Billy Ray unlatched the stall. "Hey, Clarence. I'm gonna meet you outside."

"What's a matter? You don't want to stay for the fireworks?"

"Sounds like the duck could be out of a job."

"Yeah, this might take a while."

I hope you die like Elvis.

After folding the paper carefully, he tucked the fat man's bundle into his breast pocket and hurried out of the bathroom. The building was cavernous now, empty besides two men in the far corner folding a flag with undue ceremony. Careful not to disturb them, Billy Ray gathered his belongings, tucked the six-pack under his arm and heel-toed into the night.

In the parking lot only a few cars remained, among them his Corolla and Clarence/Junior's truck, a lifted and chromed monstrosity glistening with ostentation in the weak gray moonlight. In the flatbed, Mallard Fillmore sat patiently in his cage, its breath clouding in the thin air, its eyes glowing like the truck's hubcaps, vivid green and oddly human.

Oh, duck, he thought. He knew the next move.

Billy Ray moved quickly. He loaded his gear into the car, ears scanning the stark night for the sound of footsteps. At any moment he expected the fat man to appear huffing and slobbering, shambling like a creature through the darkness and destroying the placidity. The duck cage was welded onto the back of the truck but the door was unlocked. Billy Ray lifted the wire latch and the cage came open. He pounded his fist on the roof of the cage and Mallard Fillmore fluttered off the flatbed to the dirt below. Billy Ray expected the bird to fly away, but instead, a stranger to autonomy, it waddled around the side of the truck and sat down beside the tire. Billy Ray straightened up as tall as possible and clapped his hands over his head and the duck jumped and Billy Ray ushered the disoriented bird into the underbrush toward the valley and farther the river. "Go on, get. Shoo, shoo. You're free, stupid. Time served." The duck looked back at him, unaware of the gift it was receiving, and Billy Ray barked. "Go on now," he chided. "You don't have to do this anymore." The duck took a few more steps before stopping to peck at an anthill. Billy Ray kicked a plume of sand and the duck scattered. "Shoo, goddamnit. Get to getting. Go be a duck again." The stars bearing witness, Billy Ray herded the duck deeper into the country, a big man chasing a waterfowl through the desert, stomping and swearing, growing angry at what he perceived to be a lack of gratitude, urging it forward until, at the ridge, the duck spread wing and drifted into the black expanse and Billy Ray watched it glide into the dark canyon until it disappeared from his vision and became another piece of the sky.

Going gone with the radio on, Billy Ray was more than a mile down the road devouring the asphalt moonlight at eighty miles an hour before the fat man even flushed the toilet.

He passed the night in his motel room naked, smoking cigarettes and waiting for the sun to find the courage to rise.

Between lines, he chewed his fingernails until they bled. His mouth was dry. Cocaine mixed with solitude was a whole different drug: there was no one to talk at, no one to bounce off of. With nothing exterior to absorb his energy, he went inside of himself, too deep, spelunking the caves without light where it was easy to get lost. Guided only by the ember of a perpetual cigarette, he followed his nose past the concept of Self and fell plunging into the deepest recesses of his identity, the unmapped and lawless fringe, the home of absolute truth: avast, here be monsters. The bottom was shallow.

His thoughts—disparate, erratic, condemning—buzzed with the significance of epiphany. Extremes became mirrors: in the reflection, opposites dissolved. Two ideas alternated in his head: "you cannot because you *can* no longer" and "enough is only enough when there isn't any more." Revelations, credos, silent prayers. He wished he had stolen more beer.

Somewhere around four he smoked his last Winston, killed the lights and listened without blinking to the walloping of his heart. His biggest fear was to hear it stop. He knew he would most likely die in a motel room just like this one in a town whose name he forgot, solitary and companionless and far away from anyone that might care. In the end all he would amount to was a task for housekeeping, remembered by the sheets he ruined, by a mattress thrown away. As his body blued, the maid would call the manager and the manager would call the police and someone would be summoned to collect him—his sister, his sons, maybe his ex-wife—whichever unlucky person answered the phone first—and they would be forced to come to whatever nameless place finally killed him and decide what to do with his bones. To whoever drew the shortest straw, his death would be one last inconvenience.

Or maybe not. There were other ways. He could get lucky like Buddy Holly and die in an aerial disaster or honor the statistics and go out on the highway in a tangle of bent steel. Best case scenario he'd pop an aneurysm on stage: *Thank you, Reality. That's my time . . .* At least then he would make the papers.

The room was cold. His skin felt like paper: thin, insufficient. He sat up, leaned over the nightstand and cleared a line with each nostril. "There it is," he said, and smiled. His teeth felt like dentures. The cocaine swung him to his poles. Up and down were the same direction. At the heights of his delusion, he romanticized his lifestyle, fancying himself a scion of a dying breed of restless ones, a hobo, a minstrel, an American Bedouin, an itinerant anthropologist collecting the lost histories of the forgotten. The miles he traveled, the truths he acquired, the people—he served the people. *I am a missionary. I go when others stop.* Billy Ray Schafer was not a smart man, but after years of frontline exposure, he understood people on a preternatural level: their secrets, the intricacies of their reasoning—he knew the *whys* to their *whats*. And despite his baseline loathing, he admired their toughness in the face of futility. They were indelible, as was their mercy: through them he experienced himself.

"Mamas," he sang, lighting his last cigarette, "don't let your babies grow up to be cowboys."

His logic, like the cocaine in his blood, was circuitous and racing: comedians are brave; bravery is noble; nobility is akin to heroism; comedians are heroes. Occasionally, when the chemicals were right, he was able to take pride in these elaborate equations. But here and

now—in this room, in this light—he saw this was another of his ma-
nipulations, yet more smoke rising from the ashes of his career. Heroes
don't stay in off-ramp motels. This was no Valhalla. If he was brave, he
would fit his brain for a bullet, but he was not brave, he was a mirage, a
pillar of salt frozen and forever looking back. The nineties were over.
Leno was canceled. Carson was dead. Comics like him were a vestigial
tail the industry had failed to sever. Road dog, hack—he knew what he
was and he didn't want to be alone with himself. He shut his eyes:
thump thump, thump thump. Soon the darkness was too much.

He turned on the lamp and opened the drawers in the nightstand
until he found the Bible. Ripping a blank page from the back of the
book, he tore a rectangle from the thin sheet and folded it in half. The
ashtray was laden with spent butts, the longer ones of which he emptied of their last strands of burnt tobacco until he had enough. He arranged the remnants along the crease in the rectangle and dusted the
tobacco with a flurry of cocaine. With a seasoned twist of his thick
fingers, he brought the paper to his tongue and licked it shut. Fully
nude, Billy Ray sat on the edge of the bed and lit the coolie. The resin-
ated tobacco was foul to breathe and the burnt cocaine smelled like
aspirin tastes, but the effect was immediate and exquisite. The room
became brighter and the details of the varying motifs pronounced
themselves. He could count the petals of the flowers on the dull, yellow
wallpaper and he found infinitely interesting and complex designs in
the stucco ceiling. It all made sense: symbols are meaningless, borders
are lines, land is the opposite of water and water is the opposite of air.
It went on like this, the room filling with crude freebase as the ashes
burnt the sheets; a man on the cusp of it all.

When the cigarette was gone he was meteoric and listless and dripping with sweat despite the heavily conditioned air. A car drove past his
window; slivers of headlight pierced the blinds. Two worlds: inside and
out. This is mine and that is theirs: as long as I have money, they don't
have me—this was one of the things he knew.

He retrieved his nest egg from his suitcase and arranged the bills by denomination on the bedspread. $3,743. The total was comforting: it was nice to know exactly how much he was worth.

He went to the sink and brushed his teeth until his gums were raw and bleeding. He spat in the sink and splashed water on his face and blotted dry with a towel. Catching himself in the mirror, he marveled at his nude entirety. He slapped at his chest and his shoulders: the meat sounded different. He turned sideways and inspected his barreled profile, leaning his head back until his chin undoubled and sucking in his gut.

"Look at you. Just look at you."

There was still a lot of him, but what was once hard had gone soft. He frowned: it reminded him of the armadillo.

In prison, one day on the yard, he'd joined a group of inmates gathered near the razor-wire crowned fence. He assumed they'd found a piece of contraband tossed over from the outside world or, God willing, a hole in the chain-link fence, but when he reached the front of the herd, what he saw was new and disgusting and dead. At first he assumed the creature was a mutant pig born of incestuous congress or an abominable hybrid, but Tall Terry, who claimed, before the meth really got ahold of him, to have cleaned cages at the zoo in Branson and was therefore attributed an air of expertise in all matters of biology, explained to the crowd that this four-legged abomination was nothing more than an armadillo picked clean of its shell by birds. All the inmates nodded and agreed, searching the body for a cause of death until someone kicked the carcass and a bloom of plump maggots rose from its skin. At this, the crowd cheered, calling attention from the guards who came and broke up their viewing and returned them to their monotony. The armadillo dominated conversation for the coming weeks. A few inmates memorialized the creature—they began to refer to it as Shelly—with tattoos, but the design—a muscle-bound and snarling pig-looking thing wrapped in a husk of metallic armor and puffing steam from its nostrils—failed to remember Shelly accurately. Looking at himself in the mirror above the sink, Billy Ray remembered what they'd actually seen near the fence: a weak and indefensible and hairy pink beast robbed of its hardness and filled up with bugs.

He shadowboxed his reflection until they were both gasping and wet. Breathing heavy, he collapsed on the bed and took long pulls from a two liter of Dr Pepper. The soda was thick in his throat. He checked the bottle of vodka on the nightstand but it was still empty, so he counted his money once more, meditative, covetous, stacking the cash into thousand dollar towers before returning it to the secret pocket inside of his suitcase. When that was finished, he laid back and touched himself, pulling without finesse or lubrication, not due to arousal but compelled by compulsion: this was what came next. The procedure was mechanical, gratuitous, asexual. He thought about nothing, tried to think about nothing, tried not to think about Olivia, who had been his wife. He tried to think about the girl from last night but in his memory she had no face. She was just a body, but so was he. They were ghosts last night and that was fine. It worked. He wiped the results on the bedspread.

After, unsatiated, he turned out every conceivable pocket for a cigarette. When the search came up empty, he reached for the ashtray and flipped through the Bible for another blank page.

WEDNESDAY

HE AWOKE AT NEAR NOON, HIS FACE HATCHED BY THE SUNLIGHT clawing through the slats in the cheap plastic blinds. Bars of light segmented the darkness. The room looked like a cage built for an angel.

The pillowcase was soaked, the sheets damp. He sat up and bile filled his throat. His eyes were poached eggs. His teeth hurt and his mouth was as dry as if he'd sucked on a vacuum. "Fuck," he said, greeting the day.

He stumbled to the sink and folded his body to the faucet and drank tap water in gulping slurps. He stood up bracing himself on the basin, loosed a burp, the battery taste of stomach acid registering on the back of his tongue. He repeated himself: "Fuck. Fuck." Mornings hurt: he was used to this.

The shower knobs were sticky. He twisted the knob marked *H* to its limit and stood in the blistering water until his skin went numb. The soap smelled like candles. It refused to lather. He pissed in the stream, bright yellow, almost orange, but no blood. That was good. He had had a few scares.

He dressed, packed and entered the fresh afternoon.

The sky was flat, a dull turquoise patched with thin clouds. They drifted like smears on a lens. On his way to the staircase, he passed a woman pushing a cart of cleaning supplies. "Morning," he said. She kept pushing.

There was a liquor store in the strip mall across the street. He loaded his bags in the car and crossed the parking lot. He was slaked with sweat when he entered the store. The impurities stung his eyes.

He bought a pint of vodka and two packs of cigarettes and asked the clerk for directions to the nearest McDonald's. He preferred the coffee at McDonald's because it tasted the same everywhere, a rare point of consistency in his day. Constants were a luxury in his life.

He drank coffee splashed with vodka and smoked cigarettes on a picnic table in a small park across the street from the *Trinidad Chronicle* building, killing time until one-thirty Mountain, twelve-thirty Pacific, the time when Red Haberstadt, his longtime manager and onetime friend, took lunch and started drinking for the day.

He never called Red's cellphone. It was only for emergencies: cancelations, missed flights, car accidents. Billy Ray wasn't sure but making less money than a shitting duck felt like an emergency.

He hated cellphones. They created accountability. They allowed him to be located. Over the years of mercenary travel, Billy Ray had grown accustomed to riding rogue. He preferred to be out of pocket. He called home when he needed to, otherwise he was a rumor. Now he never called home because there was no home to call.

Like most of his life's complexities, the phone was his wife's decision. When cellular phones first came out, her brother had worked for US West, and he got them a deal. "Two hundred dollars isn't much to pay for peace of mind," he'd say from behind his desk made of handsome redwood. His name was Tucker and he grinned like a date rapist. Billy Ray's wife did all the talking while Billy Ray rubbed the rich wood's smooth grain and calculated his brother-in-law's commission.

His wife was beaming when they left her brother's office.

"Now we can talk whenever we want," she'd said.

Billy Ray said nothing.

That was fifteen years ago.

A subtle breeze tickled the park in which he sat, animating the grass and the bushes and the limbs of the trees. The breeze felt good on his hangover; he took off his shirt and let the wind at his body, soaking in the radiance of the high, white sun. Billy Ray flipped open the phone and turned it on. He always expected it to be heavier; it held so much. He had no idea how it worked. He understood cellular phones as well as he understood his wife's need to own one. The coffee had gone bitter. He lit another smoke.

When the phone was booted up he pulled out his wallet and located Red's card and thumbed the number labeled CELL onto the small gray screen. The only numbers saved into the phone's memory were his wife's and the girl from Madison, Wisconsin who looked like his wife on the day that they'd met. They each had to enter their numbers themselves. He didn't know how to save them.

Before he pressed the send button, he outlined his position one last time: under the counsel and guidance of Red Haberstadt, his earnings had atrophied, resulting in the unrecognizable ramshackle embarrassment he called a career. The degradations have been extensive and disgusting: shows in midwestern sports bars during Monday night football where the ambushed locals want to skin you because you're the reason they turned off the TVs; moribund nooners in nursing homes—"they're called retirement communities now"—for crowds of abandoned geriatrics no longer physically capable of laughter. The clubs he worked were shitholes. They pushed chicken tenders and buckets of beer, filled their calendars with hypnotists and ventriloquists and "triple X-rated" magicians; C-rooms or worse, regional portals to hell—the Laff Stop in Spokane, Crackers in Indianapolis, the Jacksonville Funny Bone, graveyards with a two-item minimum. He couldn't keep screaming if no one would hear it. The stakes were too low for all the anguish involved.

Part of it was his fault for refusing fossilization. It would have been easy to lay up, set his watch for forty-five minutes, put his head down and wait for the alarm, to cash in on nostalgia, to start all of his premises with "Remember when?" and "Back in my day" but Billy Ray wasn't smart like that and he had too much skin in the game. He wasn't some petrified artifact rolling up the sleeves on his blazer: whether it was spite or pride, he still gave a shit. And unlike the hacks he crossed paths with on the Road—their notebooks empty, their acts gone ossified and lifeless, dragging their prop cases behind them like a dog's ass across carpet—Billy Ray was still good at the job. His act was still breathing, alive—more alive than him. He remained undeniably funny and his name retained meaning among a certain demographic, albeit a small one without much loyalty or expendable income. There was sweat and heartbeats in what he did and occasionally, among the easy local references and the hoary crowd work, flashes of the old Billy Ray shone through, faint sparks of brilliance, like a light in the distance seen through darkness and fog. He could still harness the moment. When he was present and realized, there were few who could improvise on his level or at his speed since Robin Williams quit cocaine. He knew how to seize The Now, how to occupy the membrane that divides Then from When. The absurd acuity of his mental machinations gave birth to moments of truly vital comedy. He was the quintessential live act: he had to be seen to be believed, like warfare or birth. When he was young he could take off on a premise running only to catch up to his own flight of imagination sixty minutes later, his clothes soaked and the air itself crackling with the urgency of what he'd done. Those days were gone, but even drunk and coked and spun and pilled, he still killed harder than the reductive drivel being peddled in theaters and arenas by the skeletons he envied. Despite his failures with sobriety, monogamy, business and fatherhood, he was still funny, and funny is the hardest thing to be.

He wrote himself a note last night. At the peak of his frenzy, he'd purged a few paragraphs, staining the hotel stationery while he smoked reclaimed tobacco wrapped in Gideon paper. Most of it was unintelligible gibberish, the disjointed mess a result of his brain moving faster than his hand. His thoughts skipped like rocks across water.

One line—a joke maybe?—said *2 many baskets/not enough eggs—2 bad you cant eat baskets.* Another demanded *hand sandals???,* the question marks writ large, underlined, imploring, then later *hand sandals = handals*. There were columns of numbers with their sums totaled beneath the banner *BLOOD MONEY*. Sketches of cowboys and crude chinamen wore similar hats.

On a separate page, in a slower, more deliberate script, he'd penned a letter to his once wife.

Early in their courtship, he had made a habit of sending her postcards, treacle-dripping gestures of long-distance longing. The dispatches were earnest and embarrassing and fat with forced, Beat-aping poetics, but Olivia liked them, and for years, he sent her one every weekend, then most weekends, then when he remembered, then he forgot. He hadn't written to her in a long time.

Dearest sweetest truest Olivia

Why can I only talk to you through dead trees? Why cant I call to you on the stars or have my voice carried express by big breasted birds? Then they could sing it to you and it would always be good news. Oh Liv, there isnt enough beer. I dont know what I got myself into. Im buried but I learned to breathe the dirt. I know where you are and I still cant find you. Im the one who needs the help this time, but thats an old song, I want to forget the words. Its all a big tootsie pop—Ive never made it without biting. Oh Liv, Liv, Lively Liv, Ive breathed too much dirt. I think Im allergic to air. Remember when we used to scream out the moonroof? Remember when our bed was too small? I remember. I want to get healthy and move to Vermont. We could grow cheese. We could ice skate all year. Where did it all fall down, Baby? When did we give it all away? I went to bed one time and I woke up alone . . . I know we had it once—I went to war for it. I took a bite from the sky. I did whatever they asked. They couldnt get enough of me and Red told me 'they can kill you but they cant eat you'. Well they ate me. They boiled my

*bones for soup. Remember my first Letterman? We watched it
from the Tropicana. They comped the room and I ate shrimp
and you had crab and you were so proud and I was so proud to
have made you so proud. Where did that guy go—the guy that
got free crab? Im too alive to be this dead, Baby, but isnt that
what all the tombstones say? Anyways gotta go. I think I hear
them towing my house.*

*With love—seriously folks
The One Known As*

*PS: "There's worse things than being broke but I can't afford to
find out." Please send money for the stamp.*

He read it twice, crumpled the paper, stuffed the ball inside of his
empty coffee cup and crushed the cup between his knees. There was a
word for what this was but he couldn't think of it. He tried to remember but the term escaped him, just out of grasp on the bleeding tip of
his tongue. The word was eulogy: the person he wrote that to no longer
existed—but neither did the person who wrote it. He stubbed his cigarette out on the table, stood up, sat back down. Never mind. There were
other things to think about, things he could fix. He opened his jokebook and jotted down *HANDALS. Perfect,* he thought, *now I can write
off the room.*

He checked his watch: lunchtime in Hollywood.

Red would be made to answer.

He would not answer to Red.

He took a snort of warm vodka, pressed his knuckles into his thigh
until they popped and slapped himself on the cheek.

Ready.

Set.

"Alright." The phone was small in his hand; it looked like a toy, looked like pretend. He pressed the green button with his thumb and put the receiver to his ear. "You aren't a pussy. Don't you go soft."

Without ringing, the call went straight to voicemail.

"Motherfuckingshit."

He hung up the phone and redialed the number and again the message repeated: "You have reached Red. You know what I said: 'If you're calling this number, you better be dead.'"

He slapped the phone shut and got to his feet. Across the park, in the shadow of a pagoda, three children kicked a blue rubber ball, playing monkey-in-the-middle with a fourth. The monkey didn't look like he was having fun. Billy Ray put his shirt back on, suddenly cold now that the sun had gone behind the clouds. "I'll be goddamned," he said and that was precisely how he felt.

Zadies was the first bar Billy Ray found when he got off the highway. Sans the few lifers hunched over their Old Styles, it was empty when he arrived.

The bartender was a shriveled black man with a frying-pan face, his spine contorted into a shape like a prawn. When Billy Ray asked him for a greyhound, the man said he only made cocktails on ladies' night. So Billy Ray, unable to imagine a woman setting foot in this dank chamber, requested a glass of vodka and a glass of grapefruit juice, making sure to flash his bankroll. Grunting, the man complied, and Billy Ray tipped well for the opportunity to mix his own drink.

The drive north to Pueblo on I-25 had been a winding hour-long descent. Mountains of red rock gave way to forests and pastures then dead drags of desiccated nothing and the gas station ghost towns of Ludlow, the site of the massacre, and Colorado City, the site of the golf course, until from the ruin appeared the first traces of Pueblo, an industrial town ringed by single story ranch-style homes arranged in polite suburban neighborhoods built within driving distance from the aged gray mills that forged the steel on which the city survived. The men who worked the mills were hard and sawed-off. On their breaks from the furnaces they drank. At four, they poured in—pipefitters and boilermakers and machinists and welders, scorched men with bulging forearms and thick red hands—and the bartender jumped to work, frantic, setting them up with shots of brown liquor and mugs of headless beer so cold steam rose when the men touched the glass. They dropped the shots in the mugs and poured the concoction into the holes in their chapped faces, paying in cash and chain-smoking and filling the jukebox with Megadeth and Thin Lizzy and Judas Priest. They walked stiffly and sat their battered bodies down slow. No one played darts or shot pool.

Billy Ray nursed his greyhound in a booth next to the bathroom while the men drank off the residue of hours of heat and labor, some ducking into the bathroom in small packs only to return vibrating and pie-eyed, rubbing their noses and slapping each other on the back, their faces more pliable, their posture less dejected. Billy Ray's toe started tapping. Over years of hardcore chemical exploitation he developed an extrasensory awareness for deviance. Not only did he know when the game was afoot, he could tell you who was playing and by exactly what rules.

With his learned eye, Billy Ray studied a man at the bar who shook many hands. The man wore a khaki fishing vest and a red Kansas City Chiefs ballcap that shaded his face blank. His cargo shorts revealed two legs—one made of aluminum, the other skin and bone and muscle. The man was popular among the crowd. Steelworkers approached him and he greeted them with an extended handshake, then he put his hand in one of two pockets on his vest and followed up with another handshake. The man was smooth, working with a magician's efficiency. He kept the interactions short. Everyone left with a smile.

Billy Ray opened his wallet and moved forty dollars to his front pocket. Then, emptying his drink, he stood up from the sunken booth and walked in a metered pace to the bar and stood beside the man.

Casual, unassuming—he came to dance, but not to lead—Billy Ray laid his hands flat on the bar and tried to appear cool. The man was looking away from him, watching sports highlights on a silent TV above the bar. On the TV, a man in a blue uniform dodged men in white uniforms as he carried a football from one end of the field to the other. Upon his arrival in the far endzone, his teammates swarmed him in celebration. The closed caption read END TO END FOR THE KID FROM SOUTH BEND AS THE BILLS STEAL A NAIL-BITER FROM NEW ENGLAND.

The man slapped the bar: "Fucking Buffalo."

"You're telling me," Billy Ray agreed. "I took a bath on that one."

"Me too," the man said to the screen. "But that's what I get for betting on the fucking Snake-triots." The man turned from the TV and when Billy Ray saw his face—or lack thereof—he caught himself before he audibly grimaced. Sausage was the first thing that came to mind, red licorice was the second: the man had been melted. The front of his head was more scoured than burnt, the ears just holes, the skin as tight and red as pepperoni, the same color as his lips; the lack of delineation gave his mouth the appearance of a puncture wound slitted in above his chiseled chin. His eyes, black and eyebrowless and lasciviously wet, bulged out of his skull, his cheekbones jutted like suitcase handles. He looked like unfinished taxidermy. "Luckily the Chiefs came through," the man said, tipping his hat.

Billy Ray collected himself, fighting the urge to look away. "Arrow-arrowhead," he stammered. "Now that's a hell of a stadium."

"If you haven't seen a football game at Arrowhead, you haven't seen a football game."

"It gets loud. Those fans are wild."

"Pound the drum, here we come," said the man through the crack in his face.

"It's like a bomb went off." Billy Ray leaned on the bar, angling for the bartender's attention. The deep brown wood was cool and polished, buffed grainless by countless forearms, the acacia or burnished oak scrimshawed with epitaphs and elegies. A carving near Billy Ray's elbow read FUTILE AND FUCKED. Another under his wrist read TWIGS SEAT and next to it, inscribed in a different hand, RIP TWIG. Billy Ray signaled to the bartender, but the bartender was busy on the other end of the room. Out of options, Billy Ray faced the man and, assuming it to be a rare kindness, locked his eyes and stared him full in the face.

"Who's your team?" asked the man.

"The Donkeys."

"Well," the man sighed. "As long as it's not the Raiders."

"Fuck the Raiders."

"Amen."

"You from KC?"

"Used to be."

"I was out there a few months ago."

"I ain't been back in a while."

"They cleaned it up."

"That's what I hear."

"It was nice. I was working downtown, near the water."

"Pipeline?"

"Actually," he said, affecting a practiced nonchalance, "I'm a comedian."

"I'll be dipped," the man decreed. "I've never met a comedian before."

Billy Ray had set this trap many times and it rarely failed, at least not with laymen: based on his experience, the only people who don't want to talk to comedians are beautiful women in New York and Los Angeles and higher-ups in showbiz. Outside of big cities, meeting a comedian was the equivalent of meeting an astronaut or a lion tamer; the novelty guaranteed at least three minutes of intent conversation, three minutes of intrigue, and three minutes was more than enough time for a man like Billy Ray.

The bartender came and Billy Ray ordered a Coors, wary of appearing high-maintenance in front of the melted man. He paid for the beer and raised the mug and tipped it toward the man: "Fuck the Raiders."

"Fuck the Raiders."

The beer was too cold to taste. When he drank, the man's Adam's apple bobbed libidinously: the pump of the abraded pink flesh reminded Billy Ray of a dog's penis on its way to hard. "Where were you playing in KC? Stanford's?"

"That's right."

"I seen a couple shows there."

"Anyone good?"

The man adjusted his hat. "There was this one guy . . . I can't remember. My ex—she got the tickets from her job. Some black guy, but he was funny."

"Must not have been that funny if you can't remember his name."

The man tilted his head as if ceding the point. "I used to bartend at this bar down by there. The owner of Stanford's would come in sometimes—now there's a character. Drank cream sherry over ice. Wore a wig sometimes."

"Craig?"

"The King of Sting."

Billy Ray nodded. "One time I was there, when it came time to pay me, he offered me a check or double my check in cocaine."

The man's eyes flared. They looked like peeled grapes set in a hamburger patty. "What'd you do?"

"I took the coke. Blow can't bounce."

The man laughed, splitting his face open like a rotten gourd. Relieved, Billy Ray looked away and smiled. Voilà. He had him. *I'm about to get what I want.*

The pink-faced man's name was Curt Fletcher and he lost his face to an exploding propane tank on his thirty-first birthday—"Not much of a story, I'm sorry to say." A snakebite took his leg. He drove a Ford Bronco, baby blue, the suspension lifted and tires monstrous. Along with cocaine, Curt Fletcher sold Valiums and Darvocets and bags of weed and he claimed to have a line on automatic weapons "just in case."

He cut out generous stripes of powder on the Bronco owner's manual and Billy Ray snorted them through a receipt while the man exhibited the power of his aftermarket subwoofers by playing Pantera at a progressively louder volume. "Everyone is moving to Bose but I swear by JBL. These are the club five thousands, five and a quarter, two in the front and four in the back." The conversation plumbed the depths of Billy Ray's apathy but the man persisted. "Listen to that bass."

"It's really something." He had to yell to be heard.

"Right? You gotta pay for power like this."

The cocaine was exceptional and Billy Ray snuffed greedily, causing his inhibitions to scatter and his own self-worth to rise as he grew more dynamic with each lusty noseload. Reality sharpened. His perception honed his senses to a fine edge that bordered on precognition. His will was paramount, definitive: nothing could begin without his consent. The cocaine spun his face cold but the source of his intuition burned like a coal in the center of his forehead: *This is important,* he thought. *I am important.* Listening to this man was a nice thing to do: Billy Ray was the one doing the favor. Inflated, his ego pulsed like a second phallus. In this warped condition he occupied the gap between knowledge and truth.

Unaware of his guest's newfound omniscience, Curt continued undeterred: "Notice how there's no rattle? This ain't no nigger-rig. They sell for twelve but I got them for nine."

"Hell yeah," hollered Billy Ray. He didn't know what he was saying.

Outside the truck, wind danced scraps of trash down streets paved with bricks as cars waited their turn at a four-way stop and the newly downed sun stained the westward mountaintops the color of wine and marmalade. The drivers of the waiting cars were reflected in profile in the windows of the storefronts lining the empty street, their faces made holy rendered in the glass aflame with the day's last light. A dentist, a pharmacy, a thrift store with a sign that read EVERYTHING MUST GO. Billy Ray, coked to the gills, took it as a warning. The residual daylight, diffuse and even, shrouded the city in imminent dusk and the early night took on a somber tone as the possibilities of day succumbed to the obligations of night. Suddenly, as he listened to Curt Fletcher prattle on, Billy Ray found himself struck with an ambiguous sense of stewardship regarding the well-being of this freak, as if he had an obligation to save him from his role in this world or, at the very least, provide succor: see his face, touch his skin, steal his pain, return his soul. It was in his power to help; this was all so big, together they were less small.

Instead, like always, he did nothing and helped no one. Instead, he sucked cocaine up his nose until he couldn't swallow, saying "Fucking A" when necessary, his ear perfunctory, listening only enough to nod at the appropriate intervals, another banal question at the ready whenever the conversation ran out of muster—"That's wild, man. How's it do on gas?"—rolling the receipt ever tighter, numb and number, unable to feel the grinding of his teeth.

Eventually he interrupted Curt Fletcher and asked to buy $200 of cocaine and six Valium. As he counted out the money, the man said he didn't have change. "That's okay," said Billy Ray, licking the owner's manual clean. "Keep it. For the hospitality."

The man gave him what he paid for and Billy Ray tucked the pellets into his pocket.

"Where's your show?" asked Curt.

"Rumors. It's connected to a hotel."

"Heh. Rumors. Haven't been on that side of town in a while. I'll try to make it."

"Alright."

"Maybe I'll bring some friends."

"Alright."

Billy Ray climbed out of the truck, out of the cocoon of cymbals and guitars, and got in his rental car and drove to the motel swimming in waning elation as the world became a bruise.

Naked, he laid in the bed with his arms crossed, the ceiling above his face craggy and peeling, the initial white gone off-gray and growing darker in the corners where the walls met. Humming with the pulse of the air conditioner, the room, grave-cold and dark, the curtains pulled tight to prevent the pervasive luster of incandescent fast food signage, overlooked a sloped parking lot, near empty besides the semi–tractor trailers ringing the perimeter of the asphalt. Beyond the lot, a curving, monolithic off-ramp delivered cars to the highway under the green glow of an LED display advertising the price of gasoline and diesel.

Bristling, exhausted, Billy Ray considered a bitter scheme. He thought in serpentine loops, the logic turning back on itself and swallowing its own tail: if he didn't show up to his gig tonight, the venue would call Red and Red would have to call him. At this point Billy Ray would have his complete attention, albeit under negative circumstances, weakening Billy Ray's bargaining power and ceding the bulge in the argument to Red, an adroit negotiator and a tactician with a skill for lulling his clients into a sense of false obligation, the sorghum dripping off his coastal Georgia accent as he trapped his prey in a homespun web of pathos, ethos and old-world guilt, a true bully of order, a real son of a bitch. "There's nothing worse," he once told Billy Ray, his head down, feet planted, squaring up to drive a fresh Titleist in his handmade Lambda shoes, "than a shark that knows it's a shark."

Billy Ray ashed his Winston on the spoiled carpet. The clock on the desk read fifty-five minutes to showtime and the showroom was in the bar downstairs, less than eighty steps away by his estimate: he had time. He needed to think this through.

When he was still married he would call his wife during periods of divisive contemplation. She, empirical and clever, knew how to talk to him. She could navigate the entanglements of his brittle ego, deftly maneuvering past his artifice to the core of the matter, her methods heuristic and above condescension. The conclusions she drew were bereft of the emotion that dominated the resolutions he arrived at by himself. She could peer through the depths of his clouding bullshit: the only hokum she couldn't parse was her own.

They'd been divorced for eleven years. He still carried a Polaroid of her in his wallet, a candid from their trip to Maine: her crouching on a dock beside a basket of writhing lobsters, her hand touching her throat, smiling, mouth agape, the highlights in her chestnut hair gone gold with the mid-August sunlight. "There're two seasons in Maine," said the fishmonger, "August and the rest of the year," and she, ever the culture slut, repeated it ad nauseum, another arrow in her quiver of trite rehashings. She talked in affected soundbites, hopped vogues for sport. Her opinions were unoriginal, adopted from magazines and the famous populists she admired. She spoke like everything she said was being recorded for posterity. While there were many reasons for their divorce, legitimate reasons of which he was ashamed, Billy Ray knew, beyond his transgressions, part of it came down to the fact that people always wanted to hear what he had to say while she had to convince them: the wife of a comedian, more than anything she wanted to be taken seriously. It drove her to bouts of hyperbole.

Once, while they were lying in bed, apropos of nothing she told him: "I wish I could talk to you, but you're not here."

"I'm right here," he said, demonstrating his vicinity. "You can touch me."

"That's not what I'm saying."

"Then just say it. You can tell me anything. I love you."

"That's the thing: if you loved me—*actually* loved me—I wouldn't have to say anything at all."

In the darkness he scoffed. Maybe that was the end of things.

Since the divorce, they'd exchanged few words. The lawyers did all the talking. Once, on the courtroom steps, he told her: "For all that pissing and moaning you do, you really don't say much at all."

She wept.

He wished she had killed him right there.

He sat up and dug his feet into the stiff carpet, shook his head, slapped himself sharp. He'd completely forgotten about Red, the severity of his professional troubles dwarfed in the forefront of his mind by a lengthy highlight reel comprised of his most monstrous acts of marital treachery—the lies, the infidelities, the isolation. The dwindling parts-per-million of the drugs in his blood compounded the mounting despair. He felt like a shell casing: hollow and burnt, waiting to go off.

Slowly in the dark, he found his way to the bathroom, turned on the light and started the shower. As he waited for the water to heat, he emptied his bladder in the warming spray and fed a key tip up each nostril.

Showers, like everything, reminded him of her.

When they first met, he and Olivia spent extended periods in hotel showers pressing each other against the tile, alive underwater, unconcerned with getting clean. They spent hours stuck together, limitless and unburdened, enjoying passion without responsibility until the water went cold. He thought her so strong then, so creative, her skin softer than any kindness, all that life in her pale blue eyes. She was beautiful and willing and generous. The memory of her at twenty-two still raised his oldest blood.

Eyes closed, head in the water, he soothed himself, thinking of her and him, who they used to be, what they used to do.

He toweled off afterward then put on his show clothes, tucking his yellowing Rockmount shirt into his pants, the chinos still pleated somehow, the fabric as blue as gas flame. Half hour until showtime: this business with Red could wait. There was nothing he could do. He needed the money; he needed the hotel room; but most pressing he needed a drink.

From the start, he knew this was going to be a long sixty minutes.

There was no host, no opener, no introduction, no buffer. The sound system was faulty. The mixer was broken. "We have a sound guy but he just works karaoke." Carried through the blown speakers, his voice sounded wet and distant, all bass drenched with reverb, as if it was coming up from the bottom of a well.

The crowd seemed surprised when the bartender turned off the house music. He watched them look around, searching for the cause of the interruption. When he appeared before them, he saw the disdain in their eyes. They weren't here to listen, they were here to try to mate. His existence upset them. This was an ambush in peacetime. There were no posters on the wall.

The tables up front were empty. The crowd, a dour collection of disinterested itinerants dudded in khakis and Lacoste and ignorant to their hopelessness, sat itself at the bar or paired off in couples in the high-backed vinyl booths far from the stage. They were impenetrable. A connection was impossible, not in this place, not with these people. Staring emptily out of their heads, their faces just masks made of skin, they scowled, they groaned, they made it clear he was unwanted. He was a disappointment, an impediment, an unnecessary evil. Time slowed, the minutes viscous and dripping into each other as he struggled to deliver, an amplified stranger demanding the precious moments of their lives.

"Pueblo. The town named Town. How long did it take you geniuses to come up with that?"

Nothing.

"I would have liked to be in that meeting. What should we call this place? City? No, that's too hard to spell."

So much nothing.

The collective apathy bordered on hostility but he continued—like a professional—not letting it show, outwardly undeterred but wilting internally, soldiering on in the face of the thick silence, feeling more and more with each failed punch line like a ghoul without a tongue. His was a special hell. It was like he told them all the dates of their deaths. Reflected in their plastic eyes he saw what they saw—a deluded man pretending everything was fine—and he hated them for it, almost as much as he hated himself.

This was before his nose began to bleed.

At first he didn't notice, so consuming was his chore, but then he felt it: the blood coming hot and fast, flowing in a gout off the tip of his chin and ruining his shirt. A table of women got up and left the bar at the sight of the deluge while a man in the back of the room hollered, "Hope you brought enough for the rest of the class." Billy Ray, unshaken—this had happened before—embraced the opportunity for self-effacement. He packed his nostril with paper napkins—"Who wants to see a magic trick?"—making a show of his single tusk as he feigned indignity: "Oh, sure, like none of you get high before work."

This drew a chuckle.

"You guys are acting like a Mormon at an orgy."

Another chuckle.

"Did you know Mormons have orgies? They don't call them orgies, of course. They call them 'youth groups.'"

At this old, trite, repurposed joke (on the East Coast, he swapped "Mormon" for "priest"), the crowd coughed up legitimate laughter and Billy Ray Schafer, like a captain finding a break in the chop, put the throttle down: full speed ahead. For the next twenty minutes, he skewered the Church of Latter-day Saints ("The church says you can bang sixteen-year-olds, but *only* if they're wearing their magic underwear, and I get it—you gotta have rules") and for some strange, unquantifiable reason—one of the countless subtle variables that make stand-up comedy the only living artform—the crowd ate it up. He ripped, he slashed, he barely came up for air. He found the rhythm of the room's particular heartbeat and fanned the embers of their meager adulation until they were on fire. Then he danced among the flames.

He adapted.

He survived.

He won.

And the whole time he was thinking: *You thought you had me, motherfuckers, but I can't be got.*

Later, sitting at the bar in his shirt wet with blood, too drunk really to keep his head up but still pounding Jameson, he considered his possibilities: they were fewer than ever. Every decision tree, rootless, bore no fruit. The options he didn't have far outnumbered those he did. *I am drowning.* Bleak rumination. Nothing was concrete. He saw it all in maybes.

Maybe he would separate from Red.

Maybe he would win the lotto.

Maybe he would kill himself.

Maybe it wouldn't hurt.

None of it was pleasant to think about. He shook his head, drank. The whiskey tasted like charcoal, wet amber in the glass.

Olivia had no taste for brown liquor. She said it made her flush. She drank vodka—Stoli or Grey Goose in a pinch—Tom Collins, screwdrivers, a Black Russian in lieu of dessert. She never wanted to taste the liquor. She masked the bad with sweet.

A memory snuck in the back door of his mind: the two of them in their first apartment, him splayed out on the couch, her sitting Indian-style beside a crate of records on the rug she bought in Grand Junction, a tumbler of ginger ale and vodka between her legs, snow falling outside their barred windows, John Prine on the turntable, her singing along, his fingers in her hair, the smell of the leather, the simple magic, the calm certitude, how warm he felt then.

"Should I play another record?" she asked, looking up at him smiling, her face impossibly bright.

"Throw it on, toots. We've got nothing but time."

More memories, more glimpses: how her nose wrinkled when she was nervous, how her blue eyes went gray-lavender in the early light of dawn, how she draped her leg across his stomach when she slept, how she picked the olives off her pizza and saved them for last, how she carried their sons cocked up on one hip, how they looked at her like a god, how she begged him to become sober, how small she was when she cried, all the words he said and all the words he didn't and the divide between them too big to scream across.

I would never do this to you. I could never do this to you.

Well, we're different then, aren't we?
We used to be the same.

He clamped his eyes tight against the remembrances, cutting them off, holding them in. He pushed his fists into the sockets. He kept his eyes shut until he was confident he had aborted the tears; when he opened them, she was gone and he was alone again, delivered back to this foreign place where his decisions were foregone and his reality was beyond his control.

All he could do was ask for another drink.

At the shake of his glass, the bartender, an aspiring actor named Todd, topped him off. Todd wore red suspenders that matched the crimson bow tie growing out of his throat like a rose. Todd was beautiful, his face perfect, his features fine, his skin clear: from stage, Billy Ray had described him as "exactly what Hitler was fighting for." After Billy Ray's set, Todd had been complimentary, fawning over the "rawness"—"rock and roll, brother." Since then, he had been hospitable to a fault. "That was legendary," he said, refilling Billy Ray's glass to the brim. "You're a legend."

"The headless horseman," Billy Ray slurred. He shoved money at Todd but it was refused.

"Your money's no good."

"My head's a fucking pumpkin."

The lounge—nothing more than a collection of wounded red vinyl booths ringing the horseshoe'd bar—was near empty and lit low enough to provide the remaining faces the benefit of the doubt. A pack of businessmen stood around the far elbow of the bar chasing shots of clear liquor with lime wedges. They honked, their puckered faces twisted around the citrus, overgrown frat boys slapping the bartop after every round until the bartender heeled, proudly paying for their Patrons on the company card, being loud—"hold the salt, doctor's orders"—their faces stretched bulbous reflected in the bar's burnished grain.

Farther down the bar, an older couple were fully engaged in a vivid display of shameless affection. Tongues probing, hands curious—Billy Ray had seen similar presentations in prison visitation rooms. Truly wild stuff. He couldn't help but stare. They appeared to be a bit older than himself but they'd maintained themselves better, their faces stretched wrinkleless by science, their skin tanned a color you have to pay for. The man was big-toothed and fit for his age, the sinews and veins of his sleeveless arms visible under the skin, sharp chinned, his hair gone the precise silver of timber wolf fur. Every finger on his left hand was fitted with at least one ring and he wore sunglasses despite the late hour. The woman was straight off the cover of a VHS porno tape, fabricated in a laboratory by an enemy of nature and death. Her measurements were quixotic, her breasts massive, as if apportioned by a fourteen-year-old boy: she would be impossible to drown. Hard and immobile and set too high on her chest, the twin globes looked ridiculous mounted on her slight frame. Under her bleached blond, hairspray crisped hair, her face was Beverly Hills grotesque, the inflated lips like nightcrawlers, her soft eyes pinned open beneath a forehead arched surgically into a look of everlasting revelation, like everything was incredible, like it was all just too much. These permanently astonished eyes caught Billy Ray leering like a deaf puppy, but rather than scowling or looking away, she matched his gaze, blew a kiss and, while still maintaining eye contact, whispered something into her date's ear. The man shrugged and laughed before returning his tongue to the inside of her mouth.

While Todd flitted between them, the businessmen cackled, the tan couple made out and Billy Ray continued to drink until he was smashed beyond self-recognition. Periodically, he thumbed the lump of leather holding the cash in his pocket, the sole tangible among the ether, the only proof he was real. Tonight he put three new hundred dollar bills in his billfold: *And all I gave them was all I had.*

"S'okay," he said to nobody. "I'm-I'm—never mind."

Illusions flickered at the edge of his vision, kaleidoscopes and faces, voices he once knew. His thoughts composed themselves in a language he could no longer understand. Delirious, undefined, neither here nor there and approaching the verge, Billy Ray—if that was his name—retained only fragments of what happened next.

He turned on his cellphone, found the number named LIV and pressed send. At the sound of her voicemail, he hung up, then called back and left a ten-second recording of labored breathing punctuated by a heavy sigh. Instead of calling again, he spiked the phone between his legs, bouncing it off the brass footrail and snapping it at the hinge. Bending forward to pick up the pieces, Billy Ray lost his equilibrium and toppled from the high stool, landing braceless on the point of his chin in a field of screaming yellow. Then he laid very still.

More blood, the darkest blood, poured in rivulets from his mouth. Todd hopped the bar, eager to help, but froze when he saw the mess: "Jesus Christ." The blood pooled in deep stains on the carpet and Billy Ray remained motionless in the flood, damaged, lame, a dripping and helpless calamity. The four men gathered around him but none moved.

"Lordy."

"Call an ambulance."

"Nwoh," said Billy Ray, spitting blood. "Nwoh cwops." He sat up slowly, the front of him slaked, new blood on old blood. He shook his head to reaffirm his wishes and the blood fell in sheets.

"Call it anyway."

"That's too much blood."

The augmented woman cut through the crowd. "Here, watch out. I used to be a nurse." Tying back her hair, she knelt beside him and put her hands on his shoulders firmly. "Can you hear me?" Billy Ray winked, still painless in the shock of it all. "Good. Listen to me, okay?" She smiled, her eyes benign, and he smiled back a twisted, leaking simper. In that moment she was Olivia, she was his mother, she was the mother of God. "Come here." She took his head in her hands and massaged his temples with her fingertips. "Does that hurt?" He shook his head. "Good. That's real good. Can you open your mouth?" He did, a thin pellicle of blood and saliva growing between his spreading lips. "Does that hurt?" she asked, her calm tone denoting experience. He shook his head. "Excellent. Todd, I need clean towels and ice. Ronny, give me your shirt. Who's got a flashlight?"

Todd brought towels and a bucket of ice and one of the men produced a small penlight. She had him open his mouth as wide as he could and peered inside with the light. "Stick out your tongue. Oh. Yep. You about chomped a hole in your cheek."

The woman instructed him to apply pressure to the wound with his tongue, packed his mouth with ice cubes and tied a bag of ice to the side of his face with her date's tank top. "You're lucky," she said, dabbing blood off his chin with a rag. "This could have been much worse."

Billy Ray nodded: this is nothing, sister. This is just what you can see.

Three of the men stood him up and sat him down on a stool. Todd brought a fresh drink. The woman sat on the stool beside him, her hand on the small of his back to steady him. She held the penlight between his eyes and traced it back and forth. "You're gonna feel like shit tomorrow." Billy Ray smiled, unable to speak. It didn't hurt that bad. He attempted to sip his drink, but most of it dribbled out. Todd was ready with a straw. The woman continued to tend to him, tightening his bandage, digging her breasts into his shoulder. He stared down her tank top. Tweety Bird was tattooed below her left clavicle, the initials *LCH* inscribed in fading cursive on her wrist. "You're gonna hurt like the devil's ex-wife," she told him, snickering. The corners of her eyes were liquid silver. *You're a miracle,* he thought. *I was lost and you found me.*

He pulled out his cash and peeled two fifties off the rind, held the bills out in front of him, not looking at them, staring down. The money seemed heavy in his fingers, sacramental: this was the best he could do. "Sank oo."

The woman, curling her eyes, looked back at her date before pushing Billy Ray's hand to the bar and closing his fingers around the money. "No, honey." They locked eyes: the intimacy embarrassed him. A feeling he hadn't known in a long time welled up from a secret reserve in the core of him, running out his pores, making brighter the dim surroundings, a sense of connectedness at once clarifying and intoxicating: her hand remained on his. "We have to help each other when we can."

"I lurv oo," he said.

She smiled, her eyes lingering. "You *are* funny."

Billy Ray, hoping to rid himself of attention, to restore normalcy, left the money on the bar and bought a round for everyone: he was eager to be useful to these people. Todd poured the drinks and Billy Ray proposed a toast: "To stwong chins." Everybody laughed. Things fell back into place.

The men were steelers from Harrisburg, Pennsylvania. They were in town selling new technology, some cutting-edge smelter—"If you smelt it, we dealt it." They said it was all very boring and no one disagreed. The woman—Tammy—and the man—Ronny, now shirtless, his skin a different orange where the tank top had covered—owned a string of rental properties up through Colorado Springs. In his free time he restored pinball machines and, in her younger years, before nursing school, she'd been a cheerleader for the Phoenix Suns. They had been married then divorced then married again. They knew people in Pittsburgh. "Is that close to Harrisburg?"

"No, not really."

Tammy gazed at Billy Ray while the men talked hockey, burning him with her shining wet eyes. She teased her straw with the tip of her tongue. Ronny didn't say much, but he seemed pleased by the situation, smiling broad like he knew some great truth. Billy Ray ordered another round, insisting Todd pour one for himself. Maybe his alacrity would help everyone fail to remember his helplessness: he wanted them all to forget he'd ever needed them at all.

Soon Todd locked the doors, removed his bow tie and the party became private. Lines were laid out on the bar, ashtrays were made available: the room filled up with smoke. One of the steelers stacked the jukebox with the Allman Brothers and Duane Allman's bottleneck slide whinnied its high melancholia as his brother warned the road goes on forever. The night mounted: everyone tried to deduce what came next. Tammy took turns two-stepping with the steelers while Ronny watched without protest, unminding, tipping his bottle of Coors toward Billy Ray and nodding toward his wife with a raised eyebrow, as if to say it's your turn, partner—make your move. Billy Ray raised his glass in return, a man teetering on the razored lip of lucidity. Events were blurred Polaroids, moments disconnected: A to C to G.

When it was his turn, he danced with Tammy, holding her close, following her, grateful for her warmth. She whispered something he didn't hear then repeated herself, pushing her breasts into his chest while her husband watched, grinning his omnipotent smile: did he want to come back to their place? Billy Ray followed her outside. Ronny carried his suitcase.

The truck smelled like hay. Patches of coarse orange rust showed through on the paneling. The passenger door handle stuck. Billy Ray waited for Tammy to open it from the inside. Spinning slowly on the rearview mirror, a fraying dream catcher hung above the bench seat, the hard vinyl wrapped tightly in a Navajo blanket patterned with blue and brown waves. Tammy sat between them, thigh-to-thigh, Ronny's arm slung around her as he drove through the empty streets. The night was pitiless dark. Between streetlights the city existed in stretches of flat void beneath a moonless sky. Staring out into the ink, Billy Ray experienced none of the novelty due a passenger adrift in an ocean of unseeable possibility. Nothing was new anymore: everything that was going to happen had already happened to him. All of this was leftovers. He'd already met these people, just their names were different. He'd been in this truck driving down this road, but it was somewhere else, in a place they had never been and would never visit. These people lived everywhere, conned by their senses into believing themselves unique and exciting, but Billy Ray knew better: the world went on without them. The smallness is what killed him. The only way these people could surprise him would be by driving off a cliff into the endless twilight or pulling into an abandoned lot and caving his skull in with shovels. Maybe his last words would be "Thank you." He'd give his life for something new.

At a drive-in burger joint, Ronny turned down a street made of cobblestones and the truck began to bounce. In the tumult, Tammy grabbed hold of Billy Ray's thigh. He looked down, assuming it was an accident, but she squeezed tighter, working up his leg toward the cardinal piece of him. He traced her hand up her arm, making sure it connected to her shoulder, verifying this was not some hallucination: it was hard to tell anymore. He stopped at her chest. Her breasts remained steadfast. They didn't bobble in the least. As he tried to envision what they looked like when she was naked on her back, he felt fingers in his hair. He could see both of Tammy's hands.

Wherever they were going, he hoped there was whiskey waiting.

The old truck topped the hill and pulled off into a parking lot and eased into a space in front of a row of nondescript apartments. He fumbled with the door handle until Tammy reached over him, shoving her alterations into his groin, adding, "There's a trick to this."

White light from a tall pole divided the asphalt into three distinct darknesses. He followed them into a vestibule and Ronny unlocked a glass door and they walked single file up a staircase coated in drab gray carpet. At the top of the second flight of stairs, Ronny opened another door and they stepped into a silent room as cold as it was dark. Entering the room, Billy Ray thought of floating through space untethered with nothing to bring you back until Ronny turned on a light and Billy Ray knew exactly where he was: a studio apartment, bed in one corner, a full bar in the other, the walls decorated with framed photographs of a fully nude Tammy pretzeled into various uncomfortable positions. Her face was different in the photos. Younger, less plasticine. More human. Alive.

They took off their shoes and invited him to do the same. "Get comfortable."

"What if I gotta wun?" said Billy Ray. He could barely stand up under the weight of his daylong drunk.

"Then we'll have to chase you."

There was nowhere to sit besides the bed. He leaned on the sill of the only window while Tammy got to work pouring drinks. Her husband, the man, brought out a mirror in the shape of a heart. The room throbbed with invisible momentum. Imperceptible. He could hear it like a dog. Billy Ray lit a cigarette without asking if it was okay to do so: this seemed like the type of place where permission was unimportant. He sat and smoked and tried to think of something to say.

Tammy handed him a glass. "Cheers." She pursed her fat lips. No one was wasting any time. They gathered around the mirror and took their turns with a straw. Ronny's cocaine was strong, fortifying, the powder fine and pearl white. After a few lines, Billy Ray found his balance. The taffy left his knees. He asked for music and when they complied he danced in slow circles, arms akimbo, free in here, relishing his movements, the space: it was nice to not be alone. While they watched him dance, Ronny and Tammy kissed with their mouths open, their lips searching, their hands disappearing. Tammy giggled and broke off to orbit Billy Ray and Ronny lit a cigar and leaned against the bar with his arms crossed passing the stogie from one corner of his mouth to the other, his eyes glinting and fiendish behind the veil of blue smoke, watching as his wife moved graceless against another man and not at all objecting when they kissed, not raising an eye, instead touching himself through his shorts while he sucked the cigar, his grin growing like a crack in the world big enough to swallow them all.

The music stopped. Tammy repeated the chorus: "More than this, there is nothing."

Tammy pushed Billy Ray to the bed and peeled off her thin shirt followed by his shoes and his pants and knelt between his legs. Billy Ray leaned back and stared at the photographs. The girl in the pictures looked happy, like she didn't need to do things like this. Without looking at him, Billy Ray felt her husband's eyes rake across his body like talons. Seconds became minutes. The smoke billowed.

When Ronny knelt beside his wife, Billy Ray shut his eyes and dug his fingers into the comforter.

He slept on the floor afterward. That was their only rule.

THURSDAY

HE AWOKE SHIVERING AND PLACELESS AND NAKED BELOW THE waist. The inside of his head was a storm without a name. This was not his hotel room. None of this was his. His back was all knots. The side of his face was a swollen cartoon. The hands on his watch said one thirty-seven.

He stood up—a prolonged and painful multitiered process that found him first on his hands and knees, then on his knees, then bent over the bed prone and cursing muffled swears into the coverlet—to find himself alone in a frigid room, his pants folded neatly and draped across the bar. Beside them he found a note.

> B.R.
>
> *Thanks for the laughs. Had stuff to do, but help yourself to whatever you want. Liquor cabinet is under sink. Cold cuts in fridge. Hope you had fun. We did.*
>
> *xo*
> *T and R*
>
> *Please lock up if you go*

He turned on the faucet and splashed cold water on his face and drank directly from the tap like a domesticated bear before bending in half and pressing his face to the imitation marble. The walls tightened immeasurably, contracting like lungs. He felt as if the gravity in the room was too high, like he was being compressed to fit in a cage of unknown dimensions, like the cell in McAlester where he learned the definition of penance.

Finding no vodka, he settled for a fifth of Carnaby's gin. Peeling off the cellophane with trembling hands, he drank in hot gulps straight from the bottle, downing the neck in one pull. Almost instantly his head unconstricted and his hands calmed. In the closet he found a shirt of Ronny's that refused to button around his distended stomach, forcing him to wear it open, exposing his hairy pale breasts. He left his blood-ruined shirt in the trash and put on his pants. The bottle fit snugly in the front pocket of his merchandise suitcase.

Locking the door behind him, he went down the stairs and through the antechamber and stepped out into stale oblivion. The day hung like a sheet, stagnant and aching with heat that made his bones hurt. Swaths of sunlight slashed from the spaces between buildings creating a checkerboard grid of light and shadow. This, this now, was not designed for the recovering poisoned. He existed in opposition: *Your honor, I object.* The pain in his head bloomed awful. Spider legs of white daggers savaged his brain, turning the world a weeping gray wound. Down the street, mirages made the street wet, the heat rising in waves like souls from the broken asphalt. There was nothing he wanted more than to disappear. Go up like the smoke peeling off his last cigarette. *I am thirsty and there's not enough water in the world.*

He followed the cobblestones back to the drive-in, the parking lot now inundated with cars and their passengers engaged in late lunch. Children brandishing corndogs. A mélange of pop hits muddling from radios. Cars parked in spaces lined off with orange paint, the drivers speaking into metal boxes crackling with static anticipation. This *is America,* he thought. Land that I love. In times like these, when his head was desperate for context, he took solace in plain people and their simple objectives: eat, drink, go. It was a relief to be reminded that meeting these easy needs connected him to the rest of the alive. Life wasn't a complex chore. It was a series of binary decisions, a matter of connecting one thing to the next. The only trick to it was understanding the rules of engagement and knowing that improvement is difficult but making it worse is as easy as breathing and dying.

He stepped up to the window where a girl with twin strawberry pigtails received orders from the masses. "How can I help you?"

He didn't know how to answer.

Inside her little booth, the girl smacked gum. She was young still, early twenties, and actually beautiful, but too old for this kind of work. She could be anywhere doing anything but instead she was here doing this: what waste. Hungover as he was—still drunk, really—he was overcome with a dour sentimentality. Suddenly he felt it was on him to rescue this girl, to escape her from the tiny booth, built as much of steel and glass as it was her limited imagination and torpor: *Let me teach you how to run while you still have the legs.*

"Sir?" She looked bored. He was boring her. She stared out without seeing him, peering through him as if he was made of the same smudged glass as her window. It made him hate her: the inaction. She probably never knew any dead people. Her life was an expansive fenceless acreage, her lifespan limitless, inexorable: there's always tomorrow, tomorrow is always. Unlike him, she had yet to be trapped in her life. There was still something she could do and defining that something was all that mattered. He wanted to slap her, to make her feel pain, to make her feel. Maybe then she would understand the stakes of this game.

"Sir?"

"Let me get two grilled cheeses, onion rings and a Diet Coke."

"We don't have grilled cheese."

"You don't have grilled cheese?"

In response, she cocked her head and flattened her gaze and

stretched her gum, turning her tongue into a lubricous pink eel. "We took it off the menu."

"You have bread, right?"

She corked her eyes back in her head then dropped them down on his face. "We have *buns*."

"Perfect."

"Buns aren't bread."

He leaned on the steel counter. "Buns *are* bread."

"I guess."

"So you have bread and you have cheese, correct? I can see the cheese." He pointed past her at a deck of sweating Kraft singles.

"It's not on the menu. I wouldn't know what to ring it up as."

"I'm sure you can figure it out."

"I'll have to ask Derrick."

"Well we wouldn't want to bother Derrick." He blinked twice, his deadpan unregistered. The rage building at her blind obstinance was sharp and clear: his ardor startled even him. "How about this: you charge me for a cheeseburger and make it without any toppings, hold the beef?"

"Hold the beef?"

"If you insist."

"What?"

"Goddamnit." He set his voice to patronize and talked to her as if she were slow. "Look, here's what we're gonna do: charge me for a cheeseburger, but only put cheese in the bun, then kind of give it a little smush on the grill"—he demonstrated a little smush—"flip it over, give it another smush, put it in the bag, I'll give you money, whiz-bang"—he clapped his hands—"we're off to the races. How does that sound? Is that kosher? Can you do that for me?"

"I'll have to ask Derrick."

"Fuck Derrick."

"What?"

"You're gonna die in there."

Billy Ray about-faced and walked away from the gleaming cube before his escalating aggravation redefined them in its wake: he didn't want anything to happen to her—he was angry and unjustified, sans dominion: the possibilities scared him. He stomped away hungry, dragging his suitcase like a child.

Above him the sun burned the hazeless sky the faint blue of flown china and Aryan eyes, the kind of blue that was easy to imagine Heaven behind. He walked down the centerline of the street skipping his suitcase across the asphalt and sipping the bottle brazenly in the abandoned afternoon. The city was quiet, paralyzed by the workday doldrums. Entire blocks laid unpopulated beyond the people working behind shop windows and the occasional pack of school children giggling their way home. He passed Victorian–Queen Anne hybrid houses with yards full of turquoise spruce and a squat schoolhouse built of pink rhyolite and a sandstone church crowned by three proud spires horning out of a stoned tracery. The sign in the yard in front of the church read

BUT THE LORD GOD
CALLED TO THE MAN
WHERE AR3 YOU?

At the bottom of the hill, he stopped to rest in a small knoll. He smoked, watching children foot a soccer ball through an arrangement of orange cones. He never understood the appeal of soccer: all the running, the lack of scoring—even when he watched his sons play, the game just seemed like tag with more rules.

The grass was cool and when he was finished with his cigarette, hidden behind a clutch of roseless bushes, he took off his shirt and laid belly down in it, enjoying the kiss of the barbered lawn on his skin. He dozed off and woke up unprepared. The initial orange sunlight felt like ice in his eyes. The children were gone.

When he got to the hotel, the clerk, a lean and sallow-faced black man with a flat nose, his glossy skin the color of eggplant, greeted him in the mandatory manner taught in corporate handbooks. He spoke in the precise English of educated immigrants, his cadence robotic and dignified in its stiltedness. "Good afternoon, sir. My name is Sahr. Welcome to the Marriott Pueblo Downtown. Do you have a reservation?"

"Just wanted to return my key."

"Is the room not to your satisfaction?"

"No. I checked in yesterday."

"Check out time is daily at noon."

"I didn't make it back last night," he said with a wink the man did not understand.

"What was your room number?"

"One thirty-eight."

The man flipped a rolodex with his long indigenous fingers. His fingernails were pristine. "What is your name, sir?"

"Schafer."

The man removed a yellow slip from its place in the rolodex. "Schafer. Room one thirty-eight. There is a note from the maids. You left behind belongings. Would you like to claim these things?"

Billy Ray bared his teeth under a thin smile, making his impatience plain. "I think that'd be best."

"Follow me, sir."

They walked down a hallway of beaten red carpet and lithographed paintings of flowers in macro. At a door labeled EMPLOYEES ONLY, the deskman knocked. A tiny woman answered with a cup of coffee in her hand.

"Sofronia, this is the man from one thirty-eight. He would like to claim his belongings."

The miniature woman looked Billy Ray up then down with bitter eyes, comparing him to the model of the man she had drawn in her head. "Pensé que estabas muerto," she said. She shut the door.

"She seems like a nice lady," Billy Ray said. The deskman studied his shoes with his hands clasped militarily behind his back. "Everyone is very nice."

The door opened and the woman backed out of the room clutching a box in her arms. She shoved it into Billy Ray's stomach: "Tómalo." She disappeared again and returned with another suitcase she placed at his feet. Billy Ray took account of the articles in the box. Satisfied, he dropped the box on the carpet and reached for his wallet to tip her. His back pocket was empty.

"No." He patted himself down, turning all of his pockets out and emptying them into the box. "No, no, no."

He began to sweat, turned dizzy, ramping into a spell of undistilled panic: it's just relentless sometimes. "I swear to God." Stacking the box on top of the larger suitcase, he ran the bags across the carpet and kicked the lobby door open. The maid and the bellman watched him flee, turned to each other and shrugged.

At the rental car he nearly broke the trunk key off inside of the lock, his vision quivering, his heart an animal escaping a grave. He remembered blearily pulling a condom from his billfold last night in the apartment where he'd slept. "Not me," he said. "Nope."

He threw his bags and the box in the trunk and crawled into the car, slamming it in reverse without looking, fearful and loathing, cursing himself and his boozing and the wanton way he lived his life. The tires shrieked when they kissed the street. He drove like a man fleeing a cloud of poison.

The city blew by as if it was caught in a flood. Retracing his steps as best he could, he found the knoll and the church and the pink school but, at the drive-in, he turned the wrong way and U-turned in the middle of a red light while the meager traffic sounded their horns. He didn't hear them: the only sounds he was aware of were the wild jouncing of his tires across the cobblestones and the outraged howling of his own black intention.

The rows of gray apartments were as undistinguished as their occupants. He drove through the parking lot feeling his pulse in his fingertips, sweating, making promises to himself. Then he saw it: the man's rust-eaten truck. As he got out of the car, he caught a glimpse in the rearview mirror of the face of a wronged man who was unaware any longer of the exact limits of his capabilities. Excitement concealed fear: it had been a long time. What was about to happen was both new and very old.

Inside the vestibule, he hunched over the callbox and rang numbers indiscriminately until the door buzzed unlocked. He took the stairs slowly like one approaching a precarious edge. Billy Ray knew he was bigger than the driver of the truck, denser where it mattered, and he'd known violence. He still had faith in his fists.

This is it. I am it.

The hallway smelled like pizza sauce: sweet and red and metallic. His feet carried him up the stairs thoughtlessly, autonomous, powered by the legitimacy of his vendetta. Everything was clearer and more brilliant under the effect of the adrenaline he could taste like copper in the back of his mouth. The lightbulbs aglow in the sconces on the walls burned bright as private stars. Down the hall, from behind a door, as if by signal or warning, came the bleating of a trumpet being learned—a herald—and he thought of war and death, hate and fire and all that had been lost or taken away.

Billy Ray knocked on the door and planted his feet: ready. The anticipation made him gag.

Here it comes. Here I come.

When the man opened the door, he was holding a towel around his waist, his wet hair plastered to his forehead, a coy smile bunched up into the corner of his mouth. He cocked his head in an insouciant gesture. "Welcome back, stud."

With all of him behind it, Billy Ray smashed his fist into the space below the man's lower lip, cutting his knuckles on the teeth. The man yelped like a shot dog. Billy Ray followed with a right to the five o'clock of the man's face, just right of the point of his chin. The man careened sideways, hitting his head on the doorframe, and Billy Ray caught him as he fell with a glancing blow to the side of the neck. Limply, the man hit the shag and went fetal, covering his face with his hands, muffling his whimpering, the sounds coming wet and unintelligible between his fingers, the towel open and exposing him in full.

Billy Ray stepped in the room and shut the door behind him. He brushed his hair out of his eyes, surveying the room and half expecting to find a translucent safe with his wallet clearly visible inside of it. From the bathroom he heard the running of the shower, faint music, a woman singing poorly. The walls still vacillated as they had when he woke up and he realized it was the flickering of the ceiling light between spinning fan blades. Billy Ray spit on the man's chest. "Give me my money." He stomped his stomach with his boot heel, heard something crack. He didn't know the name of the man on the floor sucking air in heaving dry gasps but he recognized the man who put him there: he'd been trying to forget him all his life. "The wallet or you'll never stand up again."

"Please."

Billy Ray wound back like he was kicking off and drove his toes squarely into the man's bare brisket, deflating him, rolling him onto his back. "Where is it?" He raised his fist and the man recoiled. The weakness was sickening. Disgust boiled in Billy Ray's chest like a second heartbeat: of all the things a man can be, a coward is the worst. Disheartened, he bent over and screamed in the man's face: "WHERE IS IT?" Beneath the man, a wet stain spread. "I'm gonna give you one more chance and then I'm going to kick in your teeth."

Billy Ray could smell himself: stale sex and fresh violence. His breath was rotten.

This is how monsters smell.

This is how monsters feel.

"Where is it?"

Silence.

I am a monster.

Billy Ray snatched a lava lamp from the countertop, ripped the cord from the wall and raised the lamp over his head.

"Put it down, Billy."

He turned at the sound of his name and found the woman, the one who saved him, standing in the kitchen, naked, wet, the pistol in her hands pointed at the center of his chest.

"Put it down. Now."

Billy Ray froze. Everything stopped. The individual atoms that connected this place to Time dematerialized and they were alone in this moment.

The woman sidestepped around the island to stand between the table and the bathroom door. Her stance was textbook: squared toes forward, feet shoulder-width, knees flexed, arms isoscelese'd. She'd been trained. She was glorious. Here she was, Eve after Eden, the judgment of God attached to the end of her arm. Haloed by the light pouring from the bathroom, her golden hair clinging to her shoulders like filament, she was the Madonna, she was an angel, she was Vengeance, she was The End. No living person had ever been more important. In regards to his continuance, she was the sun.

"Move." She flicked the nose of the gun away from her husband. The chrome rippled with the light from above, hot mercury, a deadly silver thing. "Now."

Billy Ray stepped back. On the ground, the man squealed behind broken teeth, whining a high-toned abattoir noise. It was awful. Billy Ray doubted she would still love him after this. But women are surprising: all they do is forgive.

He looked at her. The woman's eyes were flat stones. Billy Ray matched her stare, doing fatal calculations in his head. He wondered how quick she could pull the trigger, *if* she could pull the trigger. He knew from experience it was harder than it looked.

"I'm not leaving without my wallet."

She motioned with the pistol to the bed. "Sit down."

"I'm serious."

"Sit."

Crouching slowly, he placed the lamp on the carpet and sat on the edge of the bed, never breaking gaze with the barrel: the answer was up inside that hole. Instead of fear, he was overcome with a sense of looming epiphany. Heartbeats replaced seconds: one more, one more, by the grace of the gun one more.

The woman backed into the kitchen heels first, locking the pistol on the center of his mass as if there was a magnet in his heart. She opened the top drawer and pawed around inside without looking, her body striped with shadows. A constellation of proud pink scars stood out like topography on the plain of her tawny skin. Every inch of her was intentional: even her nipples were tan. This woman who designed her body to be an object of lust had replaced herself with the platonic embodiment of carnality, and he understood that if she did compress that trigger, moving the small piece of metal the infinitesimal distance between life and death, she would be the last thing he ever saw, and for that he was grateful.

If he knew last night that she was to be his last woman, he wouldn't have taken an inch of her for granted. He'd have kissed her sincerely, caressed and not groped, treated her careful, listened, volunteered. Last night he'd been ugly when he could have been beautiful and for that—more than anything—a bullet he deserved.

The woman opened her mouth, but her voice failed. She cleared her throat: it sounded like opening a can of beer. "Go stand by the door," she told him, her hand still in the drawer. He assumed she was looking for a cellphone with which to call 911 and if that was the case, he would rush her. Death was preferable to prison: his life was worthless, but he'd rather she take it than it belong to the state. Could be another gun in there, just in case six bullets weren't enough. Handcuffs perhaps. He knew they had a pair.

"The door."

He did what she said, backing toward the door, his eyes on the gun. "Now. Open it."

"You're gonna have to kill me." (He used to do a joke in his act: "They say there are worse things than death. You know who says that? People who aren't dead.")

She pulled her hand out of the drawer. Billy Ray held his breath. In her fingers, holding it lightly as if it were a cold, dead thing, she raised aloft a bulging brown billfold and arched it toward him, landing it between his feet. Billy Ray picked up his wallet and rifled the contents: cash, all of it, vindication green: these sons of bitches, these dirty rats. "I knew it."

The woman shook her head. "You left it here. I found it this morning."

"Bullshit."

"Get out of my house."

"F—"

"GO."

Billy Ray, glowering, reached behind him for the doorknob. He found the cold brass and stepped backward into the hallway then shut the door forever on the naked orange woman and her heavy little gun.

Down the hall, in one of the apartments, an amateur trumpeter bleated a single note: it was the sweetest song he'd ever heard.

Down the stairs. Outside. The copper reek of fall. Vomit, acrid and thin. The taste of spent matches. Bent, panting, empty.

Hallelujah.

Dots of light danced in the corner of his vision. He looked upward, mouth agape: florid sky, pinks and reds, God's blushing face. Magnificent. Swallow me, Lord. Spit me out.

Hallelujah.

A cigarette. Breathing. Smoke and air. Another cigarette. The feeling of his feet in his shoes: *What a gift. This is a dream. I am a visitor, beholden, brand new.*

Hallelujah.

Twenty minutes before his hands were steady enough to drive, twenty more to find the highway. He drove in silence, the windows down, the headlights cutting a path through the dark while tractor trailers barreled past groaning like whales; he barely noticed them, so complete was his focus on the simple victory of not being dead. He made his mind an empty vessel. An epiphany was imminent. In order to receive it, he needed to be blank.

In his experience with apocalypse, he understood near death was a precursor to wisdom and, if he was patient and quiet, revelations would speak to him: the meaning of his life was to hear them. Such confessions didn't communicate in numbers and letters, they spoke in the most basic tongue. He knew what it sounded like—the Language of Pure Knowledge, the voice of The Truth. He'd heard it before on airplanes between the sputtering of engines, he'd heard it in the screeching of tires and in the ear-ringing quiet that follows deployed airbags; he'd heard it most clearly when he overdosed in Baltimore—the voice sang in the fluttering heartbeats that followed the kiss of the paramedic's paddles. Glimpsing the depth of his frailty, verifying his impermanence—no drugs compared. In the wake of adrenaline came clarity, from clarity came conclusion. Often it presented as gratitude—thanks to the pilot, to the seatbelt, to the hooker who, before she emptied his wallet and left him to die, found it in her mercy to call 911. Having been opened up by appreciation, the lesson was made plain: there was always something to learn. All he had to do was read the bones.

The GPS had him arriving in Cañon City in forty minutes: the show wasn't for two hours—plenty of time. He took a swig off the gin, reached for another cigarette. Outside it was bright, lustrous, the landscape rendered a chroma of lavender and pearl by the chalky light gleaming off the moon. The road followed the curves of the Arkansas River. The water, rippling, flashed like mercury, running fast, racing the car. Mountains, once the floor of a dead ocean, rose from the river's far banks, their faces pockmarked by a skein of ridges and switchbacks; their peaks abbreviated the sky. Billy Ray drove with the water, listening with more than his ears, waiting for the night to strip bare and reveal itself. He went blank, smoking robotically until the filters singed his fingers. Ten minutes passed without any vast appreciation. Ten more. He began to get nervous. What if there was no epiphany to be sussed from his rendezvous with infinity? What if there was no higher purpose to the continuation of his life? Maybe there weren't any bullets in the gun. He found it insulting somehow, cheapened: I LIVED WHEN I COULD HAVE DIED AND ALL I GOT WAS THIS STUPID T-SHIRT. I'M WITH POINTLESS, a single arrow pointing to his face. If this was nothing—blood and sex and violence—then what was the rest of it worth? Zero, even less. Maybe that was the lesson: death forms in life, it surrounds you, and what happens next is out of your control, but don't worry, don't fret, because you're small and it's of no consequence either way, so take solace in the worthlessness and remember to tip the waitstaff. "Sometimes you just have a gun pointed at your face," he said. "Sometimes you're dead." The absurdity was freeing. He began to laugh. The sound sucked out the window and disappeared on the wind. Praise be to the woman with the gun for she is my new mother. This is my birthday. Hallelujah, motherfucker, hallelujah. He punched the ceiling of the car. Thundering. Tremendous. The dome light flickered with his pounding. His knuckles began to bleed from where he had cut them on the man's teeth. The air coming in the window was cold. It moved through him. He lapped at it like a dog. It tasted like iron. He licked his knuckle. It tasted like the wind. Outside, a cloud settled on the gorge. Through the mist everything was dappled. The texture played with the distance of things. He was either far away or very close.

Five more miles and the bottle was empty. Cars no longer passed. He was alone out here. Approaching a sharp bend in the road, he turned on his brights, bouncing the high beams off a wall of soaring, blank rock. Billy Ray, still chuckling, dug a bindle of cocaine out of his breast pocket and cracked it open. Coming around the curve, busy with the powder and driving with his knees, he failed to notice a trio of haggard coyotes crossing in the temporary radiance afforded by the lights. They moved across the blacktop in a slow processional, their ears arched, their eyes wild jade. Billy Ray sped up out of the curve. As its skull smacked the fender, the third coyote yelped wetly. The yowl reverberated off the walls of the gorge, tearing apart the silence, and

Billy Ray spilled the cocaine as he jerked the wheel reflexively, careening the car into the left lane before he let off the gas and fought the fishtail back across the yellow line. After a few more sharp wobbles, he regained control and pulled the car over to the shoulder.

Billy Ray exited the vehicle, choking on the kicked dust and the stink of exhausted rubber. He covered his mouth with his forearm and looked up at the sky. "What's next?" he asked the stars.

A smear of blood and fur above the right tire marked the extent of the damage to the vehicle, but behind him, the two remaining coyotes nosed at their fallen comrade, now a mewling lump in the middle of the road. The sound was horrible. He knew it needed to stop.

Billy Ray began to swear, repeating the same few words over and over to himself as if committing them to memory. The repetition gave a form to things, contained them to a more manageable realm. He leaned on the hood, trying to catch his breath and preparing himself for what he had to do.

From the opposite direction, the headlights of an approaching pickup truck ignited the surroundings an ever-intensifying yellow. The light drove the last two coyotes skittering into the ditch, leaving their ruined packmate for the crows. Seeing his stopped car, the truck began to slow, but Billy Ray waved it on past him, and the world returned to darkness.

Resigned, Billy Ray opened the trunk, found the tire iron and walked toward the source of the noise that must end.

Ninety minutes to showtime.

THE MAN IN THE BOOTH AT THE SECURITY GATE SAID THEY were expecting him.

In the clubhouse, after a security guard patted him down and another poked around inside his merchandise case, a man named George Wetland waved the overambitious guards away, introduced himself and walked Billy Ray to the bar.

George Wetland was all jaw and his eyes were the same faint brown as the scotch he swirled. He smiled like he was trying to prove he had all his teeth. He was taller than Billy Ray and beneath his starched shirt, his long bones were corded by the type of lean muscle accrued under the guidance of a trainer. The president of both the Brushfire Golf Society and the local Shriners, George Wetland dressed like a man that relished titles and designations. The cuff links plugged into his wrist were gold and heavy and obvious, just like the pin in his tie and the watch he checked frequently. The skin where his wedding ring would have been was a shade lighter than the rest of his hand.

George's voice was a raspy deep baritone and he talked in flat statements. He said he was very rich from backhoes: "I made my money excavating but we do a lot more specialty backfill these days. As far as backfill is concerned, I'm number one in the Southwest." He put his hands on people when he talked to them. He palmed the base of Billy Ray's neck as he introduced him to the barman. "Clayton," he said, reaching over the bar to seize the young man by the wrist, "this is Billy Ray Schafer. I saw him in Atlantic City twenty years ago. We're very lucky to have him. Whatever he wants, put it on my tab."

"You got it, Mr. Wetland."

Satisfied, George Wetland glanced at his watch once more. He squeezed Billy Ray's shoulder. "Enjoy yourself. I'll send for you when it's time."

As soon as George Wetland walked away, Billy Ray ordered a Johnnie Walker, neat—"Blue Label if you got it." Clayton winked like an accomplice. He said he liked Billy Ray's style. The big man shot the whiskey as soon as it was poured and nodded for another. Clayton refilled the glass and Billy Ray slid a five across the bar. "Is he always that handsy?"

"With everyone besides his wife."

The whiskey tasted of vanilla and humidors. Clayton made sure the glass stayed full. When Billy Ray reached for his cigarettes, the barman slid a crystal ashtray in front of him. Billy Ray tested its weight in his hand and decided he would steal it on his way out.

The bar opened onto a dining room at the far end and beyond that a lounge full of deep chairs upholstered in leather stained the color of rich soil. With its old oak and garish red tableclothes, the decor reminded Billy Ray of the Friars Club, tucked away up there in the Monastery on 55th. He'd never been much for Manhattan, where survival and competition leached the humanity from his bones, but he did enjoy the Friars Club and the silly old Jews that called it home. He loved to listen to them argue and accuse each other over egg creams and white fish—who was a hack, who was a joke thief, who was a secret fag. No one was expected to tip. Five-hundred-dollar games of hearts. Cuban cigars on the roof. Once he walked in on a famous telethon host getting a blow job in the sauna—*Woah, nice la-*dy.

To remember such times was to twist a knife: from leather to cardboard, platinum to tin. Once his life had been novel, rarified, an existence so unique that in 1991, Paradigm Pictures bought the rights to his story for $50,000. "Congratulations," said Red as he slid the check across his desk. "Redemption sells, kid. The sweetest peaches grow out of shit."

In a way, he owed his entire career to Officer Clito Wainwright, the hulking, pockmarked, ginger sadist that oversaw the duration of Billy Ray's stay at Oklahoma State Penitentiary in McAlester, Oklahoma. Wainwright changed the course of his life that day, blustering in front of the entire Red Block during a night of reward programming. The projector had failed and while the equipment was being fixed, Billy Ray, as was his wont, took the opportunity to start cracking jokes. After a certain point, Wainwright, who was known for carrying a telescoping asp he lovingly referred to as his "get right stick," snapped: *You think you're so fucking funny, don't you, Schafer? You think you're Bob fucking Hope.* The room went silent when Wainwright flicked open his asp. "Come up here, Schafer," he demanded, slapping the concrete with the baton's lead tip. "Come up here and tell us a joke."

Billy Ray, sans options, did as he was asked, fighting the quiver in his knees: a race riot would have been preferable. In front of nearly one hundred federal criminals, their dead eyes gone blank from staring down all the years left ahead of them, Billy Ray told his first joke to a group of men who, as a means of survival, had forgotten how to smile: "I just flew in from Blue Pod and boy is my asshole tired."

A star was born.

Billy Ray opened for movie night for the rest of his incarceration and became the de facto emcee for all prison events. He told stories and street jokes and riffed on the news. He clowned on prison life and justice and incarceration and crime. He worked on his act all week, open-micing at chow, testing bits over games of spades. He started running a workshop for other prisoners. An improv team was formed. Eventually word got to the warden that they had a regular George Carlin in their midst, and the warden, after seeing prisoner number 1975632's act before the GED graduation ceremony, leaked the story to the local news, championing Billy Ray as an example of the rehabilitative work being done in his prison. Interviews were arranged, stories were written—"Ex-Con's Comedy No Joke"—and other easy headlines that wrote themselves.

Performing for inmates embossed him with a fearlessness that served him well as a civilian. Upon his release, Billy Ray caught a bus to Dallas and quickly climbed the ranks of the open-mic scene. When Red found him at the Hyenas in Plano two years later, Billy Ray was working in a rockyard quarrying limestone with a pickaxe and sleeping in his car behind an Arby's off the interstate. Red told him: "You're raw meat, boy, but I got a taste for raw meat." Within a year of signing with Red Eye Talent Management, Billy Ray made his network television debut on the *Arsenio Hall Show*. The *Tonight Show* soon followed. Next came a *Young Comedians Special* hosted by Rodney Dangerfield, who told him after his set: "We gotta find you a wheelbarrow for those balls, kid." In a piece on the state of modern comedy, *Rolling Stone* called Billy Ray "the voice of the New South . . . Mark Twain's gonzo grandson fried out on the truth." He was edited out of *Beverly Hills Cop II* because Eddie Murphy feared he stole his scenes. He and Red became a proven entity: people answered their phone calls because they knew money was on the line. The champagne was Moet, the cocaine was Bolivian, the bank accounts held commas, the networks were in talks.

In an interview that appeared in the September 1987 issue of *Playboy*, he was asked how he was adjusting to his success: "Life is Cindy Crawford and it's sitting on my face."

Later, in the same interview: "You have a bit of a reputation as a lothario."

"As a what?"

"You've been with a lot of women."

"Oh. Sure. I'm not shy."

"That's one way to put it."

"I imagine I know all the ways to put it."

"Do you think your—let's call it your lack of shyness—is that a result of your incarceration?"

"Let me put it to you this way: if you couldn't eat ice cream for three years, when that three years is up—you're probably gonna eat a lot of fucking ice cream, right?"

"Do you ever see yourself settling down?"

"I would for the right ice cream."

"And how will you know she's the right ice cream?"

"By trying every flavor."

In the spring of 1989, on a run through Montana, Billy Ray met the right ice cream.

Olivia was waiting tables at the diner in downtown Billings when Billy Ray blew in for pancakes smothered in red chili, his favorite breakfast. Even though it was hour ten of a sixteen-hour double and she was red-eyed and grouchy and the armpits of her uniform were dark with sweat, she was the most beautiful woman he'd ever seen. He left tickets for his show that night and his beeper number beneath a hundred-dollar tip.

She attended the show.

Eleven months later they were married on the beach in Galveston. Sam Kinison was his best man. Her mother did not attend.

He brought her to live with him in Los Angeles, but after a series of failed investments involving avocado farms and laser disc pornography, Olivia said she missed her family, and the Schafers bought a condo in Colorado Springs where she finished nursing school while he continued to barnstorm. They made two boys, Walker and Jeremiah, sold the condo, moved into a house in Denver. They were busy—she worked fifty-hour weeks, he was gone twenty days a month—but they made it work: Montessori schools, holographic Pokémon cards, trips to Epcot over Christmas. The boys wanted for nothing and their parents drove new cars.

It was a beautiful life and he was proud to give it to them; it was more than he ever had. He was infuriated whenever the boys complained. They were soft, frivolous, easily bored. Olivia said it was a good thing: children weren't supposed to be hard.

"It's not how I was raised."

"And thank goodness for that."

He did his best not to bring the road home with him and in doing so he became two men: husband/father, pirate/mercenary. Keeping them separate meant brokering bargains with himself: no liquor in the house, just beer; cocaine was reserved for weekends; he neither kissed the other women nor allowed them to spend the night. Maintaining these distinctions was all-consuming but he managed for longer than most. What happened was inevitable.

When the dam finally broke and the two disparate versions of himself came crashing together at the speed of heartbreak, the realities of his road life leveled his domestic facade: total war, no survivors. His ascent was spectacular, but it was nothing compared to the fall.

He forgot the girl's name, which made it worse: to forget the name of his destruction was to devalue what was destroyed.

She was a waitress at the Miami Improv. There were prettier girls. She never told him she was sixteen but he also never asked.

When she became pregnant, he denied paternity, but she insisted, claiming he was her first, screaming her remaining innocence into the phone, making him remember how it had hurt her. He wired the money. At the clinic, she learned the state required parental consent due to her age. Her parents, good Catholics, demanded to know who it was that damned their little girl, refusing to sign the paperwork unless she gave up the identity of the sire. Her father called the house while Billy Ray was away. Olivia answered and the scorned man rattled ugly words into her ear: abortion, rape, pedophile, Hell.

She was gone when he returned.

Counseling failed. The boys stopped talking to him. Paperwork was filed. Devastation reigned.

Billy Ray quit answering phone calls. He no-showed gigs and bombed the ones he didn't. Word spread. In two months, he destroyed fifteen years of good faith. The bridges burnt to the foundation. His career was never the same. Clubs wrote him off. The *Golden Globes* rescinded their offer to host. His audition for *Saturday Night Live* disappeared. Hollywood went to the bullpen, called up another fat guy. Billy Ray slipped into an abyss of wet and dry chemicals, experimented with needles, started buying by the ounce. Red organized an intervention. When that failed, he enlisted Tom Arnold to help plan another. His colleagues placed wagers on the date of his death. The entirety of the year 2000 occupied no space in his memory. He became a punch line, a curse spoken in whispers, an urban legend managers used to warn their young clients:

"Have you ever heard of Billy Ray Schafer?"

"Who?"

"Exactly."

For her part, Olivia did her best to soldier forward. After the divorce, she sold the house and moved herself and the boys in with her sister in Edgewater. They formed a triangle from the square. She put the settlement money into two college funds and got hired on as a charge nurse at the new hospital in Fort Lupton. Her and her sister bought a house and flipped it. When the boys finished high school, she moved up north. Staying busy kept her mind off the wreckage. To acknowledge the weight of her anguish would be to admit how much she still loved him. Instead, she started taking Xanax, ran marathons on the weekends. She sheltered the boys from the extent of their father's improprieties, scolded them when they spoke ill—"Just because he's not my husband doesn't mean he's not your father"—but the paternal bonds were damaged if not destroyed outright, irrevocable, smashed to smithereens. Their lives lost continuity. Walker buried himself in his studies and sport. Jeremiah played video games, learned to huff duster. They saw their father twice a month, giving him the silent treatment for the duration of their dour rendezvous at the Denny's in Loveland and then they watched the television in his hotel room or swam laps in the pool. The family formerly known as the Schafers were replaced by four mannequins with rocks in their chests, each of their lives punctured and reshaped by a black hole the exact size and shape of Billy

Ray's recklessness, a sucking wound that consumed and incinerated everything they valued including the *they* itself, leaving a woman martyred, two children sacrificed and a man alone.

He never returned to Miami.

Billy Ray put a carton of cigarettes and a black metal Zippo on George Wetland's tab and ordered a ribeye for afterward to-go. Despondence made him petty. As the room pinched around him, he sat on a stool that was too small for him chasing whiskey with smoke, his head heavy, cumbersome, the hair falling out of it. More cigarettes. More drinks. More more. When he felt the sway of the whiskey and his tongue was too round, he stumbled into the bathroom to true himself with dashes of powder. *My liver. My liege.* Soon he switched to beer.

A recurrent thought picked at the part of his brain that still fired: what would he have unleashed on the man in the apartment had the woman not come out with a gun? He knew the answer. It was dreadful. It caused him to sweat cold. He would have been severe. Extreme. There was too much energy. The limitlessness was horrifying: the lengths he could go. Whenever he thought he had finally mapped out his boundaries, there was always the wilderness, the farther, the dregs of him—black parts—of which he was ashamed. There's no returning from some places. Maybe that was the grand realization: you are the monstrous, the abominable: you are the beast beyond love. Billy Ray mashed his eyes with the palms of his hands. Firmly, he rubbed in slow circles until he saw flares of white light. He wondered how hard he would have to push to go blind, driving his palms in until the pressure was all that was real. It came to him in the canceling numbness: two men had been saved today—one from the other and the other from himself. By saving her husband, the woman had preserved the remaining shreds of Billy Ray's humanity. He remembered the feeling of power he had standing over the man, the thrill at his vulnerability; it made him sick. *How could I do this to you, brother? Can't you see we are twins?*

"Come again?"

Billy Ray rolled his head back to find the barman staring at him.

"Did you say something, boss?" He was dipping glasses two at a time into a sink of sudsed water. He ceased his work and dried his hands on a rag that hung like a tail from his back pocket before leaning over to open the beer cooler. "Another Peroni?" Like all successful bartenders, his voice was inviting, bereft of judgment, and his eyes were sympathetic.

Billy Ray didn't hear him. "What's your name?"

Clayton closed the cooler and leaned on the bar. "I'm Clayton, sir."

"Can I call you Clay?"

"Sure. I'm malleable."

Billy Ray pointed both index fingers at the bartender and cocked his head: *Got me.* "Hey-*yo.*"

Clayton submerged two more glasses and set them on a wire rack. "Thanks. I'm here all week."

"You're alright with me, Clay."

"Thank you, sir."

"Lay off that 'sir' shit. I don't sign your checks."

"I can do that."

"And let me get another green bottle."

Clayton slid the cooler door back, retrieved a Peroni and opened the bottle in one fluid, practiced movement. "Where you coming from?"

Billy Ray ripped a burp and blew it over his shoulder. "Pueblo."

"How was that?"

"I almost bit off my tongue."

"Sounds like Pueblo."

"I tell ya—I was right there." Billy Ray measured an inch between his forefinger and thumb, held his hand up to his rheumy eye and peered through the gap. "Right there."

"What happened?"

"It was me or him, but it was both of us. You know what I mean?"

"Of course," Clayton lied.

"But nothing's different."

"It never is."

Billy Ray's head lolled in agreement. "You ain't lying."

Clayton shook his head with pancake sympathy. "If it's not one thing," he said, "it's another."

"Except when it's nothing at all."

Clayton nodded. There was nothing else to say.

When George Wetland returned, his smiling face was red and slick with a film of sweat. He ordered a tequila, shot it and sucked loudly on the lime. He tipped Clayton with a new twenty, making a show of it as he peeled it off a roll of bills before counting ten fifties into a neat pile and sliding them to Billy Ray. "Might as well get this out of the way. Shall we?"

Billy Ray followed George Wetland through a heavy door inlaid with tawny brass down a hallway lined with photos of smiling white men encased in golden frames. Their smiles, practiced and unnatural, were variations on the same grimace, as if they sat for the photo while passing a stone. The corridor smelled like spent cigars and the carpet was a design of crocheted squares the same green as billiard felt. At the end of the hall, mounted above another ornate door, a silver plaque read in looping cursive: Senior Members Only Beyond This Point. The distinct forlorn twang of country-western guitar splattered out of the room as Wetland opened the door. "Wait here a moment," he said. "I'll make sure we're ready."

Billy Ray leaned on the wall with his eyes closed, a lone inebriant— a visitor—wobbling in an unfamiliar passage waiting to enter a room filled with strangers. Without seeing them, he had an idea of the kind of people awaiting him. He hated them. They were monied, landed, the kind of men that tucked in their T-shirts and drank rum and diets and complained about NAFTA. They were proud men, high on their own assets. Four-hundred-dollar cowboy hat Republicans, concealed carriers; they bought diamonds for their mistresses and horses for their wives. Their sons were named Dakota, Austin, Dallas. Their adult daughters called them daddy. He knew them down to the opals in their bolo ties and the Copenhagen in their lips. To these men, Billy Ray was yet another migrant worker, a whore summoned here at their beckon to provide tonight's scheduled release. Once he entered that room, he belonged to them, and he would dance for their amusement, ever the good chimp. That was his job: giving himself away. There was a time, early in his career, when, eager to impress, he would have been nervous around such men. Not anymore. He already had their money. There was nothing they could do to hurt him. Only people have feelings: Billy Ray was something else.

He pulled out his dwindling baggie and snuffed cocaine until the hallway regained definition and he could stand without leaning. From inside the room he heard a woman's voice followed by a barrage of piercing wolf whistles: a stripper. Perfect. Nothing aids laughter like unrealized erections.

I could leave. I could be gone. The thought was comforting. If he ever saw Red again, he decided he would kill him slowly with his hands.

He cleared his sinuses and spat on the carpet, disgusted with what he was about to do.

What's the difference between a clown and whore?

Whores wear less makeup but a clown will let you kiss him.

Comedy was just a trick that he knew, a deceptive ruse of cadence, timing and charm. No magic. No love. He'd seen behind the curtain: the emperor wasn't just naked—he was ugly and sick. And while he was a master of his craft, a doyen, skill and passion are two separate things. What was once a calling became a stark necessity, a filthy maintenance ritual, the chasing of a long-dead dragon: he'd lived for this and it killed him. Where once he had options, now he had no choice. It was too late to become something new.

The only aspect he cared about was the cash. At least the money was good. He could fake it for five hundred dollars. He'd done more for less.

He caught his face reflected in an empty picture frame. He looked away but his eyes drifted back. His bulbous head, bloated with liquor and jowled, was a dangerous carnal pink and crowned with a pompadour piled high like coiled mounds of greasy black shit. Gray mustache, gray mutton chops, gray teeth. Fat rimmed his chin, hanging in folds on his neck. In his cheeks, old acne pits glistened with indigenous grease. Deep lines corralled the eyes blinking back a tired no amount of sleep could cure, the whites of them stale yellow, the veins showing in the sclera like red lightning shot through fog.

I need to see a doctor.

I need to fuck a nun.

He buried his nose in the baggie and horked what remained. When it was empty, he stuck his tongue in the bag like it was a prophylactic and licked it clean. Vines of cold blind nothing climbed the interior of his face. He couldn't feel his mouth. He stood stock-still, his arm cocked to the side as if frozen in spasm, and listened to the exacerbated mechanism of his heart. If I died in here, he thought, they wouldn't even cancel their party. What a life.

Suddenly, the door cracked, spilling the corridor full of music and festive conversation. George Wetland, his tie loosened to a limp noose, a fez perched atop his pate, poked his head and shoulders into the hall. "Alrighty," he said, his horse teeth gleaming like diamonds. "I'm about to bring you on."

Billy Ray snorted like a bull, tasting the cocaine dripping down the back of his throat. Wide open, his eyes looked like shotgun bores.

George Wetland's eyebrows arched. "You might wanna . . ." Deigning, he brushed his nose with the edge of his thumb.

Billy Ray turned to his reflection in the glass. White powder ringed his nostrils. "Mamma mia! I'm Tony Montana." He swept his tongue across his mustache like a giraffe. "Is that better?"

Wetland's weak smile belied his discomfort.

Billy Ray sneered in a Cuban accent: "I always tell the truth, even when I lie."

Wetland shook his head. "I'm sorry?"

"Forget it." Billy Ray licked his fingers and tamed his hair back at the temples. "I never could do impressions." Then, as he always did, he shook out his arms and rolled his head on his neck in a figure eight. "I'm ready when you are, G.W." Acronyming people was an endearment tactic he employed regularly, but tonight the feigned familiarity read of desperation. He immediately regretted his choice.

George Wetland cleared his throat and scratched behind his ear in a habit of nerves. "We can wait if you . . . need a minute."

"Let's just do this fucking thing."

Cracking the door ajar, Billy Ray watched as George Wetland approached a microphone situated beneath the taxidermied head of a panther. A poster board bearing a simple crescent and writing too small for Billy Ray to make out balanced on an easel beside the mic stand and, behind that, a single speaker rested on a bar stool pointing toward a crowd of about forty men, all of them wearing the same red cylindrical peakless hats. They sat facing the microphone in hastily arranged folding chairs, the sparse metal clashing with the lavish decorations adorning the rest of the room: a snooker table, golden trophies arranged in a showcase, a top-shelf bar cart resting on ivory wheels. On the far wall between heavy red curtains hung the preserved heads of four more large cats mounted, he supposed, to appear as if they were bursting through the wall, their mouths ferocious, their eyes dead. Every aspect of the room was a lampoon of opulence, a rakish, overtly masculine aesthetic imported direct from the lairs of Bond villains, rich with the blatant affectation common to new money spent fast. The room made him think of Teddy Roosevelt, but the men were more FDR.

Billy Ray gave the crowd a quick read. White, thirty-five and older leaning an average of fifty or so. They seemed in good spirits, pouring domestic beer from cans into their wide, red American faces, dressed down in polo shirts and khakis and loafers and cowboy boots. He saw a few flasks being passed. A fair portion of them chomped cigars.

Wetland tapped his finger to the microphone. "Check, check, check." He looked toward Billy Ray, eyes asking. "How's that sound? Check, check. One two three four." Billy Ray pointed at the ceiling and George adjusted a knob on the speaker's built-in amplifier. "That better? One two. Apple butter. Chrysanthemum. Bangkok." Billy Ray gave a thumbs-up. George nodded.

Showtime.

Turning to the crowd, Wetland held up his hands, and the men responded to this signal with an obedient hush. He was quiet for a prolonged moment, drawing the silence thin, his arms out in front of him, palms facing the ground, a conductor before his symphony. When the silence was at its peak, Wetland dropped his arms, leaned into the microphone and snapped off a sharp bark. In unison, the men in the crowd bellowed back a collective growl, a low, grumbling noise like dogs smelling meat, and Wetland returned the sound in kind, raising his hand toward the ceiling, increasing the volume by the elevation of his fingers, feeding the discord, rising, roaring, bringing the men to the peaks of their voices until, like a guillotine, he dropped his arm, severing the ceremony and plunging the room into silence. Wetland cleared his throat and began: "Imperial sirs, illustrious sirs, members of the divan and nobles, it is my honor on this night in this hall to welcome you to the bachelor party of Illustrious Sir Tommy Murdock of the Templar Shriners of Fremont County, Colorado." At this, a tall thin man stood up and bent a quick bow before a barrage of empty beer cans drove him back into his seat. "Illustrious Sir Tommy, let me be the first to congratulate you. Es selamu aleikum."

The assembled men joined in a chorus: "Aleikum es selamu."

Billy Ray checked his watch but it was on the other wrist.

"Marriage is a sacred vow but in these halls it is inviolate. Mary Anne isn't just marrying a man, she's marrying a Shriner." Wetland's voice was stentorian, his rigid posture underlining the gravity of his words. "This order has existed for over seventy-five years and this temple for seventy, built by our fathers to be used by our sons. Everyone in this room is here because they yearned to be a part of something bigger than themselves. On Saturday, our numbers grow by one as we welcome Mary Anne to our temple and our brotherhood. If either of you ever need anything, you need look no further than the faces in this room. All you must do is ask." George Wetland motioned with his upraised palm to a bean bag of a man seated in the first row. "Percy, when red blotch ate up your soy crop, who leased you land on their farm?"

The corpulent man's face blushed into a beefsteak tomato. He peered in the direction of a rawboned man in a gray chamois shirt sitting hunched over with his elbows on his knees. "Chief Rabban Gregory," said the fat man. The rawbone man raised his can to the fat man and took a slug of his beer.

"And Tully, when the city shut down the gravel pit, who appealed your case?"

"Curt Wilson's son Wyatt," said a short man, broad as a washing machine, his jaw a plug chewing the nub of a cigar.

"Damn right he did. Shriners take up for each other. We protect our own. The prosperity of one is the prosperity of all. Tommy, on your wedding day, your wife becomes our sister and from that day forward, she will share in our commonwealth. May your love grow with your money and may your money never affect your love."

"Here here!" someone shouted, banging two chairs together.

"Congratulations, Tommy," said Wetland. "Es selamu aleikum!" The crowd burst into raucous applause.

Billy Ray lit a cigarette and spat on the carpet. "Faggots." The liquor had him nasty. He zeroed in on the man who was to be wed: *Run, boy. Go before you're gone.*

He barely remembered his bachelor party but he knew it was nothing like this circle-jerk. The sincerity was disgusting. Brotherhood—no fucking thank you. No part of him, not one cell, desired to be part of something bigger than himself. Obligation is slavery: association begets dismay. Trusting in the sanctity of a small group is how he wound up in the penitentiary, and the fallout surrounding the dissolution of his marriage injured two generations. Unifying was his life's greatest tragedy.

Poor Olivia: she'd never been hurt and he changed that. She loved him too much. Her devotion was total, naïve, the unbound love of the young and optimistic. She lost herself in him, became entangled, an individual no more. The woman formerly known as Olivia Svetlana Prudholm became a Wife, a Mother. She thought in plurals—them, us, we. Their separation left her struggling to find a new vocabulary: her future was their future until it was no future at all.

Billy Ray thought different. Above all else, Billy Ray Schafer believed in Billy Ray Schafer and, unlike his wife—Olivia, her name was just Olivia now—he viewed their relationship not as a new creation, but as an extension of himself. Everything they were, everything they had, it all grew from him. His marriage failed for many reasons, all of them failings of his decency, but paramount among them was his refusal to vacate his autonomy. His inability to cede himself to true amalgamation was the cancer that ate them alive.

It was a simple thing: she loved him because he loved her—and he did love her, truly, the best he knew how. It didn't come natural. He made mistakes. He was never comfortable. He doubted himself. He always wondered why she allowed herself to be with someone like him. She was a beautiful miracle and he was the opposite of that. He used to stare at her while she slept and trace her skin with his fingers, confused as to how the woman he wanted in the deepest physical way was also his wife. He loved her like the tides love the moon and it was easy to remain faithful in close proximity, but when he was away from her, out on the road enduring the crippling solitude of the high lonesome, there was nothing to govern the crashing of his waves. He looked for her in the string of blank women he subjected to his weakness. They were only proxies, symptoms of his dereliction: at the peak of his indulgence, he called them by her name.

The only person he loved more than his wife was himself.

The woman with the gun should have pulled the trigger. For the sake of mankind, she should have blown him away.

Still in the hallway, Billy Ray wiped away tears as the men in the Theodore Roosevelt room toasted the groom-to-be. They draped

across the man's shoulders a fine yellow sash and sang a song in a language Billy Ray did not understand. At Wetland's command, two
bikini-clad women emerged from a back room carrying trays of filled
shot glasses. Weary-eyed, their plastic smiles highlighted by smears of
electric lipstick, the women moved among the men disseminating the
liquor to a sea of groping hands. Cheers were called for, another toast.
A man with eyebrows as thick as silkworms raised his glass to the bachelor: "May the Lord provide and the whores deny." Laughter. The sharp
kissing of glass to glass. Their fraternity was palpable; it filled up the
room like light and sound.

Billy Ray lit another cigarette and kicked the toes of one foot into
the heel of the other. His mouth was ashes, his tongue a parched alien
in his mouth. Peeking through the door as he was, he felt like a child
watching the secret rituals of adults, less than them. His ankles hurt
and his lower back was stiff with the memory of sleeping on the floor
the night previous. He wanted to pop a few Valium and sit in a shower
until the water ran cold. "Fuck this." He touched his wallet in his back
pocket. He came for the money and he had it. There was nothing keeping him here. What would happen if he left? An angry phone call to
Red? A lawsuit? He smiled: *I have nothing and they can share in it.*

He was halfway down the hallway when he remembered the steak
he'd ordered. He hadn't had a good steak in a long time. A good steak
was one of his few genuine pleasures. No way the bartender would
hand over the meat if Billy Ray bailed prematurely. It was probably cold
by now.

"Goddamnit," he murmured. He checked his watch again. He'd been
in the hallway for more than ten minutes, trapped between and waiting. Breathing stale air. Sweat slicked his forehead as it poured out of
his hair. Adrenaline and cocaine and liquor scoured the walls of his
veins. He was ready to explode.

Say my name, George. Let me prove I am real.

"Thank you, ladies," Wetland said from his post on stage. Their trays
empty, the women left through the door they entered. Audible chagrin

rang out as they went. "Don't worry. We'll be seeing more of them later. Lots more. But now—sit, sit you animals. Good lord. Y'all act like you never seen a titty before."

"I haven't!" shouted a man in thick sunglasses, a collapsible cane laid across his lap.

"Good point, Bo. When they come back, you're first in line for a lap dance."

"Read 'em like braille, Bo," hollered someone, and the blind man pantomimed tuning a radio as the other men laughed.

George Wetland smoothed the front of his shirt and coughed into his hand as if he found this crudeness tedious. "Okay, okay. Until then, as I was saying, it's time for some comedy."

At the word, Billy Ray's ear perked like a dog. Unconsciously, his spine straightened. He rolled his neck out once more and flexed his hands, looking and feeling like a boxer behind the curtain.

"My esteemed brothers," Wetland said, filling his voice with pomp, "it is my humble honor to welcome to the Templar Shriners a man who I've had the pleasure of seeing before on my very own honeymoon those many eons ago, a man who needs no introduction, but he's getting one anyway. Please join me in welcoming a legendary comedian— he sat on the couch next to Johnny Carson—here he is"—Wetland motioned to the curtain, genuine in his excitement—"Billy. Ray. *Schafer!*"

His name, his burden. Billy Ray breathed in, breathed out and pushed open the door, crossing the space between the door and the microphone as well as the infinite space in his head, the space between who he was and who he had been. He stared out at the group of drunk men slapping their thick palms together in welcome. Their faces disappeared. Unbeknownst to them, in the moment he removed the microphone from the stand, they were no longer individuals—they were unified, combined. In his presence, they were reborn, melted down into a single organism—The Crowd, the faceless beast with countless mouths, its hundred eyes pregnant with expectation.

Feeding time, you monster. I hope you gorge till you choke.

"Thanks, George, for the warm welcome." He adjusted the mic stand to the appropriate height, an act of muscle memory as preconceived as his next breath. "And let's hear it for the girls. I hope to see them later, sitting on Tommy's face." The men seated nearest Tommy prodded him with their elbows. A hand from behind him tousled his hair. "Now that's my idea of a wedding veil." Billy Ray bent toward the blind man. "I bet you'd like to see that, eh, Bo? Hell, I bet you'd like to see anything." The blind man nodded vigorously, shaking the sunglasses off his face into his lap. "What happened, Bo? Did they make you valet your dog? Bo may be blind but I heard his dick can read lips. It telescopes, too. He doesn't even need that cane." Rolling his eyes back in his head, Billy Ray lifted the mic stand to crotch level and tapped it around as he crossed to the far side of the stage then back, milking the crowd's propulsive laughter, and back once more. "Somebody tell Bo what we're laughing about."

It was like waking up. For the next forty-three minutes, Billy Ray's voice was the blood in their veins. Reality cooked away. He was their shepherd: they went where he led. Bewitched, they spoke in tongues: laughter, the wordless language of purest communication, the unnatural coupling of logic and primality. Billy Ray explored the space, riffing on what he saw. He chewed up the stage like something uncorralled, pushing, pulling, establishing limits before crossing them, swinging seamlessly between bits and riffs in a display of vocal trapeze. The intensity of his focus was fire and brimstone. He commanded attention like a preacher at a pulpit and the men listened to his words like they might save their souls. Although he wasn't as quick as he was in his prime, his crowd work remained tenacious, rapid-fire. All he saw were targets, bobbing from one man to the next and weaving in callbacks, operating at a high speed in multiple sectors, an expert spinning plates. He made it look easy because, for him, it was.

"This place is like my omelets—whites only."

"Sandals, huh? Are you married, sir? You are. Does your wife know you're gay?"

"Those are some tight dungarees, brother. I can see you're circumcised. Jesus, I think it winked at me. Were you a Marine, sir? I thought so. Your ballsack matches your haircut: high and tight."

In the trenches, blunt effectiveness trumped clever. These men weren't here to think. Nothing he said was profound: he did what worked. He dealt in volume and velocity, working at a fevered pace. Boom boom boom. He knew the secret: laughter begets its own inertia and, like anything temporary, it yearns for perpetuity. Like a basketball spun on a fingertip, once he had them going, it was only a matter of maintaining momentum. The feeling was undeniable: total domination. He was ruthless, precise, unpredictable. His eyes glimmered, full of blue flames: I am trying to kill you. I have your lives in my hands.

Around the forty-minute mark, Billy Ray paused for a sip of beer while the men wheezed the dry rattle of dissipating mirth. To Billy Ray, they sounded like victory, conquest. He granted them this respite: they breathed with his permission. It didn't matter what he said anymore. These men were subservient, eager slaves to the sounds he made. His voice was Pavlovian. A pattern had been established: he talked, they laughed. Enough. It was time to bring it home.

Billy Ray adjusted his pants and turned to face the groom. "Well, gentlemen, this has been fun, but let's not forget why we're here. How about a round of applause for the man of the hour." On cue, the men hooted like primates. "Tommy, where are you? There he is. Tommy, sweet Tommy. You're getting married tomorrow. How you feeling?"

The groom raised a can of beer. "I'm feeling drunk."

Billy Ray smiled. "As you should. Look. Let me ask you something: do you hate blow jobs?"

"No."

"Then why are you getting married?" Billy Ray swatted a fly circling his head. "How old are you son?"

"I'll be thirty next month."

"Thirty. Goddamn. I've got pubes older than you. Look at you. Handsome. Fit. You got a job?"

"I supervise a road crew."

"So you make good money?"

"I do just fine."

"Well don't brag about it too much. These guys are gonna up your dues." Billy Ray gathered the mic chord and walked to the edge of the stage, tingling with a pleasant delirium. Sweat dripped off the tip of his chin, staining his clothes and spreading in dark patches under his arms and down the center of his back and forming crescents beneath his breasts. He was lightheaded, his senses heightened. He felt as if he could hear sounds before they happened, as if they were creations of his will. Only he knew what came next and this knowledge gave him power. "Tommy, listen to me. As a happily divorced man, let me give you some advice from the bottom of my heart: Run! Go! Save yourself! Go while you still have time! It's not too late. I know a guy who works in witness protection. He'll set you up with a whole new identity, a new life. There's the door. Here's my keys." He fished the ring of car keys from his pocket and tossed them to the young man. "Red Corolla parked out front. It's a rental. Don't worry—I'll report it as stolen. You can be in Mexico by sunup. Hell, I'll carry you across the border like a camel if I have to. Border patrol would understand. They'd probably give us a police escort to the whorehouse. Just go! Go! GO!"

A flash of dire panic cracked the groom's face while the rest of the men laughed. Billy Ray understood the look: the young man wasn't sure if he was joking: It's Funny Because It's True And Other Deceptions. The most human part of Schafer wished he could drop the act, bring the betrothed close and whisper, *Yes, I'm serious. This is the end of you, man*, but that wasn't funny, and Billy Ray only said what was funny. So instead he lied. "Jesus, son, I'm just fucking with you. Did you see his face? He was thinking about it. He was trying to remember his high school Spanish. I'm kidding, Tommy. Relax. You've got nothing to worry about. Congratulations. I wish you and your bride nothing but the best. Here's to you. Let's hear it for him, fellas."

The crowd, a rolling tide, roared their felicitation. *You dumbshits,* he thought. Billy Ray stared. How could they allow themselves to be gulled by such cheap manipulation? He loathed their hope but he allowed the celebrants their crescendo: only a fool shunned a free applause break. Billy Ray drank his beer standing firm in the eye of the storm, dreading the moment the adulation ceased and he had to speak again.

He decided to close on an old story he hadn't told in some time. A longer version of the story appeared as the final track on his second comedy album, *White Collar/Redneck,* a record that reached number one on the Billboard spoken word chart. The anecdote detailed the day he and his son visited his father's deathbed. In the joke, he and his son were together and laughing. Outside of the joke, they hadn't talked in years.

Unlike most stories comedians told, the events he related actually occurred: the hospice did reek of death, like "urine, Lysol and held-in tears"; when they entered the room, his father was asleep, as was his mother—him in his adjustable bed, her in the reclining chair she lived in for the long three months it took her husband to die; both he and his son had seen his father's erect penis "poking out of his boxer shorts like a startled ostrich"; and the ending was word-for-word accurate—he and his son did laugh hard enough to wake his mother and her response upon waking up was her crowning contribution to the world of humor.

". . . so there we are. We're dying—well, actually, *they're* dying, *we're* laughing and the nurse is confused. And that's when my mother wakes up and sees us and she says, 'Billy Ray? Jeremiah? What's so funny?'

"My son—he's an honest kid, so he looked at his grandmother and told her the truth: 'Well, granny, I'm sorry to wake you up, but grandpa's got a b-b-boner and me and my dad are . . . laughing . . . at it.'

"Now—my mother. She isn't what you'd call a cutup, but on that day, she said the funniest thing she ever said."

Standing motionless behind the microphone in the stand, Billy Ray swept the room with his eyes, reading the faces of the supplicants assembled. He took his time, scanning slowly, increasing the force of the silence. After saying so much, now he said nothing. The tension begged to be relieved. Anticipation impregnated the room. Through a break in the curtains, he saw the world beyond the window had fallen to complete abject black. For all he knew, this was all that was left.

He waited a beat longer, listening to an internal clock that ticked in his blood. At precisely the correct moment, he opened his mouth, licked his lips and pulled the pin.

"My mother said, and I swear to God, she said: 'Oh, that's okay, honey. I've been laughing at it for eighty years.'"

The adamance of their praise was deafening. He had to yell to be heard. "I've been Billy Ray Schafer. I've got T-shirts for sale." He found himself waving with both hands like Nixon as the men rose to their feet. "Now what do you say we get the girls back out here?" The applause devolved into grunting. The night slipped into decay.

They were kind with the liquor. He became automatic. Behind his eyes was a scraped-out void, bleached by the poison that powered his machine. His head rolled on his neck like it rested on ball bearings as he lurched about as if hung on strings, a marionette piloted by crippled hands. He was an amoeba. He operated with a primal understanding, responding to simple stimuli in aborted sentences, his eyes barely open, his memory perforated, his continuity dissolved.

Still he drank.

Upside down, the small-breasted woman stood on her hands, straddled his head and butted his chin with her pubis. He clenched his teeth. Her groin was sharp and the thrusting hurt his jaw but he bore it without complaint. In fact, he said nothing: he was afraid if he opened his mouth he might bite off his tongue.

He couldn't see the other woman, the one he wanted, but he could hear the scrape of her voice as she negotiated with the other man. Her voice was too coarse to whisper.

"One hundred for that," she told the man. "Two hundred for both."

They'd introduced themselves but Billy Ray forgot. Names didn't matter. In his head he referred to them as the small one and the big one.

The small one was the girl currently tamping his chin flat. The material of her thin panties was chafing him raw. Her face was long and thin and dominated by her eyes, which were oblong and lovely, like twin almonds made of glass, and encircled in rings of sunken blue gray. Her cheekbones stuck out like awnings. She had a habit of chewing her lip in the side of her mouth, a flirty affectation that reminded Billy Ray of a raccoon. Her body was jagged, like she was made of elbows, edged where most women were supple, displeasing to his touch. She smelled like moss.

The big one was the softer of the two and the subject of Billy Ray's booze-soaked libido. While her face, with its weak mouth and small, upturned nose and brown, beady eyes set too close together, was rodential, her ample body was as wide at the shoulders as it was at the hip, not fat by any means but sturdy, built of curves both rounded and heaped. Her novelty proportions raised a giggling, juvenile kind of lust in him: by way of introduction, Billy Ray told her he wanted to put a saddle on her and play Lone Ranger. She accused him of being the comedian and he said no, he owned a circus and he was trying to fill a sword-swallowing position. This caused her face to wink even more squirrelish. He couldn't tell but he thought it was her version of a smile. Sure enough, she extended her hand and he took it and she led him this way to the back room where her and the small woman had been stationed all night. She sat him down, but before she could offer her terms, her counterpart started bouncing on his lap.

The room was windowless and lit by two desk lamps positioned on the floor pointing at two plush recliners set back-to-back. The chair she had him pinned against smelled of men grown old in the country, the stink of barn jackets—scotch and hay, manure and sweat. This place reminded Billy Ray of the mudroom in his childhood home where his father kept his boots, the forgotten room where Olly Schafer smoked his hand-rolled cigarettes and took his coffee on frigid mornings while the snow swirled outside in blinding mosaics. Both rooms were sparsely appointed, decorated in the utilitarian style of rural people. A map of Colorado pinned to the wall was the only decoration besides an empty coatrack in one corner and a card table supporting stacks of red plastic cups, a few bottles of liquor and a plastic Tupperware full of ice. Underneath the table, a CD player pumped modern country into the stale air. Unlike the main room, the antechamber was charmless and uninviting. Even with the skinny woman's sex threatening to break his nose, Billy Ray felt like a detainee, as if any second he was about to be subjected to an interrogation: it was guilty in here.

After one final jab to his chin, the skinny woman dropped her feet back down to the floor and bent over and pulled her panties to the side so that Billy Ray could see directly into the puckered pink hole in the center of her ass. "You're looking at two hundred bucks, cowboy," she said, looking up between her legs. "Three without a rubber." She slapped her cheeks with her hands then stood up and faced him. She wore nothing besides the sheer panties. Topless, her tiny breasts looked like nippled shoulder blades. Her head was near shaved, clipped with a 0 or a 1 guard to a fine brown fuzz. The haircut did her face no favors: in the wrong light, her femininity abandoned her and she became a shirtless boy with maternal hips.

"Well," she said, running her palms down her torso. She dragged the tip of her tongue the circumference of her glossed mouth. "You wanna party, baby?"

"Have to save my money," he said. "Need an operation."

Her face sagged, eyes wide. "Oh. Poor thing."

"Doctor says I need a penis shortening. Very expensive."

The other man said something to the big woman that made her laugh. Billy Ray couldn't make it out but he knew, in this room, at this time, whatever he said was desperate.

"You're funny," the small one said.

"I wanna fuck your mouth."

The girl whistled. "Fifty up front."

Billy Ray's hand went to his wallet but he stopped. He pointed toward the ground and stirred his finger. "Spin around again first. I need to check you for ticks."

As she gyrated in weak circles, Billy Ray made a catalogue of the indelible designs inked into the different pieces of her. A black bird, he judged it a crow, was drawn permanently on the blanched skin stretched tight across her rib cage. The bird held her left nipple in its beak. Empty black stars were tattooed on the tops of her shoulders and in the hollow of her lower back, written like a memory, the words "Baby Girl."

"Who does your tattoos?"

"What?"

"Who does your tattoos?"

"My brother." Bracing herself with her hands on his knees, she snapped forward like a snake and rubbed her face on the crotch of his pants. The sudden attack to his groin caused Billy Ray to flinch but he relaxed as she nuzzled his lap with her forehead. He could feel her skull through his pants. "Careful now," said Billy Ray. "Don't put your eye out." She laughed into his groin as he snuck his fingers under the elastic of her thong.

Behind him, the other man moaned.

Billy Ray's solicitor stood up and posed with her hands on her waist. She was younger than the other woman but haggard, feeble. Her body was too narrow to house the organs that sustained it. The longer he looked at her, the less of her he saw. Billy Ray figured he outweighed her three-to-one. She was frail, incapable of protecting herself. Anyone could take anything from her. Something was eating her up. She was almost gone.

"How old are you?" he asked.

She knelt in front of him and spread his knees apart with her hands. "Younger than you." Her hand found his zipper. He folded the fifty, tented it and placed it atop her head like a paper hat. She told him to lie back. He shut his eyes.

After ten minutes, she stopped and wiped her mouth with the back of her hand. "You wanna try something else? You're not even—"

"I'm drunk."

"I can tell."

"Keep trying."

"I've got other money to make."

"I'm close."

The girl returned to her task, but after several more fruitless minutes, he shoved her head back and zipped himself away. "Nope," he said. "Nope no-o-ope nope."

"It's okay."

"They got me drunk."

The girl picked a half-burnt cigarette butt from the ashtray on the card table. "It's a party," she said, lighting the refry. "We're having fun."

Billy Ray patted himself down for cigarettes and found none. "Can I have some of that?" She gave him the cigarette. "I gotta straighten out."

"We all do."

He sat up in the chair. "Can you get stuff?"

"What stuff?"

The burning cherry floated between them like a comet as they passed the cigarette in the low light. "White."

"You think you need that?"

"I'll give you some."

Using the chair for support, she stood up and retrieved a soft pack of Salems from a purse hanging on the coat rack. "How much?"

"A ball?"

She lit her cigarette and shook the match dead. "Are you asking or telling?"

"A ball," he said.

Pensive, doing math in her head, the girl searched his face for a moment until she found whatever it was she needed. "I'll see what I can do. Wait here." She opened the door, allowing a wedge of light and sound to pierce the room, stepped into it and was gone. Forgoing a cup, Billy Ray took a bottle of dark liquor from the card table and sat back down and waited. The repetitive wet plunging sound rising from the chair behind him gave the room a unique tempo.

I'm I'm I'm. Formless thoughts rolled in his head like blank balls in a hopper. *What what what. Why why why.* His body ached for sleep. *Where do I why why why.* The bottle rose. The liquor tasted like his breath.

When Billy Ray woke up, he thought he was dead.

He was shaking him—the squat man he took for the devil. His hands were heavy on him. He understood they were there to prevent him from floating up to Heaven. The man's fingers, stout and strong, dug into Billy Ray's shoulder. His face was shaped like a dinner plate. His head dug in neckless to his compressed body, the eyes dark and bored into his pink flesh like hot coals in snow. Seeing him, this fiend claiming his body, Billy Ray was compelled to scream. The women jumped back. The man laughed and let go and Billy Ray did not levitate and in remaining seated he understood he was alive after all.

"Easy, big boy," the large woman said. Her puffy nipples stood out alert against the material of her robe. "Easy now." In the corner of the room, the skinny girl alternated between dragging a cigarette and chewing the nail of her thumb. The smoke curled in wisps.

"Wake up and smell the roses," the man said, dangling a sandwich bag before Billy Ray's face. Tied off into a corner of the bag, a turnip-sized lump of white powder hung pendulant. He swung the lump back and forth in front of Billy Ray's eyes like a television hypnotist. Billy

Ray, understanding his role, reset himself in the chair. His mouth began to salivate. He looked at the skinny girl and she nodded. Billy Ray asked for a cigarette. She complied.

Next to her, the big woman leaned against the door, her arms crossed. "Make it quick, Travis. We need the room."

"Oh I'm quick." The man pinched her chin with his thumb. "You know that." He bent forward, hands on his knees, putting his face close to Billy Ray's. "How you doing there, sailor? Need a light? Give him a light, Henrietta." The skinny girl leaned forward to join the flame of her Bic to the end of the cigarette poked between Billy Ray's lips. Once it was lit, the man smacked her ass, raising her onto the balls of her feet. "Henrietta here tells me you're looking for something extra." He spoke slowly, decisive, his voice twanged through with a Dixie lilt. His breath was hot on Billy Ray's face; it smelled like cinnamon gum.

"I do—I'm—I am."

The man unbent. Upright he was barely taller than Billy Ray sitting down. His top lip raised as he licked his front teeth. Considering Billy Ray, he tucked his hands in his hip pockets, stuck out his belly and rocked on his heels, appraising the big man as if he were for sale at auction. "They tell me you're a comedian."

"'Kay."

"Is that right?"

"Yes."

"I like comedians."

"'Kay."

"What kind of comedy do you do?"

Billy Ray ashed his cigarette on the arm of the chair. "The funny kind."

The man turned to the women. "You hear that? 'The *funny* kind.' That's good. That's funny."

"Donny said he was funny."

"Well, if Donny said it." The man looked at Billy Ray, sucked his teeth. "Do you know Rodney Carrington? I seent him in Phoenix once. He didn't swear one time. I was goddamned. Do you swear?"

A knock on the door from the other room interrupted his question. The big woman cracked the door, spilling a slash of light onto her face. "I know," she said out the door. "Just a minute. I promise." She shut the door with her shoulder and turned back to the man. "Travis," her exhausted patience plain. "Come on."

"I was just trying to pick his brain."

"Look at him," she said. "There ain't no brain to pick."

The man pulled the chunk of cocaine out of his pocket and handed it to the skinny girl. "The boys out front said he was funny something fierce. He doesn't look so funny now. Why don't you tell us a joke?"

"Why don't you suck my dick?"

"Henry said she tried that already." The skinny girl untied the plastic knot and returned the opened baggie to him. "Give me your cellophane." The woman peeled the wrapper off her Salems and gave it to the man and he knelt in front of the card table. "Give some light this a-way." The big one picked up a lamp from the floor, cutting the room in half, and held it like a lantern beside the man's work. The shadow of his head became a toad's on the wall.

"He said he wants a ball."

The man bit his lip as he measured about half the piece of cocaine into the wrapper. He held it up to Billy Ray. "That look right to you?"

"How much?"

The man paused. He looked up at Henrietta. She shrugged. "One . . . fifty?"

Billy Ray counted the bills out on his lap then recounted them for the man to see. "Twenty, thirty, fifty, sev—sixty, eighty, hundred, one fifty."

The man tucked the wad into the pocket of his shirt and sealed the top of the cellophane with a lighter before handing it to Billy Ray. "My work here is done. You happy?" He leaned in to kiss the big woman but she turned her head and opened the door. "Fine," he said. "Pleasure doing business, Mr. Comedian." The man turned to the skinny girl. "I'll be out front."

"Some of that's mine."

"We'll see."

The big woman kicked the leg of Billy Ray's chair. "Hey! You too." She snapped her fingers, holding open the door. "Out." She kicked the chair again. "Let's go."

Three men filed past Billy Ray as he stumbled out of the door. Before the door shut, he heard the big woman say, "Sorry about that, fellas. He was telling us a joke."

The party crowd had thinned considerably, boiled down to the stragglers. The remaining men sat and talked in gatherings of threes and fours, their faces slack and vacant, leaned back in the metal chairs with their legs spread wide and shirts untucked, a few of them shoeless in stockinged feet, their tall riding boots removed and set in paired vigils next to crushed beer cans and half-eaten hot dogs and torn bags of store-brand potato chips and empty tins of sardines. In the corner, a man curled around a crock pot slept on the ground using a flag for a pillow. No one noticed Billy Ray collect his suitcase and go.

The hallway back to the bar seemed much longer before. He barreled down the passage knocking frames off the wall, eager to be alone with the cocaine. The need for the powder was an awful eating feeling, a gnawing he experienced in the radicles of his teeth and the cores of his bones; it made his hands sweat, this fantastic compulsion. It was all he needed and all there was.

The bartender put down his rag when the big man entered the lounge. "Taking off, Mr. Schafer?" Billy Ray ignored him. The barman tried again to get his attention but Billy Ray walked straight out into the night. A layer of fresh snow blanketed the world. He stopped to let his eyes adjust, coughing on the cold air. The untouched snowfall shimmered like powdered diamonds, flecked through with sparks of purple and blue. The suitcase carved tracks in the white.

At the car, he collapsed the bag's telescoping handle and tossed the case in the back seat. The vehicle sputtered to a start and he sat behind the wheel shaking and watching his visible exhalations fog the rearview mirror. A chrysalis of frost coated the windshield: it felt like he was encased in amber. Early in their marriage, when Olivia worked the sunrise shift at the hospital, he drove her to work when he could, avoiding the bus and allowing her an extra forty minutes of sleep. He woke up at five, fifteen minutes before his wife, often still drunk and on scant hours of sleep, to start a pot of coffee and warm up the Buick. On the cold mornings, when the light was mist and the day yet solidified, he sat in the driver's seat smoking cigarettes and toeing gas into the LeSabre, goosing it until the defrost came on and melted away the verglas. Sitting in this frigid car reminded him of those crisp mornings, groggy and hungover but proud to be of service to the woman he loved. She'd come out with her steaming coffee and her Carhartt jacket zipped up to her ears and talk the entire ride, filling his head with hospital gossip involving the names of co-workers he pretended to know and taking dainty sips from her mug and pointing at buildings she liked and him driving with his hand on her thigh and taking the speed bumps slow so as not to spill her coffee, driving until they arrived finally at the ER with its glass facade gleaming in the light of the new day sun, and her kissing him goodbye, saying *I love you, baby,* saying *Thank you, my love.*

Sitting here fighting hiccups and blowing heat into his hands, he remembered those mornings long ago when he had a purpose and a reason: this was like that only completely different.

A pounding on the roof of the car ended his reminiscion. Obscured by the rime of frost, a stooped figure called to him from outside the glass, the shape of its words undecipherable and dampened by the door. Billy Ray wondered if this was real or yet another failing of his grasp on things, but the form tapped on the glass, asserting its legitimacy.

"What?" asked Billy Ray. He tried the window crank but the glass, frozen stuck to the doorframe, refused to lower. He leaned hard on the crank, breaking the hold of the frost, and through the gap he saw the upper portion of the barman's face.

"You forgot your dinner." The bartender held up a white Styrofoam box. "The steak."

"Oh." He forced the lever down farther to allow the box passage. Cody or Clark—something with a C. "Thanks," he said.

"No problem." Cody or Clark leaned in close to the crack, blowing his breath into the car. "This weather sure came out of nowhere." He glanced at the road, furrowed his brow. "Hell of a night to be driving. Is this front-wheel drive?" Billy Ray had no idea. "There's a cab service in town . . ." He trailed off, leaving space for a conclusion to be made, but Billy Ray's eyes registered no change or understanding. The barman cleared his throat. "We could charge it to the club. Have them bring you back out tomorrow for the car."

Billy Ray didn't know what was expected of him in this moment. He grasped the words without comprehending the message. Driving was one of the few skills he had: he drank, he smoked, he drove. Without the car, he was trapped, and that wouldn't do. He opened his wallet and slipped five dollars out the slot hoping that's what this was about, but the man refused the bill.

"No, Mr. Schafer." The barman grabbed hold of the window as if to hold the car in place. "You sure took down a lot of Blue Label tonight." He cocked his head and pitched his eyebrows. "I'd certainly feel better if—"

Billy Ray rolled up the window, nearly clipping the tips of the barman's fingers. He flipped the windshield wipers and the frost moved away in a wet sheet. Cleared, Billy Ray pulled the gear selector, missing reverse by one click, and stomped the accelerator. The man jumped back as the fresh snow caught the rear tires, preventing their traction, snaking the car left then right before the tread caught the asphalt and the car plowed across an elevated island of grass smashing grill-first into the trunk of a conifer. The seams of the airbag sliced his face, breaking his nose, snapping his head back into the headrest. An explosion of stark white, drifting, lost. He disappeared for a while.

"Mr. Schafer? Mr. Billy Ray?"

He was on the ground looking up at the sky. Snowflakes landed on his face and became pink water on his skin. From the blood steam rose. "You're all cut up, Mr. Billy Ray." The barman knelt beside him in the snow, his hands hovering above the body, afraid to touch anymore. The collision compressed the front of the car. Smoke escaped the hood accompanied by the bleating of the smashed horn. The noise called the last Shriners outside to gawk at his disaster. In their tiny red hats against the serene white and made small by the distance, they looked like elves and he understood them as such.

In and out. Black to white to black again. Hands on, hands off. A voice squeezed his feet, asking can you feel that? How about this? Red and blue lights purpling in the snow. He heard voices: *I told him. I swear I did.* Then he was lifted and delivered into a room where plastic snakes were inserted into his face. Hold still. The room moved under him.

In and out.

In and out.

In.

Out.

He woke up flanked by machines of rectangular design. Their monitors told a story. Green lines moved inside of them, numbers in red. He was beeping. Tubes stung the back of his hands, either delivering blood or stealing it. There was no way to tell.

Maybe I am dead, he thought. *Or maybe I was never alive.*

FRIDAY

THE DOCTOR NEVER LOOKED UP FROM HIS CLIPBOARD.

"We ran a CT scan. No signs of brain trauma, no bruising, no bleeds. Minor lacerations, no stitches necessary. Your nose is broken but you knew that. You should be out of here today."

Billy Ray sipped apple juice from a box dwarfed miniature in his hand. Shards of light wormed through the blinds building a hopscotch on the gray ceiling. Looking up from his back he felt upside down.

The doctor seemed put out. He was older than his patient. He spoke in a monotone dirge, the way someone sounds recounting a story they've told too much. He looked like it had been years since he got enough sleep. Vines of red veins grew out of the sides of his nose and spread across his cheeks in the pattern of broken glass up into the heavy bags that pillowed his eyes. A lifetime of familiarity with the persistence of death warped his face but his hands, pristine tools, appeared to be thirty years younger than the rest of him. "Mr. Schafer." The doctor removed his glasses and looked up from his chart. "We also did some blood work. When was the last time you've seen a medical professional?"

Billy Ray cleared his throat. "The last time I had insurance." His voice came out flat beneath his squashed nose.

"And when was that?"

"I quit paying SAG in ninety-nine."

The doctor looked above his head, doing the math. "So eighteen years?"

"It was ninety-nine."

The doctor sat back in his chair and crossed his legs. "Do you have a history of hypertension in your family?"

"My daddy had fast blood."

"Is he alive?"

"Nope."

"How did he pass?"

"I heard he had a heart attack on his combine."

"And at what age did he pass?"

"Fifty-one. We were born on the same day."

"And your mother?"

"She died, too."

"How?"

"Not sure. My sister found her." Billy Ray straightened up in the bed. "It fucked her up."

"How old was she?"

"My sister?"

"Your mother."

"Fifty . . . five? Six? What's with the questions, sawbones?"

The doctor removed a pen from behind his ear and wrote something on the clipboard. "Mr. Schafer, at the time of your intake, your blood pressure was one seventy over one oh two. From a medical standpoint, those are worrisome numbers."

Billy Ray looked past the doctor to the hallway behind him. Out there, two women in sky-blue smocks laughed across a water cooler. One of them covered her face, nodding emphatically, as the other gripped her shoulder. He wondered what was so funny.

The doctor continued. "Are you a smoker?"

Billy Ray nodded.

"And how often do you drink?"

"When I'm working."

"And how often do you work?"

"Every day I can."

The doctor jotted. "What about the cocaine?"

At this, Billy Ray's brow caved. "What?"

"Your workup showed," the doctor said, flipping to another piece of paper, "a level of point eight milligrams of cocaine per liter of blood. That indicates either a sustained period of use or one hell of a night." The doctor leveled his eyes. "I understand you're a comedian, Mr. Schafer?"

"That's what they tell me." He wanted another juice box or preferably something stronger.

"That must be a lot of pressure."

"You're a doctor. My wife was a nurse. That's a lot of pressure." The doctor uncrossed his legs and planted his feet on the floor. By the angle of the light through the blinds, Billy Ray knew it was early morning. They must have kept him here all night. "Can I get another juice?"

"Mr. Schafer, you're putting a lot of years on your heart."

"Apple's fine. Or grape. If you got it."

"I don't think you're hearing what I'm saying."

"No, I heard you. You said I could get out of here today."

The doctor tucked the pen back behind his ear and stood up. He was taller than Billy Ray assumed, long in the leg. He put his glasses back on. "You're on an unreckonable path, sir."

"Did I sleep through breakfast?"

The doctor sighed and returned the chart to the end of the bed and Billy Ray shut his eyes until he heard the doctor leave. Alone, he fell into a fitful sleep. In his dream, he stood under a waterfall. The water ran over his face in a sheet, pounding him. He tried to move but the water was too strong.

When he woke up, his face was warm and sticky and his pillow was wet with blood.

·　·　·

Upon his discharge, he bought a pair of sweatpants and a T-shirt from the gift shop and changed out of his bloodstained clothes in the bathroom in the lobby. He filled the prescription they gave him at the onsite pharmacy and called the rental car company from a phone at the front desk. Fully insured with Diamond Club status, the operator said no problem when he told them where to collect the Corolla and happily transferred him to their franchise in Pueblo, where he reserved another car. He hung up, called a cab and stepped outside to smoke a cigarette he bummed off a nurse.

A sharp wind slashed the afternoon, screaming across the bright day and whipping the leaves off the trees. On the lawn, the thin snow had hardened overnight into a dirty gray crust. Billy Ray hid from the cold in the high sunlight drenching the hospital's eastern wall, flattening his body against the lee to avoid the clawing wind. When the cigarette was gone, he consulted the ashtray built into the top of the trash can but the snowmelt had ruined the butts. He sat on the curb and stared at the sun.

A corrosive anxiety rose in his breast. At any moment he expected to be accosted by deputies holding handcuffs open and hungry for his wrists. The way he understood it, the presence of an ambulance meant the police were informed automatically. Didn't they share the same scanners? The men at the club were powerful but they had no incentive to cover for him. He didn't even get to eat the steak.

In 1987, up in Maine where the sun goes down at three in the afternoon, he'd been hauled in for DUI, but, using a combination of namedropping, folksiness and anti-Canadian humor, he'd managed to charm not only his arresting officer but the entire Sheriff's office and they released him in the morning scot-free after gathering round for a Polaroid; a deputy even gave him a ride back to his car. This wouldn't be like that: you should never go back to the well. He was different, then and now. Back then he was almost famous: today, according to the doctor, he was almost dead.

All through the morning he listened for the sound of boots on the tile, waiting for that blue uniform to knock on the door and say, Billy Ray Schafer? You're coming with me, but the blue uniform never came and now he sat outside away from the entrance with his fingers crossed, praying to whatever wasn't cold and dead that the next car to turn in to the hospital complex was a yellow taxi and not a black-and-white. A DUI would ruin him but most pressing, the show in Denver started at seven: he was running out of time.

Eventually, a black sedan turned off the county road into the hospital entrance. As the car approached, Billy Ray's heartbeat staccato'd as he prepared to disappear into the thicket of black trees behind the hospital at the first sign of law. The car seemed civilian—no cherries, no bullbar, no government plates—and the driver was paunchy and disheveled. It was the words painted in white on the passenger door that finally convinced him: So. CO Taxi Co. He relaxed. "Hell yes," he said, flagging the driver. He was in the back seat before the car reached a full stop.

The cabbie was brown and fat. His eyes in the rearview were red crescents. In the corner of his mouth, a nub of unlit cigar muddled his words. "You Daniel?"

"Sure am."

"Where to?"

The cab smelled like wet socks. "How much to Pueblo?"

"Pueblo's a ways, bud."

"How much?"

"Cash or card?"

"Cash."

The cigarlette spun as the driver mulled. "I'll do it for eighty if it's cash."

Billy Ray counted the bills and laid them on the driver's shoulder. "I'll throw in some extra if you're fast. We gotta make one stop first." Billy Ray gave the man the address of the golf course and slunk down in the seat but his size made concealment an impossibility. Lowering, his face appeared in the driver's side mirror. He looked bad. In the middle of his face, his nose was a rotten potato, a crooked black tuber stuck in the center of a violet bruise under a forehead thatched with strips of white adhesive bandage. Talking hurt.

Billy Ray dug two Valium out of the pocket in his wallet, chewed them down and swallowed them dry. The car lurched as the driver geared to drive. The world passing outside the car was rendered in a weak fidelity: grainy, flat, monochromatic. Banks of plowed snow piled in two-foot drifts lined the sides of the road, the mounds built taller where the wind was most prevalent. Vehicles kicked the snowmelt from their back tires in rooster tails. An opaque sky hid the sun from the earth.

The taxi accelerated around a six-wheeled pickup hauling a long metal horse trailer and Billy Ray made eye contact with one of the horses through the slats. The big animal's eyes were rheumy, yellowed like the pages of an old book. They looked defeated, like they'd seen enough, the eyes of a wild thing captured. "Better you than me."

"What's that, bud?" said the driver.

"I was talking to the horse," said Billy Ray.

The golf course was closer to town than Billy Ray remembered. He told the driver to pull up to the security booth and he rolled down his window. The security guard leaned his top half out of the booth. His legs below him not visible, he looked like a massive sock puppet. "Howdy there."

"Hey. Uh . . . howdy. I was the comedian last night."

"What's your name?"

"Schafer."

The security guard popped back in the booth and consulted a computer screen. He shook his head. "I don't have a Schafer on my list."

"I was the one who crashed the car."

"Oh."

"I gotta get some stuff before the tow comes."

"I heard about you."

"I bet."

"Must have been a hell of a party."

The gate arm lifted and the cab pulled up the drive into the parking lot and Billy Ray directed the driver to park next to the squashed Corolla. "Pop the trunk, would ya?"

He lugged his suitcases from the wreck to the taxi before sweeping the interior. Loose belongings were shoved into a ruck he reserved for dirty clothes. Trash he collected in plastic grocery bags, getting under the seats, careful not to leave behind any evidence of criminality in case the rental company investigated the car. It was remarkable how much detritus he generated in just three days. Two bags full of fast-food wrappers and Styrofoam cartons and cigarette boxes and paper cups and napkins and crushed beer cans and water bottles and condiment packets left unused, hundreds of dollars turned into excrement, pounds of trash, the evidence of his life. Before he shut the door, he left the keys in the visor as he'd been instructed by the rental agency and, as he always did when returning a car, he rolled down the windows to air out the stink of stale smoke lest he incur a fine.

He shut the trunk and kicked the mud off his boots and returned to the taxi. "Don't worry. I won't ask," said the driver. The car began to move.

On the radio, two men with similar rancorous voices yelled about war and the economy and oil. The driver increased the volume as they pulled onto the main highway. "Let me know if you want me to change the radio." Billy Ray told him it was fine. "Good."

"You don't like music?"

"I like to hear what people have to say."

"So you're talk radio only?"

"If I'm in the car, it's on."

"You ever listen to Phil Hendrie?"

"That's the guy that does them voices?"

"Yeah."

"He's pretty funny sometimes."

RUNNING THE LIGHT 121

"He's a genius." From the wreck, Billy Ray had salvaged a half a pack of cigarettes. "You mind if I smoke in here?"

"I don't mind if you don't mind." The driver opened the glove box and retrieved a fresh cigar the same color as the pads of his fingers. He put the cigar in his mouth and chomped the head and spat the decapitated nub out the window.

"You like *Coast to Coast*?" said Schafer, already sucking on a Winston.

"When I drive at night—of course. George Noory is my guy." Holding the wheel steady with his knees, the cabbie sparked a match and plumes of rich smoke clouded the car as he puffed the cigar. "He's one of the few men that tell the truth."

Billy Ray yawned. The pills he'd swallowed were already caressing his blood, sanding the edges off the bleached afternoon. "Do you believe in all that stuff?"

"What stuff?"

"You know. Lizard people. Bigfoot. Kennedy is still alive and lives with Elvis in the center of the earth."

"I don't not believe in it. Being sure of anything is for fools."

"I think it's all bullshit."

The driver snorted. "That's what they want you to think, bud. They want you to believe what they tell you. They want us to dream we are awake."

"Who is *they*?"

"The men who own the world."

They passed a McDonald's attached to a gas station. The sign out front read ONE BILLION PEOPLE CANT BE WRONG. Billy Ray made a circle in the air with his cigarette. "You're telling me you think there's a plan for all of this?"

The driver's voice was leveled, sincere. "Top to bottom. We're just pawns, bud. We only see what they show us. We're cogs in their big machine."

"Are you fucking with me?"

"It's all a hoax."

Billy Ray tapped his ashes out the thin slit between the window and the door. "Shit. If anyone is in control, they're doing a terrible fucking job."

They drove on. The driver was aggressive. He used all the lanes, threading the gaps between the other cars and passing on the right. Once he cut off a semi and the trucker blew his horn but Billy Ray didn't notice. After so many miles behind the wheel, there was a novelty to the back seat. He stared out the window and smoked as the men on the radio answered calls from exasperated people—longtime listeners, first-time callers—watching Highway 50 sweep past the early winter landscape, past the empty fields of frostbit alfalfa and browned acres of indeterminate growth and the horses in their blankets and blinders and the cattle behind barbed wire fences gathered in groupings one hundred head deep to share their body heat against the wind, driving under the begging fast-food neon and the green signs detailing the distances to cities and the austere black billboards warning Jesus was coming, repent, repent. The roadway curved to accommodate the footprints of the mountains, the ground pitching gradually away from the car until it met the sheer slabs of ever-rising earth. The mountains, tremendous, their peaks frosted with snow that would not melt for months, were too big to see all at once. Billy Ray catalogued their individual aspects and attempted to piece them together in his mind's eye but he was unable to build the image as the pills coated his brain in a warm shellac of beautiful nothingness. His body felt unattached to itself.

Every few miles, road signs warned BEWARE OF FALLING ROCK. After the third sign, Billy Ray chuckled to himself. "Beware of falling rock," he said.

"Lots of good that's gonna do you, eh?"

"'Did you hear about Jeff?' 'No, what happened?' 'He was driving on twenty-five and a boulder came out of nowhere and crushed his car.'

'What a shame. If only he read the signs.'" The tube of fat ringing the base of the driver's neck wiggled as he laughed. Billy Ray wrote *FALL-ING ROCKS* in his Moleskine: another day at the office.

In Pueblo, the driver asked him where to and Billy Ray gave him the address of the rental car lot. "I don't know the streets up here," the driver said.

"Put it in Google."

"I don't fuck with GPS. They don't need to know where I am. Put it in your phone."

Billy Ray pulled the two pieces of his phone from his pocket.

"Oh," the driver said. The driver pulled into a gas station and Billy Ray went in to ask directions. The cashier apologized, he had no idea, he thought it was by the airport, but the second attendant gave them detailed directions. "By the airport?" he scoffed. "What a dumbass."

The directions were precise and they found the lot without incident. Billy Ray tipped the cabbie an extra ten, then, as an afterthought, dropped two Valiums into his palm, changing the man effusive—"Shit, bud, good looking out"—and the two men shook hands and gave dap. "Drive safe," Billy Ray said as he bumped the cabbie's fist. "And keep watching the skies."

The cabbie snapped his fingers. "Bet. Look out for falling rocks."

The rental agent tried not to stare at his face. His rental options were limited, she explained. The weekend rush had cleared most of their stock, leaving him the choice of a tiny Nissan Leaf or a ten-miles-per-gallon Escalade battleship. He chose the Nissan and reverse engineered the directions back to the highway.

From there he knew the rest of the way.

Driving north on I-25 behind a convoy of camouflaged military Jeeps, a strange desolate malaise seeped up through the benzo lacuna like oil through dirt. Between here and Wits End, the club in north Denver where he was booked all weekend, lay the first place he and Olivia really ever called home: Colorado Springs. Their tenure only lasted four years before she transferred to the hospital in Denver, but the place was the center of his life's greatest happiness. His life would be empty without what transpired in that timespan.

The memories seemed impossible. Phantasmagoria. Before the ugliness and the ruin, there was the constant sweetness of cohabitation in their little condo, the pride she brought him, the sound of her voice, the smell of her in everything, "dinner time" and "date night" and the days spent in bed perfecting the act that created the two little boys whose arrival changed his very definition. Those four years were the marrow in the bones of the skeleton of his history. If they made a drug that replicated the essence of that time period, he would shoot it into his jugular until it replaced his blood and killed him.

"Hello, old gal," he said to the welcome sign. Due to the artist's mistake, an extra serif on the N in SPRINGS made the letter appear upside down, a fact locals used to bore tourists—he couldn't remember how his old joke went. He slowed down to investigate whether the N had been fixed, but a passing dually truck blew a cloud of diesel exhaust too thick to see through, and immediately he remembered why he liked this place: unlike Denver, the big city to the north, with its braggadocious sports franchises and overhyped culture, Colorado Springs, home to the ProRodeo Hall of Fame and Museum of the American Cowboy and Air Force Academy, was unpretentious and wild. "Where urban living meets the mountain." The nearness of Pikes Peak encouraged frequent communes with nature. They'd hiked picnics up the mountainside, made love in the long shadows spilling off the Garden of the Gods. A recurring excursion involved taking acid at the zoo: he'd never be as funny as a penguin.

Despite the direct access to nature, the Springs wasn't all hippy-dippy like Boulder. People still feared God here. Churches were packed on Sunday. The preachers were celebrities. The military presence infected the whole city with an unhealthy respect for the flag, and the grunts on furlough prevented a man going soft. Billy Ray had found himself in many a last-call dustup with brush-cut cadets eager to field test the techniques they'd learned in the Academy. It reminded him of where he grew up, and he judged it as good a place as any to be young, fearless, dumb and in love.

He had been back many times since they'd moved, but the Valium had him sentimental. Everything he saw was a sentence on a page in the book of his life: the Mr. Donuts where she confused crullers with croissants, the Walgreens where she purchased the pregnancy test that turned into Walker. Crossing Monument Creek, he recalled the golden afternoon when an overzealous goose, hungry for the pretzel in his pocket, chased him off the shallow bank and into the water. That was the hardest she'd ever laughed, Olivia, who was most beautiful when she laughed. No joke in his arsenal compared. Spasmodic, she fell in the grass, kicking her feet in the air as she cackled up at the sky. It became the story she told at parties, her most treasured anecdote, and in the telling of it, she laughed just as hard as that day in the park, to the point where she was inconsolable, and the story was ruined and she couldn't continue.

Then he saw it.

Without signaling, he shot across three lanes of traffic, barely catching the exit for Mark Dabling Boulevard. At the end of the exit loomed the red-and-white building that always reminded him of a carton of milk: Drifter's Hamburgers, home of the boysenberry malt and the most identifiable border between Present and Past.

He parked beneath the canopy of a bulbous cottonwood with leaves gone rusted and ready to shed. Chimes announced his entrance. An eager teenage boy sporting a long ponytail of sandy brown hair greeted him through braces. "Hello, sir. Welcome to Drifter's." The menu was the same: burgers, French fries, chicken fingers, hot dogs, corn dogs, chili and Olivia's personal favorite: Frito pie.

"Y'all still do the boysenberry malts?"

"Yessir," the boy said, turning to point at the portion of the menu labeled SWEET DREAMS. Acne had made a red moonscape of the side of his face. Around his wrist, a hemp necklace dangled with small charms. "We got shakes, too."

"Well, I better have one of those."

"A shake?"

"No, the malted."

"You got it. What size?"

Suddenly he was very hungry. "Large."

The boy raised his voice and threw it over his shoulder. "I need a large berry malted. Is that all, sir?"

"You like the Frito pie?"

"I used to." The boy flicked his head and the ponytail jumped. "I'm a vegetarian now."

"Good for you, kid." The boy smiled. "I'll do a cheeseburger. No ketchup. No tomato. Extra pickles."

"Onions and lettuce okay?"

"Sure. And a Frito pie."

Billy Ray paid and sat in a booth but the table dug into him, bulging his gut onto the Formica, so he moved to a table and waited until the boy brought out his food. It was just like he remembered: the fries were well salted and shoestringed and the beef tasted like griddle and the malt was yeasty and tart with the fresh berries. Tasting the Frito pie reminded him of Olivia, tired from another twelve hour shift and splayed out on the couch in the living room of their neat apartment, her head on the armrest, her swollen feet kicked up on his lap as she ate her dinner off the ottoman ("the most comfortable of all the empires"), a splash of blackberry brandy in her malt, watching *Cheers* or *Battle of the Network Stars* until she plummeted into a bottomless sleep, at which time, careful not to wake her, Billy Ray would finish whatever she didn't eat and smoke cigarettes and rub her feet, enjoying being close to her and the bond of their simple domesticity, welling with gratitude for his wife and her love of him, staring at her, transfixed on the little miracle that was the rise and fall of her chest, the small noises she made, glad to be pinned under her and staying there for as long as he could, often through the news and Carson.

The remembering of those moments made him wish he was dead.

He could never explain it to her—he lacked the vocabulary and refused himself the vulnerability—but those were the moments he craved: the gentle, quiet times. It was the intimacy he sought in the parade of anonymous women he used to fall asleep. They were a facsimile, never a substitute, holograms, an empty needle in his arm. They were nothing and with them he was less. They gave him their bodies but they could never give him the feeling of home he derived from rubbing Olivia's feet while she softly snored at the other end of the couch. She was the only one he ever wanted. He needed her. She was like his blood.

It was all his fault—every teardrop. Their divorce was a casualty of his spinelessness: *I am weak. I say yes. I need more.* Now all the more in the world would never be enough. He was too young then and too strung out, unable to understand what he was looking for was bigger than the physical, bigger than sex: he was looking for her, because with her he was not himself. Inside of his marriage, he was able to hide from the man he was, and when it collapsed, he was crushed, buried beneath the rubble of the enormous form of their love, forever doomed to stalk the demolition, haunting and haunted by the wreckage.

He ate a few forkfuls of the Frito pie but it was too much. He had had enough. He ended up throwing it away.

As he left, the boy called out to him: "Thanks for coming in, sir. Drift back again soon."

He crossed the parking lot and purchased six Coors and forty cigarettes from a liquor store that smelled like burnt hair. He lit a cigarette and smoked it while pressing his face against the top of the car. The cold metal made his face hurt less. His nose sung with a single throbbing note that spread up into the space between his eyes. If he ate more of the pills, he couldn't drink tonight and he needed to drink. He cracked one of the beers and chugged it and hid the bottle under a bush. As he crawled into the small car, the springs yawned with compression.

He drove north. The headlights on the asphalt looked like the sky. In no hurry, he drove in the right lane, allowing the cars to pass him as he breathed through his mouth, icing his nose with a beer. Pastureland filled in the spaces between towns. The prairies swayed in the breeze like a single organism comprised of raw nerves. The wind whistled through the grass. West of Larkspur, growing out of the wide nothing, Raspberry Butte built a second horizon in the darkness, flat as a coffee table and set with sharp crystal stars. Ten miles farther, Castle Rock was an enormous black tooth. Behind it, in the distance, Denver glowed.

By the time he reached Denver city limits, four of the beers were gone along with eleven of the cigarettes. The city came on slow, manifesting as nothing more than a collection of overpasses and off-ramps trapped between retaining walls until he passed Broadway and Gates Rubber and the train yards and the corkscrewed eighty-foot yellow statue— "the Slinky" his wife called it—that marked the end of the creeping suburbs and the beginnings of the city proper, then he was in it, crossing Santa Fe and Sixth Avenue, which was a highway itself, passing Mile High Stadium or whatever it was called now, ovoid and roofless and hulking and across the highway from the dormant roller coasters of Elitch Gardens, where he spent long summer days chasing his sons from ride to ride, and behind that the college Walker attended as a man and, farther on, the white-yellow lights of downtown and the new performing arts center and the Platte River, black and smooth, carving out its space in the world, and, up the hill, the Cash Register Building, of which he never knew the real name, and Republic Plaza, the gleaming glass tower on which the city hung its hat, and the capitol building, with its dome leafed in gold and built exactly one mile above the ocean, and the spotlights on the City and County Building blinking blue and orange for the season—Denver, the Queen City of the Plains, where his sons were raised and his love had died, where somewhere, among the streets and avenues and the warm little stone houses built to withstand the cold, his family—the flesh and the blood—learned to live lives devoid of him.

An excerpt from *High Praise: Thirty Years of Comedy Works,* a retrospective serialized in *The Denver Post*

ROSEANNE BARR: In Denver, in those days, it was magic every night. We had the best club and the best owner and everyone was funny. That's all I remember—laughing. That was all we did. There was enough stage time to go around but the scene—I hate that word, scene. Andy Warhol and the hippies hung out in scenes. We were a tribe. Warriors. Comics are all loners but at least we had each other to be alone with.

We moved between McKelvey's and Comedy Works and the Brass Rail and everyone got along, for the most part. The guys would get drunk and fight sometimes—plenty of beer, plenty of blow. All that ego and testosterone. I had my moments, too. But that didn't mean we didn't love each other.

DOCTOR KEVIN FITZGERALD: One time at Comedy Works this yahoo was heckling Rosie and I could tell she wasn't having it. I walked up and picked him up by the collar—this big hick from the sticks in a cowboy hat and shit kickers—and I kindly escorted him out of the showroom. He tried to swing on me, so I put his head through the door.

RICK KERNS: Doctor Kev worked security for bands when he was younger. Mountain, the Rolling Stones. Him and his brothers were all Golden Gloves, this pack of Irish longhairs. All of them had fists like hams and they wore lots of rings. Out of all of them, Kev had the longest fuse, but it was still pretty short.

I was there that night he bounced that cowboy, but that's not even the best part of the story. The next day, the guy called the club. "Uh, hi," he says, "I was at the show last night and one of your comics shoved my head through the wall." The club was already nervous the guy was gonna sue or something, so the manager gets on the phone and says, "Yes sir, we're very sorry about that," but the guy cuts her off and says, "No, I was drunk and out of line. I shouldn't have heckled." The manager is all surprised. She says, "Well, uh, alright. Then why are you calling?" and the guy says, "Well, I had a hat."

ROSEANNE BARR: I remember. I was furious. I didn't need Kevin's help. I was roasting that asshole and killing. I used to love hecklers. You just made fun of them and you didn't have to do your jokes.

NORA LYNCH: Me and [my husband] Phil [Palisoul] used to work the road a lot, so we were at a distance from the real craziness, but whenever we came home, there was always a story or two. What a pack of knuckleheads. I heard once that Billy Schafer beat the hell out of Ollie Joe Prater in the kitchen at McKelvey's for stealing one of his jokes. He made a real mess of the guy, but no one stopped him, because Ollie Joe was notorious for being a thief. He didn't even try and defend himself. While Billy Ray was pounding on him, Ollie just kept saying, "But I tell it better! But I tell it better!"

BILLY RAY SCHAFER: Yeah, he stole it, but it wasn't even that good of a joke. I just didn't like the guy. He was real friendly whenever I had drugs, but when he scored, it was like he didn't even remember your name. I thought I was gonna get banned from the room, but George [McKelvey, the owner of McKelvey's Comedy Corner] wasn't even mad. When he found out what happened, he bought me a beer, saluted and thanked me for my service.

DOCTOR KEVIN FITZGERALD: I was never looking for trouble but I never backed down from a fight. I wasn't afraid of anyone back then. Bill Schafer was the only guy in town that I didn't want to tussle with. I don't fight with guys that did hard time. I'm dumb, but not that dumb. They don't know when to stop and Bill was no exception. He was tougher than the head of a hammer and he loved driving nails.

BILLY RAY SCHAFER: I always liked Doctor Kev. Everyone else was such a pussy. I saw him once with these two ladies after a show, pretty little things, a blonde and a redhead, and they were hanging all over him. They went to the bathroom or something, so I went up to Kev and I said, "You piping both of them gals, Kev?" and he looks at me and says—I can't do the voice, but you know how he talks, all hangdog—"You know, I like to take them to bed two at a time. That way, when I'm done, they got someone to talk to." That still makes me laugh. You know Keith Richards paid for his veterinarian school, right? Wrote him a blank check?

DOCTOR KEVIN FITZGERALD: It was actually Mick Jagger.

JOHN "HIPPIEMAN" NOVOSAD: Man, when they fought—Kevin and Schafer—it was at my house up in Boulder. It was my divorce party and I was tripping acid. It really bummed me out.

TODD JOHNSON: I don't know what it was about. Billy Ray told me Kev made a move on [Schafer's wife] Olivia, but who knows? That doesn't sound like Kev and Billy Ray was chuffing a lot of powder. *A lot of powder.* I know because I was getting it for him. His habit bought Escobar a boat.

PHIL PALISOUL: I remember Talking Heads were playing and we were all dancing in the backyard under fairy lights and—you know when the air charges with electricity and you can feel it and your hair stands up?—this was when I still had hair—it was like that. Like something broke and all of a sudden they were on each other—"You son of a bitch!" this and "You bastard!" that. It was crazy and fast. Me and Nora watched from the other side of the deck. I'm a lover, not a fighter, unless I forget the safe word.

DOCTOR KEVIN FITZGERALD: He can throw a punch. I'll give him that. Especially a sucker punch.

BILLY RAY SCHAFER: I don't remember what it was about. All I know is that I hit him first and then he hit me the rest. That mick knows how to land a punch. I was drinking beer through a straw for a month.

ROSEANNE BARR: When I got my show [multiple Emmy Award–winner, *Roseanne*], I hired a lot of the guys I came up with to write for me and some of them brought their bad habits with them. It didn't matter. The show was a success, so we hired on more. They didn't all make it. Billy Ray only lasted half of the third season. We walked into the writer's room one day and there he was fucking a writer's assistant on the table next to a pile of scripts. He looked up and said, "She's teaching me how to type."

RICK KERNS: Here we were given a golden opportunity and some people didn't know a good thing when they had it. Comics aren't domesticated. They follow their lesser desires, get used to a certain lifestyle—staying up late and sleeping until two. They couldn't leave the road behind. I was one of those people. I turned down the job three episodes in because I missed doing whatever I wanted, whenever I wanted. I didn't get into this business to punch a clock.

NORA LYNCH: I was really grateful for the job. I was young and it was my first big showbiz gig. I was the freshest face and I attacked every day. Not everyone had as much enthusiasm.

When we moved to L.A., the studio put us all up at this apartment building until we could find our own places. It was nice. Rooftop pool. Fitness center. I remember I was headed down in the morning to work out, early before work, like 7 A.M., and Billy Ray and Rick were coming in from the night before. Ricky had on one of those hats that has cupholders built in with two straws coming down to your mouth so you can drink beer hands-free and Billy was eating chili fries with his fingers. They looked *tired,* if you catch my drift. They asked where I was going and I told them and I remember Billy saying, "This place has a gym?" I didn't expect them to show up for work, but there they were, two hours later, and they were running the room. Sharp, you know? On it—and funny as hell. That's when I knew they were separate breeds. I remember being kind of jealous. Like, "I wish I could go out all night and be that funny in the morning." But then they got fired and I wasn't jealous any more.

TODD JOHNSON: Has anybody told the story of when Billy Ray threw the couch off the roof?

BILLY RAY SCHAFER: I didn't throw the couch. I tried, but it was too heavy.

RICK KERNS: We were smoking a joint and having some beers and watching the sun come up over the city. It was really something to see when you were high—the sun burning red through all that smog. I turned around to pee and the next thing I knew I heard this loud crash and a car horn. Billy was tossing the plastic furniture down eight stories into traffic. "What are you doing?" I said. "Are you crazy?" And he looks at me with this look in his eyes, holding this chair over his head, and he says, "Yeah, man. I think I am."

ROSEANNE BARR: I didn't know what to do. This was my first shot and here I get the news that one of my writers went King Kong on West Hollywood. When I heard about the couch, I called him into my office and sat him down and before I could even get a word out, he said, "I quit, Rosie. Tell them to forward my check to Denver. I'm going home."

FRIDAY NIGHT

ON THE CUSP OF WINTER, AFTER AUTUMN BUT BEFORE THE real cold sets in, the sky in Denver is a windowpane that glows with a pale indigo radiance, a pink silver vaginal color that grows darker toward the edges of the frame. When he thought of Denver, he thought of this color and that sky. It was as much a part of the city to him as the mountains to the west. Being under that sky was the closest he got to a sense of connectedness, of belonging. That sky was the color of home.

Tonight the sky was black.

Tonight a veil of weak clouds streaked the heavens like thumbprints, blotting out the stars and dampening the moonlight and turning the sky into a hole through which the world fell. Staring up at it gave him anxiety, as if he might float away and be consumed by the big black nothing above. He didn't feel good. His legs were sore and his back was coiled with knots from his tailbone to the base of his skull. His eyes burned with poor sleep and his fingers were yellow. It had been some time since he'd drank a glass of water, longer since he'd ate something green. The reflection of his face in the rearview was hideous and foreign. *This is who I am now. Maybe I've reached my final form.*

104th Ave was wider than he remembered, fat with an extra lane in each direction. Business campuses and parking lots filled in land that was grass last year. The new construction confused him and he missed his turn.

Wits End was located in the elbow of a strip mall between a pizza shop and a discount tennis shoe outlet. Pulling in, his headlights swept across an empty parking lot. Immediately he knew something was wrong.

He parked in front of the entrance. The building was dark, lifeless, and the door was locked. He checked his watch: 6:06. Surely a few early birds should have arrived. He cupped his hands to the glass and peered in between but there was nothing to see. He tried the door again, rattled it on its hinges, kicking the bottom with the toe of his boot until he was worried it would shatter, but still no one answered. Numbers formed in his head and subtracted themselves from each other. He pounded harder. The sound boomed in the unmoving quiet.

Farther down the building, a door opened and a man's head appeared. A mix of fear and agitation scowled his face, a feeble attempt at intimidation. "What? What the fucking what?" Billy Ray turned to the sound of the man's voice. Registering, the man's face squinted. "Billy?"

"Hey, Don."

Don, his head patchy with tufts of gray hair, stepped out the door, revealing an aluminum baseball bat dangling by his side. "Jesus, Billy. What the fuck happened to your face?"

"Pussy-eating accident. Did y'all change showtimes?"

"Didn't you talk to Red?"

At the mention of his manager's name, the iron in Billy Ray's blood turned molten. "Talk to Red about what?"

Don looked down and shook his head, tapping the tip of the bat on the concrete. He exhaled loudly through his nose like a horse. "Fuck."

"Oh boy."

"Come on. I'll show you."

Billy Ray, seething, followed him inside and down a hallway lit with candles. Their movement billowed the small flames, causing the individual fires to flare and recede with their passing. At the end of the hall, a yellow stand of halogen work lights lit a black plywood bar converted into a desk via the placement of loose papers and a laptop computer. "Back here." They walked through the hatch and behind the bar and the man pulled open a heavy white door. He removed a flashlight from the liquor shelf and turned it on and held the beam on the walk-in illuminating boxes of beer and cases of liquor drowned in a foot of standing water. "Freezer crapped out. All the ice melted. Fried the electricity. It happened yesterday. One of the waitresses is married to an HVAC guy. He's coming in later tonight when he's off."

Billy Ray looked from the man to the water back to the man, searching for an answer in the space between, but he didn't have any questions: nothing surprised him anymore. He wanted to be furious, to bluster, to find reprisal, but he knew it was useless, one more wasted emotion. Instead he stood very still.

"All the bar food is soaked and the beer is probably skunked. There was nothing we could do." Don killed the light and sealed the door. He took a bottle of Jameson down from the shelf and poured two fingers into a pair of rocks glasses. "I called Red yesterday morning and told him we had to cancel. I figured he would get ahold of you. I would have called you direct if I had your new number." He handed a whiskey to Billy Ray and clasped his shoulder. "Sorry, brother." Don raised his glass to the large man and drank.

Billy Ray housed a furnace. "Canceled," he repeated, testing the word for a forgotten homonym that didn't translate to the loss of $1,200. "The whole weekend?"

Don nodded. He moved around to the other side of the bar, putting the plywood between them, still dragging the bat. "Red didn't call you? He said he would call you."

"My phone's broke."

"Shit."

"It just keeps piling up." He ran his fingers through his hair, the indignancy condensing to a familiar self-pity. "I don't know what I'm gonna do."

Don raised his hand to pat his old friend on the back, but decided against it mid-gesture, afraid of provoking the big man: he knew him that way.

"My flight isn't until Monday. Can I still stay at the condo?"

"We sold the condo."

"That answers that."

"I can't believe he didn't call you."

Billy Ray poured the whiskey into his mouth and Don refilled the glass and his own. They drank, reminiscing, trading stories from their time in the trenches. When they met, they were both comics and they'd lived the blur, but Don was smart with his money—"It's not what you make, it's what you save." The club was a B room, a respite for road hacks, up-and-comers and former child actors trying to cash in on fleeting fame, but when it went up for sale, Don saw his out. He gathered investors, took out a loan and purchased the building cash. He hadn't done stand-up since. He laughed at Billy Ray's stories of modern warfare, believing half of what he heard. Billy Ray was a liar's liar, a raconteur and racketeer. He inflated his numbers, both financial and carnal, and he redacted all the bad. Don fibbed when it was his turn to talk. He bitched about the club, the staff, the state of comedy, dwindling ticket sales, the scourge of streaming services and media on demand, the comedians, the bankers, the neighbors, the city. The way he told it, owning a comedy club was a test from God, but in all honesty, business was good and he was happy. His house was paid off. Retirement loomed. Quitting stand-up was the best thing he ever did, but he could never say that to a lifer like Billy Ray.

"How long you been out?"

"Three weeks."

"That's a long time."

"What else am I going to do?"

Don had no answer. While he enjoyed listening to Billy Ray's dispatches from the old world, he didn't envy his position. Comedy was a young man's sport and Billy Ray was not a young man. Like all the old dogs who worked his club, the big man drinking whiskey like it was water was a dinosaur waiting for a comet, and they both knew it. Therefore, out of sympathy, Don pretended his life was bad, too.

It didn't matter. Billy Ray barely heard a word. Occupied by his own fresh disaster, he nodded along indifferent, devoid of any compassion for the supposed struggles of his longtime friend. "What a shame," he said. "Ain't that some shit?" he said, focused completely on money and the lack thereof. He was the one who was wounded.

Billy Ray had worked the club at least once a year for eight years but he'd known Don for close to twenty. Their kids had grown up together, their wives were close. During the divorce, Don let him stay at the condo while he figured things out. After his sons turned on him and the comedy community, thinking him a pervert, distanced themselves, Don was his only friend in the world. Still, even with all their history, a part of Billy Ray, a rank, low, ungrateful part, wanted to crack his old friend square in the jaw, to break him off some of his pain. Money and friendship are two different words and only one paid his rent.

"Where are you headed after this?"

"Back to L.A."

"You still like it out there?"

"No."

"Then why don't you move?"

"I might. I'm trying to get back on the boats. If I got enough of them, I'd move to Galveston."

"It's nice down there."

"Is it?"

"I don't know. It's just one of those things you say."

Gradually, the conversation dried up. They started talking in platitudes. Don checked his watch. Billy Ray's glass stopped getting filled. Don seemed jumpy, impatient. Billy Ray could tell he was afraid of him. What he might do, what he might ask for. The divide was evident. Don was housebroke and he was still feral. The trepidation hurt more than the lost work. He wanted to leave. Both of them were relieved when the phone rang.

"Wits End . . . Alright . . . I'll be here." Don replaced the phone on the cradle. "HVAC guy's on his way."

"I better get going."

"I'd say you could sleep at ours, but you know Gracy."

"She still wears the pants?"

"And she picks out mine for me."

"Do her and Olivia still talk?"

"They play bridge on Tuesdays. Seems like they're shopping every time I turn around." Don rubbed his finger with his nose. "She's been going by her middle name."

"Svetlana?"

"Just Lana."

"Jesus."

"I still call her Olive."

"She always hated that."

"She still does."

"Good."

"You talk to her much anymore?"

"I would if I thought she would listen. Thanks for the Jay-mo."

"Of course."

"You wanna hit me one more for the road?"

Don opened his mouth to say something but instead he splashed a shot in the big man's glass.

"Lana." Billy Ray swirled the whiskey, watching it bleed down the sides. "She's still at the house in Fort Collins. I send her money for Jeremiah's tuition but that's all I have—an address."

"I heard Walker is gonna be a lawyer."

"He always was good at arguing. He used to run his mother in circles until she was dizzy."

"They're good boys, Billy. You did a good job."

"They're all Olivia's to show for. I was barely there."

"They're just like you."

Billy Ray downed the liquor. "God forbid."

"There's a couch in the green room."

"That's okay. I'll figure it out."

"I really am sorry."

"Shit happens. Sorry about your freezer. Hope the HVAC guy doesn't bend you over a barrel."

"He better buy me dinner first."

Don walked him to the door. Most of the candles had burnt out. The night seemed colder now. They stood awkwardly, not knowing what else to say, pinned down by the leaden sky. Billy Ray lit a cigarette and offered the pack. Don waved it off.

"Gracy would kill me."

"I'm surprised you didn't bleed out when she cut off your balls."

Don laughed and the two men shook hands. "Don't be a stranger, Billy."

"There's worse things to be." Billy Ray opened the car door but paused before sitting down. "You know who's downtown tonight?"

"I think it's Norm."

"Macdonald?"

"No, Crosby."

"I'd pay to see that."

"Me too."

"I haven't seen old Norman in a while."

"Remember when he hosted for us in Ottawa that time?"

"'I'm sorry, sir, but this hotel doesn't offer bidets.'"

"'In that case, I think I ruined your sink.'"

Billy Ray laughed and Don disappeared back inside his stronghold.

Driving south on the highway, he drank his last beer. He played a classic rock station at full volume, screaming along to the lyrics. He knew every word.

On Larimer Street, the streetlights glow year round, but tonight they shimmered with new clarity against the starless sky gone a rose color that changed purple under scrutiny and populated by thin clouds drifting aimlessly like floats escaped from a parade. Through the clouds, the filtered moonlight made an ethereal haze, soupy, thick somehow. Walking through it made him feel like he was underwater.

The sidewalks were teeming with the temporary inhabitants of Friday night. Swing-shifters and waitresses and the fresh-from-work suits hustled briskly while stumbling barhoppers snickered at the tourists, their unfolded maps blocking the paths of dudded-up weekend gentlemen dragging their bored dates around packs of glory-seeking frat boys speaking in cajoling hoots like shaved chimps, weaving among the families who, weighed down by rich dinners, doddled in aimless phalanxes, the children licking bulbs of ice cream while the mothers sipped overpriced coffee and the fathers rarely smiled, and, through them all, the hopeless beggars and destitute fiends wormed apologetically, looking for miracles and asking for anything that could be spared. The itinerants and wretches helped annul any lingering dispiritedness from Don's bad news. Seeing them in their rags reminded Billy Ray that worse things, real calamity, can and does happen. While he himself was a drifter who was always a few canceled gigs away from joining their ranks, at least he had money in his pocket and a trade to ply: it was better to be a troubadour than a tramp. He bummed a few cigarettes to a man in a wheelchair pushing himself along with one leg. In return for his largess, the amputated man offered a joke: "Two fags are fucking each other when the house catches fire. Which one of them gets out first: the top or the bottom? The bottom. His shit's already packed." Billy Ray smiled. Things could always be worse.

He stopped in a liquor store and bought a pint of Wild Turkey and a can of Squirt. He crossed 15th Street and followed a bike path down to Cherry Creek and sat on a bench. He poured out half the soda and topped it off with Turkey and listened to the water lap the concrete shore. Strolling couples quickened their pace as they passed his perch, the men walking on the side closest to him. The liquor and the carbonated sugar burned in his stomach. When the can was empty, he threw it in the water and watched it bob on the current until it disappeared around the bend. After a few cigarettes, he put the lid on the bottle and started toward the club where his career began.

From the front door of Comedy Works, a line of well-dressed people unfurled like a tongue down the block and around the corner up Larimer. The building had undergone refacing. The windows were wider, taller, offering a view of the upstairs bar and the ticket booth and the stairs leading down to the showroom. The logo on the awning was bigger, the font different, modern and done in white neon, and below it, written in black letter tiles, THIS WEEKEND FROM SNL NORM MAC-DONALD. While the signage had changed, when he touched the exterior, it was still the same cragged red brick that he used to lean against as he chain-smoked nervously before sets. He pressed the side of his face against the molded clay. It felt odd to stand cheek to cheek with a memory, to feel the palpable proof of a past life, to know it was real or had been at one time. He had forgotten what reverence felt like. This is where I learned to pray.

He had never waited in the general admission line before and his ego disallowed the notion. He walked around the corner and down the back stairs under the sign that said EXIT ONLY GUESTS ENTER ON 15TH and rang the buzzer above the door and waited. A young woman dressed in all black and visibly perturbed eventually came to the glass and cracked the door.

"This door is for staff only, sir. Please enter upstairs."

"I'm a friend of Norm's."

Dubious, the girl's face pickled: she had better things to do than shoo off fans. "Is he expecting you?"

"Yes ma'am."

The girl looked him up and down, this big mangled man, assessing his legitimacy. Billy Ray tried to appear innocuous despite his bruises. He smiled at the serious girl, aiming his whiskey breath away from her face. Finally she sighed. "What's your name?"

"Billy Ray Schafer."

"If he doesn't know you, I'm calling security."

"That's fair."

She shut the door and through the glass slit he watched her knock on the door to the green room. When it opened, she said something and jerked her thumb toward the door and Billy Ray held his breath, prepared to be forgotten. The girl nodded, nodded again, and returned to him. "This way," she said, obviously disappointed she didn't get to sick her brutes on him. Billy Ray brushed past her and walked into the green room.

In a plush recliner, Norm Macdonald sat with a plate of salmon balanced on his knees. A cloth napkin jammed into the collar of his shirt shielded the front of his gray linen sport coat from his meal. His eyes, seashell blue and coruscating, flashed up to the doorway and his mouth curled at the corners, balling up his cheeks. To Billy Ray, sitting there apple-cheeked in his bib hunched over his dinner of pink flesh, Macdonald looked like a mischievous boy experimenting on a trapped animal.

"Good lord, Billy Ray Schafer, as I live and breathe."

"Normy boy."

Macdonald set his plate on a shelf and stood up, unfolding his long-boned frame like a jack-in-a-box. He was not fat nor muscular but thick, the tissue packed dense on his bones like the farmhands he came from. Billy Ray stuck out his hand, but Macdonald slapped it away and wrapped his arms around him, pulling him in to his chest. "It's good to see you, you old rake."

"Since when are you a hugger?"

"I'm not. I'm just patting you down for weapons."

Billy Ray sat down on a couch made of green leather beside a thin, spoon-faced young man in an unbuttoned flannel long sleeve. He was no older than twenty-five, his hair prematurely thinning. "Do you want the room, Norm?" said the young man, sitting forward at the ready to vacate.

"No, no, Kevin, you stay right there. Kevin, let me introduce you to one of the funniest men to ever hold a microphone: Billy Ray Schafer.

When I was just starting out, Billy Ray treated me very well. Billy Ray, this is Kevin O'Brien. He's the emcee this weekend."

"Nice to meet you."

"Put 'er there, O'Brien." Kevin's hand felt soft and unworked in Billy Ray's calloused mitt but he matched the strength of his handshake and shook vigorously.

"Would you like a drink?" Macdonald asked, returning his plate to his lap. "Something to eat? The restaurant upstairs does great work with a piece of fish." Kevin handed Billy Ray a laminated menu. Reading it, Billy Ray whistled a high tone.

"Chicken almondine? Snails in white wine? This is a step up from chicken tenders."

"The tuna tartare is really good," offered O'Brien.

"They've been taking care of me," said Macdonald. "Whatever you want. We can have the waitress grab it."

"I'll probably get something."

"Good. So to what do I owe this exquisite pleasure?"

Billy Ray pulled out his cigarettes and took an ashtray off a side table. "There's a dick-sucking convention and they needed a judge."

"I see. A *judge* for a dick-sucking *convention*?" Macdonald deadpanned. "Now why would a convention need a judge?"

"It's a competition."

"Let me see if I understand you correctly: there's a dick-sucking competition in town?"

"Correct."

"And they brought you in because you're an expert on sucking dick?"

"I see what you did there."

"Is that what happened to your face? You were giving a fella a blow job and you got a little overzealous, didya?"

"I walked right into that."

"Looks like you walked right into an active propeller blade. I think I speak for both myself and young master O'Brien when I say"—

Macdonald broke his insouciance, bulging his eyes and proceeding in mock exclamation—"good God, man! What the hell happened to your fucking face?"

At this, O'Brien cracked up, braying in a high chortle he tried to stifle with the side of his fist, and Billy Ray laughed, too, a victim of the precision timing brandished by his old friend. Macdonald, satisfied, sat in his chair cutting his fish and smiling coyly.

Billy Ray regaled them with the story of Cañon City and the introduction of the car to the tree. He punched the anecdote up for entertainment value, adding in jokes and saying what he should have said instead of what he did say, smoothing the corners and sharpening the edges. O'Brien listened genially, laughing when the old man paused or looked at him, while Macdonald interjected with bits of frayed logic and asinine questions as he smoked one of Billy Ray's cigarettes.

When the waitress came, she began to say something to Macdonald, but upon seeing Billy Ray, she cut herself off and squealed with recognition. "Is that Billy Ray Schafer? It can't be."

"Hey, Toni."

"I thought you were dead."

"No," he said, standing, "I just smell funny." Billy Ray scooped her up in a bear hug, removing her from the ground. Dangling, her feet kicked like a dog running in a dream.

"Billy," she said once she was terrestrial, "I haven't seen you in . . . must be seven years?"

"Sounds right."

"Where you been?"

"Avoiding success."

"What happened to your face?"

"It's a long story."

He ordered a Jack Daniel's, to which Macdonald said dryly, "I haven't seen such a pedestrian choice since the last time I was in a crosswalk," and everyone laughed, including Billy Ray who, even though he didn't actually understand the joke, didn't want to counteract the good-natured vibe. "Get him a Glenlivet rocks, Toni, or a Jameson, something from a green bottle that tastes like smoke. Me too, and one for young Kevin, please. And let's get the old man a steak—a rib eye if you have it. Put it on my tab."

"You got it, Norm." Toni put her arm around Billy Ray's waist. "It's good to see you, Billy."

"It's good to be seen."

"Are you doing a set?"

Macdonald answered for him: "He sure is."

"Norm, you don't have—"

"You will sing for your supper, Schafer," Macdonald said, sounding like an old movie cowboy, "or there will be blood."

"I don't want to bump anyone."

"Nonsense. Kevin, would you please tell the other guy that Billy Ray is going up before him? I would do it myself, but I don't want to."

"You got it."

Toni squawked again and clapped her hands. Her teeth when she smiled were small yellow pills. "I have to tell the rest of the girls. Brenda's going to shit." She squeezed Billy Ray once more, touching the side of her face to his chest, hearing his heart. "I missed you, Billy. I can't believe it but I did." She shut the door as she went, cutting off the noise of the amassing second show crowd and plunging the room into abrupt quiet.

Billy Ray put his hands on his hips, cocked his elbows out like handles. Though it was just the two of them, the room felt smaller than before, the empty spaces now filled out with expectation. He looked at the carpet between his feet. It didn't look new. It seemed to be the same graying green nylon he remembered crawling across on his hands and knees, mining the fibers for spilled cocaine. He'd laid with women on it when the couch was occupied, scouring their backs and burning his knees. While the rest of the room was different—the television on the wall, the mini-fridge in the corner filled with Red Bull, the furniture, once plastic, now studded leather—the floor hadn't changed and for some reason he found the sameness consoling, although from what he was being comforted he was not sure; it had been a long time since he was nervous.

He pulled out the Wild Turkey, nipped off a quick one, then lit another Winston. Macdonald, his brow bent in contemplation, sat with his long legs crossed studying a yellow legal pad and chewing on the butt of a ballpoint pen. He looked up to find Billy Ray staring at him through the smoke.

"You didn't have to give me time," said Billy Ray. "That's not why I came down here."

Macdonald removed the pen from his mouth and tapped it twice against the paper. "I know."

"I just came down to see you, say hi, shoot the shit. That's all. No pressure."

"Don't be retarded. I'm glad you're here." Macdonald's face beamed with cordiality. His eyes sparkled as if entombed in ice. "I want to see you. I haven't laughed in a while."

"I don't want to piss off Wende."

"Wende's not here."

"Well. Alright." Billy Ray's face turned pink and hot and he rubbed the back of his neck. He regretted this show of sincerity and the accompanying exposure. It shamed him that Macdonald had to reassure him of his welcome, to necessitate comforting, but the thought of his old friend thinking him a desperate scavenger was a worse feeling, lower than embarrassment: he didn't want him to think he needed this, even if he did. "Well. Alright then."

"We're going to have fun tonight, baby, just you wait. Now if you'll excuse me a minute," Macdonald said, "I have to finish my will," and resumed gnawing on the pen.

Soon Toni came back with a tray of scotch and O'Brien returned with a portly, bearded young man in an ill-fitting Hawaiian shirt, both of them red-eyed and reeking of the skunked diesel musk of sinsemilla.

The shaggy round one introduced himself as Nathan and said he was pleased to meet Billy Ray, that he'd heard his name on podcasts, and Billy Ray asked, "What's a podcast?" and Nathan and Kevin laughed in deference and Billy Ray, unsure, acted like he was joking.

"Yeah, man," O'Brien apologized. "I didn't realize you were *the* Billy Ray Schafer when we met. I read *Pistols at Dawn*. Joey Diaz talks about you all the time. You're a legend."

"A legend?" Billy Ray said softly as if tasting the word for poison.

"Like Bigfoot," piped up Macdonald. "Or a funny woman." Hearing this the two young men laughed obsequiously. Then they sat down to stare at their phones.

Billy Ray, his ego engorged, focused on his whiskey. He sniffed the glass, sipped, savoring the piquant rake of the liquid across his tongue and the burn at the back of his throat, assuming the affect of a connoisseur, an expert in elegance, all in an attempt to validate the esteem lavished on him by these fawning underclassmen. He knew they were just trying to be nice but trying was a nice thing to do. After their sanctification, he felt even more pressure to deliver, lest they appear naïve. Even though he was exhausted and hollow and brittle and burnt, if they expected a legend, he would give them none less.

Billy Ray stood up and turned his back to Macdonald and removed from his wallet his cocaine. Nathan nudged Kevin and the youngster looked up from his screen and they watched as the big man, unable to use his nose, keyed two lumps of powder into his drink, stirred the clouding honeyed liquid with his finger and licked the key clean.

Feeling their eyes on him, Schafer looked up and winked. He offered the bag and they waved it off and he returned it to his wallet, glad not to share. "So, fellas. How long y'all been doing stand-up?"

They looked at each other. Nathan said seven years, Kevin said five.

"You still like it?" Already his lips were going numb.

Nathan nodded. His beard bounced like Spanish moss. "It's the best thing to ever happen to me. Stand-up saved my life."

Billy Ray sucked an ice cube, waiting for the earnestness to clear. The innocence dripping off the fat kid's answer broke his heart. *Just wait*, he thought. *Just wait until it's all you have left.*

"How long you been doing it?" O'Brien asked, his face illuminated from underneath by the pallid blue of his phone screen. Billy Ray looked up and to the left and backward into his chronology, searching for mile markers and landmarks in the blur of his past.

Before he could answer—twenty-eight years or thereabouts—Macdonald cut him off: "Billy Ray started comedy in prison."

The young comics' eyes bulged. "Seriously?" Lit from below by their phones, they looked like children around a campfire hearing a ghost story.

Billy Ray cleared his throat. "That's not all I learned in there."

"You're right," Macdonald agreed. "I shouldn't sell you short. He also learned male rape."

"You did comedy in jail?" asked O'Brien.

"Prison."

"For real?"

Billy Ray pulled on his cigarette, playing the part. "As real as the teeth in your head. You don't know how funny you can be until you have to." The boys were silent and eager. Macdonald put away his notes. "Talk about a captive audience."

"I was waiting for that," said Macdonald.

"You boys grew up on cable, Comedy Central, the online. You're too young to remember, but when I was your age, there were like five comedians. Stand-up wasn't a thing everyday people did. It wasn't a job to be considered. Comics were like rock stars. Aliens. Richard Pryor may as well have been from the moon. I was always funny but that and a dollar got you a beer. I never thought of it as a marketable skill. More like a trick, like being good at horseshoes. Then I got in some trouble."

"What did you go down for?" said Nathan.

As quick as he said it, O'Brien elbowed him in the ribs. "You're not supposed to ask that, dumbass."

"Shit, I don't care," Billy Ray professed. The cocaine had him feeling chatty and he was enjoying the sway of his cache: holding court in the green room. It felt like old times. "I'm an open book."

Macdonald snickered. "You're a book of Japanese poetry: unpleasant to read."

"You don't have to answer—obviously," Nathan said, his fingers digging nervously in his beard.

Billy Ray put the heel of his boot on his knee, aping Merle Haggard in a photo he always admired, but squished his testicles in the process. "I was a bad kid," he started, pulling at the crotch of his jeans. "I grew up on the eastern plains, Elbert County. There wasn't much to do but get in trouble. I ran with a fast bunch, but I always pulled up the rear. We made a small career doing shakedowns, rolling dealers, working muscle for a lizard pimp, gigs that depended on size and not brains. Nothing heavy or lucrative. We were knuckleheads. One time me and my cousin made off with ten grand in fake hundreds. We traded them for fives and tens." He paused to sip his drink, relishing an audience to sound dangerous before. He tried to make himself look bored with the telling of this story, cool-handed, like it was nothing special, just one of many tales, but he couldn't help but smile as he talked. "I was out in Limon this time and this old boy I knew was moving dope in from Omaha and he knew I liked to drive. He said the money was good and quick, in and out cash, and I didn't have to use my hands, which appealed to me. I don't mind getting messy. I hate cleaning up. He sent me out in a Ford Bronco and I came back in another, out and back, out and back. I could do a trip a day if the weather was good. I ran for him for months and it was smooth, no hitches, no trouble. Everyone was getting fat. More money than I knew what to do with. I got all gold fillings, bought my mother a car. I could have stuffed a mattress with all that cash. Then one day I get out to Omaha and the Mexicans tell me the return truck is in the shop, so they packed the usual load into the trunk of a junked-out Camry. Me, being dumb, I said alright, yessir, jefe, even though the back end of that car was practically dragging with shit. I don't know for sure if it was a setup, but as soon as I got on the highway the jakes were on me. They came up to the window with guns and dogs. I was fucked. They were on one. They spent five days trying to flip me. Offered me every deal they had. Man. I've never been that quiet. All I told them was all I knew: I spill the beans, the beaners spill my guts. Keep sniffing, pigs. They didn't much care for that. The book, the bookcase, the whole goddamn library—the judge threw it at me. Trafficking, distribution, racketeering. Federal charges. Sent me up for seven to twenty down at Big Mac. It's by Tulsa. All I knew about Oklahoma was the musical because my mom liked it, but prison is the last place you wanna be singing show tunes." He lit a cigarette, filling the room with more smoke, but his words were all they breathed. The two young comics were pop-eyed, sitting forward, their mouths limp and open, while Macdonald stared at him with something like awe in his eyes.

It had been a while since Billy Ray explained his origins and even longer since anyone had cared to listen. Once it made great fodder for interviews, but typically—more recently—he only ever related this tale in verbal pissing contests with other ex-cons who in turn regurgitated the details of their own downfalls. In the past, when interviewers inevitably inquired of his penal origins, he downplayed the whole ordeal, painting the picture in simple aw-shucks strokes. He told them what he knew they wanted to hear, bullet pointing it for them, vague on the specifics and smeared with country bravado, laying it out amorphous to allow them to mold his words into whatever story they wanted to tell. Sometimes he was depicted as a duped simpleton too loyal for his own good, the good old boy forged in fire, hapless, an impoverished bumpkin lured by the promise of easy prosperity into the blind and gnashing jaws of Justice (they either capitalized justice or they fenced the word with snarky quotation marks to highlight their disdain for a court system that, as they invariably put it, "turned men into a series of numbers"). Others made him out a hardened criminal or felonious brute—the caged kind—saved by and reborn in the healing light of laughter, a triumph of salvaged humanity over ignominy and degradation.

None of them got it right.

Billy Ray saw himself as a man guilty of circumstance. He was given options and he chose from among them. At no point was he ignorant to the consequences of his task. He was paid a good wage to partake in a dangerous game defined by steep stakes. The buy-in was his freedom and he was betting on the house to lose. No one tricked him: he could have walked away from the table but he wanted to keep playing. There were other ways to make money, honest jobs for honest pay, but he wanted more. And while he had a history of criminal activity, he was not the last-ditch scourge rendered by some journalists. He was a big man with limited education and friends in low, lucrative places. Given the same skill set, size and opportunity, he doubted most men would choose the lumberyard or unloading trucks at Walmart over lumps of tax-free cash. In a way—a way that he could feel but not articulate—he was proud of his resourcefulness: he used what he had and what he had was enough. While the story of his sentencing and incarceration was a font of deep shame, he took pride in the gutsiness that put him in a position to be convicted. To risk your autonomy for a chance at something better, to literally bet your life, is both definitively stupid and inarguably brave. He gave it a shot and that's more than most can say.

What was not brave was refusing to roll over and snitch on those higher up the chain. The authors of the interviews that appeared on magazine racks tried to portray it as a defiant act, a trite example of "honor among thieves" (in their glib laziness, they almost always used that phrase), when really his silence was a matter of survival: he didn't want to be murdered. This was too simple a fact. Simplicity doesn't sell. Only Billy Ray retained the truth of who he was: Billy Ray was just a man trying to live better and there was no room in his recollection or his life thereafter for the revisionistic or sentimental.

He could see in his glass where the cocaine had attached to the ice cubes, specks of snow on square glaciers. Like all good storytellers, he knew when to pause and let the necessary question be asked.

The skinnier of the two twentysomethings had his elbows dug into his knees, leaning forward like a bird awaiting the movement of mice. He looked quickly from Macdonald to his friend back to Billy Ray. "That's fucked."

The fat one agreed: "Super fucked. What happened?"

Billy Ray slipped a smile. "I made friends with a lot of bald white guys with interesting tattoos." The boys laughed, the tension broken. Billy Ray waited for Macdonald to wisecrack but he was silent, rapt, his long fingers tented in his lap. Billy Ray thought he looked like a psychiatrist waiting to assign a diagnosis.

Nathan pulled a cigarette from behind his ear and stuck it between his lips. As he talked, the cigarette bobbed antennal. "Wait. So how'd you start doing comedy then? A talent show or like poetry night or something?"

"You think there's poetry night in prison?" O'Brien needled.

"I don't know."

Billy Ray feigned. "That's a boring story." He nodded to the man in the room he'd known the longest. "Normy's heard it."

A single corner of Macdonald's mouth curled in a charming palsy. "I love this story."

"Then why don't you tell it?"

"You've got better timing."

"Christ on the cross." He drained his glass and pulverized the ice and the roof of his mouth went numb along with pieces of his tongue. "I did six months in county waiting to be sent up. Easy time. Every month they gave us a drum of Bugler and a stack of papers and we got steak once a week. That's a better deal than lots of folks get on the outside. Prison was a different world. I'd known some heavy cats, but Big Mac is a human zoo. Every kind of man. All the different breeds just stalking their cages. Luckily I knew a few boys who knew a few boys so I settled in with a little crew and they told me who was who. I didn't gamble and didn't take what was offered besides a little pinch of pruno if I trusted the vineyard." He let the lockup jargon take hold, settling into the jungle honky-tonk patois of the immured. "I was lucky because most white boys can't move between groups. In prison, honkies are an endangered species, but the Mexicans owed me a favor and the blacks liked me because I was funny. I could run the dozens as good as any of their asses and my shit was all original off-the-top while they were running gassed street jokes they passed around like a porno mag. Soon everybody knew me as the funniest inmate, which is like being the world's best ventriloquist: nothing to brag about. Eventually I started writing burns to use the next day, getting specific, personal, weaponizing my shit, running my jokes by the cool guards before I unleashed them on the pod floor, but I still hadn't performed for a crowd bigger than ten yet.

"Then one night, while our cells were being fumigated, the trustees were rewarded with the Tyson–Berbick fight on pay-per-view but the cable failed and it was damn near a riot. The place caught fire. The inmates, the guards, we'd all been looking forward to this fight for weeks and now everyone was pissed and pointing fingers. We were getting heated but the guards couldn't just send us back to our cells because the whole block was filled with poison and the non-trustees were in the cafeteria, so they don't know what to do, and we're all hollering. It's getting hot. Somehow it's decided that the guilty party was this CO named Wainwright and we let him have it. Poor bastard had bright red hair and a harelip. I remember one time this dude said his head looked like a busted softball and that cracked me up. He was fish in a barrel. I went in on him fierce. I think I called him a tampon-headed motherfucker and he loses it and gets in my face and says, 'Schafer, you think you're so funny, don't you? You're just Mort fucking Sahl, huh?' and that got me real good—that Mort Sahl was his go-to comedian—and I started laughing and that chapped his ass even redder and he says, 'Everything is just a great big joke, isn't it? Well why don't you come up here and tell us some jokes then, you hillbilly, peckerwood son-of-a-bitch?'"

Billy Ray slit his eyes. "I'd like to say that I dusted his teeth, but that'd be a lie. I'm not that brave or that stupid—it's hard to tell. Wainwright didn't give me much of a choice in the matter. He kicked my chair out from under me and when I hopped up he shoved me to the front of the crowd and everyone shut their yapping on account of his putting his hands on me. I'm looking at them and they're staring at me and all I can hear is breathing, just breathing. Silence is the scariest noise in prison. Feels like you're swallowed. Like you're in a black hole. It's all pins and needles and I'm thinking, What's the move here? Am I supposed to smoke this cop? Will they all think I'm bitch if I don't and how bad am I gonna get whupped if I do? I was fucked from toes to teeth. There I am, on the spot, eighty-three men, one hundred sixty-six ears and all I got is this one mouth." As he always did at this point in the story, he pointed to the largest hole in his head and Macdonald mouthed along with him like he was singing the chorus of a favorite song: "So I used it." Macdonald smiled as his friend—yes, they were still friends, he decided, bound as they were by the fraternal spirit of men from the same platoon, survivors of the same foxholes—continued. "I just started talking and for some reason this old, blind, deaf and dumb Indian pops into my head, this guy named Red Leon that lived next door to me growing up. I get to telling this story about a time Red Leon got so drunk on Ripple out on his porch that he couldn't find the front door and they got to laughing, so I leaned into it, as you do, and it's working and I'm doing an impression of Red Leon, an act-out with a voice, this Helen Keller meets Frankenstein thing"—Billy Ray moaned like his tongue was cut out—"and they're eating it up and Wainwright is watching and his face is turning red as a dog's dick and I knew it right away: this is it for me. I'm home. I've landed on the right planet. I fucking killed. It was magic. I was napalm. I got their asses. I don't remember much of what I said but people were quoting back lines to me all week. From then on I opened every week for movie night, a new fifteen minutes every Saturday. I opened for all reward programming—the Super Bowl, boxing, *It's a Wonderful Life* on Christmas Eve. I did a half hour at halftime of the yearly trustees versus guards basketball game and I started a little side hustle punching up the letters dudes sent home. I racked up good behavior. Shit. When I got in front of the parole board, they asked me to tell them a joke."

The emcee snapped back straight in the couch as if influenced by a powerful magnet. He clapped his hands twice, loud blasts that cut the room. "That's badass."

"Told you it was a great story," said Macdonald.

Billy Ray leaned back and soaked in the esteem, adding cooly, "Stay in school, boys."

When Toni returned, she carried a black-and-blue rib eye with mashed redskins and asparagus. She refused Billy Ray's gratuity and sat down for a cigarette. She slipped out of her black tennis shoes and curled and uncurled her toes, cracking them against the carpet as she answered Billy Ray's questions about the comics he'd worked with at the club before his forced sabbatical: Don Battersby was dead and Ron Moore lost an arm to a train accident and Phil Palisoul and Nora Lynch got married but kept their names and Todd Jordan writes for Leno and Lori Calahan's husband died and it was killing her and Charlie Royen was mental and Dick Sterns was clean and George McPherson fell off the wagon and DJ Malone was dead, too. Hearing their names, Billy Ray, struck by a forgotten polarity, remembered each of their laughs, the unique bray and timbre and duration, the energy of it, the beautiful energy. All the hours in this room soliciting those most coveted sounds . . . even blinded men remember colors. He pictured them, their young selves, clustered in this very room, the tightness, the voracity, the bristling nerves, so close, the madness and genius and comradery as thick as the smoke trailing from their cigarettes, still rising, still hungry, their career heights unreached, the world unyet a solved and dying thing. He was unaware then, but through hindsight's telescopic lens, it was easy to see those nights were the happiest he had been as a comedian. That was the real thing. Before the agents and the managers divvied the percentages of their humanity, before they traded sanity for success, before Showbiz, the great widow-maker, the beast with its mark reading $$$. Never had he been as content as he was in this room engulfed in the laughter of the litany of maniacs in Toni's recitation, and he pined for them, all of them—the dead, the alive and the ones like him who were both.

"We're coming up on a year since we buried him."

"How'd he do it?"

"Rope and a stool. Dick found him. They lived together."

"Christ."

"Yessir."

"He always seemed so happy."

"He should have been an actor."

"Fucking DJ. Remember that Christmas when channel seven came down and did that live remote for the toy drive? It was all the girls and Wende and me, Todd Jordan, I think George Lopez was there, and for the whole interview, DJ was standing to the side with his ballbag hanging out his fly."

"Oh, I remember alright. Wende still talks about it."

"I've never seen her so mad. Not even when she fired me."

"Channel seven still won't let us do press."

"You remember what he said? 'Come on, boss. I shaved them . . .'" Toni put her hand on Billy Ray's kneecap and, in unison, they said, "'. . . For the kids!'"

Billy Ray tapped his finger on the rim of his glass. "Now *that* was funny. He had some good times," he said, saying it as much to himself as to the room. "We had some good times."

Toni blushed. "Sure did, cowboy." She danced her fingertips on his knee. "If I remember correctly, we had some good times on this very couch." Her laugh sounded like a pack a day. It exploded through her yellow teeth like snapped celery. The laughter purged the matronliness from her face, and in those gasps, he saw flickers of the woman she once was and he remembered the promises he broke in her dirty apartment on Federal, the naked thrashing intervals, the lies he fed his wife.

Calming herself, the waitress covered her mouth with both of her hands like a hushed schoolgirl. She turned to the emcee and the opener. "Don't look at me like that, boys. I wasn't always this old."

The emcee waved his bony hands. "No judgment here," he said. "I just hope you flipped the cushions over."

Billy Ray seized Toni's foot, surprised by the dampness of her sock. "I don't know about the cushions, but I definitely flipped you over."

"You dirty dog," said Macdonald.

Toni squealed and slapped Billy Ray's thigh. "I better get out of here before I get in trouble." Sliding her feet back into her shoes, she stood up and picked up her tray. "I'll be back to check on you boys in a bit. Sounds like we're about sold out."

The emcee checked his watch, an orange digital with a plastic band. "It's about that time."

His counterpart dug a joint from the tangle of black hair crowning his bulbous head. "Anyone?"

Macdonald shook his head but Billy Ray, tenderized by nostalgia, followed the striplings outside and huddled in the stairwell as the joint circled, coughing, saying, "This is some primo shit" as he watched, googly-eyed and cotton tongued, the strands of piney smoke twirl and dissipate through the staircase into the faraway blanket of pale rose twilight. "My head's a balloon." The boys laughed. He passed on the third circuit, stony bologna already. His arms felt like Styrofoam; they dangled like pool noodles. The near surroundings glimmered with a mesmeric brilliance that had him studying the grout between bricks. The smoke made him sappy, seized by a sense of heightened benevolence. He felt a kinship with the two young comics. They were all part of a lineage, connected, born in this place. As it was, he probably loved them. He thought of his sons. How long since he'd seen their faces. It was difficult to imagine them men, but they were—good men he hoped, men unlike him. He decided he would visit them while he was here, tomorrow or the next day. The thought cheered him. Sometimes it was that easy. "Primo," he repeated, lost in admiration for the length and shape of his own shadow. "Shee-it." He thanked the boys for their dope and left them to huff the roach.

Entering the building, he hoped the bathroom was in the same place. He walked past the green room down the hallway behind the stage and entered the showroom where staff, dressed in black shirts, black pants, black shoes, dealt with the growing line of attendees. The queue was a cross section of contemporary American fashion. Suburban couples gone genderless in their blue jeans and pullovers and comfortable sneakers stood behind country tourists drifted in for the weekend from the high plains, their ballcaps filthy and their ponytails taut, bunched up against hip city dwellers stunting in their Friday night best, the well-groomed men in pastel polos and starched oxfords and leather jackets and twill suit coats, herringbone, sharkskin, and pantsed in sleek dungarees or pleated khakis or slate chinos tailored tight above shined brogues or Jordans or nubucks, attired to signal their legitimacy to their meticulously styled dates, their hair teased and flattened and straightened and curled above smoked eyes and frosted lips, their earrings catching the light, their bodies contoured in satin blouses and sleeveless jumpsuits and dresses that plunged and skirts that left the eye begging, their curves accentuated by rhinestoned jeans and sheer tights as snug as skin and the shoes, catalogues full—pumps and heels and flats and knee-highs clasped and zipped and buckled to their feet—polished women and manicured men, the sex and promise reeking off them like perfume, immortal, as far from Monday morning as they were their own graves.

Billy Ray looked through them as he slithered past, hugging tight to the wall, trying to make himself small out of respect to the waitresses bearing trays fitted with as many glasses as they could hold as they moved with practiced fluidity, shouting "Corner!" as they darted to and from the bar like hummingbirds. He didn't recognize the bartender but he still nodded out of habit.

The bathroom had not moved. There was a line for the urinals. Those waiting avoided eye contact, as was the agreement. A man said, "I don't buy beer, I rent it." Another said, "I hear that." When his time came, he sidled between two men and held his breath.

Foregoing soap, he wet his hands in the sink and ran his fingers through his hair, tamping it down at the back of his head and fixing his bangs. He liked this mirror. His face wasn't that bad if you knew how to look at it, and while they were charred red from the weed, there was still fight in his eyes, a cagey, assured capability. Billy Ray made up his mind that tonight he would kill. There was no other option.

Leaving the bathroom, he cut back past the bar, mumbling "Corner" as he edged into the hallway, the narrow walls plastered on both sides with posters advertising upcoming headliners. The faces on the posters were so young and handsome and polished and prim. They weren't ugly enough for this business. He doubted they were funny—Kyle Kinane, Sean Patton, Tig Notaro, Baron Vaughn—faces he'd never seen, names he'd never heard. *And they,* he thought, *have never heard of me.*

He wormed past the backbar and through the auxiliary seating where the girl that let him in the back door eyed him with irresolution. He smiled. She looked back at her clipboard. He stepped up on the side of the stage onto the platform that held the piano and looked out through the curtain at the crowd. What were they doing here? Almost thirty years and the arrangement still eluded him. How dim were their lives that they had to pay for laughter? What was tonight supposed to solve? Whatever it was, he was ready.

This is my kingdom.

To me you will submit.

He left the piano and entered the green room and sat between the stoned openers, both of whom scribbled quietly in worn notebooks.

Seeing them, he remembered: beware falling rocks. He lit a cigarette and went over the bit in his head; there wasn't much to it beyond the absurdity of the signage. Maybe he would go into it, but only after his foot was on their necks. The inherent excitement of testing unproven material was often enough to buoy a weak bit, but tonight wasn't for trying out new stuff. Tonight was about pronouncement, dominance: he had to leave no doubts.

In the past, the mantra was *no survivors*. That was what they said to each other back then.

How was it?

No survivors.

Right on.

They talked in homicidal vocabulary, as if this thing they did was violent. They killed, they murdered, they annihilated, they crushed. Sometimes they died. Sitting beside him, the chubby feature pulled at his beard. Billy Ray felt bad about what he was about to do to him. *Poor kid,* he thought. *I am going to bury you.* His confidence was absolute: total control. He had an idea, something like redemption. Reclamation demands sacrifice. There would be collateral damage. The feature looked up from his notebook and caught the old man staring. He smiled. Billy Ray showed him his teeth. *I am going to make this hard on you. I'm sorry. This is not your night.*

At precisely 9:45, a manager came in the door and asked the emcee if he was ready. The skinny kid said he was and the manager said alright and the kid stood up and bounced on his toes, then jumped quickly three times, bringing his knees to his chest. He turned to Billy Ray and asked how he wanted to be introduced.

"I don't care, kid. Whatever you want."

"Come on," said Macdonald. "Let's give them a show."

"Fine." Billy Ray panned the span of his career for the gold. "You can tell them twelve appearances on Johnny Carson, six Lettermans and an hour special on HBO."

"Woah," the emcee said.

"And tell them I totaled my car last night."

"Can do." The kid shut the door but reopened it immediately. "And—sorry—but it's Scha*fer* right? Not Shaver?"

"Last I checked."

"Okay. Sorry. Thanks." The kid shut the door and stayed gone.

From behind the door they heard music come on the loudspeakers and the crowd went quiet. Over the music, a voice through a microphone said, "Good evening, ladies and gentlemen, and welcome to the world-famous Comedy Works. Please keep your conversation to a minimum and your laughter to a maximum." The voice asked the crowd to welcome their emcee to the stage and the voice said the kid's name and the crowd broke into ready applause.

Billy Ray's heart stormed. He looked at his watch. Ten minutes until his rebirth.

The other opener shut his notebook and rose to his feet with a grunt. "I'm gonna go watch him," he said. "Have a good set."

"No survivors," said Billy Ray.

"What?"

"Never mind."

The feature left.

Besides the sound of Macdonald tapping a staccato rhythm with his pen against his notepad, the room was silent. Billy Ray lit a cigarette and blew a cloud of smoke into the white lights embedded like eyeballs in the ceiling. The bulbs cast Macdonald in an angelic highlight. To Billy Ray, the light appeared to be pulling his friend skyward. Damnit, he thought, I shouldn't have smoked that grass. He shook his head like a dog fed peanut butter and slapped his cheek with his palm. "Last chance to take me off the show," he said. "I could pull the fire alarm."

"No, sir. It's happening." Macdonald smiled his cad's grin. "Either you'll crush or fail miserably. I'll have a good laugh either way."

"You got all the angles covered."

"Any good gambler knows a sure thing."

"So you're a good gambler now?"

"I've only lost everything twice."

"It's good to see you, Norm."

"I was thinking about you the other day. I was in Albany. They have one of your old headshots on the wall. The mullet one."

"I hated that fucking picture."

"I like it. You look good. Mischievous. Like how I remember you."

"Mischievous?"

"Like a kid with a slingshot and a pocket full of rocks."

"I probably had some rocks in my pocket back then."

"When you walked in here tonight, I took it as a sign."

"A sign of what?"

"I don't know. I don't think we're meant to understand signs. I think all we can do is acknowledge them when they appear."

"Are you stoned too?"

"Do you believe in God, Billy?"

Billy Ray searched Macdonald's face for a hint of the joke, hoping for a punch line, but all he found was a placid sincerity he didn't know what to do with. He cleared his throat and spit in a trashcan. "Do I believe in God? Like Jesus?"

"Doesn't have to be Jesus. Just a higher power. Something greater. An order. A bigger truth."

Billy Ray cocked his eyebrow. "No. I can't say I do. And I don't think God believes in me."

"Do you believe in anything?"

Billy Ray looked at the carpet. "I believe in my act."

Macdonald nodded. "Sometimes it feels like that's all we have."

"So you're a God guy now?"

"I don't know. I think about it. What's next and all that."

"It's all dirt, baby."

"I hope there's more."

"That's the safer bet. It's all house money."

"But if He knows we're hedging, why would He honor the slip?"

"You're getting heavy in your old age. And not just in the middle."

"I think I've been reading too much."

Billy Ray put out his cigarette and finished his whiskey. "I better get out there." He stood up and repeated the ritual of smoothing his hair. He adjusted his shirt in the mirror, cinched his bolo. He wished his nostrils worked. "Don't think too hard while I'm gone."

"I'm going to watch you."

Billy Ray opened the door. "Watch and learn."

"See you on the other side."

Billy Ray took his position behind the curtain and rolled his neck in slow circles. He listened to the crowd. The emcee was doing well. He talked fast, so fast he stepped on his laughs, but it was a purposeful pace. He wasn't rushing to dodge silence, he was throttling up. The crowd reacted to his punch lines but instead of waiting for them to quit laughing, he just hit them again, building momentum, pushing the tempo, increasing the fervor. It was like building a campfire: to maximize the flame, you have to arrange the sticks just so. Billy Ray could feel it: they were about to burn.

". . . and I told her," the emcee said, " 'No, that's not a clover hitch—and I'm not a Boy Scout either.' " Billy Ray didn't hear the setup but by the way the kid delivered the line, he knew this was his closer, and the crowd concurred: applause, laughter, riot.

It was time.

Adrenaline flooded his blood. Clear purpose drove the haze from his head and his spine went bolt straight. His focus crystallized, taking on weight, becoming a brandishable thing. The only sound to ever exist was the emcee's voice. "Who's ready for a comedy show?" Billy Ray cracked his knuckles. He was an instrument, a blunt object. "We have a real good one for you tonight. Norm Macdonald is here, y'all. Let him hear it. But before that, we have a few special guests. I'm really excited about this first guy. He's a bona fide legend. He's an old friend of Norm's who just so happened to be in town, so Norm told him to come down. He's a little banged up. He was in a car accident last night in Pueblo, but we all know how they drive down there: drunk." Billy Ray was lightning; he was time itself. "You might have seen him on Letterman, or he appeared on a little show called the *Tonight Show* with Johnny Carson *twelve* times. Maybe you saw his hour special on HBO. Ladies and gentlemen, we're lucky to have this guy." Now. "Please give a big Comedy Works welcome to Billy Ray *Schafer*!"

Now now now.

He floated through the curtain on skates of light. His legs ended at his knees. It felt like he was inside a memory. The crowd bayed and he saw them all at once and he remembered there are only five kinds of faces and they only exist with his sanction. Here we go, motherfuckers. Now this is me.

He found the emcee's hand and as they shook, he felt the individual bones in the kid's fingers rub together. "Have fun," said the kid. Billy Ray winked and seized the microphone and set his feet squarely in the center of the stage. The ceiling was lower than he remembered, right on top of him, both very close and distant. He placed his palm flat against it, becoming a pillar. He cocked his hip to the side. All these eyes, all these ears. He realized he was standing far back, upstage. The lights were on his chest. He stepped into them and went blind.

"Hello, Denver. How the hell are you?" Like every crowd everywhere, they bucked with rowdy pride upon hearing the name of the place where they lived. It was a cheap trick, but an effective one: he didn't come to fight fair. "Let's keep it going for Kevin, a very funny young woman. If anyone needs to clean their gutters, Kevin's torso is available. He'll eat all the leaves. Denver. Hot damn, am I glad to be home. I'm born and raised in Colorado. I started in this very room." The crowd roared: one of us. They opened their bosom, spread their collective legs: he knew precisely what he was doing. "I love Colorado so much, I got 303 tattooed on my wrist." Billy Ray pushed back his sleeve to reveal a blanched tattoo—303—gone gray as peeled snakeskin. "You guys know what that is right?"

"Area code," shouted one voice.

"The area code," shouted another.

"That's right," Billy Ray said. "It's my target weight. I'll get there one day." He stalked the edge of the stage, making a show of surveying the room. "What a good-looking bunch. Jesus. Look at the size of this guy." He motioned at a hulk in the front row. The black skin on his bald head glistened in the lights like an obsidian totem. "How'd you get off the Green Mile? Lordy. How tall are you, sir?"

The man's voice was a timpani drum beaten in the bottom of a well. "Six seven."

"Six seven," Billy Ray repeated for the benefit of the back of the room. "Do you play for the Broncos or are you just hung like one? God-damn. I bet you're hiding a hammer. You get a boner—your feet fall asleep." The man's laugh exposed a row of opaline teeth dotted with one golden canine. "And is this your date?" Billy Ray pointed to the slight white woman beside him.

"That's my wife," the man said.

"Your wife. I see. I had you pegged for her driver. Your wife. What a beautiful couple. Ma'am, how long have you been married?"

"Twelve years," she said.

"Twelve years. A year for every inch of his dick. I'm surprised you're not in a wheelchair, honey. You're just the cutest little thing. I bet you sleep in a drawer. How tall are you?"

"Five one."

"Five one!" Billy Ray slapped the mic on his thigh and affected mock stupefaction. "Five one and six seven. When you two make love it looks like a marshmallow on a tree branch." Billy Ray surprised himself: he'd never said that before. He joined the crowd and laughed at his fresh creation. "I bet when he—"

"What happened to your face?" demanded a pair of muttonchops in an acid-washed jacket.

Reflexively, Billy Ray pivoted, located the inquisitor and, faster than thought, spoke directly from his instinctive unconscious: "What happened to my face? I was in a car accident last night, sideburns. What's your excuse?" The line was neither incredibly funny nor original, but in shootouts, it was the quickness that mattered. A crash of laughter and a welling wave of percussive applause spread from back to front and left to right. The shrieking of air pushed hard through pursed lips punctured the ruckus like bottle rockets above a parade. Billy Ray leaned in. "If you're here, who's loading Metallica's gear? Why did you kill JonBenét?" He pointed to the enormous black man from earlier. "If you don't shut up, I'm gonna sic John Henry on you. But instead of racing a train, he's gonna run a train—on your ass!" Billy Ray held up a fist and forced the microphone inside of it. The giant stomped his feet. His laughter boomed off the brick walls. "Didn't you listen? As Kevin said up top, I was in a bit of a car accident last night. If you think this is bad, you should see the tree. I was in Pueblo last night—"

"I'm sorry," shouted a voice in the darkness.

Billy Ray spread his faux smile. "So I see you've been there. Anyone else been to Pueblo?" Weak applause drowned in a chorus of boos. "What the hell happened down there? Do they put meth in the tap water? The town motto is 'Turn Around.'" He was really using every part of the buffalo. Ingratiating regionalism—one of the oldest arrows in his quiver: bash a nearby city, but one far enough away that no one in the room lives there. It was like mocking the deaf: they can't hear it. "Pueblo. They really put a lot of creativity into that name. Pueblo: the town named town. Wonder how long they worked on that? What—was Adobe Shithole taken?" The laughs came unfettered now. The mix of charm and xenophobia had shorted out their judgment centers. They were defenseless, doomed: they liked him and he knew it. In this realm, the words lost meaning. All that mattered was they came from his mouth. He was in the pocket, outside of time. From this vantage point he could do what he pleased. The sense of connection, of agency— ONE.

"And another thing," he said, as alive as a man can be. "They have the dumbest fucking street signs I've ever seen. I saw one today that said beware of falling rock . . ."

He smiled. He had risen. He was home.

—ᨌ—

Chewing ice, Macdonald smiled over the lip of his glass. "What was that line? Like a marshmallow on a tree branch?"

They were tucked away in a corner booth at a bar down Curtis Street, Macdonald and Schafer and Kevin the emcee. The bar was called Becketts and appointed to every inch of wall space hung the framed jerseys of famous Denver sportsmen. Most of them were autographed. Billy Ray recognized all the names. He wondered how much the autograph increased the value of the memorabilia. He wondered what his signature was worth, if anything. He had been asked for autographs tonight.

After the show, as the crowd let out, he'd stood by the bar shaking hands hoping someone would offer him drugs. He drank three Glenlivets after his set, doubles, all of them spiked with cocaine. The cocktails and fresh triumph had him gregarious and talkative and needy so he stood by the bar leeching compliments, letting the people tell him how funny he was, how he made their night, how he was just what they needed.

A drunk man in a filthy sweatshirt swore he remembered Billy Ray from Carson and Billy Ray's ego decided to believe him. The man asked for a picture with him and his wife and Billy Ray complied, standing between them, his hand drifting lower and lower down the woman's back until it rested on the top of the curve of her ass. She tried to pull away but Billy Ray held her in place. "Smile," said the man.

A pair of couples told Billy Ray they remembered him from the club many years before. "You used to have a mullet, right?"

"It was a wig."

"Really?"

"Yeah. I sold it to Jeff Foxworthy."

Three women, clearly sloshed, attacked him in a squealing group hug. They'd won free tickets at work and this was their first comedy show. They smelled like cigarettes and hairspray. As they talked, he pictured each of them naked on their hands and knees. "You were our favorite," the leader said. "You should have stayed on longer. That last guy must have been high or something."

The women encircled him, forming a shell that separated Billy Ray from the rest of the crowd. One of them stood very close, jamming her breasts into his forearm. Her teeth were gapped. She looked like Howdy Doody. "So you grew up in Colorado?" she said.

"Born and bred." He imagined her naked, her face in a pillow, her hair in his fist, his dick in her ass.

"Where?"

"Kiowa." She would scream.

"Where's that?"

"Out east." He wanted to make her scream. He pressed into her, feeling the wire of her bra against the back of his wrist. "Where are you ladies headed after this?"

They giggled. "Gotta get home to the hubby," said Howdy Doody. "He's probably . . ." She kept talking but Billy Ray didn't need to hear anymore.

He signed a few ticket stubs and posed for more pictures but no one offered him anything besides praise. He would have taken anything. His performer's high had burnt off and the comedown was sharp, harsh, pellucid. Earlier he'd indulged himself the premise that tonight was a homecoming, a victory, a decisive return to form, but now, in the loud quiet, he understood that without stakes, nothing could be won; the game needs skin and he was a skeleton. The club was empty and so was he.

He went to the bathroom and tried unsuccessfully to force cocaine up his vitiated nostril. Frustrated, he considered boofing the blow but he decided he didn't have enough left to make it worthwhile. He dropped what he had left on his tongue and let his mouth go cold.

Now in this sports bar surrounded by noteworthy blouses, Schafer sat silently fiending. His leg bounced wildly. Every so often he kneed the underside of the table, causing the glasses to rattle. Since they sat down, Macdonald and Kevin had been talking about golf. Billy Ray wanted the emcee to leave so he could be alone with his friend, but Macdonald seemed to be enjoying the conversation. While they talked, Billy Ray scanned the room for indications of purchasable cocaine: neck tattoos, sunglasses, runny noses, jabber jaws. He kept his eye on the bathroom watching for frequent flyers but nobody caught his attention. The closest he found was a man in a mottled wifebeater standing at the end of the bar. The man was chewed up, wan, composed of evident bones. His shoulder blades, sharp as ulus, jutted like calcified wings and between them dangled a rope of long gray hair tied off into three segments with strips of leather. The man gesticulated, drawing circles in the low light. His voice rose above the electric jukebox. Whoever the man was talking to wasn't listening or didn't exist.

Billy Ray peeled himself off the vinyl and raised his empty bottle. He'd decided to switch to beer, not wanting to appear too drunk around Norm. " 'Nother round?" Macdonald shook his head but the emcee raised his High Life and said, "Yes. Please."

Billy Ray maneuvered to the bar and stood at the elbow next to the raving man.

"Don't let me catch you lying, bitch," the man said. "Just fucking watch me." The man leaned against the bar and arched backward until his nose pointed at the ceiling. "Nine years you got me for. NINE." The man rotated to face Billy Ray, holding up eight fingers. His skin was wasp paper gray, his face a spiderweb of wrinkles. Trapped in his skull, his eyes were unseeing, as blank as two busted televisions. "You got nine off me. And now what?"

"Chicken butt," Billy Ray muttered.

The madman spread his arms and shimmied back and forth on the bartop as if he were crucified. "Just fucking wait," said the man. "No one does me this way. I'll see to it. I'll see." Then he started to cry.

Billy Ray moved down the bar and ordered two High Lifes. Baby-faced businessmen—new captains of old industries—downed Jäger-bombs along the middle of the bar while three old drunks sipped red wine and watched a muted game show on a flat-screen TV. Billy Ray surmised one if not all of the young Turks held blow. They probably had a ball between them, good stuff most likely, but they wouldn't be looking to sell. Men like them didn't traffic, they shared, but they didn't share with men like him.

Billy Ray brought the beers back to the table and re-wedged himself in the booth. "Are you fags still talking about golf?"

Macdonald nodded. "Yep. We're just a couple of randy homosexuals talking about golf. Nothing I enjoy more than talking about golf with other full-fledged homosexual men. I like shooting the shit before packing the shit, that's what I like, yessir, I tell ya."

Billy Ray smiled at his friend's riff but, soured by his failed dope hunt, he failed to laugh. "I was always terrible at golf."

"Of course you were," Macdonald explained. "You're too tall for golf. Golf is a short man's game. It's all about finding your center."

"I don't have the patience."

"You would if you tried."

"I don't know."

"I think it's a perfect game."

"You still get out there?"

"Some. I prefer to watch."

"You watch golf?"

"Incessantly."

"Live?"

"Mostly on TV."

Billy Ray whistled. "Damn if that isn't some boring shit."

"Well it's not monster trucks. You have to know how to watch. It's like fencing with grass."

"All that whispering."

"You don't know anything."

"I know watching golf is some masochist shit."

"Then I'm the Marquis de Sade."

"I will say, if I was better at golf, I might still have a career. The green is where the real deals get made. Remember that, Kevin."

The emcee perked up, glad to be included. He nodded intently. "Really?"

"No," said Billy Ray. "Stand-up is dead."

Macdonald's eyes narrowed. "From what I hear, we're in a golden age."

"It's gilded."

"They call it progress."

"I call it bullshit."

"You sound like a caveman."

"I am what I am. I've seen too much to shut my eyes. You're still funny. There's still some killers. Hell, Kevin's gonna be good. But for the most part, the industry is softer than my dick. All the PC shit. No one has jokes. It's all just trying to make people think."

"Pryor didn't make you think?"

"He made me laugh."

Kevin interjected: "Did you hear he fucked Marlon Brando?"

Billy Ray's head snapped toward the young comedian. "What?"

"That's what I read."

"Huh."

The two older men exchanged glances, considering this factoid. Finally, Macdonald asked, "Who was on the bottom?"

Billy Ray waved his bottle in front of his face as if shooing flies. "Who knows. Maybe I'd have fucked Brando. That's not the point."

Macdonald cracked a wry smile. "It's not?"

"What I'm saying is Pryor told the truth is what he did. And that truth was fucking funny. It wasn't candy-coated and neutered. None of this bathwater bullshit."

Macdonald laughed. "What does that even mean?"

"Call me old-fashioned, but I like *funny* comedy."

"Old-fashioned."

"I didn't come to read the news."

"I'm sorry but—are you . . ." One of the young moneymen from the bar stood in front of their booth staring at Macdonald. He wore a visor backward and upside down. Embroidered on the visor was a cursive letter *A*. Flipped, it looked like a *V* with a line through it.

"What's up?" Macdonald asked.

The man squinted, as if assessing something. "I'm sorry to be this guy, but—". He cut himself off. His eyes expanded with excitement as he reached a conclusion in his head. "Holy shit! You're him." The man turned around to face his friends and held his arms vertically perpendicular: touchdown. "It's him!" he shouted. "It's the Weekend Update guy!"

Billy Ray straightened up, stacking every inch of himself rigid. "Alright. Move it along. This isn't a zoo."

"No," Macdonald said, patting the big man on the shoulder. "It's alright." He stuck out his hand. "What's up, man?"

"I fucking knew it." The man pumped Macdonald's hand. "I fucking loved you when I was a kid. You were the best part of the show."

"Wow, thanks, man."

"What's your name again?"

"Jim Breuer."

"That's right. *Jim Breuer.*" He turned back to his friends and yelled: "Jim fucking Breuer!" The man clasped his head with his hands as if it might explode. "I told them it was you." He looked back at his crew. "I fucking told you it was him!" The man leaned in, laying his elbow on the table. "You think you could come over and say hi to my boys?"

"Oh, I don't think so. But thanks for watching the show."

"Come on. They're all big fans. They're just right over there." The man jerked his thumb over his shoulder.

"I'm not gonna do that but, again, thanks."

"Don't be like that. Come on. Have a drink with us."

"I'm flattered." Macdonald waved at the group and they responded with thumbs-up and raised glasses. "But I'm fine right here."

"What—you're too good to come over and say hi to some fans?"

"No."

"Then come over. Just for one minute. You gotta meet my boy Donny. He's super funny. He does great impressions."

"No thank you, but thanks for the offer."

"Come on. You might get some material for your skits."

"No, I'm just—look, it's late and I'm just trying to have a quiet drink with my father and son."

That cracked Billy Ray right up. He couldn't help but laugh.

The man looked down at Billy Ray, acknowledging him for the first time. "What's so funny?"

"Oh just something my son said earlier."

"This is your dad?"

Macdonald put his hand on Billy Ray's shoulder. "Sure is. Ain't that right, Papa?"

Billy Ray struggled to restrain his laughter. He beamed at Macdonald. "That's me: Papa."

The man's eyes bounced between their faces. "He doesn't look like you."

"He was adopted," Billy Ray said.

"Great story. Come tell my friends."

"You tell them. Me and dad have some catching up to do."

"Did you raise him this way?" Looking down at Billy Ray, the man's eyes were slim red portals. He was built firm. Gym strong. Mounded traps pulled his shirt tight to his deep chest and his forearms were thick, unbreakable, but nothing about him was intimidating. Billy Ray knew scary men and they didn't wear visors. This man had never been in a fight in his life. Billy Ray could feel it, it was like a smell: the bravery of ignorance. This man had never been dominated by another. He'd never known the crude intimacy of violence, never felt the fear of laying on his back wondering if the boot would come to his temple or his throat. He was weak, of a generation of false vipers. It's easy to run your mouth when you have all your teeth.

Billy Ray rolled his beer between his palms, feeling the heaviness of the bottom of the bottle. He looked up at the man, putting the venom in his eyes. "Raised him what way?"

"To be an asshole. Mr. Hollywood won't come talk to the little people."

Macdonald smiled slyly and angled his neck to look around the man. "No one mentioned little people. You've got midgets over there?"

The man's forehead compressed. "What? No. Wait. What?"

Macdonald leaned back in the booth. "Look man, give your friends my thanks and go ahead and put a round on my bar tab. Breuer. It's open."

The man reached for his back pocket and Billy Ray tensed, automatically grabbing the bottle by the neck and lifting it slightly, but the man only held his billfold. "I don't need your money. I've got money." The man peeled back the lips of his wallet to show a sheaf of bills. "Plenty of money."

"You sure do," said Macdonald.

The man looked from Macdonald to Kevin to Billy Ray to Macdonald. "Man, fuck this." He leveled his finger at Macdonald, jabbing it in his face. "You're bullshit."

This was enough for Billy Ray. He seized the man's wrist and pinned his hand to the table. "Time to move along, son." The man tried to pull his hand away, but Billy Ray held tight. "Now."

"Let go of me."

"Will you leave?"

"I'll do whatever I fucking want. Free country." The man picked up Kevin's beer and drank from it. Billy Ray drove the butt of his hand into the bottom of the bottle, forcing the glass into the man's teeth. The bottle fell, shattered on the floor. The man staggered backward, his hand covering his mouth, his eyes alive in his skull. A noise came through his fingers. Animal. Primitive. Billy Ray had heard it before.

"Wut eh uck, an?" the man simpered. Observing from the bar, his friends put down their drinks.

Rising to his feet, Billy Ray stood as tall as he could be. "That beer wasn't yours and neither is he."

The man pulled back his hand and his eyes bulged. Dark blood stained his fingers. His lip, busted wide, leaked fresh crimson down the front of his shirt. "Udderucka," he said, sputtering blood.

Billy Ray moved forward, unsure of what happened next. His muscles danced with anticipation. The man was young and strong but Billy Ray was a veteran of violence. If his pack jumped in, the numbers would complicate the exchange, but they were still at the bar watching their friend back away from the old big man: like he thought, they were cowards. His conviction increased. Alone with this man, one on one, he had the skills to perform what was necessary. He balled his fist.

"Billy."

Billy Ray stopped his approach. It was Macdonald's voice. Billy Ray glanced back quickly, careful to leave the man in his periphery. Macdonald's face was hard, nearing plaintive, his eyes pleading, but through a crack in the grimness a grin bloomed. "Papa."

Billy Ray looked down at the floor, not wanting the visor man to see him smile. The man, his upper lip tucked under his lower lip, had positioned a table between himself and Billy Ray. Boxed in by a cigarette machine, he'd unwittingly cornered himself. No escape. The vulnerability showed on his face: I thought I was strong but I am weak. He held up his hands, cowered. The blatant recreance incensed Billy Ray.

"Ahm swowee. Ahl weave."

"I've got a mind to break your jaw," said the big man. He felt tough. It felt good.

"Ahm swowee." The visor man held his palms out flat.

"I should stomp a mudhole in your ass. But I don't want my grandson to see that." In one smooth movement, Billy Ray moved the table aside, stepped in and grabbed the man by his soaked collar. "So you're getting a pass." Billy Ray jerked the man's chest closer to him, bouncing his head off the wall. He put his mouth to the man's ear. From behind, the man appeared the victim of vampiric right. In a low buffalo, Billy Ray whispered, "Do you have any coke?"

Confusion spanned the man's face. "Wuh?"

"Blow. White. Are you holding?"

The man jammed his hand in his hip pocket but Billy Ray caught his elbow. Slowly, he allowed the man to remove his closed fist. He opened his hand, revealing a folded paper packet. "Eer. Twake ut."

Billy Ray put the parcel in his breast pocket and released his hold and returned to his seat in the booth and the man ran past his friends and out the front door. The men at the bar watched him go. None of them moved toward Billy Ray. Cowards. It was over.

Billy Ray tilted up his beer and drained it. No one spoke. The silence was a distance between them, a measurable length. A thin shame started to form around Billy Ray, a disgust with the speed with which he lapsed into barbarity. The quiet intensified the ill feeling. He was about to apologize when Macdonald said, "Thanks, Papa." Their laughter washed away the weirdness.

"That was badass, man," Kevin said. He sounded like a kid leaving a movie theater. "That was some roadhouse shit."

Macdonald agreed. "Yep. I too enjoyed that display of totally unwarranted brutality."

Billy Ray's hand shot out and pinched Macdonald's cheek. "No one bothers my baby boy."

Macdonald stroked his cheek with the back of his index finger and resumed his old sarcasm. "My favorite part was when you kissed his neck. Very psychosexual. You see, Kevin, you can take the man out of prison but you can't take the dangerous homosexuality out of the man."

Kevin shook his head. "I wouldn't last a day in prison."

"Are you kidding?" Billy Ray said. "You'd have lots of friends. They'd put a wig on you and trade you like ramen packets."

Macdonald nodded. "You'd be currency. Legal tender."

"Oh you'd be tender alright." Billy Ray slugged the young comedian's arm.

"You know what the funniest part is?" Kevin said. "Tomorrow someone is gonna ask that guy what happened to his lip and he's gonna tell them, 'I got beat up by Jim Breuer's dad.'"

They sat on the balcony, Macdonald and Schafer, burning cigars beneath a sky robbed of its stars by the city's glowing vulgarity. The condo perched forty-two stories above the sidewalk. Looking out, they could see the individual pieces of the city puzzled together as the sprawl expanded across the Platte River and farther the highway and past the new football stadium and into the Highlands and Golden and beyond, houses and buildings and roads and cars eating up all the front range, the growth only ceasing when confronted by the mountain's greater black.

Billy Ray boiled with heartburn, the cigar in one hand, a beer between his knees. After last call, they got tacos from a truck and the street meat was not agreeing with his belly full of cocaine and liquor. He was a hornet's nest. He thought he might get sick. If he did, he decided to do it over the railing so he could see what vomit looked like falling four hundred feet.

Macdonald rolled the ash from his cigar into an ashtray made of thick crystal. "Which part of the city are you from?"

"I'm from the country. Out east. Behind us."

"What was the name of your town?"

"Kiowa."

"Like the Indians?"

"Yep. The tribe used to protest at football games in their robes and headdresses. It had the opposite effect. They just looked like really authentic mascots."

Macdonald took a drag of his cigar and let the smoke stream from his mouth like it was the barrel of a fired gun. "We were the Roughriders."

"Like the condom?"

"It's a breaker of wild horses."

"Sounds like a fag porno."

"They changed it a year after I dropped out."

"To what?"

"The Cardinals."

Billy Ray loosed a tremendous burp, ripping the late quiet. It sounded like a garbage disposal. "Roughrider sounds tougher."

"Unequivocally."

"I've had a few roughriders in my day."

"Your first wife."

"Only wife." Billy Ray snorted. "She tried."

"They don't make a saddle big enough for you."

Raising his chin, Billy Ray spat through the bars of the railing and watched the arching effluvium fall and break apart. "Or she didn't hold on tight enough."

Macdonald laid his arms along the top of the cold railing and rested his chin on the back of his hands. "When you lived in the city, where did you live?"

Billy Ray pointed with the tip of the cigar. "South."

"What was that part of town called?"

"Englewood."

"What was the mascot down there?"

"Mexicans."

"You sure you have enough blankets?" Macdonald stood in the doorway framed by the light pouring out of his room. Backlit, he was faceless, a wraith.

"I'm solid," Billy Ray said.

"That couch okay?"

"Better than my car."

"You sure you don't want the bed?"

"Bed's for the headliner."

"That's what you taught me."

"Remember that time in Halifax? The bunk beds?"

"When the girl kept hitting her head?"

"You kept me up all night."

"She was insatiable."

"Can you believe that was twenty years ago?"

"I don't believe a word out of your mouth."

"The last thirty years. It's like I was fired out of a cannon."

"You're heavy artillery."

"You're a bayonet."

"Good night, Billy."

"It's Papa now."

Macdonald shut his door and pitch black swallowed the room.

Billy Ray flipped and turned for a half hour, searching for a comfortable position while the cocaine tamed. The couch, black leather, retained the heat of him. He removed his T-shirt and his pants and stripped until he wore only one sock. Fully nude and sleek with sweat, he stuck to the leather. Eventually he rolled off the couch onto the carpet and slept on the floor like a dog.

SATURDAY

THE BEAMS OF ORANGE LIGHT SKIRTING THE EDGE OF THE blinds were so bold in the darkness they looked wet, molten, like melted sugar. Bathed in the light and on his side curled fetal, Billy Ray, naked and pale pink, looked like a shrimp dipped in butter.

He'd woke once in the early morning panicked with sick and blindly bull-rushed the darkness, barely reaching the toilet in time. Tossing his festering poison served as a curative. He returned to his nest on the carpet and sank to the ocean floor of his unconscious. He remained there until twelve thirty the following afternoon soaked in the liquid light.

When he opened his eyes again, he entered the day the victim of a demanding thirst. The inside of his mouth felt drywalled. He went to the sink and slurped. The water soothed the skin of his ruined stomach. In his reflection in the surface of the stainless-steel stove he could see there was vomit in his hair. He was wordless in his mind. He felt like he should be embarrassed or disgusted but he had reached deeper bottoms. There was no more embarrassment or disgust left in him. He had exhausted his reserves. All he felt was a remoteness, as if he were far away. He smiled at his reflection. The day was too long to hate himself immediately.

"Good morning." Macdonald was seated on the balcony with a book in his lap wearing wraparound sunglasses that replaced his eyes with mirrors.

"Morning."

"There's coffee in the pot."

"Where's the towels?"

"In the closet in the hall."

Billy Ray turned the shower to scalding and stepped under the spray and let the water burn him clean. He redressed in his old clothes, stinking of dead cigarettes, and inspected the toilet and the vicinity for errant puke. Finding none, he left the bathroom and made a cup of coffee and brought the pot to the balcony. "Need a warm-up?" Macdonald held out his cup and Billy Ray poured slowly, struggling to control the quiver in his hand. "Whatchya reading?" Macdonald flattened the book and Billy Ray read the cover. "*The Plague*. Sounds light."

"How'd you sleep?"

"Alright. I made a few mistakes."

"Is that Woody Allen?"

"Steven Wright."

Below them the city breathed and bled. Cars pumped up and down streets made arteries by the distance. From here the entire circulation was laid bare. The buildings were the organs and the people were the blood. Denver, a creature with no head. The people were small, insignificant. He wondered where they were going, where they thought they had to be. Billy Ray lit a cigarette and sat down and drank his coffee and studied the cycles of the city. He never located the heart.

Billy Ray ate breakfast and Macdonald ate lunch at a diner in the lobby downstairs. Billy ordered eggs over easy with bacon and well-done hashbrowns and sourdough toast and Macdonald had a club sandwich with no tomatoes and onion rings. In the habit of the reconnected, they talked about people they knew and whether they were alive or dead.

"Did you hear Mitch Janowsky killed himself?" asked Macdonald.

"How'd he do it?"

"Shotgun in the chest."

"In the chest?" Billy Ray dabbed a puddle of yolk with a toast point. "That never made sense to me. The head is where you want it. It's not a fucking trick shot. It's right there." He rested his chin on his water glass. "Boom. Easy."

"Perhaps he wanted to save face."

"Mitch didn't have a face worth saving."

"It's less of a mess."

"Where'd he do it?"

"Hotel room after a show."

"He probably didn't want to lose the deposit. Cheap bastard."

"You know the old adage: speak ill of the dead."

Billy Ray pointed his fork at another table. "Look at this."

"What?"

"Ranch dressing."

"What about it?"

"This whole fucking country is crazy for ranch dressing. It's the new ketchup. It's disgusting."

"What are you, Andy Rooney?"

"It's a fucking epidemic."

"Did you hear about Jordy Stickle?"

"Jordy Stickle. I haven't thought about him in years."

"He ran over a kid."

"Fuck."

"They sentenced him to thirty years."

"So the kid died?"

"No, he lived."

"And he still got thirty years?"

Macdonald nodded.

"That seems a little extreme." Billy Ray had a habit of fondling things as he talked. "Fiddling" his wife called it. She said it was because he was nervous people might actually hear what he said. Sitting here with his friend—he hoped that was still the name for what they were—he re-arranged his fork and his knife like they were cards in a monte scam, his fingers working at their own game while his lips played another. He wanted a drink but the diner didn't have a license to serve. He was embarrassed when the waitress informed him. She had soft eyes. She seemed sorry, like she knew it would help.

"Was it Stickle who had that bit about wire hangers?"

"I don't know."

"Something about how they made your clothes look like a ghost was wearing them."

"I don't remember."

"Olivia always liked Stickle. She always said I should write more jokes like his."

"Bland and toothless?"

"She liked that stuff. Observations. She thought my act was too mean."

"Good comedy is truthful and the truth is mean."

"She never thought you were funny."

"I wasn't that funny back then."

"She hated Kinison."

"Then her opinion is moot."

Billy Ray arched the pitch of his voice feminine. " 'He's just yelling up there. People don't want to be yelled at on a night out.' "

"He had to yell so people would hear what he was saying."

"I think I'm going to go see her."

"Your wife?"

"She's up north."

"Where are your sons?"

"Somewhere around here." Billy Ray looked out the window at the primetime Saturday streets. A woman and a girl stood at the crosswalk waiting for the light to change. In one hand she held a burden of heavy shopping bags and in the other she clutched the child's mittened hand. A group of young men attired in black-and-gold jerseys moved around them like a school of fish and crossed against the light. The lady shook her head and leaned down to say something to the girl, a warning, nodding toward the young men, any one of which could have been his sons. He realized he didn't know what either of his boys looked like anymore. In his head, they were still as big as the girl. The light changed and the pair marched forward, little hand in bigger hand. *Hold on tight, lady,* he thought. *Don't let her get away.* "I'm gonna look them up, too."

"That's good."

"How's your boy?"

"They say he's a genius. He wants to be a writer. A poet."

"So he's gay?"

"I don't care what he is as long as he's not a comic."

Billy Ray leaned to one side and pulled his notebook from his pocket. He flipped through the pages until he found the right one. "What are your plans for today?"

"Go back upstairs and read, take a nap before the shows. You want to do the guest sets tonight? I think Wende is going to be there."

Billy Ray stirred his cold coffee. "You sure she'd be okay with that?"

"It's been years."

"She's like an elephant."

"Prized for her ivory?"

"Exactly. Could I borrow your phone?"

Billy Ray stepped outside with his notebook and Macdonald's phone and struggled to light a cigarette against the licking of a sharp breeze pushing bits of trash along the gutter as it tried to muster the strength to become wind. He found an alcove by the diner's side door and sat down on a ledge to transfer the numbers on the page to the phone's screen. Written next to the number in his blocked script was the name JERM. He stared at the ten digits. Added together they totaled twenty-two, the same age as his youngest son, one of the signs Macdonald spoke of. He pressed the green button and held his breath.

"Hello?" The voice rang in his ears like a gunshot. The sound had the effect of a smell. It returned him to a place. "Hello?"

"Jeremy?"

"This is Jeremiah." That's right—he was Jeremiah now. Only Billy Ray called him Jeremy, even when he was little. But he wasn't little anymore. He was a man named Jeremiah. "Who's this? I don't have this number saved." Behind his son's voice, other voices clashed with the sound of a television. Billy Ray wondered if he was in a bar. The apple doesn't always fall; sometimes it stays on the tree.

"Jeremiah. It's your father." The word hung in the air as if it got trapped in the line or lost somewhere in the immeasurable space between them.

"Dad?" Jeremiah's voice cracked, or maybe it was the connection or the word itself. He hadn't used it in a long time. "Are you okay?"

The worry in his son's voice set like a hook in Billy Ray's heart. "I'm fine, kiddo." Why had he said kiddo? No twenty-two-year-old wants to be called kiddo. Now that he thought about it, he might have been twenty-three. "How you doing?"

"Let me step outside. It's loud in here. Hold on." *That's all I'm doing.* "Is that better?"

"Crystal clear."

"Okay."

"What are you up to?"

"Watching the Buffs game at this bar. Where are you?"

"I'm, uh, I'm in Denver. I'm having lunch with Norm Macdonald."

"Oh."

"Yeah."

"The Weekend Update guy?"

"Yeah. This is his phone. Mine's broke."

"I saw his movie. It was funny. Dumb but funny."

"I'll tell him. Dumb but funny."

"You can leave out the dumb part."

"He can take it."

"You're in Denver?"

"Yeah. Until Monday. I don't know how I ever lived at this altitude. It's like the air isn't there."

"My roommate freshman year couldn't take it. He got really sick. He had to transfer."

"I feel like I'm drowning." The side door opened and a tired man in a filthy white apron stood there holding two trash bags. The man looked startled. Billy Ray mouthed the words *Sorry, am I good?* The man said nothing. Billy Ray spun his legs to the side to allow him a path to the dumpster. "What are you doing tonight?"

"Nothing. There's a party later. If the Buffs pull it off, it'll probably be big. Or if they lose. Either way."

"What time is that?"

"Later."

"Want to have dinner?"

"Tonight?"

"I mean if you've got plans . . ." Billy Ray trailed off. If his son said no, he felt like he would split in half and then split in half, disintegrate, break down to his component parts. "I could drive up. I have a car." Nothing. Billy Ray checked the phone. The call hadn't dropped. Jeremiah was thinking. He prepared to hold himself together. There was a bar across the street.

"Yeah."

"What?"

"Yeah. Sounds good."

Billy Ray stood up, raised by his son's agreement. He pumped his fist as a tear snapped free from his duct. He slashed it away with his wrist so the dumpster man didn't see. "Cool." He never said cool. "Very cool."

"What time you thinking? The game's in the fourth quarter."

Billy Ray flicked his butt and started back toward the front door. "I'll leave now."

"Where should I meet you?"

"I could pick you up."

"Sure. Do you know where I live?"

The answer shamed him as much as any evil he'd committed in his fifty-three years. "No. What's your address?" He wrote the numbers and words in his notebook and repeated them back.

"Yep."

"Okay. I'll be there in an hour."

"Alright. See you soon. Oh—Dad?" Dad. He let the word wash over him. "I've been drinking all morning. Game day, you know? I'll probably still be a little drunk."

The warmth of the tears was made short by the wind. "That's alright."

"Okay. See you in a bit."

"Go Buffs."

"Go Buffs."

He hung up the phone and practically ran to the booth. Their plates were cleared and Macdonald was counting out singles from a stack of bills. Billy Ray sat down and slid the phone across the Formica. "What's the damage?" He was brimming. The room seemed brighter, more real.

"I got it."

"Let me get the tip then."

"I got it. I'm very famous."

"Oh yeah, I forgot. You're Jim Breuer."

"How'd the phone call go?"

"Good. Real good. I'm gonna head up to Boulder. My youngest is up there. We're gonna have dinner."

Macdonald's mouth U'd magnanimous. "That is good, man."

"Yeah. Yeah it is." Billy Ray downed the rest of his coffee.

"You still want the guest spots?"

"Pencil me in."

"Bring the kid if you want."

"We'll see. He said he saw your movie."

"Did he like it?"

"He said it was dumb but funny."

"Smart kid."

Walking down 15th, he moved like Bluto, bowlegged, his arms stiff at his side and going fast as he braced against the northerly wind blowing full bore now and kissed with the stink of cooked blood and industrial slaughter, gifts of the dog food plant in Commerce City and the slaughterhouses to the north, the smell of impending storm. He ducked into a liquor store on Champa and left with more cigarettes and a flask of vodka and a tall boy of Mickey's he opened and brown-bagged and drank as he walked.

At the car, he smelled his wardrobe for freshness and assembled an outfit and stripped down to his boxers on the sidewalk to change. Passersby gawked and hurried past, some of them crossing the street at the sight of him, but he was oblivious to their concern, to the day, to the cold: he was on the way to see his son. The exhilaration moved his blood like a second heart. In the scrapheap of shit that was his life, rarely did he ever receive the opportunity to mend. This dinner was new England, a second chance on a second chance on a second chance. Their history was filled with cankers. He'd done his son dirty since the day he was born.

Trapped in Burlington International as the runway caked with snow, Billy Ray had missed Jeremiah's screaming nativity. His wife had begged him to cancel his dates that weekend, sure that the baby would burst forth any moment, quoting her mother's folklore about "Prudholm women push them out as soon as they can," but Billy Ray, cavalier and at the peak of his fame, sided with their doctor's avowal that their son would not come for two more weeks and he flew to Boston that Thursday confident in his decision.

He was in Sunapee, New Hampshire when her water broke. As soon as the caterer handed him the note, he flew from the ballroom without getting his check and braved the driving snow to Burlington, whispering "fuck me, fuck me" for the duration and daring the tires to hold the asphalt. He bought a seat on the next flight to Chicago that connected into Denver, getting him home in seven hours—five with the time change—but the snow fell and the flight was delayed and he screamed "fuck me" with all the wind in his lungs. He went to the bar and bribed the bartender twenty dollars for the rights to the phone and drank Canadian Club while he waited for updates from his sister-in-law. By the time the runways were cleared, Jeremiah David Schafer was prenatal no longer: he was a seven-and-a-half-pound wedge between him and his wife, a newborn trump card in every argument thereafter. His father's absence at his birth was the first crack in the thin veneer that was his parents' fragile marriage and, in the ugliest recesses of his judgment, Billy Ray never forgave his son for being born.

Out of clean socks, he wore his cowboy boots bareback. He brushed his teeth over a trash can and rinsed his mouth with beer. Speer Boulevard was empty in the dwindling afternoon. He found I-25 and sped north at eighty miles per hour, chain-smoking and drinking the vodka and concocting a lie to tell his son when he asked about his face. At Highway 36, he exited on the left, toward Boulder and his deliverance.

He'd never cared for Boulder. A thick layer of neo-hippie pretension hung over the city like smog, choking the citizens humorless. The college brought in fresh minds descended from wealthy coastal families, spoiled young Californians and New Englanders who only knew Colorado as the land that surrounded Vail and Aspen. They chose Boulder for its proximity to the slopes and they lived in constant conflict with the locals, a judgmental breed of Earthshoed, Subaru-driving, granola-totaling yuppies that pined for the sixties and spent their retirement fighting for bike lanes and recycling programs as if they were civil rights. In his low opinion, the only admirable aspect of Boulder was the Flatirons, five slashing juts of silver-veined indigo earth that served as the city's de facto welcome sign. He lowered his speed to admire the peaks glowing in the embrace of the sun's last few hours of light. To Billy Ray it always looked like the tallest of the peaks had its arms around the other four, cradling them as if it was their shepherd and the sky was their pasture.

When Highway 36 turned into 28th, he pulled over at a gas station on Canyon Boulevard and asked the counter boy for directions to his son.

"What?"

"Can you tell me how to get to Pine and 21st?"

The kid sighed and rolled his eyes, obviously perturbed that Billy Ray had the audacity to interrupt his consumption of a comic book titled *HATE*. "Pine is up on the left," he said, pointing with a painted black fingernail. He covered his gangly torso with a tattered black Megadeth T-shirt, an affront to the city's peacenik affectation and rich with the smell of torched weed. Billy Ray found it endearing. "Keep going till you hit 21st. It's right by the elementary. What's the address?" Billy Ray read off the numbers. "Yeah, right by the school. I think I partied there before." At this tidbit, Billy Ray experienced a twinge of odd jealousy. Had this surly little skidmark really been allowed in his son's house? Were they classmates? Friends? Did his son wear dark nail polish? Did he smoke dope before work and treat strangers with contempt? Did this greasy stoned reprobate know his boy better than he did?

"Thanks," Billy Ray said. For some reason, he wanted the kid's approval. "You like Megadeth?"

"Oh. Wow. Geez. What gave it away?"

Billy Ray smoked a cigarette outside the car and when it was spent he applied deodorant and sprayed himself liberally with a bottle of cologne he kept on hand for extemporaneous trysts. He threw away his empty cans and gave the car a dowsing then, after smelling his breath in his cupped hand and deeming it tolerable, he entered the car and turned out onto Canyon drumming a beat on the steering wheel, sweating and more nervous than his first appearance on Carson.

At Pine, he turned left and followed the descending street signs to 21st. He turned right at the school and trawled a street of neat craft-style homes for the address he'd received, repeating the house numbers as he passed. "2216, 2220, 2222." He parked the car in front of a yarded single-story home outfitted with a covered front porch and sherbert green siding. "There it is."

The driveway housed two cars: a cream, late-model Buick Century and a maroon Pontiac Sebring convertible. Walking up the drive, he hoped one of them belonged to his son, preferably the convertible. Girls love convertibles. He hoped girls loved his son.

On the porch, a coffee can overflowed with cigarette butts and empty beer bottles rolled in the light wind like toppled bowling pins. The doorbell was canned chimes. The electronic tones were incongruous and barely audible over a thumping boom-bap beat emanating from inside the house. He rang it once, waited, then rang it again, then again, reluctant to knock: he didn't want to sound like the cops. After the fifth ring, the music turned down and he heard a female voice yell, "I got it." A young woman opened the door. Her face was fine-boned and subtly Asian and crowned with a tangle of asymmetric hair bleached a dull white. She wore shorts that ended well above her knee, revealing a tattoo of a jet-black panther down her right thigh, and her small breasts, the nipples undoubtedly pierced, pushed unrestrained against the thin cotton of her tank top. She was shoeless. She looked like she just woke up. "Hello?"

"Uh, hiya. I'm sorry. I might have the wrong house. Does Jeremiah Schafer live here?"

"Yeah." The girl crossed her arms against Billy Ray's wandering gaze.

"Oh." He stuck out his hand. "Billy Ray Schafer. I'm his father."

"I'll get him." She neglected his hand. "Jeremiah," she bellowed. "That guy is here."

He stood there awkwardly on the threshold—that guy?—the girl not inviting him in farther and Billy Ray not knowing how to talk to her. She was beautiful and original and intimidating. She looked like she was from the future.

"Lovely house," he offered.

"It's a rental."

"Great location."

"I guess."

"Is that your convertible?"

"Yeah. I got it when my mom died."

Billy Ray was relieved when he heard footsteps and around a corner came a tall young man with a face much like his but improved upon by the addition of Olivia's clear blue eyes. His chestnut hair was cropped tight at the sides and parted down the middle; it looked exactly like the tip of a penis. Billy Ray breathed a sigh of silent relief when he saw his fingernails were unvarnished. Dressed in a blue sweatshirt and black denims over red Chuck Taylors, his son appeared healthy, untroubled—normal.

"Hey, Dad."

My son is a stranger to me. Billy Ray wanted to weep. Who is this young man? How did I let it get so bad? His son's maturation proved evidence of all the time squandered, of all the memories left unmade. Yes, Billy Ray wanted to cry, to bawl, to rip his eyes out and swallow his tongue, to fall on his knees and beg forgiveness for all the evaporated time, to apologize for every forgotten birthday, for every missed swim meet, for the way he misused his mother and the resulting years he wasted dwelling in his own pit of solitary degradation while he and his brother grew into men without guidance or love. Instead he smiled like God told him a secret.

"Hey yourself." He stuck out his hand and to his surprise, Jeremiah took it and yanked the old man into him and, while the girl watched, hugged him, the two of them patting each other's backs, Billy Ray feeling the dense meat of his boy's new body and smelling his son's hair and wishing he could stop time and be buried in this moment.

"Lulu, this is my father," Jeremiah said, his arm around the old man's back as if he were showing him to a buyer.

"We met."

"Lulu. Now that's a great name."

"What happened to your face?"

"I slipped on some ice."

"You're a comedian or something?"

"Or something," Billy Ray agreed.

"Jeremiah showed me some of your videos on YouTube."

He looked at his son, unbelieving. "He did?"

"I could see how people could think you were funny."

Billy Ray laughed. "Well, that's high praise."

"Come on," Jeremiah said. "I'm hungry." He bent down and kissed the girl with a loud smack. "See you at Todd's?"

"I'm going to Janeane's first."

"Oh are you?" Jeremiah squeezed the girl to him and kissed her again, harder, lips parted, and she opened her mouth to allow his tongue access. Billy Ray caught himself staring like some kind of sick zookeeper as his boy, all grown up, fed his tongue to this new species of woman with white hair and feline features, gawking until he realized what he was doing and fought his eyes to the floor and studied the grain of the boards beneath his feet and surged with paternal spirit: *Attafuckingboy.* "Text me," Jeremiah said.

She cocked her eyebrow, the fine hair most dark against her sunless skin. "Maybe," she said. "We'll see."

Jeremiah bounded down the driveway in a kind of duck walk, his haircut bouncing like a poorly tethered wig, long feet attached to long legs, his hands jammed in his pockets and his chin tucked tight to his chest against the chill. Walking behind him, Billy Ray took note of how his son's shoulders filled out his sweatshirt. He was a Schafer alright: broad, big, handsome. Billy Ray's father was six foot in a time when that was gigantic and when the tailor last measured him, Billy Ray was pushing six three, but here walking next to Jeremiah, his shadow was shorter than his son's. He'd always tried to guide the boy toward brutish sports where he could use his body as a weapon—football, wrestling, basketball—but Jeremiah took to swimming and this was the result: lean, elongated muscles packed to a wide back that tapered slim at his waist.

Jeremiah spun around. "You want me to drive?"

"Nah, my car's across the street," Billy Ray said. He pressed the button on the keyless entry remote and the horn honked and the headlights flashed.

"What happened to the T-Bird?"

"I sold it. This is a rental."

They climbed in the car and Billy Ray put on his seatbelt, following his son's lead. "Don't you get tired of driving?" Jeremiah said.

"Not yet."

"I think I would." Compacted in the seat, Jeremiah's knees were bundled and pressed against the glove compartment. Billy Ray reached between his son's legs and pulled the lever below the seat and the seat slid back.

"That's better." He turned on the car and turned the radio off. "Where to?"

"I could really go for some barbeque."

"Wherever you want."

Billy Ray pulled onto the street and followed his son's directions below brown and leafless trees, their branches picked barren by autumn's persistent fingers. The neighborhood was quiet on this Saturday afternoon, the occupants idly passing the time between now and nightfall in their garages or on their porches, gangs of college kids in sweatpants and gym shorts and all of them with a drink in their hands as they sat in plastic chairs or spiraled footballs across yellow lawns or stood on the opposite ends of Ping-Pong tables tossing table tennis balls at designs of red cups. Jeremiah waved at some of them and some of them waved back. Driving through this collegiate picturesque, Billy Ray smiled, proud that he could provide his son this experience he never had. In his job, the product was so ephemeral. There was no tangible result of his labor beyond the money in his pocket. It was good to know that while stand-up killed his relationship with his wife and his sons and would eventually kill him, at least it had allowed his son to live.

Jeremiah pointed out a house with trash bags taped over the windows. "That's where the party is."

"That the one you're going to?"

"I don't know. Those guys are a bunch of assholes, but their parties are always off the chain. Turn right down here. It's a couple miles down."

It was going better than he ever imagined. Billy Ray assumed his youngest would simmer with the same contempt as his brother and his mother but, for the time being, that wasn't the case. If he did harbor those sentiments—and why wouldn't he? Billy Ray knew what he did—Jeremiah was keeping a lid on it. He was the picture of geniality. The conversation flowed without effort or lulls. Jeremiah navigated the discourse, keeping the topics surface and broad.

"Lulu seemed to like you."

"She did?"

"Yeah. If she doesn't like you, she doesn't talk."

"She's a firecracker. She's got that voodoo beauty."

"She can be a real handful."

"Is she some kind of Chinese?"

"Laos. She's adopted."

"Pretty little thing."

"And smart, too. She speaks four languages."

"They didn't make them like that when I was your age."

"Like how?"

"They were either pretty or scary and that Lulu is both."

Jeremiah laughed. "Thanks, I think?"

Billy Ray drove slow, savoring the closeness and the sound of his son's voice and wondering if right now meant as much to his son as it did to him. He couldn't remember the last time he had been this content. It was hard not to smile like his brain was broken. Afraid to jinx it, he didn't want to appear remorseless. He worried expressing too much happiness might seem flippant, serving as a reminder to his son to be angry, but he didn't want to be somber, either. He wanted his son to know he was proud of him while also communicating he was aware he had no right to take any credit: it was a fine line. Above all else, he didn't want to queer this piece of heaven. The mood could turn plenty easy without him helping it along. They both knew what was coming—the honesty, the admissions—but that could wait for dinner. Right now, things were good and Billy Ray would rather cut off his genitals and eat them than dissuade this sterling panacea.

They crossed 28th as the sun retired. The peach sky waited for the moon. Kids Jeremiah's age crowded the sidewalk in giggling packs wearing beatific smiles that seemed to say they were never going to die. Billy Ray envied them. Their lives were still unwritten. Nothing they did mattered yet. They weren't old enough to hurt anyone forever.

When Jeremiah said so, Billy Ray turned right into the parking lot of a nameless strip mall and parked in front of a restaurant called Big Jim's Smokehouse.

Crossing the space between the car and the front door, Jeremiah said, "I hope you like brisket."

Billy Ray stopped walking. "Oh, I forgot to tell you—I'm vegan."

Jeremiah scoffed. "Bullshit." He sounded like his father, sounded like his father's father.

"You got me. I'm gonna eat a whole hog."

A lip-ringed hostess led them to a table. Following, Billy Ray nudged his son in the ribs and nodded toward her ass while jerking his eyebrows up and down.

"Is this alright?" she said, standing in front of a booth. The table was covered in sheets of butcher paper. On the paper, she wrote the name SHELLY with a red wax pencil. "Your server tonight is Shelly. She'll be right with you."

"We're in no hurry," Billy Ray told her. "Thank you . . ."

The girl pointed to the name tag affixed to her right breast. "Meredith."

Billy Ray squinted and moved his head in close to her chest. "Ah there it is. Meredith. Looks like I picked the right night to forget my glasses." Billy Ray winked at his son. The girl walked away sighing.

The restaurant was bare-bones, colorless, vaguely military. The walls were wood paneled and empty besides a few framed newspaper reviews hung behind the register and a gold-and-black flag bearing the logo of the University of Colorado. Above the kitchen window, a long metal sign read IF IT DON'T SMELL LIKE SMOKE THEN THE BBQ'S A JOKE. Big Jim's was no joke: the sweet acridity of fired mesquite filled the room, riding on a primal undercurrent of roasted beef that spoke to the reptile part of Billy Ray's brain. "Something smells good," he said.

"This place has the best brisket in Boulder."

"Go ahead and order for us." Billy Ray slid out of the plastic booth. "I'm gonna go wash my hands."

"You want anything in particular?"

"Whatever's good. I trust you. And order plenty so you can take some home."

The bathroom was floor to ceiling blinding white. He turned on the faucet and splashed hot water on his face. The mirror was etched with curses and epithets: FUCK. COKSUKER. BITCH. In his reflection, they looked like they were carved into his face. He tested his nostril and finding it sealed no longer, he removed his keys and the bindle of cocaine from his pocket and opened it and dug out a bump and sniffed the key clean, not much, just enough to calm down: a lot was at stake. He was nervous and the cocaine helped him relax, or at least that's what he told himself. He checked his nose from every angle until he was sure he was powderless, fixed his collar, then, bracing himself on the sink, he implored the scarred face in the scarred mirror: "Don't fuck this up."

Back at the table, Jeremiah was talking with a Roman-nosed girl with sloe eyes and blond hair streaked through with honeysuckle highlights. Billy Ray walked around her and snuck in the booth but as he scooted, his hand skidded on the plastic, and the resulting noise sounded like a massive screeching fart. Billy Ray smiled up at the waitress. "That was the booth, I swear."

"Sure it was," said Jeremiah.

The girl's eyes were raccooned by dark circles. She looked defeated. She was too tired to be so young. "You must be Shelly," said Billy Ray.

Her mouth smiled but her eyes stayed dead. "That's me. But she spelled it wrong. I spell it with an I and an E."

"How're you doing tonight, Shellie?"

"I can't complain."

"I bet you could."

She blew an errant curl off her forehead. "It wouldn't do any good."

Jeremiah ordered a pound of brisket and a half pound of pulled pork and two hot links with sides of macaroni and cheese and baked beans.

"Anything else?" Shellie asked.

"What do y'all have on tap?" asked Billy Ray, the menu open in front of him.

"Coors, Coors Light, Bud, Busch, Killian's."

He looked over his menu at his son. "What do you want?"

"Coors."

"Coors? I'm more of a Busch man myself."

"Oh my God," Jeremiah said. "That's such a dad joke."

"I'm a dad."

"But you're also a comedian."

"I can be both."

"Can you?"

Can I? Interpreting through chemically altered optics and already hypersensitive, Billy Ray, receiving the query as a subtle barb, flinched, nothing noticeable, just a small fleeting recoil he hid behind his menu. He left the question rhetorical. "Give us a pitcher of Coors, please, Shellie with an I and an E."

The room was empty besides them and a table full of men in softball gear. Billy Ray kicked his leg up on the booth, attempting casual, but really he was terrified. There was so much to say and even more to hear. He got the feeling neither of them knew how to proceed. The situation lacked reality. This morning, getting his son on the phone felt like a Hail Mary but here they were across from each other, acting friendly, Billy Ray joking and Jeremiah smiling and laughing and calling him Dad instead of the cruel and accurate titles Billy Ray expected and deserved. Driving up today, he prepared for a fight. And not just any fight, but an eye-gouging, fishhooking, curb-stomping slobberknocker rife with emotional warfare, repressed truths and cruel reminders landed with the viciousness of steel-toes to the ribs. And worst of all, in this particular fight, he had no legitimate cause to go on the offensive: he couldn't throw any punches: the boy had never wronged him. Hands tied by his previous transgressions, Billy Ray had no legs to stand on nor a cause to stand. If Jeremiah decided to start wailing, Billy Ray had to take it. He'd practiced his parries and feints, designing rebuttals and defenses to every accusation he could imagine, creating intricate mazes of logic that transferred the blame to comedy, the road, the industry, the loneliness, to chemicals and temptation, to Olivia and sacrifice and lack of understanding, to his own upbringing and the holes it left in him, even to the idea of money itself, building these arguments painstakingly like ships in the bottle of his mind. He'd prepared for every outcome but this: peace. The waiting was eating him alive.

They talked about the events of the Buffs game until the waitress returned with their beer. Billy Ray poured their glasses full and raised his. "Thanks for coming out with me, Jerm. You didn't have to, but you did, and I'm grateful." They touched glasses and drank. The beer was cold needles. It felt good going down.

"When you called, I almost didn't pick up because I didn't have the number saved. I'm glad I did. It'd been a while."

"I know. Trust me. I know."

"Mom never tells me anything about you."

"We don't talk much. I just send her money."

"I never got to thank you for that."

"Don't mention it. It's the least I can do."

"I know how much tuition is."

"What else am I gonna spend it on?"

Billy Ray refilled his glass and topped off his son's. Shellie walked by with a loaded platter and set it down in front of the softballers. The food smelled good but he wasn't hungry. Robbed of his want to eat by discomfort and cocaine, all he wanted was one hundred cigarettes and for the shit to hit the fan. He looked at his son sucking foam off his beer. *Just hit me with it already, boy. Drop the damn hammer.* Billy Ray decided to put his toe in the water.

"How's your mom?"

"She's good. She's pretty high up at the hospital. She's been coaching volleyball. We talk every Sunday. Want me to tell her you say hi?"

"I think I'm going to go see her tomorrow."

Shock and concern yanked Jeremiah's hairline upward. "You are?"

"That's the plan."

"Have you—have you talked to *her* about it?"

"I don't think that's a good idea." He rotated his beer with his fingertips. "Think I'll surprise her."

Jeremiah scooted forward on the bench and lowered his timbre, changing the tone of the conversation along with the tone of his voice. "Dad, if I ask you something, will you be completely honest with me?"

Billy Ray sat up straight, gripped the sides of the table and prepared to be particled. "Shoot."

"Are you . . ." Jeremiah inhaled. The exhalation puffed out his cheeks. "Are you dying?"

Billy Ray smiled, the tension cracked like an egg across his face. "Jesus, kiddo. No."

"Oh," Jeremiah said, seemingly perplexed.

"I'm fine." He thumped his sternum. "Strong like bull. Why would you think that?"

"I don't know. Just the suddenness I guess. We haven't talked in three years and then you're calling me from a strange number, saying you need to see me, then you're here out of the blue with your face all fucked up telling some story about how you slipped on some ice and you're being all lovey-dovey and soft and shit. Then you say you're going to see Mom, who we both know hates your guts, and for good reason—fuck. I don't know. I just figured you had to be sick or cancer or something."

Billy Ray laughed, but it came out sounding weak and hollow. "What—I gotta have AIDS to want to see my son?"

"Well, sorry, but you haven't exactly given a shit."

Billy Ray's anger flashed white, a private explosion. "I give a shit! I give twenty grand a year worth of shit."

"Tuition is fifteen grand. Nice try."

"Who pays your rent? Your phone?"

"Whatever."

A flash of insight wrenched the big man's stomach. "Wait. Is that why you've been so sweet on me? Because you thought I was here to say goodbye?"

Jeremiah threw up his hands. "What am I supposed to think?"

"It's fucked up that your brain goes right to death."

"Well, newsflash: *I'm fucked up!* You might know that if you were ever around."

Billy Ray winced internal. "You don't think I want to be around? I'd love to be around, but someone's got to—"

"Oh, please. You can save *that* fucking shit. Like I haven't heard it all before. You used to spout it at mom until she cried. We were at the top of the stairs. Walker wanted to kill you. Did you know that? When I told him you were coming up here, he said I should punch you in the fucking face, but I said, 'What if he's dying?' and he said, 'If he's dying, someone's been listening to my prayers.'"

Billy Ray pushed air out his nose and smirked, trying to act tough, trying to appear unfazed, trying not to let on that hearing this admission had smashed his heart into fragments as fine as powdered sand. The pain was too real to allow it to be felt. His defenses compensated, flipping it, distilling anger from the hurt, raw from the crude: implode or explode: combustible, he caught fire. "Is that what it is? You wanna take a swing at me? You wanna push in my nose?" He stuck out his chin. "Well here it is, boy. Swing." Snarling. "SWING."

"I'd break your jaw."

"I'd like to see you try."

Jeremiah sneered, a shadow of his father. "I could take you."

"You couldn't take me to a movie if I bought you the damn tickets."

The younger Schafer laughed. "What does that even mean?"

Billy Ray slammed his fists on the countertop; the tableware skittered. "I don't know! I saw it in a movie!"

The restaurant fell quiet in the shockwave of his outburst. Embarrassed, blindsided, hurt, Billy Ray slammed his beer, refilled his glass and downed it again. The anger was a hot glowing thing pressing into the walls of his skull, making him sweat. Despite its intensity, the rage was confusing; in all the scenarios he'd ran, this one escaped his simulation: one son, thinking him dying, shows him compassion while the other son prays for his death. Gauntlets. Harshness. Threats. How did we become this way? So bent. So mangled. He was lost.

God, you bastard. What have I done?

He watched his son out of the corner of his eye, afraid to look him full-on. He yearned to reach out and touch him and apologize with his hands, but he stopped himself: the boy was too fragile, long wounded, and the cause of his impairment had the same name as his father. Billy Ray choked: his son was an orphan.

In his history of negligence, of selfishness, of avarice, of evil, he'd left his son without the proper aperture to experience paternal love. The result—pervasive cynicism—damned him to walk alone. When it came to his father's attempt to reenter his life, Jeremiah automatically assumed there was an ulterior motive, an alleviation. Clearly the old man was here to beg absolution before shipping off to hell. Why else would he surface this way? His father's love was never altruistic. Affection was always a function of his shortcomings, a sloppy poultice applied to previous damage. Tenderness necessitated a precipitating failure: if he forgot a birthday, he came home with a suitcase full of action figures; if he missed a baseball game, he made it up with a trip to the big-league ballpark. On the various occasions his mother kicked him out, his father would go on a bender before inevitably groveling back three days later, forever bandying a gold necklace or diamond earrings or pellet rifles or go-karts, all of it wrapped in promises to be better, to get sober, to stay home, to be good. But as soon as she caved, there he was, drunk when the boys came home from school, the Zappa cranked loud enough to drive the dog into the basement, a full ashtray in his lap, seething and bitter that he wasn't out on the road—"I'm just sitting here on my ass losing money"—as if spending time at home with his family was a penance to be paid. "Never get married, boys." That was his refrain and he sang it constantly, sitting on the porch in his boxer shorts, beer in hand, staring blindly into the middle distance before the mail even arrived. Even when he was there he wasn't *there* and now, decades later, here he was repeating himself, putting their history on a treadmill.

The awful was plain.

Through his son's eyes, he saw the holes in himself, and if he didn't do something, this would be the last time their eyes ever met.

"I'm sorry." Billy Ray reached out and snagged his son's wrist. "Alright? Okay?" There were tears in his beard. Trembling, his voice neared breaking. "I'm real fucking sorry."

Jeremiah eyed his father's hand on him like it was a snake crawling up his arm. He was tired of the tricks. "For what?" he said.

"For making you think this way. It's not your fault. I was shit as a father. Am shit. I still am shit."

Jeremiah tried to pull his arm back but his father's hand was a pink vice. "Can you let me go? People are staring." He handed him a napkin. "And stop crying. No one wants to see that."

Billy Ray dabbed his eyes and blew his nose, filling the napkin with blood. They sat there, hushed, drinking their beer and avoiding each other's eyes until the softballers stopped pretending they weren't watching and went back to their meal. Jeremiah drummed his fingers on his glass. He straightened out his leg and reached in his pocket and produced a pack of cloves. "I'm gonna smoke."

Billy Ray looked from his son's face to the small box of black cigarettes. "You smoke?"

"Save the lecture. You're in no fucking position."

"Can I join you?"

"Whatever."

Jeremiah told the hostess they were going for a smoke and the two generations stepped outside. The air bit, stiff with cold, like vaporized glass. Billy Ray flicked his Bic and held it up and Jeremiah leaned into the flame and breathed in and the big man lit his own and they smoked, wordless, pumping fat clouds into the stationary night. Billy Ray walked a few steps into the parking lot and stared up at the unlimited twilight. "Y'all got a real nice sky up here."

Jeremiah held his cigarette like a baton between his thumb and pointer. "It's different than Denver." Boulder was only two hundred feet higher than Denver but bereft of the light pollution of the capital city, the sky felt closer, like an awning shot through with holes concealing the greatest light.

Billy Ray reared back his foot and sent a rock skittering across the asphalt. "How long you been smoking?"

Jeremiah sat on the lip of a planter box full of dead frosted flowers. "Since I was fifteen. I used to steal them from you outta those cartons you kept in the freezer in the garage."

"Does your mother know?"

"She's caught me a few times."

"What'd she have to say about that?"

Jeremiah ratcheted his voice shrill and plucked the vowels: " 'Jeremiah, when you're dying in a cancer ward, shriveled up like a raisin, don't look for me to take care of you because I won't take pity.' "

Billy Ray smiled. Smoke leaked through his teeth. He sat next to his son in the flower graveyard. "That's a pretty good impression."

"Walker does it better."

"How's he doing?"

"Still the same old Walker. All business. He's almost done with law school. Says he's looking at salutatorian."

"Good for him."

"Gina's pregnant."

"She is?"

"Shit. I don't know if I was supposed to tell."

"Who would I tell?"

"Mom."

"I'm sure she knows. They were always closer than ass cheeks."

A turning car cut its headlights across them and for a moment they were only pure light. "Are you gonna try and see him?"

"I don't want to distract him."

"Probably a good move."

"When did he get so smart? When he was little, he used to call pancakes 'flat waffles.'"

"No he didn't."

"I swear."

"That's retarded."

"He was a little retarded. He ate a glue stick once."

"The whole thing?"

"Not the plastic, just the insides. We had to go to the emergency room. He didn't shit for a week."

Jeremiah tossed his butt. When the filter hit the asphalt it erupted in a shower of sparks. He stood up and breathed his fists full of hot air. "I'm glad you're not dying."

Billy Ray touched his chest in a show of false sentiment. "That's the nicest thing anyone has ever said to me."

"I'm serious. It wasn't like that's what I was pulling for."

"I know. You weren't crazy for thinking it." Billy Ray hocked up a wad of phlegm and spat it toward the car. He didn't see it land but he heard it. "Did he really tell you to punch me?"

"Yeah."

"Well I'm glad you didn't. I would have had to take it."

Jeremiah shoved his hands in his pockets and toed a crack in the asphalt. "He says he hates you, but I don't know. He sends me clips of you sometimes. Stuff he finds online."

"He does?"

"Yeah. You were funny."

Billy Ray had never received a better compliment. "Thanks."

The boy looked down at the man. His eyes glinted like solid moonlight. "Do you still like it?"

"What else am I gonna do? I can't dance anymore."

"I showed some of your stuff to Lulu."

"She told me."

"She didn't laugh." Jeremiah projected his lower jaw and touched his forehead. "I don't know why I said that."

"No. It makes me like her more. How long y'all been a thing?"

"Going on two years."

"Do you love her?"

"Shit, I don't know." Jeremiah held his arms tight to his sides and bounced from heel to heel, either from the cold or the question. "Maybe."

Billy Ray looked up at the boy whose face was so much like his own. He felt compelled to say something profound, as if the moment called for a touch of the sage. "Do you like her for more than her pussy?" That wasn't it.

Jeremiah burst open with nervous laughter. "Jesus, Dad."

"When she's not there, do you wish she was?"

"I guess."

"When me and your mama first got married and before your brother came along, I used to drive everywhere. I missed her so much that when I went out, after the last show of the run, I would walk right off-stage and directly to the car and start driving home right then. Didn't matter where I was: Boston, Tampa, Charlotte. I would just hop in the car and go and I didn't stop until I got home except to piss and refuel. Twenty hours from Cleveland, thirty-five hours from Buffalo. I did that for years."

"Didn't you get tired?"

"I missed her so bad, I couldn't sleep. Couldn't eat. Couldn't pull my pud."

"Damn."

"I drove because I knew that when I made it home I could fall asleep for as long as I wanted in my bed in my house with my wife. Love kept me awake." Billy Ray stood up and brushed dirt off the ass of his pants. "Love and handfuls of Dexedrine, but mostly love."

"It's funny to think of you and mom all lovey-dovey. I can't imagine you two holding hands."

"Shit, I used to write her poetry. I'd call her long distance collect to read them to her and she'd cry like a baby."

"Gross."

"Gross? I'll show you gross." He lassoed his son with the crook of his elbow and sucked him up in a headlock. With his other hand, he licked his index finger and plugged Jeremiah's ear. Feeling the invasive dampness, Jeremiah pried Billy Ray's arm from under his chin and swiveled and yanked his father's forearm down and around his waist and wrenched it up behind his back until Billy Ray's wrist was between his own shoulder blades.

"Motherfucker," Billy Ray yelped, hopping up on his tiptoes.

"Say it," Jeremiah said.

Billy Ray struggled but the boy was too strong. "Uncle, damnit. Uncle."

Jeremiah released his hold and his father spun away swearing and rubbing his elbow. Jeremiah smiled proudly. "I've been taking self-defense on campus."

"They taught you a hammerlock in self-defense? Goddamn. Who's your instructor? Verne Gagne?"

"Remember when we used to watch wrestling?"

"Of course."

"Remember how Walker used to cry when the bad guys won?"

"Yeah."

"I think that's why he became a lawyer. Come on. I bet our food's out."

Billy Ray held open the door for his son and they sat down and tucked into the mounds of steaming meat. The brisket was premium—thin slices of paprika'd beef smoked until they were nearly jelly—but the pulled pork was dry and the sausage was overcooked. Billy Ray ordered another pitcher.

"What'd I tell you about the brisket?"

Billy Ray refilled his son's glass. "You weren't lying."

Jeremiah drank a third of the beer, covering the glass in greasy fingerprints. "I'm fixing to be drunk after this one." He burped.

" 'Fixing to.' I haven't heard that in a while."

"I sound like Mom."

Billy Ray dragged a slice of white bread through au jus and popped it in his mouth. "How is she doing?"

"I told you. She's coaching volleyball and—"

"I mean really though. How's she *doing*?"

Jeremiah dabbed his mouth with a balled paper towel and sat back in the booth. His long arms spanned the length of the vinyl. "She's fine I guess. She works all the time and drinks wine when she gets home. She has lots of nurse friends. They went on a cruise last year. Oh yeah—she was on a God kick for a minute. She started going to church down in Longmont but it didn't last very long. I think it was for a guy."

Billy Ray looked up from his plate. "So she's not with Doug anymore?"

"Doug? No. They broke up. I don't know all the details, but I think he stole some money from her."

"She always knew how to pick 'em."

"Walker almost kicked his ass at Thanksgiving last year."

"That's too bad."

"Fuck that guy."

"The macaroni is good, too."

Shellie with an I E brought them more napkins. "How is everything?" she asked.

Billy Ray connected the tip of his index finger to the tip of his thumb and held it up to her. "It couldn't be better."

When they were done, they ordered pie and Billy Ray paid the check and the girl brought them to-go boxes and, as requested, a large soda cup. They ate the pie and Jeremiah packed the leftovers for Lulu who he admitted, after the third pitcher, that he did in fact love, and Billy Ray poured the remains of the beer into the tall paper cup.

"That was good," Jeremiah said, tapping the filter end of a cigarette on the table. "Thanks for dinner."

"Good pick. We should do it more often."

"You gonna be in town again soon?"

Billy Ray looked out the window. "I think I'm moving back."

"Woah."

"Yeah. I gotta get the fuck out of L.A."

"I thought that's where the action is?"

"I'm barely there as it is and I haven't been on an audition in years."

"Are you still with Red?"

"Unfortunately."

Jeremiah smiled. "Do you remember when Mom threw that drink in his face?"

Billy Ray's jaw sank. "Fuck. I forgot about that."

"Remember what the manager said? 'This is not the environment we encourage at Chili's. Chili's is for families!'"

Billy Ray slapped his forehead. "That's right. I used to do a bit about it. I did it on Arsenio Hall and she was pissed."

Out front, the moon looked like a squinting eye. Beneath it they lit cigarettes. Billy Ray told him they could smoke in the car but Jeremiah declined, saying he preferred to smoke in the open so he didn't reek like smoke. "Lulu doesn't like it. She's always telling me to quit."

"That's a good woman."

"I think you'd like her."

"She likes you, I like her."

"You think you'll ever get married again?"

Billy Ray shook his head and signaled incomplete pass. "I hung up my jersey."

"Don't you get lonely?"

"Now come on. I'm not celibate."

"Gross." Jeremiah pulled out his phone and looked at the screen. "Damn. It's almost eight."

In the car, Jeremiah cracked the window to air out further and Billy Ray drove with the to-go beer squeezed between his thighs. The cops were out in force, cruising for Saturday night DUIs. He split his eyes between the rearview and the road going five under in the right lane as his son talked through his options for the night.

"Both houses will have a keg but I think the Lamdas are charging at the door. Those guys all sell Molly. They'll probably have foam or some shit."

"What's Molly?"

"It's like X but purer. Kyle's will be more chill but Lulu hates Kyle, so we'll probably just end up drinking at Janeane's again."

"Who's Janeane?"

"She's Lulu's best friend. Her boyfriend OD'd on Halloween."

"Heroin?"

"Everyone is on Xanax up here. Heroin would have been better. I'm gonna call Lulu and ask her the plan."

A black-and-white pulled out behind their car while Jeremiah fingered his phone. Billy Ray's hands automatically clenched tight on the wheel as the cruiser pulled closer to his bumper.

"Hey. What's up? Just finished dinner. Good." Jeremiah stole a glance at his father. "Really good actually. Brisket. I have some leftovers for you."

The car was close enough that Billy Ray could see the cop's face in his rearview. He had a forehead like a saddle. Billy Ray focused on the yellow lines, regretting intensely having brought the beer with him: in a college town, an open container was asking for it and he knew better. As always, he let his thirst get the best of him.

"I thought you were going to Janeane's. Oh. Sure. We're driving back that way."

Jeremiah was oblivious to the cop but Billy Ray's heart was hydraulic. He hated the police and the power they had over normal folks, hated their false righteousness and counterfeit jurisdiction, loathed their governance over the parameters of his freedom. They made him feel helpless: they were going to do what they were going to do and he hated that autonomy most of all.

"Just a couple beers. Not yet. I was thinking about it. Jed and Kristen are going. Want to meet me there or should I just come back to the house?"

Ahead, the traffic light switched from green to yellow. Billy Ray hit the brake, applying a touch too much pressure, and the car came to a jerking halt.

"Fuck," he whispered. "Fuck fuck fuck."

His hands began to sweat: I'm going to have to eat a bag of cocaine in front of my son and then I'm going to jail. It was all over: he didn't have the money to pay for another DUI and he'd surely lose his license and without a license, he was done on the road and not even Nevada would grant a permit to a repeat offender and no one would rent him a car without a license and after jail came breathalyzers, classes, fines, the confines of probation, the court-ordered job. His options in this instance flashed in his mind, but his son's presence negated the possibilities: he was finished. He was all but resigned to his new life as a Burger

King employee (did they hire felons? did anywhere?) when a car in the lane beside him blew through the light and the cruiser followed, flying past, charging the intersection with salvation red and blue.

Jeremiah tilted the phone's receiver away from his mouth and pointed at the traffic stop: "Busted."

Billy Ray's hands stopped quaking. The tension left his muscles, the color returned to his knuckles. He sighed, knowing true relief. "Better them than me."

"Okay. See you soon." Jeremiah hung up and set the phone in his lap. "You can just take me back to the house."

"No party?"

"We'll see. I think Lulu is ragging."

"She's probably just mad you didn't punch me."

Jeremiah rolled up his window. "I still have time."

All up and down Jeremiah's street, on porches and in front yards, college kids readied for the night. Shrieking, laughing and talking so loud, they drank beer and passed bottles of liquor—"pre-gaming" Jeremiah called it. The smell of pot was pervasive. They drove past more than one small bonfire and a couch on a lawn and a couple kissing aggressively on a roof and a shirtless boy in gym shorts splayed face down in the grass and all around them a pulsing mélange of music blitzed the evening, mostly hip-hop and rap but, passing one house, Billy Ray heard traces of the Silver Bullet Band.

"Is that Seger?"

Jeremiah nodded. "That's like a thing up here. Seger. Kiss. Foreigner. Fucking *Journey*. All that butt rock. It used to be ironic but now I think they just like it."

Billy Ray guffawed. "Bob Seger is not butt rock."

"Dude. Bob Seger is the *definition* of butt rock."

"What are you talking about? Seger wails, man."

"You sound one hundred years old."

They stopped at a stop sign in front of a two-story house. In the driveway, four boys sat on a junker drinking beer. "Hey, Dad, hold up a minute." Jeremiah rolled down the window and hung his head out the sill. "Hey, Bonzo, are you going to Kyle's?"

"Hell yeah, bud," responded one of the boys.

"Alright," Jeremiah shouted. "I'll see your ass there." He rolled up his window and Billy Ray drove on. "That guy owes me money."

Billy Ray stomped the brake. "How much?"

"Not a lot."

"Want me to get it from him?"

Jeremiah looked at his father as if he was behind glass. "You're crazy."

"We could get it right now." He shifted into reverse.

"Yeah, that'd be a good look. Have my dad beat up my neighbor for twenty bucks."

Billy Ray looked back at the one called Bonzo before digging his eyes into his son's. "It doesn't matter if it's twenty bucks or two million. It's the principle."

"Drive, Dad."

"You can't let people fuck with you." Billy Ray's eyes were snakelike, his face transformed into the one he learned in prison, the face Jeremiah never knew. It was horrible.

"Dad, drive. Please."

Begrudgingly, Billy Ray put the car in drive.

Less than a block down, he brought the car to a stop in front of Jeremiah's driveway. Seeing the house, a swift sadness took root in him. He turned off the engine and asked his son if he could use his bathroom, desperate to prolong their time a bit longer: "I gotta piss like a greyhound."

They got out of the car and he followed his son up the drive and onto the porch and into the house. They didn't lock their door. "Make yourself at home," Jeremiah said. "I'm going first."

He stood in a living room. A television rested on a shelf facing a couch on the far wall. Between them, someone had made a table out of a STOP sign and on the sign sat a bong and a hairbrush and paper plate smeared with ketchup. A television remote and a PlayStation controller rested on a stack of *National Geographic* magazines; the cover of the top issue read THE DEATH OF A SPECIES and below the words, a small, silver monkey stared out of the picture through shiny black eyes.

"How was dinner?" Lulu appeared from the kitchen, a bowl of cereal in her hands. She leaned against the wall, one foot flat, the other kicked up on its toes like a ballerina, her pale skin rendered almost translucent by the fluorescent light. Billy Ray thought she looked like an alien.

"We had a fine time. That Big Jim can smoke some meat."

"Good."

"We brought you some." Billy Ray scanned the room for the doggie bag, desperate to give the girl some kind of offering: she made him nervous. He wanted to feel necessary. "I don't know where he put it."

"I'm fine. I've got Rice Chex."

Billy Ray cleared his throat. "Jeremiah told me a lot about you."

"Great."

"Sounds like y'all really got something special."

"Oh does it?"

"Do me a favor would you?"

Lulu stirred her cereal, purposefully distracting herself. "What?"

Braving her otherworldliness, he looked the girl square in her cat/Martian hybrid eyes. "Take care of him. Okay?"

She looked up from her bowl and opened her mouth but before she could respond, Jeremiah wrapped his arms around her waist and laid a smacking smooch on her sharp cheekbone. "Jerk," she said, leaning backward into him. "You made me spill my cereal." Jeremiah turned her around and kissed her on the lips; after the initial contact, she pushed him away "Why does your mouth smell like hand soap? Were you smoking?"

"I smoke," Billy Ray interjected. He pulled out his Winstons and shook the pack like he was enticing a dog. "You're probably smelling me. I better hit the head."

The bathroom was decorated in a pastel theme and thick with the smell of patchouli. On three staggered technicolor shelves, waterless fish bowls glowed with neon inserts. Above the shelves, Bettie Page posed in a cheetah-print bikini inside of a picture frame studded with Heineken bottle caps. Billy Ray put down the seat and sat on the closed toilet and pulled out his coke and poured a small line on top of the tank and selected two bills from his wallet, a twenty and a hundred, and rolled up the twenty and, after turning on the fan and the faucet, he took the line as quietly as he could and unrolled the twenty and wiped the tank clean then checked himself for residue in the circular mirror that looked like a porthole and flushed the toilet and washed his hands.

Lulu and Jeremiah were together on the couch, him sitting upright with his feet propped on the table, her recumbent, head on one end, her miniature feet nestled in his lap. She picked from the contents of the Styrofoam brisket box laying open on her stomach while Jeremiah finished the last of her cereal. On the television, a man in an office chair spoke directly into camera.

"I gotta say," said Billy Ray, "that bathroom is really something. Did you decorate in there, Lulu?"

"I added the fish bowls."

"I like it. It's got a real B-52's vibe."

"What time is your show, Dad?" Jeremiah asked, his eyes on the TV.

"In an hour. I gotta skedaddle."

Jeremiah patted Lulu's feet and she drew them to her chest like a drawbridge. He stood up and put down the bowl. "It was great to see you." Jeremiah hugged his father and Billy Ray hugged him back. The embrace lingered awkwardly while the old man catalogued his son's smell, the feel of him, the space he occupied in his arms. Finally, they released, and Billy Ray put out his hand to shake, the hundred-dollar bill secured to his palm in the crease of the ball of his thumb. Detecting the money, Jeremiah looked down at their handshake then up at his father. Billy Ray winked. "For a rainy day."

"Are you sure?"

"Take whatever is free."

"Thanks." Jeremiah slipped the bill in his pocket and walked his dad to the door. "I'll talk to you soon?"

Billy Ray stepped out on the porch. "Definitely. I'll call you when I get my phone fixed. It's the same number."

"I've got it saved."

"Tell your brother I'm sorry I'm not dead."

"I'll do that. Are you still gonna go see Mom?"

"Might as well."

"Good luck."

Billy Ray made the sign of the cross and Jeremiah smiled. "Pray for me." He poked his head around the door jamb. "Nice to meet you, Lulu."

Lulu covered her lips, her mouth full of beef. "Drive safe."

"Ten-four." Billy Ray gripped his son's shoulders and squeezed the muscle, enamored, enchanted, indebted, impressed. "Take care of yourself, alright?"

"You too."

Admiring Jeremiah one last time, an acute sadness set upon him like the sun descending on a graveyard. Every molecule of his creation screamed to profess an intensely sincere declaration, to be grand, to pronounce, to cut himself open and lay himself bare, to tell his son he loved him, that he was proud of him, that he was sorry for being who he was, to beg his forgiveness, to promise that things would be different this time, so trust me, please, just trust me one more time because I'm telling the truth—I know what I did—and as long as you'll have me, as long as I'm living, not once more will I ever disappoint you, never again will I let you go.

Instead, he said, "Well. Alright then."

"Night, Dad." Jeremiah closed the door.

Billy Ray lit a cigarette and walked to the car, thinking the only thing that carried him forward was the air in his lungs.

At the end of the block, instead of turning left toward the highway, he pulled into the parking lot of the elementary school, parked the car and wept.

SATURDAY NIGHT

HE DROVE BACK TO DENVER WITH THE WINDOWS DOWN. HE WAS having difficulty staying awake. He was uncomfortably full and emotionally wrung out and drunker than he planned on and the dashes of white paint dividing Highway 36 eastbound were hypnotic and the road itself was very dark between the high masts. Intermittently, he caught his chin tipping to his chest, his eyes snapping off milliseconds of unconsciousness. He wanted to pull over for coffee, but he'd wept besides the school rocking the car with his heaving violent sobs for twenty minutes and now he was running tight on time.

First he tried the radio at full volume. When that failed, he'd fumbled the parcel of cocaine between the seats. As a last ditch, he bit the inside of his cheek until it was raw and bleeding, but that proved an ineffective antidote to the beer and meat pushing on his diaphragm; the meal pulled at his eyelids like lead weights. He tried to make himself burp to relieve the pressure but in doing so, he almost caused himself to vomit twice, so he rolled down the windows and smoked, hoping to cull sobriety from the fast cold air. When he still caught himself nodding, he punched himself in the thigh until he was numb and bruised and finally awake.

Just south of Thornton where Highway 36 met the interstate, traffic thickened to a blur of red and yellow lights. Weaving through the herd of Saturday night migrants, Billy Ray asserted himself, finding gaps in the deluge and changing lanes without signaling and barely avoiding a few instances of death by machines. He exited Park Avenue and ascended with the road as it rose up over the train yards and warehouses of Globeville, driving beside the high-rise balconies sprouting off the glittering apartment towers and the million-dollar condos and descending down past a procession of three-wheeled motorcycles and a lime-green Bugatti and the redbrick and neon of Coors Field to penetrate the part of town dubbed LoDo by chicken-hawking developers, trying to envision what it looked like before the ballpark, before the rebranding, remembering when this part of Denver was a nameless skid row, a bombed-out and uninhabitable nowhere, a dangerous territory ruled by junkies, hustlers and whores, entire blocks abandoned, the roving bands of homeless scaring polite citizens too much to ever cross 20th Ave. Taxis didn't pick up here. This was the place one went to be forgotten, to get lost.

He'd spent many nights he didn't remember lurking among the refugees, scoring from them whatever he needed to get him to tomorrow. While they were desperate and without honor, he understood the binary maxim of their jungle: be strong or be gone. It was like prison, and he felt at home with them, because unlike the terrified, he trusted his hands. Now they were gone, victims of progress, gentrified into extinction. A few indigent holdouts still flew signs at red lights, but their begging went unanswered by the bar-crawling hipsters and loft-living professionals flitting between the nightclubs, beer gardens and bars. Twenty years ago they would all be at knifepoint, their pockets empty, their pants full of shit.

"Glory days," he said, remembering back when: the simplicity of violence, surviving by taking, existing on the merit of what you were willing to do. Seeing his son had cored him out, and in the vacuity, a swirling anonymous cruelty formed. He felt bare and delicate from exhaustion, weak, disabled. He detested the helplessness, the incensing vulnerability. He wanted to transfer his pain through convection, to go blind and hand himself over to force. He yearned to inflict, to punish, to maim, to bleed. By losing himself in barbarity, maybe he could go clean. And though he knew beneath the frenzy, below the underlying blankness with which he saw the world, that lashing out was no remedy—it didn't matter: it wasn't about feeling better, it was about feeling different than bad.

He turned on Larimer. Farther down the block, a gaggle of miniskirted bachelorettes crossed against the light, tottering in platform heels. Maneuvering left around a stopped cab, his attention absconded by his rage, Billy Ray nearly clipped the last two of them.

"Watch where you're going!" screamed the one nearest danger.

Billy Ray drove his forearm into the center of the steering wheel, wishing the horn a Gatling gun, wanting to chop them all down. "Get out of the road, bitch!" The women scattered. He felt a bit better.

He stopped at the light on 21st and blew his nose into a napkin. On the corner, a filthy woman panhandled meekly, holding a sign that simply said PLEASE. Wrapped in what appeared to be a swatch of uprooted carpet, her spine humped, her hair hanging over her face in lank tendrils, the woman appeared medieval, bubonic. The wretch transfixed him. He wanted to hate her, to detest her impotence, to burn her away in the fires of his disgust, but he was unable. While he roiled with contempt for the world at large, this woman was not his enemy. They were each other. Like him, society had chewed her up without having the decency to swallow. Now she stood out here in the cold, draped in flooring, half-masticated and indigestible while all of humanity made a point to not see her. He hoped they all died of colon cancer while their families watched. No matter what happened to him, he was closer to her than he was to the eye-averting majority. They had never known the pain of asking for help and being ignored. They are not like us, he thought, and thank the two-by-foured Jesus for that. He found a five in his wallet and held it out the window and she hobbled over in a limp-legged skip to take it while the light changed green.

"Oh, thank you. God bless you."

"Get the good stuff," he told her, winking.

"All the good stuff is gone."

The car behind him honked. Billy Ray's eyes snapped to the rearview. The occupants of the car were at least two young men, midtwenties, their hair styled stiff with product, their faces brusque. Their mouths formed the word *GO*. It was just about enough.

Billy Ray put the car in park, opened the door and stepped out into the street. He stared down the driver as he approached, arms tight to his side, his eyes level and anticipatory and perverse. In his pocket, his hand balled around his lighter. All the eyes in the car watched as the big man lumbered toward them with rage as visible on his face as clown paint. He slammed his fists on the hood of the car. The passengers jumped in their seats. The top half of the driver's side window was partially open. Billy Ray lowered his mouth to the crack. "If you are in such a fucking hurry," he said, "then you should have left earlier." He tried the door handle, but it was locked, so he pounded the roof. He dropped a fist on the side mirror and cracked it from its mount. "Everyone is in such a fucking hurry with nowhere to go." He kicked the door but it hurt his toes, so he rained more blows on the top of the car. Inside of the cabin, his fists against the roof echoed like localized thunder. "No one has anywhere to go." The driver searched for an escape route, but traffic was a wall on his right and he was blocked on the left by the sidewalk suddenly full now with halted pedestrians watching this large, menacing man attack the car like a rhino charging a safari Jeep. Billy Ray tried the back door and it came open and he reached inside and swung at the driver but the driver dove into the passenger's lap, yanking the wheel with him and the car darted into the neighboring lane, causing a taxi to slam on its brakes and the car sped away with the back door still open and flapping like a lame wing. The shocked bystanders watched in silence as the large man raked his fingers through his hair, ambled to his car and continued on.

He turned down 15th and found a spot on Market a block from the club. His hands throbbed. Sweat stung his eyes. He felt his heart, the opening and closing of the valves. He got out and stripped nude to the waist and let the steam rise from his torso as he gulped at the air with his hands on the back of his head. The cold was sharp on his skin but it served to calm him: the feeling was something real to focus on. He dried off with his undershirt and changed out of the trunk, applying deodorant and cologne and a fresh T-shirt and over that a snap-button rodeo long sleeve, jet-black and embroidered across the shoulders and pockets with a floral pattern done in silver thread. Above the city, the hands on the face of the clock tower read a quarter past nine. Almost showtime.

He paid the meter and speed-walked down 15th and cut the line of people at the box office and down the stairs and past the bar and yelled "Corner!" around the corner and past the line for seats and crossed by the piano until he was backstage. The green room door was closed. He stood in front of it a moment, catching his breath, steeling. Then he knocked.

"Come in," said a voice.

He knew immediately who it belonged to. The sound of it raised the finest hairs on his body. The voice snagged in him like a trawl and dragged him back twenty years, back to when he was young and unbroken, back to when stand-up was still his greatest passion and life's work, his raison d'être, back before repetition pared the magic away and the business shit on his chest and comedy turned into a crude ruse, a cheap con, a trick he turned for money, back before it was all he had. What that voice said used to mean everything; what it didn't say meant even more.

He opened the door and sitting with Norm Macdonald and Kevin was a slender woman in a sleeveless blue blouse and gray editor pants, her arms and legs crossed, a Tory Burch espadrille half off her foot and dangling from her toe. Her face had changed, smoothed and tightened by what looked to be a very skilled doctor. She had no crow's feet and her chin, bulbous when he knew her, was reduced to a perfect dimple. The lines around her eyes—shrewd and almond and exactly the color of fire-kissed marshmallows—were all that gave away her age, along with a slight sag in the hollow of her neck. The imperfections were only noticeable if you knew what she looked like before. For all he could tell, she'd aged backward. Even her hair was improved: formerly mousy brown, it was now a brilliant flax. Hanging from her ears, two strands of diamonds quivered in the lowlight like soft icicles.

"Hi, Billy," she said flatly, neither invitation nor salutation in her voice. She sounded like she was learning a new language and she wasn't yet confident with her pronunciation.

"Wende. You look good."

"Thanks." She smiled mechanically, her eyes rocks. "You look like shit."

"But I feel like at least ten bucks." His mouth was dust, his tongue wood. It adhered to the roof of his mouth like Velcro. Scanning the room for a bottle, he found none and even if there was, he knew he shouldn't reach for it in front of her, not right away. There was nowhere to sit. The space on the couch between Wende and Kevin seemed a bit familiar based on her greeting. He didn't know if he should shake her hand or wait for her to stand up. Fifteen years ago, she would have come to him and hugged him and stood there with her arm around his waist and he would have squeezed her shoulder and savored her maternity but that was not going to happen now, not after how he left it. Whatever did happen, he didn't want to act first, so he planted himself and bore down and she stared at him and he stared back and Macdonald and Kevin observed this standoff in complete silence while the moment elongated uncomfortable. Neither flinched, the window for a physical greeting closed and a decided nothing transpired, leaving him standing awkwardly in the doorway doing a masquerade of calm sobriety, feeling like an interloper and not knowing what posture to take. He leaned against the doorframe and put his hands in his pockets. "Sorry. I didn't mean to interrupt."

"You didn't interrupt," Norm said. "We were actually talking about you."

Billy Ray rocked on his heels. *Fuck,* he thought. "Whatever she said—it's all true." He could feel her eyes on him, assessing, judging. It felt like a parole hearing, like a decision was pending. He knew there existed a perfect string of words that could cut through the last twelve years and deliver them to a new moment unimpregnated by that which came before. The right amalgam of charm, humility and cool delivered just so, self-deprecating and penitent without being excessively apologetic or venal, an offering of wit bereft of acrimony but yet still sharp enough to slice this cloud of billowing tension currently choking the room like the opposite of air. However, in his current state of seething rattled inebriation, such a phrase was beyond his configuration. His brain was an hourglass that needed to be flipped: he would have to think about it. Besides, this wasn't the time or place: repentance abhors an audience. Billy Ray didn't want to appear contrite in front of his fellow comics and Wende, empire incarnate, couldn't show forgiveness in front of her employees. For the time being, Billy Ray had to take whatever she gave.

Wende put her elbow on top of the couch and rested her head on her hand like a pinup. "Norm was just telling me you had a good set last night."

"He killed," said Macdonald.

Billy Ray feigned. "This place on a Friday night? It's pretty hard not to."

"He said Nathan couldn't follow you."

"The kid did fine. Norm draws a good crowd."

"He drew four sold-out crowds. Which reminds me." Wende slapped Macdonald on the knee. From her purse beside her, she pulled out an envelope and dropped it in his lap. "There you go. There's two checks in there. One of them is the bonus."

Macdonald tossed the envelope on top of his notebook. "Excellent. Now that I've been paid we can break out the crack cocaine."

Wende laughed, concealing something deeper behind the noise. "Now I get it." She glanced at Billy Ray, putting that deeper thing in her eyes. "*That's* why Billy's here."

Outwardly, Billy Ray smiled at the dig. Inside, he flipped his mental thesaurus to the word bitch and thought all the most awful synonyms. He knew what she was doing. She was trying to make him snap, to give her an easy excuse to have him removed. Instead of burying the hatchet, she wanted him to fall on it. Never. He parried: "Come on, Wende. I don't sell crack anymore. Just angel dust."

Macdonald clapped his hands. "Perfect. I can only perform when every face in the crowd is a flaming skull screaming the date of my death."

The powerful woman creased her brow. "Is that what it's like?"

"PCP?" asked Macdonald.

"Yeah."

"How the hell should I know?" He raised his chin toward Billy Ray. "Ask Dr. Gonzo."

The three of them waited for Billy Ray to speak, even Wende, despite herself. "I tried it once when I was opening for Parliament. I thought it was weed but after a few tokes my arms disconnected from my body and whenever anyone talked, it sounded like they were inside my mouth. Everything went two-dimensional. I thought I was going blind."

"Sounds terrible," Kevin said.

"Oh, it was, but the music sounded great. Speaking of terrible: Wende, do you remember that time Tommy Chong made those brownies on New Year's?"

For a moment, a genuine smile sprouted on Wende's face, but she caught it before it could fully mature. She forced her mouth demure and began to blush. "I wish I could forget."

"He got so high that he started the New Year's countdown an hour early. Then we all ate them after the show and Wende forgot how to walk."

Wende covered her eyes.

"All night, me and Fitzgerald and Chuck took turns carrying her room to room. She was like a baby. A very stoned baby."

"'That was the last time I ever ate edibles. And the last time I ever booked Tommy Chong.'"

"I might have had my issues, but I never got so high I started a year early."

"Yeah. You were a saint." She laid her hand on Kevin's shoulder. "Kevin, when you were in—I don't know—fifth grade probably, we used to do slushy drinks at the bar. The kind with cherries and whipped cream and umbrellas. We discontinued them. Do you know why?"

"They didn't sell?"

"No. We took them off the menu because we couldn't keep Billy from sucking the nitrous out of the whipped cream."

"I did you a favor. Those drinks were liquid diabetes. You could have got sued."

"Right. You were always looking out for me." Wende checked her phone and sat up. "Gentlemen, we're about five till show. Normy, you want Billy on the show, right?"

"If that's okay with you."

"Alright. Kevin, find Nathan, please. Tell him you're bringing him on first. Tell him to do fifteen and don't worry—I'll pay him for the twenty. After Nathan, bring on Billy. Billy, do fifteen and don't go long. Think you can handle that?"

"Yes ma'am."

"Good."

Wende stood up. Macdonald, genteel, stood with her. She took his hands and squeezed them like a doting mother. "Break a leg, handsome." She stood on her toe tips and kissed him on the cheek. Kevin left to break the news and as Wende made her exit, she stopped in front of Billy Ray. "To be clear: the only reason you're on the show is because Norm requested it and the only reason you're featuring is because that's what's best for the show. Have no delusions. Don't get any ideas."

Billy Ray mounted his best cocksure smile. "It's good to see you, too. And I meant what I said. You do look great." Once she was out of earshot, Billy Ray mumbled, "Worth every penny." He plopped down on the couch and found his cigarettes.

In the floor-length mirror, Macdonald fixed his tie while Billy Ray sat behind him smoking. Reflected in the glass, the two of them were separate species, a portrait of Triumph and Warning. Macdonald, clean-shaven and boyish, his cobalt suit crisp and angular and tailored to hug his slim frame, his eyes clear as spring water and his shoes gleaming black, looked further evolved than Billy Ray, the haggard, wrinkled, hunched-over troglodyte with his bloated belly spilling fat onto his thighs, his eyes red and yellow like the sun through smog. Billy Ray looked like the personification of Macdonald's malevolence, the devil on his shoulder breathing smoke and glowering at creation.

Festering on the couch, Billy Ray tasted acid in the back of his throat. His hands were shaking. Somewhere in the conversation with Wende, the anger that polluted his entirety had turned inward; now it ate him up like cancer. The rage burned away the superficial, allowing him clear vision of the root cause of his failure.

As much as he enjoyed believing he did it alone, his success was a team effort, a coordinated assault plotted by Red and carried out by a battalion of agents and lawyers. The prosperity led him to believe he was special, an irreplaceable talent, but really Billy Ray was simply a product they sold, and for about ten years he flew off the shelves. Money fell off him like dandruff. When his downfall came, he was alone in his unmaking.

Even before the girl in Miami, his demise was forming like a storm: high pressure on high pressure: the affair was only the breaking of the sky. In showbiz circles, he'd already earned the poisonous label of "difficult." He showed up to jobs late and high. SAG labeled him uninsurable. He swore on live radio, walked out on interviews. The corporate bookings dried up. On more than one occasion, sleepless and reckless, he threatened the hosts of affiliate morning shows. He harassed weather girls with lewd entendres. He started to wear sunglasses no matter the hour. He missed nightclub dates and when he showed up, his performances were mercurial at best: he exposed himself on stage in Houston, walked an entire showroom in St. Paul. In an industry built on accommodating narcissism, he was still too much. He left a lot of people wanting their money back and that was the greatest sin.

While he was sliding, spending his money on powder and companionship, it was difficult to understand what was happening. He blamed everyone around him: *I'm being mismanaged, the clubs are fucking me, no one watches television anymore.* In reality, his team did everything in their power to stem the tide, and for good reason: he made them a lot of money. There was nothing altruistic about their work. A tenth of Billy Ray Schafer was worth fifty percent of his peers. Public relations experts were hired, but even the top firms couldn't buffer a client intimating he slept with Cher while presenting her a Grammy. Despite the diligence of Hollywood's finest, Billy Ray drowned in the fetid juice of his debauchery and everyone fled to higher ground. Only Red remained, chained by their contract, forced to shuffle Schafer between the Hell gigs his other clients refused. After so much promise, Billy Ray was forgotten, relegated to trivia answers and cautionary tales. He became a ghost story whispered around mahogany desks. America scratched his name from their memory. Whatever happened to that guy? I don't know. I don't care. Eventually the only person that remembered the greatness of Billy Ray Schafer was Billy Ray Schafer. He became his own telltale heart, a totem, a relic doomed and entombed, forever buried alive with the corpse of his career.

Schafer studied his friend perfecting his tie in the mirror, seeing not what could have been, but what was and was lost. There was no jealousy in his vision. He looked at his protégé with tenderness and pity. Does he know how sweet he has it? Does he know they can take it all away? Fear the speed of the guillotine, old pal. And hold on. Hold on, Normy boy. Hold on until your fingers break. Don't let go until they cut off your hands.

Macdonald noticed Billy Ray glaring hungrily in the mirror. "What's a matter?" he asked the reflection.

Billy Ray, startled, surfaced from his loathsome cocoon. "What?"

"Why are you looking at me like that?"

"Like what?"

"Like you want to fuck me in the ass."

Billy Ray smiled. "Sorry. I'm just thinking."

"It looks like you're thinking about fucking me in the ass."

"Sorry." His cigarette was burnt to the filter. He dropped it in the ashtray and sparked another.

"Man, I don't know what you did to Wende, but it must have been a real doozy."

"I sold cocaine to her nephew."

Macdonald paused his grooming.

"I didn't know he was struggling. He relapsed. Fell pretty hard."

Macdonald whistled. "That'll do it."

"Yep."

"I love you, buddy, but I think I'm with her on this one."

"Yeah. Me too." Billy Ray remembered the vodka in his pocket, took it out, swallowed the last inch. "Honestly, it went better than I expected."

"You expected worse than that?"

"She didn't spit in my face."

"True."

"She didn't cut off my balls."

"It's all in the perspective." Macdonald turned around. "Does this tie look alright?"

"It looks great."

"It's not too long?"

"You look great."

"Thanks. Now bend over so I can fuck you in the ass."

Soon the show started. Billy Ray went to the bar and ordered a shot of whiskey and a Budweiser. He slammed the shot and brought the beer with him into the bathroom stall where he shoveled a key load of blow up his snout. The cocaine centered him, a familiar feeling in an inconsistent existence. He dug out another gagger and snorted with gusto. On his way out of the stall, the man waiting for the toilet held up a fist with the pinky and index fingers extended. "Party," he said.

Back in the club, the laughter was cacophonous. The crowd was decidedly younger tonight and, as was the rule for Saturday late shows, much drunker. Whoever was onstage was really cooking.

He entered the showroom and watched from the back row as Kevin sang an updated version of "The Wheels on the Bus." "The wheels on the bus go round and round, round and round, round and round. The people on the bus go 'Give me five dollars or I'm gonna cut you up, white boy.'" The crowd shrieked. It was a good bit, so good the cynic in Schafer wondered if he stole it. No, he decided. The kids are just funnier these days.

When he finished the joke, Kevin had to wait for the clapping to die down before he could introduce the next comic. The crowd laughed as soon as Nathan walked onstage. It made sense: cherubic, his curly hair teased wild, he was the prototypical endearing schlub. He rode the free laughter into his first joke, propelling the energy into an applause break after his third joke—"Is it just me or have all of our black presidents looked exactly the same?"

"Now that's funny," Billy Ray said, his highest compliment. After decades in comedy, instead of laughing at solid jokes, he simply said when they were funny.

He walked toward the stage, stopping midway to press against the wall and suck in his gut to provide leeway to a waitress with an overloaded tray.

He opened the door of the green room. Macdonald was on the phone. Billy Ray resealed the room and paced up and down the hall. He peeked through the curtain and looked at the crowd. They were stunning. He pulled the curtain closed, feeling the velvet with his fingers for what seemed to be the first time. Unlike some comedians, he was not a poet: his world was hard, literal, and in it there was no use for symbols. But inside his current mania, he saw the curtain for what it was: a portal, a cloth guarding a threshold. Passing through it transformed the traveler: on this side he was one man, on the other side he was someone else. *Goddamn,* he thought. *I'm losing my fucking mind.*

Backstage he paced and listened to the feature. Billy Ray didn't understand all of his references but the crowd did, and that made him nervous: he was old and they were young. Compounding the uneasiness was Wende's presence in the building. He wanted to do well, not to spite her but to show her he still had it, to show her what he'd learned. He missed her, her club, her stage. While it was doubtful that she would watch him, if she did, he needed to be undeniable. Maybe then he could begin the complex process of apology.

He went over his setlist in his head. He knew how to open and he knew how to close; he wasn't sure about the middle. All of his best bits were at least seven minutes and full of moving parts. On a night like this, he was hesitant to test their attention span, especially given their age. He doubted young people their ability to follow breadcrumbs. It was probably best to keep it punchy and quick. He wanted to play with the crowd, mix it up like he did last night, but breaking the fourth wall invited unwanted interactions. It was hard to talk to them directly without ceding authority. And if Wende was watching, he needed her to see him crush with honed material. She thought crowd work was easy, and she was right, mostly. Some people raised the form to artistic heights, but in the hands of most comics it was a lazy and unskilled artifice learned to survive conflicts with hostile bar crowds. Billy Ray was better at it than most, but he didn't want to look like he'd been on the road too long. She'd be looking for any possible out and it was his job not to provide her one. He wanted tonight to destroy their past, to force her to behold the legitimacy of his craft—crowd work wasn't going to cut it. Besides, there was the matter of Norm and Billy Ray's role as the feature. It was bad form to go into the crowd before the headliner. You were supposed to leave that for them. And as much as he yearned to kill, he didn't want to bury one of the only friends he had left. Billy Ray was already hard to follow but when he turned it on he was weaponized.

He was getting ahead of himself.

Billy Ray twisted at the waist, one way, then the other. *Just do your job. That's all you can do.* Of course he could always bomb. He hadn't bombed in years but he also couldn't remember the last time he cared if he did. His overall apathy acted as a shield against disappointment. *Wanting is dangerous . . . Eat shit. Wear the leather. Who knows.* Twenty-five years of experience didn't mean it couldn't happen. The possibility of failure was there every night, that's what made stand-up so pure. If just one of the countless intangibles needed to facilitate laughter is miscalibrated to the smallest degree, fifteen minutes could feel like a lifetime up there, alone, choking, dying the slowest death.

He filled his lungs with air and exhaled slowly. He was overthinking things. *Look at you overthinking. You'll be fine. All you have to do is not swallow your tongue.*

Kevin came around the corner with a beer in his hand and stood at attention behind the stage. He pulled back the curtain. Slicing through the gap, the light of the showroom split his face in half. Billy Ray watched him watch. His arms were thin pipes, as thick at the biceps as they were at the wrist. When Nathan got a big laugh, Kevin's smile fattened with fraternal pride. Billy Ray remembered watching his friends with the same approval: *we're all going to be big stars.* He envied his innocence. *Just wait, kid. If you're lucky, one day you'll never see him again.*

Billy Ray opened the back door and power-smoked half a cigarette, his legs inside the building, his head and torso outside.

"This is his closer," Kevin said.

The crowd popped hard at Nathan's final joke. Billy Ray couldn't hear it, but whatever he said, the response was as loud as hail on sheet metal. Nathan came offstage appearing postcoital, glowing, dewy, strands of hair stuck to his forehead. He removed his phone from his back pocket and turned off the recorder.

"Nice set," Billy Ray said, doing his head a figure eight.

"Follow that, Pops." He didn't look up from his phone, walked away. Behind him, Billy Ray pretended to smile.

Through the curtain, Kevin instructed the crowd to give it up for his good friend Nathan Lund and the crowd redoubled their previous effort. Billy Ray cleared his sinuses and swallowed.

"Are you ready for your next comic this evening?"

Where are you, Wende? Are you in this place with me? Maybe she was in the back of the room, martini in hand, ready to bask in the deliciousness of his failure. Perhaps she was on the highway, gone already, unable to care less. He didn't know which was worse.

Maybe he would die instead. Maybe someone would shoot up the place, save them all.

"He's a close personal friend of Norm's. You might have seen him . . ."

He did not want to be here. His head hurt. The inside of his mouth tasted like metal from where his gums bled. A dull pulsing pain surged up and down the wiring that connected his eyes to his brain. It would be nice to go to sleep for one thousand years.

Forgive me, Wende.

". . . or his one-hour special on HBO . . ."

Suddenly he felt like he might cry again. The compulsion was alien and disconcerting. Water gathered in the corner of his eyes and his jaw became very stiff. He slapped himself. "Pull it together," he said. He slapped himself again. He had to pull it together. All this over comedy. How silly. What a joke. He started to laugh. He experienced it as a lightening. Absolution. Somewhere deep within his infrastructure a load-bearing fetter snapped and the urge to weep lifted, as did the disquiet. Maniacal, feverish, he was laughing. Uncontrollable, it came in explosive torrents; they bent him over. He braced against the wall. Reasonless, as loud as madness—nothing mattered. Not tonight nor any night since the inception of time. Not a thing that he or anyone had ever done was of any value or worth. Fuck her. Fuck me. Fuck this building. Fuck this town. Nothing can't change nothing. Your position is no position. Existence isn't topographical. You're off the map. No one knows you anymore because there is no you. We are made of paper. Behind our mask is another mask. What are you worried about? You've survived for twenty-five years out there on your own chasing dollars on the wind and you will continue to ramble until the blood won't move in your veins. This is what you do. This is it. Tonight is tomorrow is yesterday. How'd the old joke go? The only difference between life and death is that death doesn't hurt. Jesus saves but the Devil buys beer. God, instead of mercy, I'll take cash or check or money orders.

". . . let's hear it for Billy Ray Schafer."

Nothing can hurt me because I am nothing and that is what makes me more real.

He strutted onstage inviolate. Instead of a handshake, he snatched Kevin by the wrist, ducked down, stepped in and pulled him across his shoulders in a fireman's carry. He spun in quick circles, high-stepping and pouty lipped, modeling the bony young man like a stole. After a few laps he dropped him down on his feet and sent him on his way stumbling with a slap on the ass. Billy Ray snatched the microphone and kicked over the stand and stared into the crowd, eyes blazing, the tip of his tongue exposed, craving new blood. Nuclear. A new energy created.

"What's up, motherfuckers? It's me—Nathan Lund from the future. I've been sent here to warn him: gout is coming. If you want to see more of Nathan, just wait a few weeks—he's getting fatter every day." Intimidating, a blustering giant, sweat-stained and wild-eyed and appearing huge in the lights. He stomped on the base of the microphone stand and it shot upright and landed directly in his hand like it was on a string. "What a great show so far. Keep it going for Kevin and Nathan." The crowd clapped amicably. "I love those two. Kevin lives in Nathan's beard. Have you ever seen two more different body shapes? They look like the number ten. Speaking of different shapes—"

He pointed to a couple dead center, front row. The woman was skeletal, her face avian and drawn, her long neck attached to slim shoulders that turned inward at the breast. The man was corpulent, balloonish, his beady eyes buried in the mounds of his fleshy pink cheeks. The way his hands rested on his massive belly gave him the appearance of a manatee on a beach. "How are you two tonight?" Neither of them said anything. "Where'd you two meet? A circus?" The man smiled but the woman's face tightened. "Sir, you are a big man. Me and you and Nathan could be the offensive line for an arena football team. We should team up tonight. Go flip some cop cars. Rip some fire hydrants out of the ground. The three of us would be unstoppable. We can do whatever we want—besides have sex on top." At this, the woman sniggled and the man laughed, causing his jowls to wobble like aspic. "I'm just fucking with you. You're beautiful, both of you. Don't ever change." The man smiled a sweet, sexless, heartbreaking smile. Billy Ray had to look away.

He bent down to address two women in matching business suits. Aside from their haircuts—one wore her blond hair straight and pulled back behind her ears, the other had a severe gray buzzcut—they could have been twins. "Good lord. If you're here, who's coaching that softball team? Could you two be any more gay?"

The blond woman pointed at the buzzcut. "She couldn't."

"I'll say. I bet you've bumped your head on more boxes than Mario."

Set in front of the couple were red plastic baskets lined with wax paper.

"What are y'all eating?"

"Chicken tenders," said the buzzcut.

"Looks good."

"Do you want some?"

"I can have anything I want in this basket?"

"Have at it."

"Alright then." Billy Ray reached down and picked up a clear plastic ramekin filled with ranch dressing. He raised the cup in a toast—

"Salud"—and shot the dressing like liquor. He licked out the ramekin and when it was empty, he held the cup up to the women. "How was my tongue-work, ladies? Did I turn you on?"

One of the women tapped her chin with her index finger. "You've got some white stuff on your chin."

"No one's ever said that to you, have they?" The crowd cheered. "Perfect." He placed the cup in front of his crotch. "Now I've got a condom for later." He thrust his hips, humping the ramekin sailing to the floor. "Condoms go on penises, ladies," he said to the two women. "But y'all wouldn't know anything about that."

So much for no crowd work, he thought.

As the crowd laughed, he took a moment to read the amassed faces, noting traces of bewilderment. He felt unwhole, like a collection of small things. Atoms, protons, electrons. They rubbed together, building friction. The mood in the room was combustible, almost dangerous. Electric expectancy charged the air. It felt like any second, invisible accelerants floating around his head would catch fire and consume the room in blue flame.

He had an odd feeling. Loose and emancipated, bizarre and rash, he had never been this close to himself. At this proximity, he was able to see himself for what he was. Coherence befell him like sickness. *Look at you,* he thought, his mind drifting out, abdicating, floating above the showroom to join the ranks of the crowd. Peering down, separate from his dilapidated husk, the soul outside the flesh, he saw himself, the sweating beast, Pagliacci without makeup. At this height, broken away, he saw what they saw. It—he—was disgusting.

Twenty-five years in comedy and you just drank a cup of ranch dressing. This is how you squander your precious numbered heartbeats. This? This. What have we become?

The moment unfolded and he saw his stitching, the shoddy threadbare patchwork of him. Privy to the individual threads, he realized how poorly he was assembled. His jokes, every one of them—they trivialized his humanity. They were just lies and he saw them as such, aglow

in the light of It All, the ugliness, how tawdry; these falsities that defined him said nothing. He had become his act and his act was bad.

You need to say *something,* he said to himself, because in twenty-five
years of talking, not once have you said a goddamn thing.

He decided tonight would be different.

If I am worthless, I can give myself away.

If everyone knows you're a liar, you might as well tell the truth.

He replaced the microphone in the stand and blotted his forehead
with his shirtsleeve. *Alright,* he thought. Then he stopped thinking all
together and opened his mouth.

"Now," he began, "I could stand up here and drink ranch dressing all
night but that's not what you came to see. You came to be entertained,
to connect, to forget about yourselves. So let me tell you a little about
myself. My name is Billy Ray Schafer. I'm not a William Raymond, I'm
a Billy Ray. Ain't that some redneck shit? My name sounds like a serial
killer that drives NASCAR. People ask me 'Billy Ray, why are you
named Billy Ray?' and I tell them 'Because my daddy's name was Billy
and there was this other guy in town named Ray and my mama, well,
let's just say she was covering her bases.' A name was all she could ever
afford to give me and she thought 'hell, might as well give him two.'
They were second cousins, my mother and father. You heard that right.
Our family tree is an aspen. At their wedding, all the guests sat on the
same side of the aisle. They had my sister and they had me and they had
my brother, but he died when he was just a baby. He barely got a name.
He was premature and he had Down syndrome. People ask, 'What was
it like to have a brother with Down syndrome?' Let me tell you—it has
its ups, but it's mostly Down syndrome.

"My father was an alcoholic. He used to drink a case of Natural
Light a day. Y'all had that shit? It tastes like weekend custody. Natural
Light—the official sponsor of getting a DUI on a tractor. My mother
did her best to cover for him. She did a real good job but I think it kind
of backfired. I don't know. When you're a kid and your dad is always
lighting fireworks off indoors, you don't think 'my dad is a reckless

drunk,' you think 'my dad is the funnest man alive.' It wasn't fair to her. She looked so uptight in comparison to that madman. When one of your parents is always showing his ass to bank tellers and the other is always locking herself in the bathroom to cry, it's easy to have a favorite. One time, my dad left me alone at a pool hall when I was ten years old. Eight hours, just me and a sock filled with quarters. It was badass. They had pinball machines and a claw machine and the soda was free refills. A bus driver paid me to let him watch me eat hot dogs. It was a great day. When the pool hall closed, I had to call my mama to come pick me up. She was furious. 'He left you at Shooters all day by yourself?' she said, and I said, 'Yeah, it was awesome!' I heard her crying through the phone and she said, 'That son of a bitch. I would never leave you alone at a pool hall,' and I said, 'No shit. Why do you think I hang out with Dad?' He left when I was thirteen. It didn't change much. Our food stamps went up. Anyone here grow up with food stamps? Good luck mailing a letter with those. It might surprise you, coming from this pristine upbringing, but I dropped out of high school when I was fifteen. But don't worry. I got my GED—in prison. I did three years. If you've never been to prison, first of all, congrats. It's not as much fun as they make it seem. The food was terrible, but the sex was great. I'm kidding! The food isn't that bad. Hey there! When you say you've been to prison, people look at you funny. They always want to know one thing: did you drop the soap? And the answer is: of course I dropped the soap! Soap is slippery, dumbass. It's soap. But that's not what they mean when they ask that. We all know what they mean and to that I say—a gentleman never tells. Nah. It's not that bad. If you keep your head down, you'll be fine. It's a different world is all. You just gotta learn the rules. Everything is upside down. For instance: lockup is the only place in America where being white is a disadvantage. In prison, white boys is a dying breed. When I got sentenced, I started doing push-ups, sit-ups, shadowboxing. What I should have done is gone tanning. Prison is like Boy Scout camp only less gay and there're black people there. It teaches you how to survive in the wilderness. Everyone has a hustle. Some guys do tattoos, other guys cut hair. I sold drugs. I could get anything. Heroin, meth, cocaine. They're all bad news. But you know what the most dangerous drug in prison is? Viagra! My man right here is laughing at that. Sir, you look like tough stuff. Have you ever been to prison? No? I just ask because you're Mexican. Come on. I'm kidding. Sangre por sangre. I was with quite a few señoritas before I met my wife. A few after. Hell, there was a few during. We got a divorce. She gave me two beautiful sons and I gave her the three H's: a house, a Honda and herpes. Not in that order. We were together for thirteen years but we're done. It was amicable. Neither of us were at fault. We just wanted different things from the marriage, you know? *She* wanted me to stay home and spend more time with the kids, clean up my act—quit smoking, exercise, eat better—that kind of stuff, and *I* wanted to have sex with other people. So as you can see, like I said, neither of us were at fault. We got married because I was horny and she was Catholic. Any Catholics in the house? That Catholic God is a real cockblock, but he's cool though. Catholic God is like, 'Look. No sex before marriage. If you have sex before marriage, you're going to hell. The only people that can have sex before marriage are priests and choir boys, alright? But listen, I'm not heartless—I'll make you a deal. If you can refrain from having premarital sex, once you're married, you never have to wear a condom again! How's that sound to you? If you can promise me that you'll just dry hump and nut in your pants until your wedding night, I'll let you raw-dog your wife for the rest of your life. I guarantee it. How can I guarantee it? Fine—if she makes you wear a condom then *she's* going to hell. Boom! How's that? Is that cool? Alright. Good luck. And remember: anal doesn't count.'"

In the sound booth behind the crowd, a flashlight blinked on and off. He checked his watch. 10:20. They were lighting him early. *What's a matter, Wende? Is that not enough blood?*

The flashlight flickered faster, signaling his disgrace: really, that's enough. He stared at the flashlight and the crowd stared at him. Earlier they were laughing, now they were silent. He hated how they looked at him. If I had a gun, I would empty it of bullets and your eyes would stay open forever. Finally, in that chaos, you might see what I mean.

"Yeah, that God is a real tricky son of a bitch. It's hard to believe that this is the best he can do. This world, us, you and me—we're his crowning achievement? You know how when your kids come home with a shitty piece of art, like a turkey hand-tracing, and you have to lie to them and tell him it's great and hang it on the fridge, even though you know in a few years they're gonna create something much better once they quit pissing the bed? To God, we're that turkey hand-tracing. He just never had the common sense to take us off the fridge. Are you Catholic, honey? You are? I knew it. You don't like what I'm saying, do you? That's that fear. We've all got it. That fear that God is gonna see you laughing at him, put you on his naughty list and bang, you're spending eternity in hell for giggling. What bullshit, but I get it. I don't think God can take a joke. He sure can't tell one. Fifty-three years I'm still waiting for the punch line. Damn, that got heavy, didn't it? I'm sorry. You don't have to laugh, but you can smile. You're beautiful, honey. Smile. There it is. To me, Latin women are the sexiest women in the world. And I can tell you why: nothing turns me on more than fearing for my life twenty-four seven. Is this your husband? See how hard he's laughing? It's because he knows I'm right. He has to enjoy himself because he knows any day could be his last. Women are like that. Scary. My wife caught me cheating one time and I swear, I thought I was going to have to go into witness protection. I was trying to confess to crimes I didn't do just to get me off the street. Oklahoma City? I did it. Nine eleven? That was me, too. Take me away. Cheating on her was the worst thing I ever did, and I've done some *bad* shit. I've robbed. I've beat people up. I've used guns. Shit, I was in *Fletch Lives*. The worst thing I ever did was bringing kids into the world. I fucked that up something fierce. I had no right being a father. Today I went and saw my son for the first time in three years. The other boy, I don't know if I'll ever see him again. He wishes I was dead. I get it. I never told them I loved them. I tell you what, if I had it to do over I'd have said it every day. I'd say it until my tongue fell out. Until it lost meaning and I had to invent a new word. Fuck. This isn't funny anymore. Well, y'all, I've got to run. I'm due back to the halfway house by midnight. I'm sorry. Norm is gonna come out here and make it all better. Goddamnit. Goddamnit it all. I'm sorry. Good night."

He nearly trampled Kevin as he crossed through the curtain. Macdonald stood waiting.

"Easy, tiger. Easy," Macdonald said.

Billy Ray attempted to sidestep the headliner but Macdonald caught him and held firm. Billy Ray looked away, hot tears stinging his cheeks. He didn't want to be seen this way. He didn't want to be seen. "I'm . . . I'm sorry. I don't—I'm sorry."

Macdonald affirmed his grasp. "Sorry? Sorry for what?"

Billy Ray flicked his chin at the curtain. From behind it, the crowd mumbled a confused, obligatory applause. "For that."

His voice gentle, his eyes blue and beneficent, Macdonald cocked his head and smiled. "What are you talking about?"

"I don't know what the fuck that was."

Macdonald shook his head. "What that was was beautiful, baby. You were singing for the angels."

Billy Ray ripped his body from Macdonald's hold. He noticed, with alarm, his hands balling into heavy, tight fists. Below him, his knees were both weak and impossibly stiff. He felt if he didn't move they might shatter. "That was shit."

"No, last night was shit. *That* was marvelous. Never apologize for telling the truth. You told me that."

"I said a lot of bull. You'd be better off if you never heard a word."

Behind the curtain, Kevin worked to restore the crowd's enthusiasm. "The winner of tonight's raffle . . ."

The two men stood in front of each other. The space between them rippled and hummed. Billy Ray was dizzy. His muscles twitched, begging to remove themselves from here. "Move, Norm."

"Don't leave. I want to talk to you."

"Go earn your bonus."

"Don't be like that, Billy."

"Go earn that second check."

"Just stay until I get off."

"I'm gone already. I was barely ever here."

"What do you mean?"

"You know everyone thinks you're this smart motherfucker, Norm. But you're not. You're just Canadian and you talk slow."

Having reset the room, Kevin announced Macdonald's entrance, but the headliner remained immobile. His hands still outstretched from his aborted mollification, Macdonald failed to move, overcome with crippling empathy at the pain on the face of his lost friend, helpless to the sorrow.

The emcee repeated Macdonald's name, waited, said it again: "He's coming, folks. I promise."

Overpowering his natural instincts (comfort this man lest you lose him again), Macdonald dropped his arms. "Duty calls."

"I know."

"I'm sorry."

"Me too."

Macdonald stepped aside. He watched as the big man punched open the back door and walked out of the club, feeling the coldness come in.

Beset by a prescient dread, Macdonald took the stage, aware somehow in the core of his being that never again would he see his friend alive. The crowd noise intensified. He went into his act.

Billy Ray took the stairs two at a time. Five steps and he was on Larimer. Hands in his pockets, not feeling the cold, he charged down the sidewalk driven by a self-loathing butchery he recognized from darker days. Disobedient to his will, the rage carried him forward, fully a passenger now. He shouldered pedestrians, bulled, collided, begging objection, hoping someone foolish enough to question his supremacy. Then he could pour out his violence. Pulp them or be destroyed.

Crossing Market, he saw his car was still where he left it and he went to it and retrieved his burly Carhartt from the back seat. He climbed in the passenger seat and sat unnaturally still, watching his heavy breath spread like flattened ghosts upon the windshield. Holding his keys in his hand, he considered driving to Fort Collins to confront Olivia tonight, but it was only a fantasy. Even in his state of cockeyed inebriation, he wasn't yet drunk enough to think driving a good idea. And in the unlikelihood he made it without killing anyone, there was no way she would receive him; it would be messy. Cops. He knew she had a gun. Better to wait for tomorrow, when he had the benefit of daylight. He didn't want to make her afraid.

The cocaine was nearing its end. He'd done a lot today. He poured the remnants out onto a CD case and formed the entirety into a single fat caterpillar. The wide line froze the back of his throat and turned off his sinus. In the initial stoned moments, as the cocaine broached the barrier between his blood and his brain, he enjoyed a perfect thoughtless silence, neither pleasurable or epiphanous but a vacuous antifeeling under the spell of which he excised all desire besides for the emptiness to last forever. He closed his eyes, savoring the fleeting calm. He knew it wouldn't last: the state of paralyzed consciousness grew shorter with each dose and awareness of the half-life hastened the erosion. Still it was nice. He moved his lower jaw in a semicircle, hearing the joint click in his temple. It's all falling apart, isn't it. When he reached for his cigarettes, the reprieve was over, and his thoughts returned to gluttony and perversion.

More was the name of the game. More liquor. More blow. More more. His yearning was frantic. It howled like wind through the holes in his brain. He longed to penetrate and excrete, to fuck and be fucked, to violate, to be ruined. He groped the root of his lust through his pants but it was unresponsive beneath the rough denim. Half-heartedly masturbating, he sat in the car smelling his breath, pulling and pushing stale air through the gaps in his teeth as he considered his next move.

Priorities were as follows: locate then purchase then do more cocaine, followed by drinks at a bar peopled by enough women that he could entice one of them into allowing herself to be subjected to his obscenity, likely with the aid of said cocaine. The final step was unachievable without accomplishing the first. Things had to go in order. One thing led to the next. He didn't have the patience for wooing. He needed an arrangement, a simple, unadorned exchange where both parties were complicit and everyone got what they desired. This wasn't, however, a job for a professional. If that were the case, he would head to East Colfax and hire one of the fractured girls off the Avenue. No, his partner had to be an amateur. Enlisting a civilian was paramount for an elemental reason: beyond the ache of his pudendal urge, he needed a place to stay, a place with a roof and four walls. What did Kerns call it? Hobosexual? Bed, couch, bathtub, floor—any indoors was better than sleeping in the car. And any old gal would do.

But which way does the wind blow? That was the question. The old wasteland near the ballpark was bleached clean and he didn't trust the selection of the scoundrels on Colfax, home to purveyors of fifty sacks of baby laxative and ten-dollar slivers of bar soap. At this hour, Federal was too hot and Bruce Randolph was too heavy and he couldn't go to Civic Center because he wasn't looking for crystal meth. There was always Cheesman, but last he heard, in the park these days, the only thing the boys sold were their mouths. That left Five Points, the black citadel north of downtown where the dope boys still worked an honest corner. He looked in the rearview mirror, licked his thumb and wiped white residue out of his mustache. "I taut I taw a puddy tat."

Billy Ray got out of the car and counted out a collection of bills large and small, one thousand dollars in total, and hid the rest of his bankroll in the trunk. He crossed the street to the south side and flagged down one of the schooling taxis.

"Where to?" asked the ruddy-faced driver, his nose a constellation of burst capillaries.

"Twenty-sixth and Stout."

The driver's eyes screwed weary.

"My girlfriend lives over there. I've got cash."

"Whatever," the driver said, putting the car in drive. "But I drop off. I don't wait."

The cab worked left on 14th and turned at the first light. Arapahoe Street was an ant pile. Up and down the sidewalks, carousers moved in bustling queues. Billy Ray watched them with an ire-edged jealousy. He imagined commandeering the wheel and veering through a clump of them, jumping the curb and scattering pedestrians across the hood and under the tires until they smashed through the lobby of the Rock Bottom Brewery in a microburst of blood and raining glass. It was a scenario he often envisioned while a passenger in metropolitan taxis. He'd considered it so many times he began to believe there was a possibility he could get away with it if he blamed it all on the driver. I don't know what happened, officer. He just kind of snapped. Frame the driver, claim himself captive to the madman's rampage and sue the cab company for damages. His word versus the man with his hands on the wheel. It seemed too easy. He assumed the cab companies outfitted their fleets with secret cameras to prevent exactly this kind of creativity. He sat on his hands.

The business district ended at 20th Street. From there on converted warehouses flanked them on both sides sporting homeless bivouacs nested in their doorways. Outside of the car the city swirled and he felt a part of it, a piece of dust caught up in the churning cycles of urbanity. Tumbling, thrown. You claim this place but it no longer claims you. Seething turning to melancholy. The billboards peel.

The cabbie maintained a slow but constant speed, timing the lights with a master's precision and making it to 22nd without stopping once. At the light, a voice crackled over the radio.

"Car four-twenty, come back."

The driver picked up his walkie. "Copy."

"We have an airport run from MLK and Josephine. Do you want it?"

"I can be there in ten. Dropping off in the jungle now."

At Park Avenue the neighborhood began. Recessed, postwar Victorians abutted neat townhomes, the narrow rectangles built tight to each other like boxes of cereal on a shelf. Sprinkled among them, modern architectural designs marked the encroachment of development. The new growth was markedly unassimilated, the glass-walled, exposed-metal, nouveau riche cubes looking like space vessels run aground.

The streets were quieter than ten blocks previous and darker, beyond the reach of the lights of downtown. Besides a few occupied porches, the neighborhood was empty. Below a murky aubergine sky, no boulevardiers strolled the ash-canopied sidewalks. Billy Ray spotted no entrepreneurs.

"Stout and what?" asked the cabbie.

"Actually, go right. You can drop me on Welton."

The cabbie eyed him suspiciously, but he flicked the blinker and turned the wheel and after four stop signs he pulled over in front of a cellphone repair shop. "Last stop, slick."

Billy Ray handed two bills forward and opened the door. "Keep the change."

"Wow," the cabbie muttered, "seventy-five cents," but Billy Ray was already out and walking, eager to replace his memory with chemicals.

The clouds were crepe paper in front of the moon, thin as snakeskin. Streetlights burnt patches of white in the black. Billy Ray beelined toward a dark figure leaning against a building like a decorative wooden cowboy. The man met all the markers in Billy Ray's head: young, black, a hood pulled up over his head, rangy but not intimidating, his dark eyes actively sweeping the streets and his hands busy in the pouch-pocket of his poncho. Schafer, adopting a stilted strut, approached in what he perceived to be a smooth, streetwise manner, but viewed by the man on the street, his affected walk made him look like his legs were without joints.

"What's up, brother?"

The young man continued to bob his head, ignoring Billy Ray.

"Fine night for some candy."

The young man unplugged a pair of cordless earbuds from his head. "What?"

"I said, what's up, young brother?" Billy Ray, having palmed a fifty before he left the cab, raised his hand up for a swooping hand hug, but the young man left him hanging.

"What you want, man?"

Billy Ray flashed him the bill. "Snow."

The young man's nostrils flared. He made a sound with his tongue against the roof of his mouth. "Man, you corny. Beat it."

"Come on. I'm not a cop."

"Man."

"Two twenties is fine."

"Are you for real right now?"

"Oh, I'm real."

"This is some bullshit."

Billy Ray, alarmed, scanned the street. Something was off. "I'm not law enforcement."

Pronouncing his agitation, the young man turned his head and pursed his lips. "Man." He snapped his head back and Billy Ray's muscles tensed defensively. "I'm not the one, motherfucker."

"What?"

"You think every young nigger is just out here pushing?"

A blanket of goose pimples scaled Billy Ray's skin: oh no.

"Is that what you think?"

"No, I just . . . I thought . . ."

"You thought what? Whatchu think?"

"Well. Yeah."

"Why? Because I'm black?"

"No," he stammered, "because you're . . . outside and . . . it's night-time."

The young man squinted. "So a black man can't stand outside at night without work in his pocket?" Despite his stringiness, the young man's hands made big fists. He stepped toward Billy Ray, his elbows bent. "Is that it?"

Billy Ray, understanding his egregious trespass, retreated, his hands at the ready. Shit. Fear smothered his lust for mayhem. In his glory days—sure, no problem. But now, even with his formidable size advantage, this wasn't a fight he thought he could win. He was no match for youth and athleticism fortified by righteous indignation, not without a weapon. He scanned the man's waistband for pistol-shaped lumps. "I'm sorry. My mistake. No need to be sour."

The young man continued his measured approach. "Whatchu think, motherfucker?"

Billy Ray increased the rate of his backpedal. He wanted to run but the kid was definitely faster and for that reason he didn't want to turn his back. "I don't think anything." He gathered distance until he deemed there was enough space to spin and turn, at which point he set off in a lurching bowlegged gallop. As he ran, he listened for footsteps but all he heard was the youth yelling behind him: "Yeah, you better run, bitch. Go on. Get out of here with your fat racist ass."

In front of the Roxy, a clutch of vapists laughed as the big man doddered through their clouds. Billy Ray made it half a block before his beleaguered heart forced him to slow to a loping speed-walk, and on the corner of 27th, he stopped and steadied himself against a lamppost and struggled to corral his breath. Sweat clung his shirt to his back. His boots pinched his feet. He looked up and lost his vision to the spotlight, humiliated. Dead center inside the cone of harsh light, he presented as an abductee.

Once his breathing normalized, he lit a cigarette and looked around. He stood alone at the crossroads of 26th Avenue, 27th Street, Welton and Washington—the direct confluence of the five points. Between each street the city wedged off in five slices, the result of a failed grid system. It was unrecognizable from the apex he knew. As a young man, upon his release from prison, he'd lived down the street in a halfway house near Curtis Park, one of the few whites interspersed among the

Latino and black majority. His neighbors viewed him as an anomaly, this country boy who knew how to play dominoes, but his sense of humor won them, and over cash games of spades, at cookouts and quinceañeras, he learned of the Isley Brothers, Santana, Sly and his Family Stone. They played for him Redd Foxx and Freddie Prinze. Taught him The Dog. He felt brave and adventurous then, a sponge for culture, and a fifteen-minute chunk of his first album was about this neighborhood. But since then, this namesake intersection and the neighborhood surrounding, once the Harlem of the West, had been developed into ubiquity by the arrival of the light rail. The train tracks along Welton allowed the gentrifiers easy access to downtown and the crossroads reflected their vapidity. Apartment buildings replaced the landmarks he knew. Coffeeshops with verbs for names. CrossFit garages. Their newness underlined his sense of unbelonging solus. Only one of the points had yet to be built upon, a small brick building on the tip of 26th and Welton. In front of the building, a wrought-iron fence made a patio of blank concrete and inside of it, dirty young people drank beer at long picnic tables. Gun-shy, abased and out of ideas—a stranger completely—he resigned to crushing his craving with liquor and crossed the tracks.

At the door to the bar, a doorman with tattoos on his hands asked him for ID.

"What's this place called?"

"Seven one five."

"I thought it closed in the eighties."

"It did." The doorman flipped his license and inspected the reverse. "Now it's back."

The bar was dimly lit inside and very busy. The overriding aesthetic was an uncle's garage. Greasy hipsters dressed like low-budget rockstars in cheetah print and denim packed themselves tight to the bar. When they weren't looking at their phones, the clientele, their hair styled elaborately unkempt, tried desperately to cultivate an apathetic air, as if they just woke up in their vintage T-shirts and distressed designer jeans. The men looked like lesser Ramones while the women, fans of eyeliner, aped different iterations of Joan Jett. They drank High Life bottles and looked bored and most everyone was androgynous and beautiful. Through the house speakers, a repetitive throbbing synthetic bassline slashed with shreds of no-wave guitar pulsed sans melody.

By a span of decades, he was the oldest person in the room.

He spotted a gap in the row of people lining the bar, muscled between two leather jackets and bellied-up. When one of the three bartenders finally came, he ordered a shot of well whiskey and a High Life. The bartender, slim, towheaded and efficient in a peach cardigan, poured stiff.

"Five bucks," the bartender shouted, pushing the tiny glass across the reclaimed wood. Around his neck, he wore a boar's tooth on a gold chain.

Billy Ray laid a twenty down. "You know where I can buy a ski pass?"

Making a show of rolling his eyes, the bartender made change and moved down the line.

Billy Ray fired the Ten High, feeling the burn all the way down. The whiskey was foul but he didn't mind: he was well beyond opinion. He leaned against the bar sipping his beer, his eyes among the young things culling for the slowest member of the herd.

He snagged his eye on a pair of girls talking loudly in a nearby booth. He watched them for a while. One of them was moonfaced and cat-eyed, not fat but substantial, bountiful, full in the places women are taught should be flat. The weight looked good on her; it gave her a fecundity that spoke to the reptile in him, the neurons that begged to breed. Her hair was what attracted his attention: electric orange, she wore it short in a tapered bowl. When she talked, she punctuated each word with her right hand, the palm downward and the fingers wiggling like tarantula legs as if she were playing an invisible piano. When she listened, she toyed with a cigarette, pulling it from and putting it between two lips painted the same neon as her hair. In the middle of her pale face, they looked labial and dramatic. The other girl was thin, lithe-necked and swimming in an oversized hockey jersey, her head shaved aboriginal on one side, the remaining hair long and crow-black and satin. He couldn't tell but he assumed she was very tall. Her face was long and elegant and epicene: nu beautiful. Billy Ray decided they were dykes, but he couldn't help but stare at their mouths as they talked.

"I know it's one of those books you were supposed to read in high school or whatever, but—I don't know—I really dug it," said the skinny girl.

"I get that," said the other.

"It's like, I get it's old and for teens, but that doesn't mean it's wrong, you know?"

"Exactly."

"There's still lots of phonies."

"Totally."

"Right?"

"I wonder why they never made a movie out of it?" said the neon redhead, pinching her face in exaggerated contemplation.

The thin girl responded as if this was a revelation: "I know!"

They didn't always look like this, he thought, feeling the age disparity between them as an intense, unattainable longing, as if he were drowning and they were the shore. They made him feel unworthy, disentitled, ancient, unevolved, as if his knuckles were dragging. Looking around, they all looked so happy. Everyone was hugging, even the boys. No one hugged when he was their age. He could feel the promise rising off them, the glowing hope. Their fire turned him cold. He wanted to gather them in his arms and warn them: this is as good as it gets. Your victories still outweigh your defeats. Your disappointments aren't looming specters. You are as yet unhaunted. You are reborn every day. Their lives stretched out in front of them like endless swaths of red velvet and they strolled the carpet like guests of honor waving and blowing kisses. They were never going to die, not this version.

Youth doesn't perish, it mutes. It would happen to them just like it happened to him. Their lives would ossify and their lights would languish, growing dimmer and dimmer until the day they could no longer see themselves. Rendered unrecognizable by the darkness, they would forget how bright they had shined.

Look at me, he thought, *I'm you. So live it up before you're me.*

Billy Ray pulled himself off the bar and worked down the wall and found a place to stand. He stood awhile, shrinking, trying to be out of the way, but he kept having to move himself to accommodate the constant expansion. Penned in by the crush of young faces, he felt surrounded, claustrophobic, queasy. It occurred to him that he was wasted. The possibility of vomit. He decided he needed air.

Wobbly, he wormed through the bar out onto the patio and leaned against the fence. Exhaling opaque in the cold, he focused on his breathing until the Tilt-A-Whirl feeling passed, then he lit a cigarette and finished his beer.

Around him kids smoked in clumps. Laughter. Effusive noise. Bits of their conversations fell on him like shrapnel.

". . . they're more death metal than black metal . . ."

". . . that's what they drink in Portugal . . ."

". . . she says she's gay now but I don't know . . ."

On the farthest reach of the patio, the neon redhead stood by herself staring into her phone. Underlit by the blue of her screen, her face was rendered divine. A cigarette burned near her ear. Between drags she chewed on her thumbnail. Billy Ray watched her. After a few minutes, he knew she was perfect, and he started toward her, his eyes on the concrete carefully picking his steps, drawn not by lust but by boredom: he wanted to talk to someone and she had ears.

"Excuse me. Do you know what the time is?"

Her eyes, a diffident hazel that ran chartreuse around the pupil, peeled wide when she saw the bleared face standing before her. Inside the bar she looked older but at this distance her youth was pronounced. Not a single line creased her face. Her skin was unblemished talc. Twin dimples framed her mouth when she smiled, which she did after the initial shock of him lifted. She glanced back at her phone. "Just past midnight."

"And what time is last call?"

Her breath was lime and tequila and smoke. "One-thirty usually. One-forty if Cam's in a good mood."

"Damn. That's early."

"Welcome to Denver."

"I thought it'd be later."

"This city dies at 2 A.M." She dropped her cigarette and stomped it with her Doc Martens and pulled another from her pack.

"Here." He flashed his lighter and cupped the flame for her.

"A gentleman appears."

"That one of those Spirits?"

She nodded.

"Them are those healthy cigarettes, right?"

She tilted her chin down and pursed her lips into a perfect bow through which she pushed a thin stream of smoke. "That's what my doctor told me."

"My doctor had a stroke. He lost his whole left side."

"Oh no."

"He's all right now."

"I've got to remember that one."

"It's an oldie."

"What do you do with a sick pig?"

"I don't know."

"Put him in a ham-bulance."

"That's pretty good. You should be a comedian."

She sat on the edge of a wooden table and crossed her ankles. "I'm fucked up but not *that* fucked up."

He nodded at her boots. "Those are some real shit kickers."

"I kick a lot of shit." She stuck out her hand. "Erica." Perplexed, he took her hand and shook.

"That's some shake you got, Miss Erica."

"Your turn."

"My turn."

"What's your name?"

"Oh. Billy Ray. Billy Ray Schafer."

"You must be from the south."

"I grew up here. I've been gone is all."

"It's rare you meet a native."

"Where are you from?"

"Here."

"So then you're rare, too."

"We're just a couple of fucking unicorns."

"I'd say you're more of a dragon."

"Why's that?"

"Because unicorns aren't scary."

She looked up at him. "I'm scary?"

"Terrifying."

"I'll take that as a compliment."

"It's how I meant it."

"Well thanks. I like your sideburns."

"Thank you kindly."

"What are you doing out here?"

"Smoking."

"I mean in Denver."

"Visiting family."

"And how are you liking it?"

Billy Ray focused his limited faculties on preventing his words from slurring. "I'm shit-faced and talking to a pretty girl. I've had worse luck."

Erica touched her fingers to her collarbone and batted her eyelashes in mock flattery. "You sweet talker, you."

"I saw you. I was over there and I saw you and I just thought you looked nice so I came over."

"Yeah. I was just kind of zoned out on my phone, as always."

"I don't have a phone."

"You don't?"

"Yeah. I mean nope."

"How do you talk to people?"

"I don't really."

"Lucky," she said.

Billy Ray looked around for his beer until he remembered he didn't have one. "Looks like I need a drink."

"You better get one."

"Can I buy you a drink?"

"I have a boyfriend."

"Can I buy him a drink?"

"He's not here."

"Well tell him I offered."

"I will."

"It was nice talking to you, Miss Erica."

"Yeah. You too."

And with that, he used up all he had left.

He fought to the bar and ordered another boilermaker. He pushed his fists into his forehead. *I don't have it anymore.* The conversation emphasized his incongruity. This place wasn't for him and very few places were. If the doorman had any empathy, he wouldn't have let him in. A dragon? *Fuck me,* he thought.

He leaned on the hardwood, a man far beyond tired. Exhausted. Depleted. All dried up. He felt miserable and bitter, flammable, a pile of straw looking for a spark before it blew away. He looked around. Everything about the bar was a razor to his nerves. The music. The tough guy chic. The shit on the walls. Even the way the bartender poured: too precise, inhuman. The previous bartender was generous but this one— yet another kid, brown hair messy, his boyish face still handsome beneath a padding of beer bloat—he poured like an accountant.

"Five bucks." That's all they knew how to say.

Billy Ray gave him a ten and waved off his change. He leaned in and tapped his nostril with his index finger. "Do you think you could help me out?"

Beneath bent brows, the bartender's eyes iced over. Billy Ray popped the whiskey, trying to appear casual instead of desperate. The bartender's gaze stiffened. The moment dragged until the bartender's arm shot out and snatched away Billy Ray's beer. "You gotta go, bud."

Billy Ray was too tired for jokes. "I paid for that."

The bartender pushed the tenner back to him. "Out. Now." He pointed toward the door. "Spencer." The doorman rose off his stool. The bartender raised his chin at Billy Ray. "He's gotta go."

"What did I do?" Billy Ray demanded, his eyes incredulous, his face pleading *can you believe this*? The surrounding onlookers, heeding the barkeep's call, offered no sympathy. Instead they signaled their allegiance, raising their chins and squaring their shoulders, hardening themselves in a cabaret of manhood.

"You can't come in here and ask the staff for drugs," the bartender said. The circle of young bodies tightened and Billy Ray found himself chest-to-chest with a smirking, bleached-haired face. The youth's eyes glinted with meanness.

"Want to dance?" the face said.

"I don't have the time to teach you."

"Come on," the doorman said, working his body between Billy Ray and the wall of patrons. He took the big man by the wrist and tugged him toward the door. "Let's go, old-timer."

Billy Ray stopped dead. "I'll leave but I'm not going to hold your hand." The doorman faltered, unable to match the big man's intensity. He let go and Billy Ray marched, brushing the shoulder of the boy who offered to dance.

The bleached-head boy raised his hand an inch from Billy Ray's face and waved. "Later, faggot."

Enough.

The room turned every shade of red. The day's failures calcified.

Sharp jagged shards rupturing his long-ballooning rage. His son. Wende. The girl outside. Billy Ray raised his boot and stomped down hard, crushing the instep of the bleach boy's Vans. The boy howled. Billy Ray spat in his face.

"Not cool," said the doorman, leaning his shoulder into the big man to push him from behind. Billy Ray spun sideways and the doorman toppled forward. As he stumbled, Billy Ray shoved him, sending him face-first into the wall. He turned and snatched the hem of the bleached kid's T-shirt, yanked it up over his face and pistoned a jab into his rib cage before tossing him sprawling to the floor. He kicked him in the stomach, spat on him again. One of the bartenders said he was calling the cops.

Two hard-looking boys in matching denim vests started at him but Billy Ray found an empty High Life and broke the bottom of the bottle against the edge of a table. The pair of vests froze as Billy Ray slashed the space in front of him with the jagged bottleneck, his eyes burning, collapsed stars. "Who's tough?" he said. "Who wants to stay young forever?" He backed toward the door holding the shard in front of him, barking aspersions, hoping to be tested, aching to spread skin, but nobody moved against his madness. As he butted open the front door, the last thing he said before he started running was, "All I wanted was a taste."

The night was still. Sounds failed to echo. Through it he moved like a cloud, totally mindless and roving, his legs churning ungoverned. No one followed but still he ran. All he knew was he had to get away.

On Welton, a train passed, a blur of chimes and lights. He went north, following the train, pounding the vacant sidewalk. Panting. The slap of his boots reporting off the pavement. When he stopped, bent over and heaving at the light on 30th, his throat stung with bile. Dizzy, his vision contracted with his pulse. He was still holding the shattered bottle neck. He tossed the weapon into a bush, found a bench and collapsed. His heart was pneumatic. He figured he might die.

Artificially bright and choked of stars, the sky filled his vision but he stared without seeing as his chest rose and fell, alive despite himself, thoughtless, detached. He turned his head, vomited. Laid back down. Another train passed. To the passengers he looked dead. He remained like that until the nausea passed. He thought of water. Drifting. His legs hurt. *You've really done it this time, fella.* He was almost asleep when he heard the whistling.

From down the block across the street, seven notes repeated, growing louder on every recurrence. Billy Ray recognized the melody, sang along in his head: *Cel-e-brate good times. Come on.* The tunesmith wore a duster, black leather and too long for his stocky body, a sausage in excess casing. He walked funny to avoid stepping on the tail of his coat, kicking his feet out in a prancing goose-step, his knees unbending, moving his legs like a pair of scissors. *Cel-e-brate good times. Come on.* Billy Ray sat up to see him better. The man stopped and cocked his head.

"You a vampire?" the man said. He stepped off the sidewalk. In the streetlight Billy Ray saw him better. He looked unwell. Deep hollows carved out his cheeks. Gray-mauve circles enclosed his eyes. He was bald, ash-skinned and appeared to be completely bereft of teeth. On his chin, a thin goatee further exacerbated his gauntness; an itinerant magician. Billy Ray hoped he stayed over there.

Billy Ray laid back, lighting a cigarette. The man was a moth. *Goddamnit,* he thought, realizing what he'd done.

The man crossed quickly, scissor-stepping, the coat flapping like broken wings. "Think I could bum one of those?" *Goddamnit.* Billy Ray handed him a Winston. The man's lighter was clear blue plastic and the flame shot three inches long. Despite his sallow face, the sleeves of his jacket bulged when he flexed his arm and his hands were gnarly with work. "You popped up on me like a vampire." His eyes never stopped moving. They danced across Billy Ray's body down the street to the sky, darting, curious, seeing everything all at once. "I'm glad you're not one. A vampire, I mean." The man smacked his gums. "Looks like you were sick."

"I don't have any money."

"That makes two of us." The man squatted on his heels. "We might could make some. Bars are about to let out. People's more generous when they's drunk." The man pulled his cigarette hard, burning it quick. Five drags and it was spent.

Billy Ray watched the man out of the corner of his eye. He wished the man would leave him be but he lacked the energy to assert himself again. A part of him still expected to be descended upon by the mob from the bar and if that happened, he would have to take the beating. His tank was empty. He didn't have any more to give.

The man scratched at the sidewalk with a rock, the tip of his tongue exposed. Billy Ray couldn't see what he was etching, but he found the noise not unpleasant. The man scraped at the concrete, whistling his song, working with an artist's flourish. When he stopped to consider his work, he nodded. "That'll do," he said, skipping the rock across the street. "I drew a vampire."

Billy Ray grunted.

"I used to draw caricatures on the boardwalk in Hollywood, Maryland. One time this guy asks me to draw his wife and I do and he pays me and he says why don't you come back to our house and I do and then he pays me some more to lay down with his lady and he says I'm gonna draw you two and he does and his drawing was much better than mine. I told him he should have my job and he says I should have his wife and I said deal and every Wednesday I went over there and he drew us and it got to be a pretty nice little gig and they started buying me things and soon it was like we were a little family. Turned out he was a famous artist and he had a gallery opening and made me the guest of honor and all these rich people bought up them paintings of me boinking his ol lady and they all wanted to meet me and I shook their hands and he made a speech and said I was his inspiration and he gave me some of the money. He thanked me for helping him with his art and I said all I did was boink your wife and he said that was what he needed to make art and I said if I had to watch someone fuck my wife to make art I would get a new hobby." The man laughed. "We didn't talk after that."

The man rose from his haunches and smoothed his duster down in the back. "I'll never understand art. But I don't think I want to."

Billy Ray said nothing, not wanting to encourage him.

"Can I have another cigarette?"

Billy Ray sat up. The man, constantly twitching, stood very close. Everything about him made Billy Ray uneasy. He'd known men like him in prison. Bizarros. The unpredictability made them dangerous. Billy Ray got to his feet to show his size.

"Lordy. You sure got a lot of bones." The man made a show of observing him from head to toe. "If you're fixing to rough it, you're gonna need a bigger bench."

"I wasn't sleeping," said Billy Ray.

"Stargazer, huh?" The man craned his head backward. "Ain't much to look at."

"You got to know what you're looking for."

The man snapped his chin down as if catching a scent on the wind. His demeanor changed, serious now, no longer squirrely. The jerking subsided. He managed to lock his eyes on Billy Ray, squinted. "You say you're looking for something?"

Billy Ray thought he detected something in the man's question. It would explain the jitteriness, the breathless sentences. Billy Ray matched the man's stare, extrapolating, running the numbers. "Depends."

The man picked a cigarette butt off the ground, inspected it, tossed it away. "Well, if you're looking, look no further."

A train approached, the chimes growing louder, bathing them in light. They both watched it pass. Billy Ray swallowed, his mouth watering. Between his feet, the man's vampire sketch looked up at him. He covered its eyes with his heels.

The man looked left then right, put his hand to his mouth and spit.

He held out his hand and revealed a palmful of small knots of tied-off plastic. Billy Ray's heart sank. "Oh," he said. So close.

"It's fire. I whipped it myself." Contained in the knots were tiny lumps of a dull substance that looked like miniature marshmallows. "Ten a rock. You can try it first."

A car turned onto the street and the man shoved the wet pearls back in his mouth, pushing them down in his lip with his tongue. "If I'm lying, I'm dying." Billy Ray hesitated, said nothing. The silence was all the man needed to hear. "Come on, chief. Step into my office."

The man turned, his coat flaring, and Billy Ray followed him back toward the city. The man's gait was even odder up close. His knees never bent, as if his legs were lead pipes. They turned at 29th and then again at the alley. Behind a graffitied garage, the man stepped between two dumpsters and Billy Ray joined him, the pair invisible from the street. The man's hands worked quick, his thick fingers stuffing a glass tube with a piece of Brillo before nesting on top of it a chunk of grayish wax the same color as the moon. "Here," he said, offering the pipe.

Blank, Billy Ray put the pipe to his lips and the man torched the tip in quick intervals. He sucked slow, milking a massive hit, filling his lungs with euphoria. He held it in, exploded dark smoke. It was immediate. It came on like a concussive rush, like he'd stood up too fast. Feeling it first in his legs, it ran the length of him, an electric wave of rhapsodic pleasure; it shot out his fingers and the world fell away. His blood evaporated. His veins welled with life itself. *Oh,* he thought. *Oh oh oh.* The deepest sensuality, cosmic understanding—it refused to be defined, and it was beautiful, this unknowable knowledge, blasting away all uncertainty, ears ringing, eyes wide. This was heavy fuel, burning clean, burning. The very manna of existence. It felt like getting fucked by God. Seeing in soft-focus and breathing crushed velvet perfume: miracles. We are miracles. We are why the angels sing. Infinity. All Of It. All. Of. It. Oh oh oh.

The stranger watched with a certain kind of pride as the big man hacked and coughed. "I told you," he said, taking the rest of the pipe load. "Fire."

Completely gone to the moment, Billy Ray knew only one word: more. He pulled his wallet from his pocket and removed three tens, unaware of the way the man's eyes stoked when he revealed his bankroll. He gave the man the money and seized his purchases. He didn't mind they were wet with the stranger's slobber. He used his own teeth to untie the knot. In his frenzy, he didn't notice that the man had given him four rocks instead of three. The scorched glass burnt his fingers but he didn't feel it. Nothing mattered besides having more. This was why he was alive. The flame on the rock was conception. This is it. Bingo. We have a winner. He sucked and sucked. Inflating, deflating, inflating. Replacing himself. Oh oh oh. There it is. Here I am.

Billy Ray cashed the pipe. Untied another bundle. The man picked up a chunk of loose brick, judged the weight in his hand.

While the dead moon stared down at the dying planet, Billy Ray packed an entire rock into the end of the tube. He was searching for his lighter when the brick connected with the back of his head and absolute black shattered all the lights in the world.

SUNDAY

AS THE YAWNING SUN CRESTED THE CITY FILLING THE GLASS
windows with gold, the trash picker nudged an exploratory toe into the
body between the dumpsters.

"You dead?"

He'd worked through the night wrapped in his blankets, fending off
the cold via locomotion as he hunted treasures. Sunday mornings were
the best time for picking. On Sunday mornings, the dumpsters
brimmed with bottles and cans, vestiges of the weekend. His shopping
cart was loaded with plunder; it had been a fruitful night. Earlier, he'd
stripped a washing machine of its precious copper and later, behind a
church, he'd found a trash bag full of old *Hustlers* and fireworks, but
that was all just another day at the office. To date, this body on the
ground was his most interesting find.

The body was breathing. Snoring actually. Pants pockets turned out,
the crotch a darker shade of blue. The body was big. Whatever had put
it face down must have been bigger. The picker toed the body again and
then stepped back, putting the cart between them. He was afraid this
big body would come to life mean. He didn't want to catch a quarrel.
"Hello," he said. The body remained prostrate. Creaking on old joints,
he knelt down by the body's head and yelled in its ear. "Hello?"

Like an animal coming out of anesthesia, the body jerked awake
violently. The picker jumped away and grabbed the handle of his cart,

ready to ram the body if it charged. Slowly, the body rolled onto its side, gathering itself, its eyes bleary and searching for some marker to alert it to its whereabouts.

The picker leaned into his cart and found one of the sealed water bottles he'd scored. He cracked the top and extended his arm to the body slowly, careful not to spook it. "Here."

The body sat up to cough and touch its face and the man thought of it no longer as a body. Billy Ray looked up and saw the picker for the first time, trying to make sense of who he was and what he offered. The man was old, wise-eyed, his skin the cooked adobe color of a life lived outdoors, his hair a madman's curly white. He looked like a shepherd. With the man standing over him, a halo of sunlight burning around him, Billy Ray understood he was dead and this man was here to broker his passage. "Take it," the shepherd said. He did as he was told.

"Where am I?"

"Denver," the stranger said.

"Okay."

Billy Ray opened the water and drank in small sips. He felt like he'd been dropped from a great height. His head was a basket of raw meat stuffed with snakes. Vicious, they snapped at the walls, filling his skull with venom. Opening his eyes hurt but so did closing them and his forehead was studded with embedded pebbles from lying as he had. He had no memory of this place. He vaguely remembered running from somewhere but after that was a great empty canyon. The holes in his memory were scary black places. What transgressions lurked in that darkness were best not to think about. What he had done and what had been done to him. *Had I deserved it? Probably. Yes. Yes I had.*

"How long have I been here?" he asked the shepherd, shielding his eyes from the excoriating sunlight.

The shepherd shook his head. "I don't know. I just came up on you. I thought you were dead."

Billy Ray twisted and his stomach turned mutinous. He was still drunk and increasingly disoriented. He had lost his jacket somewhere.

As so often happened, Drunk Billy Ray had shanghaied Current Billy Ray and abandoned himself in this low place, leaving them with a heavy tab to pay. There was no one to blame really. Rough trade was the cost of doing business. There was nothing new but the packaging. It could always be worse. He touched the back of his head. The hair was sticky. On his fingers looked like jam.

He looked at his wrist and stared uncomprehending at the pale band of skin where his watch used to be. Realizing what was missing, his hands shot to his pockets, but they hung out of his pants like dog ears. Worse indeed. He looked up at the shepherd and the old man gave him a solemn nod.

"You been picked clean," the shepherd said. "You done pissed yourself, too."

Billy Ray touched his crotch. "Fuck."

"Yep."

Billy Ray watched a pair of magpies alight on a gutter. He coughed. Spat brown. "You got any cigarettes?"

"I got me a pouch."

Billy Ray struggled to his feet, joints popping, and rolled a cigarette from the shepherd's tobacco and stood huffing rough smoke as the old man picked over the bins. The sun, nascent no longer, burned with a punitive intensity that Billy Ray couldn't help but take personally. He moved into the shade of the garage and stripped to the waist and drank water and smoked, watching the trash picker assemble a very small fortune of glass and aluminum. Knowing the amount of money stolen from his wallet collapsed his lungs but he received a nonzero amount of comfort in knowing that he and the mystery bandit were two-sides of the same opportunistic coin. He'd made evil moves against the weak and unsuspecting. The perpetration of such acts had defined him for a time. And while he would never call it karma—he refused to believe the universe was organized in any way nor did he believe a super-cosmic matrix connected him to anyone else—he understood Newton's laws: actions, reactions. The momentum created by his past iniquities had simply boomeranged on him and today it was his turn to wake up with nothing. He'd been playing with markers for years and last night the house had finally come to collect what was theirs. The mystery bandit and Billy Ray were links in a chain as old as the concept of property and he harbored no resentment toward his mugger. The only person to blame was himself. It was he who left himself open to be victimized (in the scenario he envisioned, he assumed he'd come to the alley to relieve himself and some enterprising assailant had snuck up with a blunt object and scored a jackpot while his dick was in his hands) and it was he who decided to be his own bank. No one should carry that much cash; he knew that. It was foolish and gauche, the result of his impoverished upbringing. There was nothing he loved more than the bulge of folded money. The impotence he felt as a poor youth dangling without a safety net had twisted his perception of the importance of physical currency, an idea further warped by the dignity-stripping effect of prison's mutant economy. Having a thousand dollars on him ensured his autonomy. A man with money is just that: a *man*. And as long as he's got the cash, he is forever free. Now a healthy portion of his net worth and the legacy of his labor for the past month, along with his driver's license and his credit card, were in the possession of someone stronger than he. And while thinking about the actual money gave him the spins, inside of his wounded mind, on the scales he used to measure legitimacy and justice, he viewed the crime itself as a small piece of the natural order of things. The powerful plunder and the weak are ransacked, so it is written and so it goes.

"Well lookie here." Billy Ray surfaced from deep within himself to see the shepherd emerge from the dumpster, hopping out of the metal box with a practiced efficiency that contradicted his age. "Are these yours?" He dangled a set of keys on a steel braid.

"Fuck my big old ass."

Smiling, the shepherd tossed the big man his keys. "You never know what you'll find until you start looking for it." The trash picker set to work smashing the cans he'd found and Billy Ray joined him. They worked wordlessly, the old man setting the cans upright and Billy Ray dropping his boot and the old man loading the aluminum discs in a trash bag. When the cans were done, Billy Ray held open the trash bag and the old man filled it with bottles. Billy Ray loaded the bags in the cart and rolled one last cigarette while the old man secured his bounty with bungee cords. Billy Ray held out the Bugler but the old man waved it off. "You take it."

Billy Ray started to refuse but stopped himself. "You sure?"

The old man nodded. "I can buy more."

He didn't know what to say. Moved by this morning's succession of unnecessary kindnesses, Billy Ray felt a pressure from within to say something poignant. If this was a movie, this was the time for his character to communicate his gratitude. When his grand statement was over, punctuated by a lingering hand-hug, the old man would turn to leave, but not before imparting him with a few arcane final words that Billy Ray would ponder as the old man disappeared in an orchestrated lens flare. But Billy Ray wasn't a movie star anymore: he was a penniless and shirtless and piss-soaked destitute, incapable of poetry with gravel in his hair. In lieu of anything meaningful, Billy Ray said, "Thanks," and the old drifter said, "Yep," and recommenced his task, leaning into his cart to return to his lonely circuit. As he watched his shepherd grow smaller down the alley, in his addled, semi-conscious mindstate, Billy Ray half-expected wings to emerge from the old man's back and for his shepherd to ascend in a beam of austere light and for he himself to wake up and be rescued from this nightmare.

Instead he started his trudge.

He stuck to the alleyways. All around him the new day formed. Squirrels chattered in the branches of trees. Bird sounds. Mice busy in the leaves. A dog in a backyard followed him along the chain link, its bark choked by its leash. "Fuck off, mutt," he said. He found a hose and drank from it. The dog ran back and forth.

His belly swayed as he walked, flopping in front of him like an un-filled bladder. The sunlight felt pleasant on his chest but in his jeans, his thighs chafed, brined in urine and rashing. Chemical liquid bled out his pores. The stink was sharp and inorganic. He tied his shirt around his head in a turban. "Death to America," he said, still drunk. He sat down on a concrete embankment and removed his boots. The feet in his moist socks were pink, almost purple, and swollen. He was sur-prised when they didn't stink. He crossed his leg and rubbed his toes until the color lessened then returned them to his socks and pulled on his boots. He slapped his thighs and stood up. "Alright," he said.

At the light on Park Avenue, he crossed the diagonal and continued his parade south, snaking past the herds of well-dressed churchgoers, Judas among the Philistines. In a churchyard, children stopped what they were doing to stare at him. He waved. The children turned away.

While the clock tower on Arapahoe rang nine times, he crafted a cigarette at the bus stop on 20th, sharing his tobacco among the desti-nationless. Assuming he was one of them, they offered tips on fresh beds in exchange for his papers and none of them asked him for any-thing more.

"I can't eat no more of that soup, hear."

"The chicken and rice isn't that bad."

"A man needs more than soup."

"They have bologna."

"Bitch, I got your bologna right here."

He stood with them and smoked and listened to their nonsense, enjoying the anonymity, the small stakes of their lives. His raw-dog headache had dulled to a persistent pulsation centered in the roots of his eyes. His teeth felt loose in his gums and his stomach alternated between a burning cauldron and a heavy leaden thing. The hardest part was not answering the quivering in his hands. His addiction didn't un-derstand commerce. *Motherfucker*, he thought. The treachery. He thought he spied a bottle circling among the transients but it never made it his way. He was about to ask if anyone had a sip to spare when a transit cop came and the group dispersed. His hands continued to shake. He put on his shirt.

He walked Stout Street slowly, trying to keep his thighs from rubbing. His hand reached under his shirt periodically to wipe the sweat from beneath his breasts and on top of his head, his scalp burned in the spots where his hair was sparse. A line of young people queued at a breakfast restaurant, their phone screens reflected in their sunglasses. A group of patrons rose from their table on the patio and off their plates he stole a half-eaten sandwich and a handful of home fries and downed the remains of two champagne flutes. He opened the leather bill book but found no cash. He ate the sandwich in three bites. A train passed. His face in the windows looked displeased. Farther ahead, he saw what he assumed to be a street fair. It wasn't until 18th that the zombies appeared.

They were legion. Their numbers clotted the streets. It was worse than he could ever imagine. The dead alive. Risen. The locks of their sepulchers broken. Empty hell. Apocalypse by the thousands. The streets blocked off to accommodate the rotting herd. They lurched mechanically, petrified, somnambulistic, gnashing and groaning full-throated when they bumped into each other. Some wore jerseys and some wore rags and some were stylish and some were near nude. Color-coordinated in matching outfits, groups of monsters moved together in formation while others who had clearly been families before the outbreak stayed close to one another, mother and father zombies pulling their undead children on leashes. Zombies holding hands, others stopping to kiss or snap selfies. His brain scrambled to make sense of the disparate inputs. The ghouls outnumbered the living, but of the unturned, only he seemed to be alarmed. It was like a block party. Hawkers peddled bottled water and T-shirts and music blared from a bandstand and hot dog carts did busy business, unharassed by the shuffling horde and serving up franks to the zombies who waited patiently to pay. The dissonance was incomputable. *I am asleep*, he thought, *or the shepherd was a liar and I have joined the ranks of hell.*

He turned to a man standing on a park bench filming the macabre display with his cellphone. Billy Ray had to yell to be heard. "What is this shit?"

The man turned to answer him. Half of his face was a cherry-red scab. "Zombie crawl, dude." The man pointed and Billy Ray followed his finger. A banner above Stout Street read 5th Annual Denver Zombie Crawl. "Bra-a-a-ains," the man hissed. Billy Ray moved away from him, shaking his head.

Zombie crawl. He had never heard of such a thing but it made sense. As a species, humankind was bored and ever increasingly bullshit passed for fun. Their mirth disgusted him. Their happiness was ostracizing. Numb to inorganic novelty, he pitied them their false calamity. Their lives—staid, monotonous—were so safe and predictable these people were forced to organize chaos and pretend they were dead. It was disappointing. For a moment he thought he'd made it to Armageddon. He'd always maintained a fantasy that he would live long enough to see the end of days. It seemed like the best way to go: bearing witness to the last breaths of mankind, licked to death by the same flames that consumed existence. The quiet afterward . . . In his mind it was beautiful. The last humans, unalone in death, dying shoulder-to-shoulder, as close as the species will ever be. Bound by extinction, a part of the ultimate Something—Ragnarok, The End. In their final moments they will know true bravery and they will die united and noble. No caskets. No survivors trapped in mourning. Their ashes the soil from which the next nature grows. He envied them. To be swallowed by annihilation. The purest form of death. It was the most he could hope for. At the very least, holocaust is original. This fraudulent hell was only more purgatory.

"What will they think of next?" he asked, but no one was listening. He considered going around. Decided what the hell. I'll show them a monster. He stepped off the sidewalk and entered the fray.

Portions of faces. Shoulder blades. Hands. Feet on feet. Knees colliding. Shins hammering shins. Crevice odors. Fingers. Mouths and teeth and tongues. They moaned. They cackled. Billy Ray hated them all, these pieces of this larger thing.

Despite an initial push that left him turned around and unsure of his direction, he found a rhythm and matched the flow. After a few panicked moments he located the clocktower and adapted to the swirl of the crush. The trick was to never stop moving forward. He surged through gaps in the mass, darting like a running back, picking his holes and anticipating their movements. Having already walked a dehydrated mile this morning, he felt every step in the large muscles of his legs and the arches of his feet. His height was an asset, allowing him to see above the heads and find breaks in the unrelenting wave. Patterns became evident. The crowd seemed to enclose and expand simultaneously. Gelatinous contractions. The throng moved like a jellyfish. He bobbed, he weaved. Inside the bedlam, his headache became a crown of nails. His eyes burned. Still they came.

By 17th Street, he exhausted the reserves of his consideration. He became violent. His pace increased. He fought. He muscled. He clawed. When they reached for him, he slapped away their hands. He stomped on their toes. If the procession ceased momentarily, he lowered his shoulder and shoved the back of the person in front of him until progress was restored. His eyes silenced any protests. *I am the monster,* they said. *You're pretending to be me.*

The intimate quarters afforded him an anonymity that was rare to a man of his size. It was thrilling to be so close to so many without being noticed. He could do anything in here. It reminded him of the orgies in the Valley, the ones with masks and tarps, a bucket of Crisco by the door. The closeness surfaced a licentious debauchery from the darkest depths of his id and he succumbed to the whispers of his lowest craven impulse. Ever the explorer, Billy Ray tested the floor of his bottom.

At first, he experimented with the back of his forearm, brushing quickly against the breasts of passing women. His wrists. His fingers like feathers. When none of them challenged his touch, emboldened, he switched to his hands, disguising his clandestine assaults as accidental contact forced by the crowds' constant compressions. He palmed. He groped. He initiated gratuitous friction. Rising. *Oh boy,* he thought. They were all here. Seventy-two virgins. A terrorist in heaven. The ease of the debasement possessed him. The monster became the beast. He squeezed a woman's buttock, smelling the rose oil in her hair. A hand caught his wrist and the woman spun around. Seeing the behemoth, the dead eyes in its skull, the joy melted from her face.

"Oh," he said.

She shoved him, her hands strong against his chest. "Sicko," she shrieked. "Dirty fucking bastard." She slapped him, clawed for his eyes, fingernails against his neck drawing blood, but her attack went unnoticed in the sea of moaning. Despite the volume, her outrage melded with the overall din, her remonstration presenting as more counterfeit madness. Billy Ray wriggled backward. Bodies filed between them and they were separated. He escaped into a crease in the mob and followed the slipstream until it shot him out on 16th Street.

He leaned against a Starbucks window pulling in air. Outside the swarm, his humanity returned and the former rutting brute was confronted by his own stench. The stink of old urine was overpowering. *That's me,* he thought. *That's the smell of me.* Feeling the rigidity between his thighs, shame both sudden and complete set around him like personal midnight. *If I'm not dead,* he thought, *I should be. My God.* He turned to the window and touched the cool glass. He imagined driving his face through the pane and cutting his neck on the shards. A shuttle bus stopped at the intersection and he considered laying down in front of its wheels. Nearby, a group of police stood in a half circle observing the revelers. *I could go for one of their guns. That would do it.* He found comfort in the thought of dying but the momentary solace was canceled when he remembered he was a coward and there was nothing to be done.

The event thinned out the farther he got from Stout. Placidity replaced fervor. It was Sunday after all. Pastel-clad women sipped wine on patios. Buskers warbled over untuned guitars. Outside the Cheesecake Factory, families of tourists stared at their phones, a new breed of zombie. Granted invisibility by his filthiness, nobody saw Billy Ray.

From a block away, Billy Ray spotted a yellow envelope tucked under his wiper blade. Unwilling to subject himself to yet another insult, he tore the ticket in half without opening it and let the pieces be carried away by the wind. He opened the trunk and found his cache and counted what remained of his money: less than he needed, more than he was worth. It was all he had in the world.

He took off his boots and his pants and his overshirt and stuffed them in the trunk and climbed into the driver's seat and peeled off his underwear and dropped them out the window. Completely nude, he attempted a cigarette but his hands failed him and the tobacco spilled all over his naked stomach. He slammed his fist into the roof of the car: that was something his hands could still do. He pressed his forehead into the steering wheel and made a list of all the things he needed to accomplish: he needed cold liquor and he needed cold water and he needed hot food and he needed soap and he needed to get clean and he needed to get off the road and he needed Red because he needed the cruise ships because he needed more money because he was getting too old and he needed to forgive comedy because he was not a martyr and he needed to be grateful because he'd had a good ride, he needed to forget about what he had been and come to terms with what he was and he needed to be a father and a grandfather and he needed to apologize to everyone that ever loved him and needed to remember that once he had been loved and he needed to see Olivia's face, to smell her perfume, to hear her laugh because he needed to reconnect to a time before the reign of desperation, before he succumbed to the ugly and dark, and he needed to remember once he had been a good man, that once he was whole and he needed to remind himself life was precious because above all else, as it stood right now, he needed to convince himself that he didn't want to die.

There were a pair of sweatpants in the back seat and he found them and put them on. He slipped on a crewneck and his boots sans socks and, taking a deep breath, Billy Ray emerged from the car and walked the two blocks to the liquor store, swollen with nausea and a mounting, free-range anxiety that drove his heart against the bars of its cage. He caught his reflection in the window of a café. He looked like a ward of the state, like a mental patient or one of the sad, broken men in prison who couldn't be trusted with a belt or shoelaces. The outfit made sense: it reflected how he felt.

He arrived at Champa Street Liquors, a prophet at the gates of mecca. His fingers calmed as they met the doorknob. He pulled the brass. The door refused. You gotta twist it, stupid. He tried again, yanking with all of him, but the door remained shut. He cupped his hands on the glass and peered inside. The store was empty. Despite the obvious vacancy, he banged on the door. "Hello?" He stepped back, checking around the side for an alternate entrance. A sign on the door offered the hours of operation. Reading it, his despondency red-lined. "No," he said. "Come on." It was Sunday. When he was a child, the Centennial State prohibited the sale of liquor on the sabbath, but for the law to still stand in this age of gay marriage and pot shops seemed impossible. He tried the knob one last time, shaking the door on its hinges. "Fuck me running," he said. He spat on the door. His saliva looked like paste.

He didn't have enough money to drink in a bar. He knew what he needed and he knew what he had and one was less than the other. There was rent and renters insurance and the car note and Jeremiah's tuition. He couldn't float any of it. Last he talked to the creditors, they said he had to start paying a portion of his credit cards down or else they were going to take him to court. After last night, he had about eighty dollars to spare, and that wasn't enough for bar prices. Even riding the rail, his war chest would run empty before he remedied himself. This was real pain. His nerves were hot wires, his bones were made of glass. His eyes felt like they were constricting, as if they might burst, and in the space behind them where his brain used to be, a Detroit of rusted machinery begged for lubrication as it showered his interior skull with sparks. This wasn't a hair of the dog situation. He needed every bit of the dog: the lungs, the heart, the teeth; total obliteration: he needed to drink until he disappeared, until he abdicated the title of Billy Ray Schafer and devolved into something without a name or a past.

He assessed the entrance. Even if he smashed the glass, the door was mounted with a second steel security door. He'd need tools to remove it. The windows weren't barred but they were high and narrow and Billy Ray was low and fat. Larceny wasn't an option. His knuckles were white. "Goddamnit it all."

Focus, he thought. What he needed right now was a double whiskey stopgap and to sit and think until his reality ceased pulsing. He scanned his surroundings. Across the street, two bars with ampersands in their names shouldered each other for attention. On one patio mimosa seekers emptied carafes. On the other, young people posed in self-conscious smiles while their waiters captured their memories on smartphones. These places were not for him. He felt too dead to be around so much life. A block down in front of a steakhouse, a sandwich board advertised five-dollar vodka and oyster shooters. Reading it, he gagged. The office buildings lining Champa offered no succor. He spun around and searched the storefronts—Indian restaurant, improv theater, cupcake shop, hot dogs—his eyes finding nothing, his anxiety swelling to a symphony of asymmetrical noise. Then he saw it: the familiar red awning, the cursive letters stained a dirty off-white. *Of course,* he thought. *There's my foxhole.*

With grim purpose, he walked to Walgreens.

The store, like all chain pharmacies, was sterile and white, a retail designer's vision of hospital chic. Soft jazz and softer light. The conditioned air's faux-cold sealed his sweat-soaked shirt to his back like a second skin. His fellow shoppers shifted listlessly, dragging behind their shopping carts, blank, lifeless, as if they too were designed and installed in this location. A group of Latino children in backward hats rummaged through bins of candy beneath a sign for diabetic testing supplies. A stooped woman, gray and muttering, studied a coupon insert with a magnifying glass as if it were a map of her destiny. In the supplements aisle, two men compared the prices on bottles of vitamins, one of them legless in an electric wheelchair, the other tethered via tubing to a rolling tank of oxygen while zombies from the parade filled tote bags with Gatorade and salami and sunscreen. Billy Ray saw all of this, standing in the middle of it, a hybrid, near dead but not yet, a filthy, wet, last-chance man burping his shirt and searching the store directory for the oral hygiene aisle.

The Listerine was less than a penny per milliliter and it came in two flavors: mint or ultraclean. He settled on ultraclean. The blue hue looked more refreshing.

The clerk was a large woman with heavy braids and long fingernails painted the color of honeydew melon. She looked from him to the mouthwash, puckered her lips to the side of her face and scanned the bottle, her eyes askance and knowing. "Is that it?"

"What are your cheapest cigarettes?" His voice sounded like snapping twigs.

When she turned around to face the cigarettes, the clerk's hair swung like a coil of shining black pendulums. "Pall Malls is buy one, get one."

"Okay. The reds." He slipped a candy bar in his pocket as she bent for the lowest shelf.

He laid a twenty on the counter and she held the bill up to examine it by the light, making a show of verifying the bill's legitimacy before adding it to her drawer. Carefully, begrudgingly, she picked out his change with her talons and handed him the remainder. Billy Ray collected his sundries and thanked her. The woman shouted, "Next!"

He stepped outside and opened the cigarettes and asked a tie-dyed stranger for a light. He lifted up his pullover and leaned against the building, pressing his back into the cold gray marble as he smoked, watching the light rail fill up with undead. The sun was at full peak, beating the city and filling the sidewalks with fire. He regretted not buying water. He missed the air conditioning back in the store. If only he had a hotel room. He could go there, turn the thermostat to its lowest setting and freeze as he drank himself to death. When the train stop was empty, he cracked the mouthwash.

If he pinched his nose it wasn't that bad. With a bit of imagination it tasted like peppermint schnapps or the liqueur bartenders toast with in Chicago. The mouthwash was room temperature and it stung his throat going down. The blue liquid scoured the walls of his empty organ, acid on acid. The reaction felt like he was splitting in half. He drank some more.

After a few long pulls off the bottle and another cigarette, his head quit screaming and the quiver went out of his hands. He recapped the bottle and went back inside to buy a jug of water and a handful of Slim Jims, taking his time, enjoying the cool air, letting the steam rise. In the foyer he removed his sweatshirt and walked to the car with the sun on his back.

He smelled awful, a gamy, metallic, roadkill stink. If he was going to see Olivia—and he was, it was his only purpose—he needed to be clean. He dug through the trunk and found a plastic bag full of hotel soaps and a clean T-shirt and his pair of Levi's and packed them in with his sustenance. Then, in the car, he removed his boots and his sweatpants and slipped on a pair of boxers before redonning the sweats. Shoeless and gumming on a Slim Jim, Billy Ray walked up 14th to Larimer and down the stairs to find himself alone with the Cherry Creek.

The creek was fat and clear with the last of the summer melt but it still ran slow enough for Billy Ray to stand still in the current without fighting. The water barely reached his thighs. He walked down until he was far from the path and stripped to his boxers and knelt in the silt, letting the water cover him to his neck. The creek was cold and sharp and rich with the rusted metal smell of wild water. He dipped his chin and let the water fill his mouth. It tasted like pennies.

He stood up and lathered himself with soap and dipped back down and repeated this process until he was raw and clean, then he worked the bar through his hair, careful around the tender spot where the brick connected, and scrubbed his face and submerged totally, disappearing beneath the rippling silver, becoming a secret from the world.

Under the water, he couldn't help but smile. This was a level of freedom very few men achieved: pure communion. He welled with a sense of renewal. Even in the throes of a brutal hangover and on a pauper's budget, he'd figured out how to heal himself and get clean for less than five dollars. There was always more money—cash was liquid, inconstant, it came and went like rain—and he knew how to live while he was waiting for more. At least he still had his wits. He spit a fountain of water. He splashed. He peed. He forgot about his calamitous night and his empty pockets and his weeks of work pilfered. He didn't have much at this time but he owned the present and later tonight he would attest for his past and improve his future. It wasn't about winning her back—he wasn't delusional. It was about vocalizing his understanding of his misdeeds and failures, about taking responsibility for his long-term interpersonal vandalism and apologizing, hopefully offering closure on what he knew to be her deepest of wounds. If it was too early for olive branches, maybe they could at least plant the tree. He didn't know what he was going to say; he'd figure it out on the drive up. He worked better against a deadline and the words were of small consequence. It was the doing of the thing that mattered. It felt good to have a plan.

High on his conviction and the water and the sunlight, he decided it was proper to get fully nude.

He looked both ways up and down the bike trail that hugged the creek's edge. When he deemed it clear, he crouched down in the water and liberated himself. A nuthatch honked. Billy Ray shut his eyes and enjoyed the buoyancy, relishing the weightlessness and the relief to his overburdened joints. It was narcotic, akin to beer and Somas. He grabbed a handful of love handle and squeezed. It wasn't always this way. Once his body had been a collection of stones hewn together with straps of leather. He was a solid 220 going into his eighteenth year, lean and strong. Once, when Anthony Sandrin, misjudging the hairpins and washboards on Missile Base Road, spilled off his Harley, Billy Ray pulled the chopper off his pinned friend with one arm. Prison had further fortified his conditioning. At the end of his sentence, he emerged from lockup a slab of concrete, as sturdy and hard as petrified wood. What he'd give for that body, that youth. Pulling at his gut, he decided tomorrow he would start a diet. It would be nothing for him to drop thirty pounds if he hit the weights. Back when he was in demand as an actor, he learned how to drop mass quick. Egg whites and green beans, vodka instead of beer. Easy as that. Get into shape, meet someone normal, live a life less lonely—tomorrow: what a beautiful word. As the clouds bound the sun like poached whites around egg yolk, Billy Ray laid back against a boulder and made a mental note to go swimming more often.

A *ka-thunk*. A splash. He opened his eyes and looked for the fish, but another *ka-thunk* behind him and a clutch of young laughter made him understand he was under attack. Standing up, exposed completely, he looked above to Speer Boulevard.

"Holy shit. He's fucking bareass."

Above him on Larimer leaning against the guardrail, a group of teenagers whooped and pointed from their vantage point on the pedestrian bridge. None of them appeared old enough to buy cigarettes but a few of them were smoking. They were dressed for outdoor exertion—basketball shorts, gownish T-shirts, thick sneakers with puffy, wide tongues—sportswear that clashed with their punked haircuts and stick-and-poke tattoos, the lot of them either standing on skateboards or holding their decks by the nose.

"No way."

"Look."

"I can't see it."

Billy Ray forgot about his lack of trunks and stomped toward the youths, high-kneeing through the water, his scrotum flopping between his thighs. "You think that's funny, you little shits?"

"Woah."

"Holy shit."

"I told you. Fucking bareass."

The boys clucked. A few of them slapped their boards against the rail.

"Hey, mister," called down a kid with a bushy red afro. "Where's your dick?"

Billy Ray looked down to see a less than flattering length of himself exposed. Covering up with his hands, he considered deferring to the water temperature but he decided to greet hostility with hostility. "I left it in your mother's cunt, faggot."

The youth recoiled, obviously surprised at the quickness of the naked man's retort.

"Her bush looked like your hairdo and her pussy looked like your face."

A tremor of tremendous laughter seized the group of skateboarders as they fell over each other laughing. Only the redhead refrained, any further rebuttal silenced by his peers' decisive glee. Instead he scowled and shrank.

"This guy rules," one of them said, a black kid with a hoop in his nose.

"Maybe he'll buy us some beer?"

"It's Sunday, retard."

"We can still get three-two."

"Fuck three-two."

"Fuck you, Colby. Hey, man, will you buy us some beer?"

"Go fuck yourself," said Billy Ray.

"We're not cops."

"We're just trying to party."

"Go fuck yourself," he repeated.

"Damn."

Billy Ray turned and walked back to the shore and wrapped himself in a pullover. "If you wanna get drunk," he offered, "go buy some Listerine."

"Mouthwash is for hobos, man."

"Suit yourself." Billy Ray bent over, brought out his bottle and drank. The skateboarders reacted with a collective awe bordering on admiration.

"Gnarly."

"Savage."

"I told you this guy rules."

The stiff Levi's cut into his stomach but the dark denim complimented the powder-blue snapshirt tucked into his waist. The belt was unnecessary but he fancied the buckle and the way the strip of rich red leather divided his body. He slipped on socks and, after administering a quick spit shine with an old T-shirt, he pulled his boots on over them and neatly cuffed his jeans. *I'm getting shaggy,* he thought, amassing the length of his hair into a ducktail at the base of his neck. He was overdue for a razor and the middle of his face was healing around his broken nose in a graying-purple, but, assessing himself in the darkened glass of a high-rise window, he thought he looked like he gave a shit, and he hoped Olivia would agree.

He took off the shirt and put it on a hanger and hung it from the grip handle in the back seat so as not to wrinkle it or sweat it through on the drive. He smoked a cigarette, holding the butt away from him and blowing the smoke off his body. Olivia hated the smell.

When they first met she smoked Virginia Slim Superslims, as long and narrow as the stick of a tootsie pop. She smoked on weekends and she smoked when she drank but her habit was a weak imitation of Billy Ray's two packs per day obsession. When she quit, it was easy for her and made easier by her nurses rounds and her daily glimpse into the long-term effects of carcinogens. She begged Billy Ray to stop and he tried while he was home with her, having weeks of success, especially when she used her body as incentive. But as soon as he was back on the road and dependent on willpower to govern his various intakes, the spell broke and Thursday morning came and he woke up with a carton in his hotel mini-fridge. Eventually he quit quitting because he didn't like feeling weak and Olivia, succumbing to another nonconsensual compromise, quit asking him to quit because she didn't like feeling stupid. Instead she changed her attack and enforced what rules she could. At her request, before he got into bed beside her, he scrubbed his hands and face with LAVA soap or else she wouldn't let him near her. The pumice was like washing with sandpaper but it was the only soap that did the job and it was worth it to smell the back of her head, to kiss her on the base of her neck where her necklaces closed, and he washed like this every night until one night, after an argument, he refused as a sign of protest and the habit was broken, joining his ever-growing list of petty defiances.

Olivia had few needs and she asked for very little and Billy Ray denied her out of habit, viewing compliance with her simple demands as a signal of surrender and submission to what he saw as a pervasive crusade to domesticate him completely—to wring out all of his wild: he'd live in the barn and he'd fight with the rope but he wasn't ready to be fit for a saddle. To give in to her was to lose another inch of himself and between the travel and the radio and the shows and the crowds, Billy Ray didn't think there was much more of him left to give. He fought for what remained with a blindfolded fury that rendered his wife his enemy.

You fucking idiot.

If he had a time machine, he wouldn't go back in time and kill Hitler. He'd return to that night he didn't wash his hands and scrub them until they bled.

He got in the car and turned it on and joined Arapahoe and fought over right to turn onto Speer and followed it across the river and out of the city until he was northbound on I-25. He drove with the radio on classic rock, happy to hear something familiar. Less and less he understood the things people said and that confusion carried over into modern music. The bottom end was too thin and the lyrics, abstruse, tried too hard at profound. He liked songs that said what they meant. Songs about fast women and weak men and the results of their coupling. He slapped the steering wheel along with Keith Moon as Roger Daltrey promised he wouldn't get fooled again and when Billy Gibbons posited that women loved a sharp-dressed man, Billy Ray agreed by opening up the throttle to beat a merging big rig.

Within two song lengths, Denver was gone, replaced briefly by suburbs until the retaining walls of Thornton and Northglenn ended and the enterprise zone began, a leftover expanse filled with the black-topped acreages of office park parking lots and faceless, bland rectangles of postindustrial architecture, unapologetically brutal in their adherence to form following function. It looked like New Jersey. He drove past car dealerships and grocery wholesalers and depots pertaining to both office and home, past fast-food drive-thrus and fast-casual dine-ins and the patriotic big-box stores flying massive American flags selling goods straight from China, past a movie theater with twenty-five screens and a Putt-Putt course with laser tag and a sporting goods store with an indoor lake. Finally he drove past more than a mile of furniture outlets and the land thereafter became unfenced barren pastures of brittle, golden grass.

In his opinion, all the Colorado north of Boulder was southern Wyoming. The land up here was barely fit for grazing cattle. Unzoned and unwanted, the Bureau of Land Management oversaw the majority of the I-25 corridor between Longmont and Fort Collins. Besides the sporadic truck stops and the telephone poles, the land was unadorned and empty. For stretches of tens of miles, the world outside of his windows was bereft of the hallmarks of civilization, surrounding him with twin seas of monotonous yellow, the most exciting feature of which was the wind. Unimpeded by buildings or mountains for miles east and west, the wind blew faster in the north, startling the alfalfa fields frenzied as if they were haunted or on wires and lashing the car in harsh gales that pushed Billy Ray across the white line. Fighting the wind consumed his focus until he passed a sign that read HIGH WINDS POSSIBLE. "No shit," he muttered, making a mental note to add it to his chunk about falling rocks.

Craving a cigarette and food beyond Slim Jims, Billy Ray pulled off at a truck stop twenty-eight miles from Fort Collins. At the entrance to the parking lot, he missed his turn and found himself in the lot reserved for long-haulers. He felt small weaving his car through the jungle of resting chrome hulks, miniaturized by their enormity. A woman in a glaring red miniskirt walked among the trucks. She knocked on the door of a wine-colored rig and the trucker inside the cabin rolled down his window and said something Billy Ray couldn't hear and the woman frowned and skulked along.

He crawled out of the car at the pump and massaged both of his fists into his lower back as he arched backward to stretch. The sky above, unhampered by smog, burned brighter than it did in the city, a vivid blue like the color of the mouthwash he'd been sipping. He had to squint against its intensity.

The gas station was expansive inside, stocked with a menagerie of goods that spoke to the odd needs of those that lived on the road. There were racks of men's clothes—electric orange long sleeves, cheap flannel shirts, long underwear in sizes up to XXXXL—and baskets of socks and wool gloves and, arranged neatly inside of a glass case, pocket knives with handles made of elk horn laid beside blackjacks and telescoping batons and brass knuckles labeled as novelty paperweights and, on the shelf below, jet-black BB pistols glistened like the real thing. Foam beer koozies and snow globes and postcards and shot glasses— every kind of souvenir, six for ten dollars and available in unique designs for each of the fifty states.

Billy Ray perused the bric-a-brac hoping to find an absurd gift to bring to Olivia, something silly to break the ice. He considered a T-shirt that read FART COLLINS, COLONRADO but he didn't know her size and guessing seemed like a minefield. An apron proclaiming GRANDMAS DO IT IN THE KITCHEN opened him up for skewering. A can of mace was probably the most practical gift but it wasn't funny enough. And even though he thought it was hilarious, he doubted she would laugh at a Confederate flag towel. He was about to buy her a singing wall-mounted fish when, laying on top of a bin of miscellaneous CDs, he spotted a two-disc set of the Pretenders' greatest hits. Olivia loved Chrissie Hynde. On many mornings Billy Ray had woken up to Olivia butchering "Brass in Pocket" in the shower. "I'll Stand by You" was their first dance at their wedding. "Well I'll be damned," he said, putting a voice to the serendipity raising the skin on his neck. He thought of Norm Macdonald and his soothsaying. Even filtered through his hardened cynicism, it was hard for him not to interpret the availability of this semipopular British New Wave band's greatest hits inside this rural gas station as a nudge from the universe. Some cosmic wink. He wasn't sure what it meant but he was sure it meant something and something was more to grasp at than the nothing he had before.

Triumphant and brimming with new confidence, he put the singing fish back on the shelf.

He selected a turkey sandwich and a couple of prepackaged hard-boiled eggs from the grocery cooler, pausing for a moment in front of the open door to enjoy the refrigeration. Taped to the glass on the next cooler over, a handwritten sign read NO BEER SALES ON SUNDAY. Behind the sign, six-packs and forty ounces glowed under the fluorescent light. The cans and bottles reminded Billy Ray of the jewels in the *Pink Panther* movies. He coveted them the same.

Billy Ray looked around. The gas station had filled up since he'd come in. At the front of the store, the two cashiers were busy with a line of customers and he hadn't seen any other employees stocking the shelves. Casually, he scanned the ceiling and the corners of the building for cameras. Once, twice. Spotted none. Blocking his actions with the width of his body, Billy Ray opened the beer case and freed two sixteen-ounce Millers from their plastic rings. He tucked the beers under his arm and walked to the bathroom, holding his arm tight to his body like the victim of a stroke.

The bathroom smelled of disinfectant and poor digestion. Billy Ray hurried past the row of men filling the urinals and found an empty stall. He sat down on the toilet and cracked one of the cans, coughing loudly to cover the hiss. The beer tasted like water. He finished it with three long swallows. The second beer he savored, pressing the can to his forehead between sips, enjoying the kiss of the cool aluminum. *I should have brought the whole six pack,* he thought. In another stall, it sounded like someone was sobbing. *Been there,* he thought. When the can was empty, he ate the sandwich and the eggs and hid the evidence of his meal behind the base of the toilet. He left the stall whistling.

He filled a Styrofoam cup with ice and Sprite and got in the line for the counter behind a woman and a child. The woman's face was pulled, the beleaguered tired specific to motherhood. Below a furrowed brow, she stared forward stone-faced, ignoring the child yanking on the hem of her dress and begging in Spanish.

"Por favor, mami! Por favor!"

The woman remained indifferent as she stepped up to the cashier. Seeing his window closing, the child collapsed to the linoleum in a thrashing, squealing tantrum. Billy Ray looked on without empathy, appalled by the woman's indifference. It wasn't right to make this his problem. Billy Ray wanted her to slap the boy, to end this havoc and make him shut up. Over the woman's shoulder, Billy Ray's eyes met the cashier's, a stout white man with a knobby shaved head. While the woman typed in her pin number, the cashier smiled at Billy Ray and stuck out his tongue while at the same time pointing his finger to his temple gunwise and pulling an invisible trigger. Billy Ray nodded.

When her transaction was complete, the woman collected her bags with one hand and in a movement that was obviously practiced, she yanked the boy's wrist without looking and dragged him mewling out the door.

The cashier shook his naked head. "What a scene."

"I don't know how she takes it," Billy Ray said. "If I ever acted that way, my mama would have slapped the bumps off my tongue."

"Mine, too."

"Must be a Mexican thing."

"These fucking wetbacks. You never can tell." The man scanned the Pretenders CDs and Billy Ray noticed the number 1488 crudely tattooed on the inside of his thick forearm. "I won't charge you for the soda, brother."

Billy Ray wanted to ask the man where he was locked up and for how long and to tell him he understood, to trust him, he understood, but he knew he couldn't: that wasn't the kind of thing people talked about, even people like them. Instead he added gas to his total and counted out a portion of his measly bankroll and the cashier gave him his change followed by a slow nod. Billy Ray sensed fraternity in the gesture—along what lines, he wasn't sure, but he returned it anyway—and as he left, the neo-Nazi wished him a nice day.

While the gas pumped, Billy Ray leaned in the car and splashed a few fingers of Listerine over the ice. When the pump clicked, he replaced the hose on the stand and moved the car to a parking space beside a small plot of fenced-off Astroturf where people took their dogs to shit. He got out of the car and lit a cigarette and stirred his cocktail with his finger and let his mind drift like the clouds becoming shapes in the sky. He was glad he didn't have any cocaine because if he did, he would do it, and he didn't want Olivia to see him that way. She could always tell. He had no idea what to expect. Maybe she would invite him in for a cup of coffee and they would sit at the kitchen table they bought on that trip to Pittsburgh, the one where they danced on the Amtrak and she ate lamb for the first time, and maybe they'd talk in civil tones about times less sour and she'd break out a bottle of wine and after the second glass he'd make her laugh and he'd ask her if she remembered where they got this table and maybe she would say Pittsburgh and he would say do you remember on the train? When the dining car was empty and we danced without music? Do you remember when I asked you why you were crying and you said it was just all too perfect, baby, that it didn't get any better than this, and I, too, shed a tear because I knew you were right? Do you remember before we forgot how to love each other? When you were my everything? Do you remember me when I was me? Because I remember you and you were beautiful. We were beautiful. Do you remember where we got this table he would ask her. And maybe she would say yes.

Most likely he would never get close to the table. He'd be lucky if she let him onto the porch. There was no reason for her to subject herself to him. From what he understood, she was happy in her life and if she asked him to, he would turn around and leave her to it. For once in his life, it wasn't about what he wanted, it was about what she needed, and if she needed him to fuck right off and disappear forever again, then that's what he would do. He owed her that and so much more.

He went into the diner attached to the truck stop and sat at the counter and ordered a cup of coffee. When it was empty, he motioned to the waitress and she came with the pot. Her fingernails were chipped.

"You want anything to eat?"

"I wouldn't mind a bite of you."

"Wow. I've never heard that one before."

He drank the coffee slow. He was in no hurry. Truckers chattered in a nearby booth.

"I won't get home until Thanksgiving."

"The money isn't at home."

"Amen."

Amen.

He took his third cup to go and left a five-dollar bill.

Back in the car, he rolled down the windows to release the baked air. His head was beginning to hurt again. He drank the rest of the water and massaged his eyebrows with his palms. He was exhausted. He didn't remember the date. All he knew was tomorrow he went back to L.A. and he could sleep until it was time to leave again. That's all he had to do, that and go see Red. Hopefully the cruise ships came through. He knew the guy at Carnival liked him. It was on Red. Red hated the boats. He called them "a retirement home for hacks." The "AARP"—the

American Association for Retired Prop-acts. It wasn't like that any-more. Billy Ray knew lots of boat guys and some of them were still funny. Phil Palisoul, Black Louis Johnson—they did boats and they were as funny as anyone. Besides, Billy Ray didn't give a shit what Red thought. It was easy for Red to be judgmental from behind a desk. Red wasn't the one driving to Spokane from Calgary in freezing rain. Red never had to check his mattress for bedbugs. The road was built for young men, the hungry and excited. Billy Ray deserved better. The boats were easy work and the money—forget about it. Five days, five hours, three grand plus travel and in the downtime, a life of leisure on a floating buffet. Fuck Red. What did he know about integrity? He rep-resented ventriloquists. Integrity and fifty cents can buy you a phone call. Stability though . . . Just show him where to sign.

In the distance, faintly, like an echo of an echo, a train whistle blew. Billy Ray started the car.

On the highway again, Billy Ray put on the Broncos game and cruised in the right lane doing five over the limit. Traffic was light and consisted predominantly of tractor trailers. Billy Ray passed them be-fore he got too close. It was best to give them plenty of room. The road curved and suddenly he was driving directly into the sun. Even with sunglasses, the daystar burnt holes in his vision. He tried to blink them away by shutting his eyes tight but the imprints persisted; orbs of pure white floated across the blackness like sparks.

He knew Olivia's address and he knew she lived in Old Town be-cause she lived on the same block as the house in which she was raised, the house where they celebrated every Christmas, Thanksgiving and Easter, a modest ranch-style home her father bought on the G.I. Bill. Olivia loved her family and her family tolerated Billy Ray. Their mid-western roots were too strong to allow them to be naked with their disapproval. They asked him the same questions at every gathering and in between answering them Billy Ray slipped away to drink whiskey in the bathroom and smoke cigarettes in the garage. During the divorce, her mother died, "probably of happiness," he joked. Olivia didn't find it funny. She stopped laughing toward the end. That's when he knew it was over.

Since the divorce was finalized, they'd seen each other twice: Jeremiah's high school graduation and Walker's wedding. On both occasions, she'd maintained decorum even when he tried to hurt her. Billy Ray attended the wedding with a girl Jeremiah's age: Yvette, an actress from Long Beach whose interests included white witchcraft, Valium abuse and borderline personality disorder. Yvette was his midlife crisis, a piece of all-expenses-paid arm candy who, when Billy Ray broke up with her, keyed the word LIAR into the door of his Thunderbird. Even he couldn't stand Yvette, but she filled out a dress and she didn't object when he asked her to watch him masturbate. He courted her with the specific intention of making Olivia jealous, but she greeted the girl with grace and charm, even laughing when Yvette described her dress as "quaint."

In the wedding photos, Billy Ray and Olivia stand next to their son. Olivia is beaming, radiant, ever the proud mother. The picture of elation with her arm around Walker, her smile swallows half her face. She is beautiful. She pulls focus from the bride. Beside her, Billy Ray's hollow eyes refuse the light. They are a shark's eyes, black and beady, and they stare out empty above a strained smile. He appears disingenuous, captive, his forced grin like that of a man in a mugshot whose jailer just told him to smile. It is clear that one of them is overjoyed to be in the photo and one of them is heartbroken to no longer be in this family. His despair is palpable even captured on film. Their son looks tired. When the photo is developed, he doesn't have it framed.

FORT COLLINS 21

CHEYENNE WY 67

He was having doubts.

In an hour, he could be in Cheyenne, frozen Coors in hand, sniffing around the roughnecks for the go powder that kept the rigs moving.

Maybe he would meet someone, have fun, feel less alone. Maybe he would drink himself brave enough to lie down on the train tracks. Either sounded better than this ambush. The more he considered his plan—or lack thereof—the more it seemed like so much shit: *Hello Olivia. Remember me? The man you cut out like cancer? I'm here to rip open your stitches and poke around in the wound. You'll feel better afterward. Trust me. I promise.*

Olivia was bad at confrontation. She got messy. Tears. Violence. She had the mean in her. He could see her throwing a coffee mug at his head or lunging at him with a garden tool. She'd taken swings at him during their tenure, busted his lip with an ashtray once. Anything was possible when she felt cornered. He never held it against her. It was just more proof she cared.

He rolled down the window, filling the car with new air, bright and clean and rich with the loam smell of industrial agriculture. The wind made a storm of the paper trash polluting the passenger floorboards, kicking up a flurry of receipts and napkins before sucking the flotsam out the window. Turning his face to the incoming air, he allowed the wind to lash his face. The barrage pulled his mind off the looming task and for a moment his anxiety abated and he was present entirely, alone in the bitter echo chamber of underlying pessimism that he feared deep down was his true personality. This was a waste of time, he thought, but so is everything. At least this way he could say he tried. It was going to be unpleasant and it was going to hurt but the good news was she already hated him—even he couldn't make it worse. The totality of her disdain was a positive. Rarely did he know exactly where he stood with people. The awareness gave him strength. Knowing the odds allowed him to play to his outs. He strangled the steering wheel until his fingers went numb. None of this matters, he assured himself, and nothing has for eleven years.

On the day she told him she wanted a divorce, he'd flown in red-eye from Madison, Wisconsin; he was still drunk from the night before. Olivia, shattered by the conversation with the father of the waitress in

Miami, was living with the boys at her sister's. They'd tried couples therapy but the sessions were utter failures. Billy Ray blamed it on the therapist, a hippy-dippy Phish-head from Boulder who alluded to his famous clientele by their initials and talked in the convoluted buzz-words that peppered the titles of the books that he wrote. The lynchpin of his system was something called "emotional excavation," a series of brutal inquests that only served to remind Olivia that her husband had always been an asshole. Forgotten transgressions were brought to the surface and Billy Ray spent the majority of each $700 hour tied to the whipping post, apologizing for mistakes from ten years ago while Olivia emptied boxes of Kleenex and the therapist repeated, "You're hearing her, but are you listening?" On the ride home from an especially ugly session (which included the remembrance of a forgotten birthday in 1991, his long history of mocking her brother's speech impediment and the multiple times he promised their sons he would quit smoking), Billy Ray expressed his frustration thusly: "He's got me on the fucking cross, Liv, and you're handing him the nails. You and that hack won't quit until I'm begging on my goddamn knees. Is that what you want? I can do that. Just tell me. I know I fucked up. I don't need to be reminded. We don't need new evidence. I'm red-handed. I plead guilty. So why don't we skip the trial and proceed straight to sentencing? That way I can get to work on my fucking appeal." They attended no more sessions after that.

On the day she told him she wanted a divorce, he drove straight from the airport to pick up the boys for soccer practice. He arrived twenty minutes late, blamed it on a baggage snafu and rushed his sons to the park in Englewood while sipping whiskey and 7 Up from a Big Gulp cup. When they'd separated, Olivia spared the boys the details at Billy Ray's request. Walker, his mother's champion, had eavesdropped on enough of their arguments to know that whatever transpired, it was definitely his father's fault, and he sided with Olivia. He'd said little to his father since they'd moved out, but Jeremiah was too young to understand what was happening. He was accustomed to his father being gone most of the time and staying at his aunt's felt like an extended sleepover. He talked excitedly the entire drive, announcing the breed of every dog they passed and when they arrived at the park, after Billy Ray promised them post-practice Dairy Queen, Jeremiah gave his father a long hug. While the boys scrimmaged, Billy Ray sat down in the grass and chain-smoked until practice was over. Then the three Schafers got soft-serve and ate it in the store because he didn't trust them with ice cream in the car.

On the day she told him she wanted a divorce, Billy Ray remembered Olivia was wearing a peasant blouse with the sleeves rolled up and a pair of cutoff jean shorts. He remembered noticing the tone of the muscles wound around her arms, her tightly packed quads. She had been working in her sister's garden and the planting had raised a thin sheen of sweat that plastered her bangs to her forehead. She looked healthy and vital and unlike him. She came to the car and told the boys to go inside because she and Daddy needed to talk and he remembered receiving her use of the word "Daddy" as a good sign. Before she climbed in the car, she patted the dirt off her and he thanked her and she smiled queerly like the sun was in her eyes and she told him to drive and he said where and she said it didn't matter. She looked out the window as he drove, away from him, and he watched her in the side-mirror out of the corner of his eye. Around her neck she wore a bandana bandit-style. She always complained that her neck was too masculine, lamenting the coils of muscle that stood as pronounced and sharp as vertical collar bones, but he loved the length of it, the elegance. Between her neck and her shoulder blade existed a declivity just big enough for his face. It was his private space; of all of her, he missed that expanse the most. As she often did when doing housework, she'd tied her hair back and as she stared out at the passing starter homes she absently twirled the tip of the pony around her finger. He'd always described her hair as brown but he saw now, as she pulled her hair tight and let it relax, that the color changed in the sunlight from chestnut to dark honey and back again. She smelled like soil and Dove deodorant.

I love you, he thought, *and I abandoned you. Please dear God let me find you again.* He wanted to touch her, to taste her, to feel her skin, to know her warmth, to apologize without words, but he'd forfeited tenderness long ago. Instead they rode down the side streets saying nothing, Billy Ray afraid to speak while the woman whose love he let atrophy gathered the courage to begin.

On the day she told him she wanted a divorce, finally, loud as birth in the bloated silence, Olivia cleared her throat. She turned to face him and he saw she had been crying. The tears cut streaks down her dusty cheeks. Eyes wide, lips drawn white, she looked confident, certain. He knew whatever she was about to say would define them. He held his breath.

"I've been thinking," she said. "I've been thinking a lot." Then she began to weep.

FORT COLLINS NEXT THREE EXITS

Passing Harmony Road he dropped his speed five below the limit before the truck weigh station where the state troopers roamed. After Prospect, the interstate shrunk by a lane. He checked his blind spot, flipped on his blinker and took the last exit.

Once a dedicated farm road, the state added the exit to Highway 50 in the nineties to accommodate the beer trucks entering and exiting from the Anheuser-Busch brewery. Standing a mile back from the roadway, the massive facility, which looked like a cream-colored prison, dominated the horizon. From the brewhouse, new clouds belched into the bright blue void, making the day smell like burnt oats. At first whiff, the smell set Billy Ray into an intense panic as he interpreted the toasted odor to be the first sign of a stroke. Terrified, he pulled over to the shoulder. He knew the typifiers. He checked the rearview mirror to see if either side of his face was sagging while talking as fast as he could with both of his arms raised. "I'm talking. Talking. Talking. Here we go. Time to talk. No slurring, no worries. Talky talk. One two three four

eight seven six five. Five alive. Drink and drive. Time to thrive and realize. I'm talking," until he realized it was just the stink of cooking Budweiser. Relieved, Billy Ray exhaled sharply, his alarm replaced by
foolishness. He smiled. "Pull it together, old man." Then he stepped out
of the car and fed a cigarette to his nerves.

Her house wasn't far from here. He recognized a barn in the field to
his left and he knew there was a gas station in less than a mile and at
that gas station he turned right and then left and then left and somewhere on that street his ex-wife lived her new life.

In the ditch, a pack of late-season sunflowers, a few taller than him,
tottered in the breeze. Billy Ray dug in the glove box until he found his
pocketknife, severed three of the fat flowers and laid them in the back
seat. He sat on the trunk and finished his cigarette and lit another.
When the driver of a passing minivan gave him a wave, Billy Ray
flipped her the bird and laughed at the juvenility.

He reapplied deodorant. Spritzed cologne. He applied paste to his
toothbrush before he remembered he'd been drinking mouthwash and
put it away. He stretched his arms out to the side and moved them in
small circles. He kicked his heels like showtime. He needed to be ready.
He needed to be sharp. The feeling in his stomach reminded him of
performing on live television. Alright, he thought. "Okay then." He returned to the car.

The road had been widened recently and the construction was unfinished. In the left lane, oncoming vehicles drove on fresh asphalt, the
tarmac wet-looking in its blackness, darker than any color in nature.
Billy Ray drove slowly, navigating an alligator-cracked roadway of un-
paved red dirt and feeling the bump of every rut in his lower back. The
gas station was shuttered, the parking lot eaten up by crabgrass. He
turned right past a herd of doofy alpacas, then he turned left and left
again on Friar Tuck Avenue. Déjà vu consumed him fully. The houses
were as he remembered them: squat, asymmetrical, ubiquitous. All
that was new was the paint and the models of cars in the driveways.
Walker learned how to ride a bike on this street: Christmas Day, 1997,

Billy Ray holding the seat while the boy gathered balance, confidence, speed, both of them squealing, running behind until he couldn't keep up and he let go and the boy drifted away. Being here tugged a string tied to a long-dormant sadness, a sentimental melancholy. Obsolescence. It felt like getting old. The continuation of life, he suddenly understood, was the ultimate betrayal.

He hoped she offered him a glass of something stronger than wine.

The house numbers were painted on the curb. He knew the address from years of writing it on an envelope. 719. 721. 725. He stopped the car in front of a tidy split-level shed-roofed house with porthole windows and a birdbath in the yard. Topiaried bushes framed a brick walkway that led from the sidewalk to the stately front door. Parked beneath a basketball hoop attached to the garage, a seafoam Subaru with a bumper sticker that read WOMEN FOR HILLARY looked as if it had just been cleaned. He looked up and down the block. It wasn't the largest house but it was the most well maintained—classic Olivia. He thought it would be smaller—hoped, actually, prayed. This was a castle compared to where he lived. He wanted worse for her. He wanted vinyl siding or Navajo white, plastic storm windows, a battered screen door. But no—even the lawn was perfect. This was a nice house in a nice neighborhood where a nice woman raised her nice sons. Happy fucking birthday and the Fourth of July. Did they know where the money came from? Did they know that this house cost exactly half of his heart? He caught himself: no, you don't. If you were wearing a hat it would be in your hands. Instead of an altar to his failures, he tried to see the house for what it really was: the building in which his sons grew into men. He was glad to know that the divorce provided enough for his sons to grow up in a place like this. It didn't matter if they knew where the money came from; honestly, it was better if they forgot. This house was more than he had as a child and for that he could be proud.

He collected the sunflowers and the Pretenders CDs and double-checked his hair and, after downing a stiff swig of Listerine, he got out of the car and put on the overshirt.

The neighborhood, torpid in the malaise of Sunday afternoon, was quiet and still. The street was empty besides this trespasser. Even alone he got the feeling he was taking up too much space. He took a deep breath of air that smelled of meat cooked with charcoal. *Well*, he thought, and that was all. Well.

Crossing the street, he hoped to be run over and crushed and saved. No part of him wanted to proceed, but still, there he was, stepping up on the sidewalk, his legs autonomous of his fear. "Remember," he muttered as he pulled at his collar, "you're the bad guy." The recessed door created a small veranda she'd decorated with a large pot of lavender asters flanked by a pair of ceramic gnomes, the pair of them portly and still smiling despite their chipped and broken faces. The welcome mat read WELCOME. It looked clean and unused.

Through the windows, the house appeared dark and empty but from behind the door he heard the noise of a television. Olivia the conservationist—she never left the TV on when she wasn't home. "Fuck," he said. "Fuckin' *al*right." He pressed the doorbell but it made no sound. He tried it again: nothing. Reluctantly, he knocked—shave and a haircut—on the red painted wood. The bark of a dog, the skitter of claws on hardwood.

"Oh yes, Gordy. Get 'em." *That* voice. "Get 'em, buddy. That's right. Go get 'em." Like a memory, it came closer, as did the paws.

Billy Ray, resigned, nodded. Pushing up on his toes he watched through the transom as a wiggling puff of curly white fur scurried down a long hallway followed by her, by Olivia, HER, Olivia, wearing sweatpants and shoeless and brushing her bangs out of her eyes, Olivia, formerly Olivia Schafer née Prudholm now Prudholm again, pulling her shirt down, smoothing it flat over the stomach where his sons had lived, Olivia Svetlana Prudholm—they said she went by Lana now—Lana Prudholm, coming right at him, walking down the hallway of *her* house, cooing after *her* dog, condescending, maternal—*her* voice, the voice he heard in his dreams: "Oh yes, Gordy. Oh yes, you killer. Get 'em, buddy. Go get 'em. Tear 'em to shreds."

"There she is," he muttered.

The door opened.

There she was.

"Hey there, Liv."

She squinted, her mouth hung open. Billy Ray smiled, aiming for harmless and friendly but appearing instead like he had just now shit his pants. The dog, a little poodle-terrier-looking thing, jumped up on his shins and Billy Ray, saying "And hello to you, sweetness," bent down to pet it, but, at the reach of his hand, the dog hid behind her feet and growled from the back of its throat and Billy Ray stood up and faced his ex-wife. Olivia looked puzzled, contemplative, like she was trying to remember a piece of trivia, like she wasn't sure if her answer was correct.

"I was in the neighborhood," he offered weakly. "Here." He held forth the flowers and she received them without saying anything. "And check it out"—he flicked his wrist like *ta-da*—"Pretenders." She took the CD, handling it as if it were boobytrapped. "It was only ten bucks," he explained. "It's got all the hits."

"Walker put all my music on the computer."

"You could listen to it in the car."

She stared at him.

"Music always sounds better in the car."

"What are you doing here, Billy?"

"Like I said, I was in the neighborhood and—I don't know. I saw Jeremiah yesterday."

"He told me."

"Oh. What'd he say?"

"He said he saw you."

"He asked if I was dying."

"He said you weren't."

"I'm not."

"Too bad."

"Have you met his girlfriend?"

"Yes."

"She's pretty. I think they're in love."

Olivia itched the back of her leg with the toe of her other foot. The dog sniffed Billy Ray's ankle. "What are you . . . How long have you been here?"

"I just pulled up."

"I mean in Colorado."

"Since Friday. I'm supposed to be working Wits."

"Oh. Right. Grace told me."

"No one told me."

"Told you what?"

"That the freezer broke."

"The freezer?"

"The freezer broke at Wits. Don canceled the shows."

"Oh. Poor Don."

"He'll be fine." Billy Ray squatted down and let the dog lick his fingers. "He told me you were going by Lana."

"That's what they call me at school."

"Coach Lana."

"It's better than Coach Prude."

The dog's tongue felt like a slug on the back of his knuckles. Fur overgrew its eyes, rendering the pup just a mouth and a nose. Billy Ray scratched its haunch and the dog's leg started to thump. It reminded Billy Ray of air guitar. Scratching its belly caused the dog to roll over and expose itself. "There's my ChapStick," he said. Billy Ray looked up at Olivia and smiled, hoping to parlay his effectiveness with the dog, but her face maintained its veneer of impatient distaste. *Come on,* he thought. *Work with me.* The small talk made him nervous. This wasn't sustainable. He wanted to be asked inside. He felt unacquainted out here, lesser than: I'm not selling magazines. "What's the dog's name?"

"Gordy."

"Hello, Gordy. You're just a little coconut, aren't you?"

"What do you want, Billy?"

He stood up. At his full height, her eyes met his sternum. Without makeup, her long hair streaked with veins of silver-gray, she looked tired but not sleepy. She seemed reduced somehow, lacking substance, frail, but she was still beautiful. It was a hard thing to stay beautiful. He hoped she knew. "I don't want anything."

"You drove a long way for nothing."

"I go back to L.A. tomorrow. I don't know. I just thought—I don't know. I feel bad."

She sneered. "*You* feel bad."

"Yeah."

"Poor thing."

"That's not—"

"Don't expect me to cheer you up."

"I feel bad about it. How I did you."

Olivia closed her eyes and opened them, not blinking but purposeful. Through her nose she exhaled loudly then crossed her arms, the flowers under one arm, the CD under the other. She leaned against the doorframe. "How much have you had to drink today?"

He held his forefinger an inch from his thumb. "Just a scootch. I had a long night."

"Your nights are so long it's a miracle you ever see the sun."

"I'm getting better."

"Right. What happened to your face?"

"I fell."

"You fell?" Olivia's eyes rolled back inside her skull. "From how many stories?"

Billy Ray stepped backward, put his hands on his hips and turned away from her. He hated that she thought she had to act this way. "You're making this hard," he said to the street. An airplane raked a white line across the sky.

"Fuck you, Billy. Don't get me started on hard."

"You don't have to yell."

"You don't get to tell me what I have to do."

"I should just go."

"I don't give a shit what you do. I worried about what you did for thirteen years. Worried sick. Is he alright? Is he okay? Is he alive? Is he dead in a ditch? I worried every night you were out on the road, worried until I couldn't sleep, but I worried worse when you got home because I saw what you were turning into. I wasted thirteen years of my goddamn life worried over you because I thought that's what love was. Guess what? I'm not worried anymore."

"I'm sorry—"

"Fuck your sorries, Billy. You were always sorry. Motherfucker, if I had a nickel—'I'm sorry, sugar.' That was your fucking catchphrase. You should have put it on a T-shirt. You could have bought another house." Her composure was waning. Slapping the side of the house to accentuate her sentences, she snarled in an exaggerated whisper. Her eyes were wet, from fury or lamentation he couldn't tell: she was ready to break. He'd forgotten how anger put the sailor in her tongue. They'd tried to implement a swear jar when Walker was in kindergarten, but she kept filling it up too fast. She made a fun bit out of it around the house wherein, whenever she cussed, she would slap her hand over her mouth in faux embarrassment and say, "Did I just swear? Shit. I thought I fucking did. Goddamnit!," stringing curses while Walker kept a running tally on his fingers of exactly how much she owed. It always got a laugh out of Billy Ray and the boys but she did it too much; then it wasn't funny anymore.

Billy Ray was unsure how to continue. He wasn't good on defense; he preferred to serve and control the tempo of the volley. If she kept it up with the hardcase, he was bound to slip up and go somewhere too far. He didn't want to say anything. Forgetting about her disdain for the act, he dug out his cigarettes and sparked one. Puffing tough, he snorted out the smoke like a bull and stared up at the sky.

Olivia waved her hand in front of her, fanning the smoke away from her face. "Billy Ray Schafer's got nothing to say. Wow. I should have bought a Powerball."

"I'm thinking," he said.

"Don't pull a muscle. And don't ash on the porch."

"I didn't come up here to fight, Liv."

"Don't call me that. I always hated when you called me that."

"Alright, *Lana*."

"Fuck you."

"I know. You said that."

"What the fuck did you think was gonna happen coming up here? Did you think it was gonna be cake and ice cream? Even you're not that dumb. You ruined me, Billy Ray, you broke me right in fucking half, and since then I've worked hard to pick up the pieces of me I can find, the parts I can identify, and I've persevered and held it together and did my best for the two boys you let grow up alone. I took care of them and you know what? They turned out great. They're smart and loving and beautiful—and it was easy, because before them, I took care of you— you, the drunk, the cokehead, the egomaniac, the womanizing bastard who couldn't keep his dick in his pants—I took care of you because I *loved you,* you son of a bitch. I loved you and for thirteen years— thirteen fucking years, the good years, the ones you don't get back— I dealt with your mood swings, your mania, the complaining—Jesus Christ—'Why didn't I get this? Why did he get that?'—I coddled you, damnit. I changed your fucking diaper. I was there for the highs and I was there for the lows, every one of them. I lived my life filtered through you. And while I was taking care of you, no one was taking care of me, and now I can't have a relationship, I can't go on dates. I won't let anyone close to me because I forgot how to be soft. You sucked the soft right out of me. Now I'm hard. I'm brittle. And it's all because of you. So when you show up out of nowhere drunk in the afternoon, don't act surprised when I don't invite you in for tea."

At this time she began to shake. In her armpit, the flowers quivered, shedding petals. From her glassy eyes tears escaped. She buried her face into her folded arms and all he could see was the top of her head and the tip of her nose. Her shoulders moved up and down. Standing there, her arms wrapped tight like a straitjacket, he wouldn't have been surprised if she shot off like a rocket or exploded into shrapnel, so was the intensity of the emotion burning off of her. It was like waves of heat. Billy Ray's instinct said to reach for her, to bring her into him and hold her there, but she was likely to kill him if he did. He wouldn't fight it. That would be good, proper. Tit for tat. And as she destroyed him, he'd go out with his fingers crossed that she got away with it. Because she would get away with it if justice were real.

He pulled his hankie and held it out: "Here."

She eyed it like it was a snake but she took it and emptied her nose inside of it and held it balled in her hand with just a corner exposed as she continued to shake. Below her, the dog sniffed at the gnomes. He seemed indifferent, like this was nothing new. *Do something,* thought Billy Ray, but the dog was like him—powerless—and Billy Ray understood she was completely alone.

"I don't know why I'm crying," she said.

"I do."

"Crying never fixed nothing."

"There's no fixing some things."

"I didn't know all that was still in there."

"It's good."

"No, it isn't."

"It's good it's out. You weren't lying." He flicked his cigarette to the sidewalk. "I was shit. I know it, too."

"Don't."

"If I can't apologize, at least let me say it." His stomach was tight. He wished he had something to drink. "You're a good woman. You didn't deserve me."

Shaking her head, she dabbed her face with the hankie and handed it back to him. "No one deserves anything. You just get what you get. Stay here." Then she went inside the house.

Not knowing what to do with himself, Billy Ray squatted down to be nearer the dog. His knees popped with the effort. The joints sounded like gravel. *I should go,* he thought. One of the dog's eyes was green, the other blue. Billy Ray itched under his collar. "You're the new baby, huh?" The dog was small enough to fit in a microwave. *Maybe I should get a dog,* he thought. But then he remembered that he was never home and that a dog was one more thing he couldn't have.

Her footsteps were loud in the hall. She returned with a tumbler poured full of ice and wine and a bottle of beer.

"Here." She handed him the bottle. "I couldn't find a church key."

"Two Hearted," he said, reading the label aloud. "Never heard of it."

"The boys like it."

Holding the bottle by the neck, Billy Ray wedged his lighter between the bottlecap and his index finger and pried the beer open. The beer was sour, but in a pleasant way. He thanked her and put the cap in his pocket.

Gently, Olivia toed the dog in the house and shut the door then sat on the lip of the planter pot, leaning forward with her elbows on her knees. "I'd invite you in, but I don't want to."

Billy Ray nodded. "That's okay. It's nice out here."

"I was watching the Broncos game."

"I was listening on the drive up."

"What a mess."

"Is it over?"

"It's over. We lost. That's why it's so quiet."

"Damn."

"We're just not a good team. There's no chemistry."

"We need a quarterback."

"We need a miracle."

A family, two little girls and a man and a woman, rode past the front of the house on bicycles. One of the girls pushed hard on a tricycle while the adults, in matching sweatsuits, worked together on a tandem. The eldest of the girls rode out in front of the pack. "Hurry up," she called, circling back to her family. "We're gonna miss it." Then she was off again.

"Walker is having a baby."

"You know?"

"*You* know?"

"Jerm told me."

"It's gonna be a little girl."

"Uh-oh."

"That's what he said."

"Girls are different than boys."

"I'm excited. I've had my fill of boys."

"Makes sense."

Olivia held her glass up to the sky. "They say it's going to snow."

"It was hot today."

"Fall in Colorado. You know what they say: if you don't like the weather, just wait five minutes."

"They say that everywhere."

"That doesn't make it not true."

"I forgot how pretty the Novembers are."

"I hate it. Look. It's already getting dark."

Billy Ray leaned against the house and crossed his legs at the ankles. They sipped their drinks, quiet for a while. The night was setting in, erasing another day. As the sun closed in on the earth, the sky grew darker, from an almost colorless lavender overhead to, skirting the horizon, a saturated electric orange, the color of fires and fruit. He looked at Olivia's face. Her eyes were closed. Her lips purple with wine. She probably had to work tomorrow. He got the feeling that she was waiting for him to say something. He let the silence go on until it got weird.

"You been getting the checks?" he asked.

"You'd know if I wasn't."

"When's the baby due?"

"End of April."

"Spring chicken."

"He's freaking out. Have you talked to him?"

"Not since the wedding. And we didn't talk much there."

"You know how he is."

"No, not really."

"He was older. Jeremy has different memories."

"They're grown now."

"Jeremy likes to say he is."

"He sure is a handsome kid. He's got that long muscle. White people don't usually get that long muscle."

"Here we go."

"I'm just saying."

Billy Ray tilted up the last of the beer and tapped the bottle against the side of the house, hoping she'd respond to the hollowness with a fresh one. His bladder was full but he wasn't about to ask to use the facilities. This was fine. He could hold it. On the street, snow began to fall. "You remember when Jeremy had to dress up as M.L.K. for that history project?"

"I still don't know where he got that shoe polish."

"What a knucklehead."

"He almost got expelled."

"I wish I had a picture of that. I don't have any pictures at all." Billy Ray pulled out another cigarette and tapped it on his lighter. "Do you remember when Walker—"

"Don't do that."

"What?"

"I don't want to play 'do you remember.' I haven't forgot."

"Okay," he said. He'd pay her for another beer. "I went to Drifter's the other day."

"How was it?"

"Tasted the same."

"Did you get a Frito pie?"

"Yeah. And a shake."

"I loved those Frito pies."

He opened his mouth to say yep or you sure did or some other simple acknowledgment that he remembered her affinity for corn chips dressed with red chili, but instead, without his consent, usurping preconception, the words escaping like captives toward daylight, he said: "I loved you, you know. I really did."

Amazed, her mouth ajar, she stared at him, looking through him, peering back in time, back before now, before before, *way* back, trying to remember when his head was pompadoured and his cigarettes were rolled up in his sleeve, back when he made her laugh until she cried, back when they were happy and unfractured and his muttonchops were still only sideburns, trying to picture what they were like, what she was like, trying hard to envision *them*, trying because, despite everything he'd become and contrary to his actions for the last fifteen years, he was right: he had loved her. She'd felt it, she'd known him when he was sweet. His was a powerful love; she spent a decade as a satellite trapped in its orbit and when the gravity became too weak to hold her, she drifted away, not just from him but from herself. Yes, she hated him, and no, she would never be with him again, but there was a time when he was everything, when she planned after death to be buried beside him, to be consumed by the same worms. What happened to that man? She would never know. It was impossible. They were all that way—comedians. She didn't pretend to understand them. All the ones she knew were mutated. Something to do with the pressure: it changed them, like the fish that adapt to survive at the bottom of the sea. She saw it eat him up. There was nothing to be done: he was good at it. You could say what you want about him, but he was excellent at his job. His talent was both the cause and cure. With stand-up, Billy Ray was only happy onstage. He lived for the hour; the rest of his life was just filler. Abeyance. In the face of such nothing, he tried to feel something else, filling the empty times with chemicals and imprudence, but nothing compared. The thrill was as inimitable as it was ephemeral. *Mamas, don't let your babies grow up to be comics.* Stand-up—his passion and her albatross. He was married to comedy before he was married to her.

It was the weight that hung perpetually over their relationship, dangling on a strand as thin as his ego. It was too much. Eventually they were crushed by the shadow and now they existed as ghosts.

"I know you did," she said.

"I'm sorry."

"I know."

"Okay."

"That's what made it so hard."

With that she finished the wine in her glass and pushed to her feet. "I have to work in the morning."

"Yeah, I've got an early flight."

"From DIA?"

"Sí, señorita."

"Well vaya con dios."

"Where should I put this?" He held up the bottle.

"Here," she said and he handed it to her.

"You think I could have one more for the road?"

"Sure. Hold on." The dog was waiting for her when she opened the door. "No walk tonight, buddy. It's snowing." The dog reared up on its hind legs, bringing its forepaws together. It looked like it was clapping.

Alone again, Billy Ray watched the snow fall. It was picking up. Already a thin film of crystalline white shimmered like powdered diamonds. Refracted in the surface, silvering light painted phantom rainbows atop the accumulation, turning the street into a glinting borealis of swirling pink and purple. He wondered what Walker would call his daughter. He hoped he would name her after his mother. It was good luck to name a baby after a saint.

Olivia returned holding two bottles of beer and a couple slices of pizza wrapped in paper towel. "Here," she said.

"You didn't have to do that."

"No shit. I'm not gonna eat it. It's old."

"Alright." He was famished. He stacked the slices and took a bite out of both at once.

"And here." She pulled a photograph from under her arm. "You said you didn't have any pictures."

In the photo, Billy Ray stands shirtless in a swimming pool holding his sons aloft, one in each arm. The boys are young—Jeremiah sports water wings—and dressed in trunks. Pink with sunburn, Billy Ray's body has yet to go to seed. His chest is solid and pert, his arms are thick and defined; wrapped around his sons, they make the boys appear even smaller than they are, more precious. Jeremiah, either shy or asleep, buries his face in his father's biceps but Walker hams it up, smiling a big goofy grin that is minus two of its front teeth; the tip of his tongue pokes through the gap. Only Billy Ray looks into the camera. His eyes are clear, his smile sure and relaxed. Everything about him says *I got this*. They are ideal. They could be actors in a commercial for a water park or term life insurance: *Who will take care of them when you're gone?* Reflected in the bottom left corner, Olivia's face hides behind a camera. Only her mouth is visible. She is smiling.

"Where is this?" he asked.

"Glenwood Springs. I think it was Memorial Day."

"Look at that body. I should go to prison more often."

"You can have it."

"You—thank you. And for the pizza and everything."

"Like I said, I'm not gonna eat it."

"Alright then. I better get ahead of this snow."

"It's supposed to keep coming."

"Damn."

"I hope we get buried."

Billy Ray turned to leave but then he turned back. "Will you let me know when the baby comes? I'd like to send a card."

"Sure," she said.

"Maybe I'll fly out."

"Maybe," she said.

"Okay then." And with that he left.

On the sidewalk, the smooth soles of his boots struggled for traction in the snow. "Easy," he said. "Easy." After a few precarious steps, he switched to sliding his feet along the pavement, moving through the wet slush like a skater on a pond and hugging the beer bottles tight to his chest.

The wiper blades easily removed the snow from the windshield. As the car warmed up, he chewed pizza and marveled at the version of himself in the picture she gave him. "That's it," he said. "Tomorrow I'm doing push-ups." He secured the photograph in the visor and nipped a bit of the mouthwash before cracking one of the beers. The only light in Olivia's house was the pulse of the TV. He hoped his son named the baby after her.

The neighborhood was abandoned at this hour, the only sound the crunch of the snow beneath his tires. Driving through the emptiness, Billy Ray hummed to himself, enjoying the notion that the rest of humanity had been seized by a sudden rapture, leaving him alone as the last man on earth. The evening had played out much better than he expected. She hadn't attacked him with gardening tools and he'd avoided saying cunt. *Progress,* he thought. He'd achieved what he set out to do, allowing her an opportunity to vent directly to his face, to drain her residual poison on the cause of her ailment, and he'd managed to keep his mouth shut, to listen, to accept, all while avoiding the woe-is-me martyring he'd relied on in the past. Not once did he employ the clichéd rhetoric of the vilified breadwinner: *I work hard to provide for this family and this is the thanks I get?* How many times had he screamed those fifteen words? The refrain was the bedrock of his defense because, at the time, that was how he saw himself—underappreciated, sacrificial, selfless. But now, seeing with vision afforded men who live wasted lives, he understood his former position to be a fiction concocted to allow himself, the legendary wild man Billy Ray Schafer, to continue to act with impunity despite his growing responsibilities.

In truth, he booked two hundred plus days a year because, at the root of it, he liked his job and further, he was afraid to say no. The travel, the party, the admiration of strangers, it was all very exciting for a man that grew up in a small and violent world. And yes, he loved the income and he got off on dominating crowds, but of all the trappings of his lifestyle, he most coveted the sense of validation that came with success. After so many years of turmoil, from criminal to prisoner to felon, it was vindicating to find a home in a semi-legitimate industry; once he tasted self-worth, there was no going back.

Of his many titles, more than husband, father, homeowner, or sane, it was most important to Billy Ray that he be defined as a comedian, and a good comedian at that. The pursuit of that denotation decimated three innocent lives and, in maintaining it, wounded countless civilians. And here, in the end, it was the only name he had. His life's work destroyed him, left him embattled and bitter, an infamous ronin with no spine and a weak heart. There would be plenty of open seats at his funeral, and of those that attended, he doubted many would shed a tear. But still, despite the carnage both foreign and domestic, when he reflected on the events that comprised the total of his life, beneath the overwhelming regret, Billy Ray felt a strange and reluctant pride. As a father and a husband and a man, he was an undiluted failure, but as a comedian—in the span of their lives, few men are afforded the opportunity to put a price on their soul. In a lifetime pockmarked by failure and gluttony and greed, he was grateful to be of the minority allowed to choose their own worth.

"A girl," he said. "We're having a girl."

At the main road, he pulled over to answer the call of his bladder. Behind the forgotten gas station and out of sight of the highway, Billy Ray unzipped himself, carved his initials in the snow and underlined them—B R S—three steaming letters spelling I EXIST, at least temporarily. When he finished, he lit a cigarette and walked out a few steps into an undeveloped clearing that filled in the space between the gas station and Olivia's neighborhood. Across the field of undisturbed white, the houses appeared small and inconsequential, two-dimensional, like the backdrop to a film set in which nobody lived. Above him, behind the waves of snowflakes falling like ticker tape, the Big Dipper pointed at Polaris, and from that brightest of stars, Billy Ray divined true north.

Standing in the stalks of broken crabgrass, alternating lungfuls of hot smoke with cold night, Billy Ray swelled with an unfamiliar optimism. A baby was coming, his granddaughter. With her arrived a new future. Reclamation. She will be his second chance. On the day of her birth, he will be waiting, pacing the waiting room with a pocketful of cigars. From the moment he sees her his life will be different. To her he will keep every promise. To her he will never lie. In his presence, she will want for nothing. He will buy ice cream, he will purchase toys. For her he'll quit smoking. Because of her, he'll want to live. She won't know the man who destroyed her grandmother, she won't know the man her father detests, she will only know Grandpa and she will love him completely and for the rest of his days he will love her the same.

"A little baby girl," he said to the emptiness, trying unsuccessfully to thwart a creeping sanguinity. Embracing hope was dangerous. How'd the old joke go? *I'd rather get my hopes up than my dick up. At least I know if I get my hopes up, I'm definitely getting fucked.*

When his cigarette was spent, he finished his beer and tossed the bottle in the field. When it landed without a sound, he knew the drifts were getting deep.

He'd parked in a bad spot. Fighting the wet snow, it took him a few attempts to get the car moving and once he rocked it loose, he had to gun it to break through the slush. The excess speed caused the car to fishtail sharply as he turned out onto Highway 50, sending the taillights wagging across the road as the rear wheels struggled to catch on the unplowed asphalt. Billy Ray, despite his buzz, finessed the steering wheel, yanking the wheel in the direction of the skid, and the car straightened out. He drove to the interstate without further incident.

He was tired. He didn't know what else to do but drive to the airport. There, after returning the car, he could soak up free drinks in the

United Club and sleep until check-in. His flight was at 9 A.M. tomorrow. All he had was time.

The snow was unrelenting. In the tunnel of light his headlights bored in the darkness, the onslaught of swirling flakes was dizzying and hypnotic. Staring into it, his eyes began to play tricks with depth. Anything beyond fifty feet became an educated guess. It was hard to know where he was out here. He settled in the right lane and navigated by the white line that marked the shoulder of the road and listened to two men on the radio talk about aliens. They called them extraterrestrials.

"They keep saying I'm crazy, but I know what I saw, Art."

"Crazy isn't necessarily a bad thing. In a world built on lies, only madmen tell the truth."

Occasionally, drivers braver than Billy Ray cruised past in the left lane before swooping back into the right. When they pulled back in front of him, Billy Ray keyed on their taillights and followed the leader until they got too far away. He wasn't going to race to keep up. In these conditions, even sixty miles per hour was pushing it, and some of these cars must have been going seventy. Billy Ray set the cruise to fifty-five, about five miles faster than the truckers he passed. They drove with their hazards on, caravanned in long chains like elephants holding each other's tails. In times like this, he envied them their CB radios. With a CB, he could talk to drivers farther ahead and ask if it was getting better or worse.

"They weren't no taller than an infant."

"What color was their skin?"

"Gray like wax."

After fifteen minutes, he'd had enough of the snow. The constant barrage filed his nerves to a fine edge. He decided to get off at the next gas station he saw to give his eyes a break. Until then, he cracked his window for a cigarette. The wind shrieking through the thin breach drowned out the voices of the radio. He turned them up. He was interested in the things they were saying.

"Of course the government knows."

"Then why won't they tell us?"

"They're afraid of what we'll do."

"You're talking about mass hysteria."

"I think so."

"Really?"

"Imagine if the whole world found out there's no God."

Ahead of him, a tractor pulling two trailers labored in the deluge. Divided into three sections, it looked like a giant metal centipede. The truck trudged along in low gear, driving slowly to accommodate the weight of its cumbersome payload. When he got within five car lengths, Billy Ray signaled left to pass.

"So what you're saying is it's too late for us."

"We cannot be saved."

"But surely we can hope?"

Coming around the front of the truck, Billy Ray took his final drag and fed the cigarette into the narrow break in the window, but the wind refused it and threw it back into his lap. Billy Ray flailed, swatting wildly at his thighs, and his knee jerked up into the steering wheel. The car swerved left and Billy Ray yanked the wheel back to the right and the tires skidded across the snow, sending the car sliding sideways into the right lane perpendicular to the oncoming truck. Through the passenger window, the big centipede truck's headlamps filled the car with light, pure white and impossible—all the light in the world. The radiance exploded his vision and he was swallowed by the light and the infinity beyond.

He laughed.

ACKNOWLEDGMENTS

The author (me, Sam Tallent) would like to extend his sincerest gratitude

. . . to Dan Kirschen for taking the rock and doing some damage. Keep those Spirits coming, buddy. You succeeded where others failed.

. . . to Ben Greenberg for the cool Random House tote bag and making my dream come true.

. . . to Harriet Poland for enhancing my life without having to be asked.

. . . to Lee Brackstone for unleashing this book upon the world.

. . . to Dave Tallent for always being so excited about whatever I'm doing. You're a dude, Dude.

. . . to Doctor Emily Tallent for her immense patience. Thank you for sharing your life with me.

. . . to Sophia Tallent for being a woman her mother would be proud of.

. . . to Mel Cooks for being my brother and keeping Lizard warm.

. . . to Joe Hatfield for improving everything he touches.

. . . to the Fernandezes and Halverstadts for being the first to laugh at my jokes.

. . . to Richard Ingersoll for the cover art. We did it, Elizabeth.

. . . to Stanhope for championing this book and changing my life. Bingo: I'll keep the shorts short for you.

. . . to Mishka, who told me I wasn't wasting my time.

. . . to Gborie, Bobby, Lund and Charpentier for making me want to be funnier and keeping me humble, against all odds.

. . . to Wende Curtis and everyone at Comedy Works, one of the only places I ever feel at home. How has Tonya not been fired yet?

. . . to Adam Eget for talking me down, and that whole Texas crew for talking me up.

. . . to anyone who has ever sat quietly and listened to me.

. . . to all the comedians who let me sleep on their floors: we've already made it.

The author would also like to express his sincerest ingratitude to his mother, Lisbeth Patricia Tallent, for dying. What the hell, Mom?

Read on

for an excerpt from

Sam Tallent's

forthcoming novel

BRUT

AT EXACTLY NINE O'CLOCK THE FOLLOWING MORNING HE watched from the mouth of the alleyway as the silver Karmann Ghia parked in the spot reserved for L. HARRIMAN. He snuffed out his cigarette and checked the license plate against the photo of the silver Karmann Ghia. Swiped to the next photo. The driver was the man on the screen.

He was taller than he appeared in still-frame but it was him down to the suitcase and he walked with a brisk self-importance up the stairs, pausing in front of the glass door to adjust his tie in the reflection before disappearing inside. He opened the door himself and, noting this, Beaujolais grunted: no doorman.

He preferred not to operate in an office building, but the blueprints he'd been provided depicted a straightforward floor plan. Compared to his private residence, with its gates and private security patrols, this was the better option.

There was the matter of the secretary, but the dossier stated that on the third Wednesday of each month, she took an extra hour of lunch— leaving at ten and returning at noon—in order to get her teeth whitened. He often wondered who gathered this intelligence and what credentials they had, but in his seven years of arbitration, the information had never failed to be anything but precise.

There were the less pleasant options, both of them messy. Bag-and-tag was his least preferred method. Too many variables, too many opportunities for complications, like in Nebraska, but those were his orders. It was best to commit one crime at a time and, legally speaking, kidnapping was kidnapping no matter the duration: five minutes, five miles, it was all the same time.

There was also the matter of absconding cleanly with a live human being—trunks were getting smaller, people were getting bigger—an unpleasant task often involving physical brutality. In his experience, if one was going to incapacitate a target, it might as well be permanent and quick, which he considered in this instance—on the street in broad day—but there was a natural grocery store around the corner and the clientele who shopped at such places were nosy by nature, the kind of people who run toward the sound of gunshots because violence remained an abstract idea. Not that they'd be able to hear anything: the length of the suppressor was cold against his ribcage.

After they'd used each other he'd cast the man from the bar into the night and fallen immediately to sleep. At six he rose to the wake-up call and ordered a pot of coffee, two croissants, sausages, butter and marmalade, then showered and cleaned his gun while he ate (the pastries were dry).

He disassembled and then reassembled his firearm, a Beretta M9A3 joined via threaded barrel to a Wolfman silencer—his mandatory assemblage—a process that was as close as he came to meditation. He'd learned the weapon as a Marine and he valued the tools size, the heft, how the wide grip fit in his large hands. Squeezing the trigger on smaller pistols felt like crushing a bird, but the Beretta was substantial and in close quarters made for an effective bludgeon or, as he learned last week, an auger.

Once the action slid to his liking, he holstered the gun and concealed it beneath his oilskin coat and called down to the valet. He didn't have to search long for parking. A good omen, he thought, briefly. Then he remembered there was no such thing.

He rolled his balaclava into a cap with his gloved hands and crossed the quiet street. The building smelled of a chemical approximation of lavender and lemon. Two women were waiting for the elevator. He oc-

cupied himself with the building's registry until they were gone. The
stairs were concrete and his tennis shoes upon them created little
noises similar to a pug dog breathing. One, two, three flights. He
paused on the fourth with his ear to the door. The time was fourteen
past.

At fifteen past he compressed the bar on the fire door and entered a
hallway decorated on each end with potted aloe plants. Opposite the
elevator, above two chocolate leather easy chairs, a mass-market painting of a stallion in a meadow hung askew on the slate blue wall.

From the provided blueprints he knew the farthest door opened on
a receptionist's office that was currently unoccupied today due to van-
ity. Inside the office were three additional doors. The first door on the
right led to a kitchenette. The second contained a toilet. The door on
the left was where L. Harriman received his clients, and it was in front
of this door where the arbiter now stood, at seventeen past the hour,
gun in hand, safety disengaged.

The conversation on the other side of the door was muffled but one-
sided. L. Harriman was on the phone. As he fingered the safety, it occurred to him that never before had he known any part of the name of
the person he was to kill. Somehow this knowledge seemed a trespass,
a transgression greater than the act he was about to perform. To know
the surname of his target was to understand a lineage. There were previous Harrimans, potentially subsequent. Was that to whom this Harriman was speaking? A son. A daughter. Would they still be on the line
when the bullet entered his head?

He put his ear to the door. Laughter.

He took a breath and pulled the balaclava down over his face.

The door opened inward. Behind a desk sat a man who looked like
a wolf. On the man's face, as his eyes transferred the image of a masked,
gun-wielding, black-clad intruder to the parts of his brain that registered such stimuli, his lips transformed from carefree smile to open-
mouthed puzzlement to gaping gawking outraged terror in the time it
took the arbiter to level the pistol and point it at his face.

He managed one word—"But"—before a pâté of his teeth, lips and tongue exploded out the back of his skull. As the chair on which he was seated was of the wheel-mounted variety common to offices, the force of the bullet sent him skittering into the bookshelf behind him. The arbiter fired a second bullet. Propulsed by the spring-loaded mechanism in the chairback, Harriman rebounded forward violently, bouncing off the side of the desk and onto the floor.

The smell of cordite. That's what it all came down to. A life replaced by an odor. In his mind, burnt gunpowder signified relief, satisfaction, like the smell of a lover's perfume: a job completed. Success. Refractory in nature. A moment of silence, fleeting and profound. He rerolled the facemask and secured the gun over his heart.

On occasion, when the contract was a business decision or the client was particularly scorned or vindictive, a trophy was expected. A talisman of proof to be collected and delivered. A driver's license, a necklace, a finger, a nose. In this instance the client requested Harriman's cellphone and Beaujolais searched the desk and the floor, finally finding it underneath the overturned chair. He knelt to gather the phone, careful to avoid the blood. Emanating from the device he heard a faint whisper. He held it to his ear. A woman's voice.

"Dad? Hello? Did I lose you?"

He ended the call, turned off the phone and secured it in his jacket before exiting the room and closing the door. As he was reaching for the knob to the hallway, the door opened, revealing a thin woman with hair the blue-black of crows feather. In her left hand she held a drink carrier plugged with twin paper coffee cups. A lime-green Michael Kors bag dangled from her elbow. The purse matched her eyes.

She stared at him, her lips pressed tight beneath a single elevated eyebrow. "Oh. Um—hello?"

Automatically, sans thought, he stepped aside and she entered the room and set the carrier and purse on her desk. She sat and pressed a key on her keyboard then looked up at him, the light from her awoken computer screen highlighting the annoyed furrows in the skin below her hairline. "Okay. Hello. How can I help you?"

He felt his hand rise but he prevented it from reaching inside his jacket. From her viewpoint, as he stood silently with his wrist bent oddly, it appeared some kind of tic, and, assuming him to be neurologically impaired (the firm had a history of representing accident victims), she untensed her face and smiled, speaking slowly: "Hello, sir. How may I help you? Do you have an ap-point-ment?"

The arbiter started to nod but aborted mid-tilt and the resulting head shake seemed yet another symptom of his cognitive damage.

This one's laying it on pretty thick, she thought, expecting the drool to fall at any moment. "Are you here to see Mr. Harriman?"

He remained still.

"Alright. Let me see if he's in."

She spun in her chair and tapped on the door. "Mr. Harriman? I'm—my appointment was canceled. I know you don't have anything scheduled until after lunch, but there's a man out here. I'm assuming personal injury. Mr. Harriman?"

She stood. As soon as her back was turned, the gun was in his hand. She opened the door, he raised the pistol, but in the second between aim and fire, she stopped herself and turned back. "I forgot. I got us frappucin—"

Gun.

Scream.

Trigger.

At this distance, as if detonated from within, the side of her head burst, painting his face with its contents, and through the wound, whatever it was that kept her body upright escaped and she crumpled like a marionette cut from its strings. He stood over her. Another bullet evened the symmetry of her skull.

He took the stairs at top speed, bounding, leaps. As he hit the third stairwell, he heard another scream.

He was out the door and onto the street by the time the accountant in the neighboring office dialed 911. He ran, feeling the warmth of the prenoon sun as it met the blood on his bare face. At the car he attempted to reach in his hip pocket for the keys. It was at this time he noticed the gun was still in his hand.

In the nascent period of his career he worked in big trucks. Murdered out Navigators. Lifted Broncos. Ostentatious holdovers from his private security days. But with experience, his preferences changed. Now for metropolitan operations he chose small vehicles as his means of conveyance, and as the Fiesta emerged from the tight spot without needing to reverse and disappeared easily into the flow of traffic, he would have, had he not been so absolutely discomposed, commended his own foresight.

He found himself on Beale Street. The water to the left of him meant he was driving south. He knew, even through the haze of lamentation and inward disdain, that at this moment it was his job to mitigate liability. The gun, the car, his clothes—he was covered in blood.

"I'm covered in blood," he said.

He wiped at his face with the sleeve of his jacket but the waxed cotton only spread the mess. He couldn't remember a time when his situation had been this truly utterly fucked.

Beale ended at Bryant and he turned toward the water. At a red light at Embarcadero he realized he wasn't breathing. You need to be here right now, he thought. He closed his eyes and dug his palms into his eyelids and dragged them down his face, smearing blood like warpaint.

"Okay," he said, exhaling loudly. "Alright. Okay."

He opened his eyes and focused his attention, reducing each moment to the novel component parts. It was very simple: seconds become minutes and those minutes become your life. Now was the time for binary decisions.

Black or white.

Yes or no.

Live or die.

Left or right.

He looked both ways. To the left the Bay Bridge spanned the gap to Oakland. To the right more San Francisco and the greater south Bay. His initial instinct was to flee the city, to head inland across the water and ditch the car in the abundant roughness looming on the other side, but the bridge was a bottleneck, one with tollbooths and cameras, and while he didn't know if the murder of a prominent lawyer and his secretary merited a roadblock, if one existed, it seemed like an obvious placement would be at the end of the nearest bridge.

He signaled right, but turned it off after one click: driving deeper into the populated peninsula didn't interest him. I'm covered in blood. Again he wasn't breathing. A horn honked behind him, then another. He looked up. The box truck in front of him turned, revealing a third choice, an option: a prayer in one word.

Through the traffic light, abutting a boardwalk, a massive parking lot extended into the water like an abbreviated runway, and he drove forward through the mostly empty blacktop and parked the car in the farthest corner where the asphalt overlooked the ocean.

He turned off the engine and got out of the car and leaned against the guardrail inhaling great gulps of the wet air as if he swallowed enough of it he might lift and float away. Between drifts of white foam, the water rolled in a humping patchwork of cerulean and cobalt and cornflower and cyan, shades and hues infinite and unnamed, the total palette of blue and its variations augmented by the differing intensities of daylight breaching the cloud cover above. Below him, against the concrete wall, waves crashed and bloomed, and he leaned into the resulting sprays, letting the sea lick him clean.

When the blood was gone, he peeled off his jacket and his shirt and his shoes and dropped them off the platform before returning to the car for the gun and depositing it likewise, piece by piece, into the roil, followed by the paper license plates and the contents of the glove box.

He gave the car a final once-over, then, as was customary at the end of a job, he sent a text to the only number saved in his work phone before tossing it in as well.

The cool planks of the boardwalk came as a relief after crossing the asphalt barefoot. Other than a triad of homeless men passing a bottle down a bench, the promenade was empty at this hour. In just his chinos he walked past shuttered stands advertising cotton candy, lemonade, fudge, braided hair, past pole-mounted binoculars offering views of Treasure Island or Yerba Buena and machines that flattened pennies into keepsakes for the price of four quarters.

The only open business was a small café attached to a souvenir stand where the weary proprietor eyed him as he selected a pair of flip-flops, board shorts, a San Francisco 49ers ballcap and a hooded sweatshirt bearing an otter curled around the word MONTEREY. He bought the new outfit with a damp hundred-dollar bill then put on everything but the shorts and ordered two fully dressed hot dogs and a cup of hot chocolate from the café. While the same proprietor prepared his meal, he went into the bathroom and changed into the shorts, burying the pants in paper towels in the bottom of the trash can.

He ate the hot dogs in a total of five bites but lingered over the cocoa. He removed the lid and blew on the contents, sipping the warm sweetness, sitting in a white plastic chair at a white plastic table beneath an umbrella branded with the logo of Anchor Steam beer. Occasionally his fingers touched the place on his chest to the left of his sternum where his jacket pocket formerly resided and where L. Harriman's phone was supposed to be, feeling the emptiness there on the surface and internally, both on his skin and deeper, somewhere below the flesh.

SAM TALLENT is a comedian. For the last decade he has performed more than forty weekends per year across America, Canada, Australia, Europe, and Japan. His writing has appeared in *Birdy* magazine, *Denverse Magazine*, and on Vice.com. He lives in Detroit with his wife. This is his first novel.

Instagram: @samtallent

X: @TallentSam